Kathlyn Starbuck lives in San Diego with her husband, fantasy author Raymond E. Feist, the requisite two cats and a horse.

D1310094

KATHLYN S. STARBUCK

Time in Mind

Grafton

An Imprint of HarperCollins*Publishers*

Grafton
An Imprint of HarperCollins*Publishers*
77–85 Fulham Palace Road,
Hammersmith, London W6 8JB

A Grafton Original 1992
9 8 7 6 5 4 3 2 1

A catalogue record for this book
is available from the British Library

ISBN 0 586 21101 2

Set in Times

Printed in Great Britain by
HarperCollinsManufacturing Glasgow

For Rich, Kent, Michele, and Ray with love

Acknowledgements

No book being a truly solo effort, I would like to thank the following people for their patient and enthusiastic help: Linda Burton, Barbara Carr, Diane Clark, Martin Corden, Carolyn Ding, Malcolm Edwards, Michele Gillaspie, Felicia Herman, Pat LoBrutto, Jonathan Matson, Andy Montalvo, Bridget Quinn, Kent Quirk, Bunny Sisson, Debbie Smith, Glenn Smith, Don and Eleanor Smith, Rich Spahl, Dawn Wilson, Hugh Wilson and Janny Wurts. P.S. Happy Birthday, Mondie. Sorry it took me so long . . .

Prologue

'You must listen, and remember this exactly as I tell it to you, because you will have to tell your children and grandchildren when your turn comes. Remember it so that *they* can remember it and understand.'

The man paused in his speech and looked around the circle of small faces lifted to his. Firelight cast flickering shadows across childish features. Drove Gardner's face cramped into a smile and the children sat up straighter, putting what distance they could between themselves and their elder without actually moving away from him.

Gardner was aware of this, and his smile broadened. He leaned forward from his place on the hearth before them and gestured with one arm, sweeping the air in a wide arc. As a wave, the children leaned away from his open palm and sat straight again.

'Do *you* understand the importance of tradition?' Gardner asked, fixing first one, then another with his small, bloodshot eyes. Timidly, each nodded. No one wanted to be singled out for special attention.

'Once upon a time, in the Time Before, the People lived in a way that displeased the Higher Souls. They had grown away from the land and from the practices that the Higher Souls wanted them to observe,' Gardner said. He scrutinized the upturned faces in the circle before him, making sure everyone was paying attention. Raising one hand above his head, he shot a bolt of blue lightning into the corner. A small mouse that had been passing through squealed as it burst into flame. The children shivered and huddled closer together before the hearth. Gardner lowered his hand and rubbed his palms together, energy crackling between them. He shot a challenging look at the men and women who shared the room with him and the children.

Many of the Keep's adults sat on cushions against the walls under the sconces of the huge meeting room. They used the torchlight to repair tack, knit stockings and whittle toys for the children. Those near the burning mouse made no attempt to put it out, or remove it. They avoided Gardner's gaze and worked intently on whatever project was in hand.

Gardner smiled and returned his attention to the children. 'After many warnings, which the People From Before did not heed, the Higher Souls rained plagues upon them, killing the unbelievers,' Drove continued.

'That's not right,' Ian murmured under his breath. 'That's not how it happened at all!' The boy was small for his nine years. His pale hair and fair skin made him look fragile and young. He sat by himself near the front of the group. Several of the children nearby made silencing motions with their hands, hoping not to draw attention to themselves in the process.

'Most of the People From Before didn't pay any attention even then, but a few listened and were spared and were taught to return to the ways they had abandoned long ago. "You must once again practise the rituals of speaking with us in meditation every day, eat only foods grown and prepared in holistic methods and relearn the uses and powers of crystals and stones," the Higher Souls said to those chosen few.' Gardner had risen and was pacing back and forth in front of the hearth. He was a tall man, with a long stride. He dominated the front of the room both in size and presence. 'You will leave the cities and live apart,' he continued, gesturing with a heavily muscled arm. 'You will shun strangers who might carry disease into your midst. It is not healthy to be so close to so many.'

'No! That's not it!' Ian exclaimed. He heard several grown-ups hiss their breath in, but he knew they wouldn't get involved.

Gardner turned slowly to face him.

Ian squared his shoulders and stared defiantly up at Gardner. 'That's not how it happened,' he repeated.

'Don't contradict your elders.' Gardner waved carelessly in his direction.

Ian continued to sit tall in the face of the implied threat.

'To those chosen few,' Gardner continued, turning his back to Ian, 'the Higher Souls said, "You must be extremely careful in the people you get near and those you choose to mate with."'

'It wasn't that way at all,' Ian said loudly. He now sat completely alone, as the other children had edged away from him while Gardner spoke.

Gardner turned to him. 'Are you saying that they didn't die of plagues?' he asked with much amusement.

'No, they did. That's not what I meant,' Ian protested, flushing as the other children giggled. Only Sarah, he noticed, didn't laugh at him. She reddened and looked away.

'Well, what do you mean, then?' Gardner asked with exaggerated politeness. He was backlit by the fire, but Ian recognized the tone of voice, and knew that the expression on Drove's face was not pleasant.

'It wasn't the Higher Souls that sent the plagues,' Ian said, standing. 'They don't do that kind of thing. They instruct, they don't order,' he finished, sounding braver than he felt.

'Oh, I see,' Gardner replied, sounding extremely pleasant. 'We are to believe a boy who is a Deaf; a boy who can't talk to them, that the Higher Souls don't involve themselves in our petty little lives?' An unseen hand pushed Ian roughly to the floor. 'Someone should teach you obedience, boy.' Turning away from Ian, Drove

Gardner continued, 'It was the grandmas and grandpas of your grandmas and grandpas that heard the Higher Souls and got the message. They were told to carry glass beads because glass is pure and germ-free, and will prevent the transmission of diseases. Also, blood smears must be taken on them to be sure that the genes are undamaged, so babies will be healthy.

' "You must study and meditate to relearn the skills that belonged to you many centuries ago," said the Higher Souls. "There are powers of the mind that you possess, but have forgotten. They will be your salvation."

'And we have been studying ever since, trying to live as our Higher Souls dictate,' Gardner finished, regarding the semi-circle with a satisfied expression.

'No, no, no!' Ian yelled again, jumping to his feet. 'They never meant for us to stagnate! They didn't want this! They wanted us to relearn lost skills to help us build a better life. They didn't send the plagues, those came as a result of too many people living too close together. It was bound to happen, it – ' His breath cut short and he held out his hands, as if to prevent Gardner from cutting off his wind.

'Silence!' thundered Gardner. 'I have had enough of you and your backtalk! Your ideas are madness and where you get them, I don't want to know!'

Ian was struck by the invisible hand and knocked to the floor, whacking the side of his head hard against the flagstones.

'Now you are picking on other people's children, Drove?' Cia's voice cut through the ringing in Ian's ears. With a gasp of pain, Ian sat slowly and watched Cia as she left the doorway and entered the common room. She looked briefly at the people sitting along the walls, but they kept their eyes on their work.

'He was disrupting the lesson,' Drove protested. He crossed his arms over his broad chest and levelled his chin defiantly. Cia regarded him silently for a moment. His small, watery eyes were close-set under a heavy brow-ridge. His wide, thin-lipped mouth contained crooked and badly stained teeth and his nose was large, fleshy and very red.

With an impatient flick, she pushed her long silver-white hair off her shoulders and shook her head slightly. 'You mean he disagreed with what you had to say?' she asked.

'Yes!' Drove shouted. 'You memorized those stories, we all did! Ian cannot be allowed to question tradition. I punished him as an example to the others. This sort of thing can get out of hand.'

Contempt flickered across Cia's sharp features and thinned her lips. 'So you beat him?' she asked. 'In front of witnesses? I thought you were smarter than that, Drove.'

The children sat riveted by the scene. Terrified by both adults, they were secretly rooting for Cia because she never hurt them. She made them work hard, but she was always fair. They felt her influence in the beauty of their centres and heard her voice patiently repeating their lessons to them until they understood. A hard taskmaster was different from a cruel one.

Gardner growled low in his throat and raised his hand to Cia. She swayed gently from side to side as she stood before him. She was taller than most of the men in the Keep and Gardner was no exception. Slender as a child, she didn't appear to be able to stand against Gardner on her own, but she saw his gesture and laughed outright. 'Are you threatening me?' she asked.

'This is all your fault!' Gardner shouted. 'You encourage your son's lunatic ideas and prevent reasonable punishment for disruptive behaviour.'

'Beating a child is reasonable punishment for disobedience?' She turned her appeal to the silent adults, but no one would risk agreeing with her.

With an inarticulate cry of rage, Gardner flexed his fingers and stabbed blue lightning at Cia.

She stood still. The bolt struck her aura and crackled harmlessly as the energy was deflected. Colours coruscated about her as the bolt shattered on the flagstones at her feet. Tiny balls of blue fire rolled about the room, showering sparks and leaving small carbon burn marks on the stone where they touched. The children took great pleasure in batting them out with bare hands and feet.

'Drove, you should know better by now,' Cia sighed. The colours in her aura subsided and she once again stood clearly before him. 'Leave my boy alone. He can't harm you. He can't even defend himself.'

Turning away, Cia held out her hand to Ian. 'Come with me,' she said. Without looking back at Gardner, she connected to his mind. *Don't try to intimidate me, Drove, I won't be bullied.*

Ian had been about five years old when his mother first brought him to the Old City. He'd also been terrified. Stories of the horrors to be found in the Old Cities were favourite hearth fare for rainy nights' entertainment. Nevertheless, Cia took him to the library and introduced Ian to the world that had existed Before by teaching him to read their books and papers.

It never occurred to Ian to wonder why his mother knew how to read this ancient and unknown script. Children of his age were expected to heed their elders, not question the knowledge being imparted. Ian was fascinated by the stories Cia read to him from the delicate, yellowed pages. They opened for him a place and a time far beyond anything he could comprehend – a place where fear was an external condition; where strange and wonderful vehicles whizzed on and above the earth at speeds that were unimaginable to his young mind; where the population teemed in extravagant numbers doing all manner of exotic things with one another, the very names of which stirred his curiosity.

The fact that Cia drilled Ian over and over on grammar and vocabulary didn't seem to register. There was too much wonder and excitement to discover in the process to worry about the stringency of lessons. Ian was a quick learner in any case. The words and phrases fired his imagination and he learned what he needed so he could read more about the people who had killed themselves centuries before his birth.

These people had left behind an unbelievable amount of words pertaining to their lives. The sheer volume of printed information about their comings and goings puzzled Ian. It was as though they knew they were dying, and wanted to leave something behind that would tell others about themselves.

Ian had grown up with an oral tradition in the Keep. The elders told stories of their lives by the hearth at night so the children would learn history and be able to tell their own children and grandchildren some day. Some of the oldest stories had to be memorized so they could be passed along intact, but no one ever wrote them down.

The idea of writing intrigued Ian. He thought these people from Before must have been very vain and mistrustful if they had to record their stories in such a fashion, instead of passing them along to the children in the comfortable companionship of the Keep.

As he had grown older, Ian became aware he was unique in his ability to read. No one else, it seemed, was able to do these things his mother had taught him at such an early age. With this discovery (which he kept to himself), he began to wonder what had happened to cause the transition from written communication to oral tradition. He searched out all he could find on the period just before the most 'recent' dates on newspapers and in books; just before the writing stopped.

The people from Before started dying. They contracted dreadful diseases which they couldn't cure. Ian didn't understand the names, but they were deadly, wasting illnesses that leached life from the body slowly and painfully.

It began almost imperceptibly, but as the plagues became more widespread, those who were still healthy found it increasingly difficult to care for those who were sick and dying. Difficult, and distasteful it seemed, for they began rounding up those who were suffering and penned them away from the rest of society, walling them behind glass and sterilized, germ-free barriers. Still more sickened and died. Some chronicled their illnesses at great length. As he read the books and articles, Ian was appalled at the pain they expressed as their bodies rotted from within, their minds succumbing to inexorable madness; the rage at their powerlessness to make it stop.

As greater portions of the population became afflicted, trade and travel restrictions were placed on those trying to leave their own countries, or do business with other countries. By that time, there wasn't a nation that didn't have a significant percentage of its population quarantined 'for its own safety'. Politically unstable nations began experiencing border skirmishes and internal dissent.

Throughout the escalation of hostilities, they continued to print vast amounts of material communicating the events to each other on a daily basis. Death announcements became body counts. Those not ill were killing each other with bombs and bullets instead.

At about this time, small articles began appearing for 'communal living in a holistic environment' in strange places like Sedona and Four Corners and Ayers Rock. The people in these places maintained that better living could be achieved through organic foods and crystal meditation. No one took them very seriously at first, but they did seem to report fewer deaths and gradually, more and more people were writing about how life on the commune changed them for the better.

The rest of the news was as dismal as ever. Body counts stopped because no one could tally them that quickly. The dead were piling up because they couldn't be removed and burned fast enough. The decay was causing more illness, especially in countries where they had been lobbing grenades at each other instead of tending to the disposal of corpses. Still they managed to tell each other about it in their articles and books.

The sprawling cities were becoming increasingly dangerous. There were so few healthy individuals left to run the societal machine, that lines of communication began to falter. The cities soon became impossible to maintain. All who were able left with what they could carry. Businesses closed, and with them, the organizations that published the precious papers that Ian read so avidly.

The agricultural industry broke down along with the machines that had made it possible. People fled the cities and the suburbs in search of land to farm on an individual basis. Most of the buildings that were in existence prior to the breakdown of society were designed to function only with full power supplied. These homes and other buildings were impractical for the needs of the emerging society. Many suburban houses were razed for their land, but some of those that were better constructed were saved and converted for more practical use.

Gradually, there was a return to a horse and plough, torch and outhouse mentality. Handwork and holism became the operant conditions. No one wanted to risk another disease-ridden society.

Finally, the great cities of those from Before were completely abandoned to the corpses and rats. The world-wide social infrastructure had collapsed. The bombing stopped; society was in tatters. The survivors had to struggle to build a new way of life. They impressed their children with the fact that the cities were dangerous places to be avoided at all costs: only death lived there now. It would be a long time before anyone could return there safely.

The writing stopped.

What had impressed Ian most about the first visit was that neither he nor his mother sickened; neither of them died. No retribution of any kind was visited on them and no one found out they had been in that evil place. When Ian questioned his mother about that, she shushed him and told him he was never to mention it. Then she did something that he would never forget.

She knelt in front of Ian and placed her hands on his shoulders. She looked deeply into his eyes and spoke into his mind. *Ian, you must never speak of what we've done, but when you want to return, just think of it and I will know to take you there if it is at all possible. Do you understand that what I have done is dangerous for us both if anyone were ever to find out?* Ian nodded solemnly. He was a 'Deaf-Mute', although usually they were just called Deafs. He couldn't talk in anyone's mind. He'd tried to make his mother hear him, but he hadn't been able to. He had never heard anyone else's voice in his mind. If Mother could make him hear her, she must be very powerful indeed. This frightened Ian.

He never spoke of the library, but he returned there often to pore over the dusty, long forgotten volumes in the silent security of the old building.

Rain beat against the windows of the common room, but a large fire cracked and snapped on the hearth and torches hung in sconces on the walls. Mareki stood before the hearth, shivering even in the warmth of the blaze behind her. Her shawl was drawn tightly around her shoulders.

Drove Gardner sat on the hearth near her, and the children sat on the floor at her feet.

Ian sat on a pillow by himself at the back of the circle now that he was fourteen and almost a grown-up. Sarah also sat at the back of the circle with the older children, but she sat far enough away from Ian that anything which might befall him wouldn't affect her.

Mareki had been called to recite a story, but she was so terrified of Gardner that she stood and mumbled.

It was a story that they had all heard hundreds of times before, but she was forgetting whole passages and spoke so quietly that even the small children in front couldn't hear or understand her.

Gardner prodded Mareki with the unseen hand. 'Come on, girl, speak up! What's the matter with you? Cat got your tongue? Fill the room with our ancestors' wisdom.'

She shrank away from him. Her speech ran down. She stood silent before the group, head bent, tears bright on her eyelashes.

Ian jumped to his feet and ran to her. 'Why don't you pick on people who can defend themselves?' he asked conversationally. He led Mareki back to her pillows at the edge of the circle.

'Perhaps you would honour us with the retelling of that story, then,' Gardner suggested, equally pleasantly.

Ian smiled and returned to the hearth. The adults shot glances at each other that didn't escape Ian's notice. None of them dared move, but none of them wanted to be in the room any more, either. Facing the group of children, he could read fear in their eyes. He wasn't sure whether they were more afraid of Gardner, or of himself.

'Once upon a time, a long, long time ago,' he began, 'there were people who lived together without fear. They built vast cities so that they could live more closely with each other. They built fast vehicles to travel on land, over water and in the air so that they could go to a great many

17

places and see how other people lived. They shared ideas for growth and development and dreams of how they would like things to be.' Ian could feel Gardner tense behind him.

'I told you to tell the story, boy,' Drove growled.

'I am,' Ian responded. 'At the peak of their civilization, their cities were clean and beautiful. The people had enough to eat and their health was well looked after. They all had jobs and families and they were happy.

'But things got out of control. They became dissatisfied with what they had. They wanted more. There were too many people, and not enough jobs. There wasn't enough food, and medicines became an expensive privilege. Some people had lots of things, and lots of people didn't have anything.'

'What nonsense is this?' Gardner demanded.

'I am telling the story,' said Ian. 'Sicknesses appeared that their healers couldn't cure. Because there were so many of them living together, they spread those sicknesses rapidly among themselves. Many, many people died.'

'Those sicknesses didn't just appear!' Gardner exclaimed, jumping to his feet. 'They were sent by the Higher Souls to punish Those From Before!'

'No, sir,' Ian said, turning to look at Drove. 'The Higher Souls have nothing to do with the diseases that killed the friends and relatives of our ancestors. Nor did they encourage the hostilities that led to the bombings.'

'You're lying!' said Gardner. 'You have heard the story many times. You have twisted the facts with the intention of twisting the minds of the children in the Keep. You're sick and ought to be shut away!'

'No, sir,' Ian said again. 'The facts have been turned, over time, to serve the purposes of people like you who fear change.'

Drove Gardner's face reddened. He said in a danger-ously low voice, 'I will not stand here and be insulted by you, nor will I allow you to spread your dangerous and malicious lies.'

'Well then why, sir, do you keep insisting that I recite before the group?' Ian asked. 'You know I will say things that make you angry so you can justify attacking me.'

'That's a lie!' Gardner sputtered. 'I try to teach you the history of the Keep, which everyone needs to know, and you call *me* a liar. You *insolent* – !'

Ian gasped and lunged away from Drove Gardner's outstretched hand. Children scrambled away from him as he staggered through their midst. The adults stayed where they were, but reached towards the children as if to offer them some safety. Gardner stood in front of the hearth, arms raised, hands outstretched. Blue fire crackled on his palms. Red-faced and eyes bulging, Gardner cast a bolt of energy after Ian as he fled through the common room.

'You see?' Ian turned and glared at Drove, watching the blue bolt shatter on the stones near Ian. 'You aren't interested in what really happened. You are interested only in punishing me, or anyone else who reminds you that you're also a Deaf. You may be psychokinetic, but you can't hear what the laughter is about any more than I can. You don't really care what our history is, only that our versions differ. You have all of these people so terrorized that they won't dare defy you. Well you don't scare me! Frightening children is a cowardly thing to do!'

'You – ' Gardner screamed, almost incoherent.

Ian fell to his knees, feeling again the invisible hand closing on his throat. 'It doesn't matter,' he gasped. 'If it isn't me, it'll be someone else.'

'No!' Gardner roared.

Breath gone, his peripheral vision closing in, Ian smiled. 'There is nothing you can do to stop it,' he said. Then he fell forward on to the stone floor, unconscious.

PART ONE

The Keep

1

Ian was late coming back to the Keep. The sun had set by the time he had rubbed down his horse, fed him and stabled him for the night. In gathering darkness, Ian crossed the barnyard.

The Keep was an odd assortment of buildings that wandered about the landscape in a seemingly random fashion. It had begun as a house in the Time Before, but as the people who lived there outgrew its space, they added on to it.

The first additions were made with wood and brick scavenged from the other houses in the area that were torn down during land reclamation. These were mostly single-room additions made directly to the original house, but as the materials were exhausted, stone replaced them. The stone portions were sturdier and more sprawling, connected to the older portions of the Keep only as a matter of function. Some of them were not connected at all. The buildings had been arranged according to the compass points, the orientation of sun and moon, and the location of the local power vortices so that they would be in balance. The overall effect was haphazard.

The barn stood at the far north corner of the buildings, near the river that ran through the 'back yard'. The river was their life. It had been coaxed into an elaborate irrigation system that fed the fields surrounding the Keep. The farthest cultivated fields were no more than half a day's ride from the Keep to the west. Beyond that, there was nothing. The country became wild and for several weeks' travel in any direction, there was no one; nothing except overgrown heaps of rubble that were the useless parts of the old houses that had been demolished, and the Old City uncomfortably nearby.

An old shepherd trotted stiffly towards Ian from the front stoop, tail wagging in greeting.

'Hi, yourself,' he said, scratching the dog behind the ears. Pushing the door open, he was immediately knocked off balance by a small child running through the hall. The children who had been chasing her skidded to a halt when they saw Ian. The little girl who had crashed into him was scrambling to get away. The strand of glass beads she wore around her neck caught on the quartz crystal ring Ian wore on his right hand, and the stringing fibres broke, scattering beads all over the floor.

With a collective gasp, the other children began backing away from the disaster in the hallway. The little girl started to cry as she frantically grabbed for the tiny glass spheres. They rolled away from her.

'Here Nina, let me help you,' Ian suggested as he scraped a few of them together. 'Hold out your hand.'

With a low cry of fear, Nina leapt to her feet and ran after her playmates as fast as her legs could carry her.

With a sigh, Ian swept the glass beads into a pile and picked them up off the floor. Nina wouldn't be back for them until she knew they had been cleansed of his touch. He put them into a pocket of his leather trousers to give to his mother later. She would clear and restring them for the little girl.

Nina was an extremely sensitive empath and couldn't bear the touch of a person who didn't possess psychic ability. Ian could understand intellectually that his hand felt cold and dead to her because it lacked psychic vibration, but emotionally, he was hurt by her fear of his shortcoming. Her tolerance would increase as she grew older, but in the meantime, Ian had to accept that she would avoid him when at all possible.

Absently tugging at his soft, rather scraggly blond

24

beard, Ian passed through one of the common areas on his way towards the kitchen. These large rooms were among the first wooden additions made to the Old House. They had fieldstone fireplaces with wide, low hearths. At this time of night, most of the Keep's population were gathered here, but as Ian went by, few people greeted him.

Sarah looked up from her place on the floor by the fire and smiled at Ian. Rising, she followed him out of the common room towards the kitchen. The disapproving stares that followed her bothered Ian, but Sarah ignored them.

'You were so late I was beginning to worry,' she said, once they were out of earshot.

'Been talking to my mother again?' Ian asked. His voice sounded less lighthearted than he had wanted it to, but Sarah always knew what he meant.

'Come on. Let's get you some dinner,' she said.

In the kitchen, over a plate of cold meat and the end of a loaf of bread, Ian watched Sarah as she moved about making a pot of tea. At this time of night, the kitchen was deserted. The sounds of the teapot bumping in the sink and on the hearth echoed hollowly in the large room. The kitchen had been one of the first additions to the Old House.

It ran the entire length of the original building and was almost as wide. The centre of the room was dominated by a long butcher's table with a neat row of stools lined up on one side of it. The walls were lined with cupboards above and below smooth stone counters. There were deep stone sinks set into the counter at either end of the outside wall that had pumps connecting to the outdoor well. Both end walls were entirely taken by walk-in fieldstone fireplaces. Built into one side of each were two large ovens. A spit was set up in one fireplace and spider arms for pots were in the other.

Sarah bent over the latter and hooked the teapot on to one of the spider arms to boil the water and stirred the banked coals to a small flame beneath it. Turning around, she pushed a stray wisp of black curl out of her face.

'That should be ready by the time you've finished your dinner, if you quit staring and eat,' she said, settling on to the stool beside him with a grin. 'Then you can tell me what you learned today, OK?' Unconsciously, she reached into her bodice for the strand of glass beads she wore about her neck, and rolled them between thumb and index finger.

'You know, Sarah, you really hurt my position by insisting on wearing those,' Ian said, nodding at her habitual gesture.

'Better safe,' she responded, tucking the necklace back into her dress.

'But damnit, that's my point!' Ian slammed his palm against the table for emphasis. 'There's nothing dangerous in the Old City any more. Those silly baubles won't protect you from anything!' he exclaimed.

Sarah sighed and slid off her stool, using the pretext of checking the teapot to put some distance between herself and Ian. As she stirred the small fire and adjusted the spider arm from which the pot hung, she thought about the strange man she had fallen in love with.

It was unusual for an empath to become attracted to a Deaf but Sarah had always loved Ian. Even when he talked of his strange ideas and frightened her, she loved him. Their one point of contention was her unwillingness to let go of the things he was certain were useless, or worse, damaging to the Keep's society.

'No one else knows I wear them,' she said in a low voice without turning around.

'*Everyone* else knows you wear them!' Ian said in frustration. 'Sarah, how can I convince you that you aren't going to die if you take those off? I haven't worn mine in years! I haven't died yet.'

'No,' Sarah said, turning to face him. 'No, you haven't died yet. But everyone in the Keep is certain you've lost your mind. Isn't that worse?' She knew her words stung him. She heard the whispers behind her back, felt the anger directed at her by people who thought she was encouraging lunatic behaviour. It hurt her, and right now, she was feeling petty enough to want to inflict some of that pain on Ian.

Ian counted ten several times. 'Sarah, do you think I've lost my mind?' he asked. He watched the pain in her face, seeing the darkening in her eyes and the tension around her mouth as she fought to keep the tears out of her voice.

Finally, she shook her head. 'No,' she whispered. 'Oh, Ian! I'm sorry, it's just . . .' her resolve broke. She ran to where he sat and threw her arms around his neck. 'I love you,' she said, kissing him. 'I didn't mean – '

'I know,' Ian said, kissing her in return. He stroked her tangled curls from her forehead. 'I love you, too.' And he did, but Sarah was a mystery to him. In so many ways, she seemed to understand him no better than the others in the Keep. At the same time, she knew his feelings before he voiced them. Sometimes, her empathy seemed very selective. Ian knew this wasn't the case, but he couldn't help but feel slighted when the one woman in the world who should know how he felt, missed the point entirely.

'I found a letter in the library, today,' he said to distract her. 'It was addressed to me.'

Sarah pushed herself out of his arms and held herself stiffly away from him. 'What?' she asked.

'It mentioned you and Cia.'

'What's a letter?' Sarah demanded. The fear was returning to her eyes.

27

'Nothing,' Ian murmured pulling her to him again, regretting having mentioned it. 'Just something I read this afternoon. Nothing at all.'

'Then finish your dinner while I make some tea. Cia wanted to talk to you when you came in,' Sarah said, gently disengaging herself. 'Maybe I should tell her you're here?'

'No!' Ian attacked his meal with renewed enthusiasm. 'I already have to find her for Nina.'

Cia watched Ian as he emptied his pocket on the table beside her. The tiny glass beads scattered across the wooden surface. She let them roll, looking instead at her son. His blond hair stuck out wildly and his cheeks flushed in embarrassment. Her son looked much as she did: tall, angular, slender. He was not quite as tall as she, owing to his father's slight build, but he possessed a muscular strength that she did not. His features could not be called handsome, but they were pleasant enough. His blue eyes had the depth of a cloudless summer sky.

Ian's hands were gentle and sure on a horse's mouth, yet he scrabbled clumsily at the tiny ornaments on the table that eluded his grasp.

With a small gesture of exasperation, he said: 'Nina dropped these.' Abandoning his attempts to reclaim the beads, Ian dropped his hands to his sides and stepped away from the table.

Cia already knew this. She nodded.

'Will you please clear them and restring them for her. I can't touch them any more.'

Again, Cia nodded. She watched Ian shift from foot to foot in discomfort.

'Sarah said you wanted to see me when I got in?' he asked finally.

'Yes.' Cia rose from her chair and stood over him,

swaying slightly. Her silver-white hair fell over narrow shoulders and brushed against her robes at her hips. She regarded Ian with pale grey eyes. 'I'll cleanse and repair Nina's beads for her,' Cia said. Then she muttered to herself, 'That girl needs to learn that the Keep doesn't exist for her ease and comfort.'

Nina was one of Cia's most promising students, but she was undisciplined, and her mother encouraged her. So, for that matter, did the rest of the Keep. Cia often wondered what the point was in trying to teach the children, when the elders were only interested in the perpetuation of mindless tradition.

'Thank you,' Ian said, looking up. 'What did you want to see me about?'

Cia looked Ian up and down before replying. He withstood the implied criticism in silence.

'You found the letter,' she said.

Ian jumped, surprised. He nodded.

'Philip told me you had. I wasn't sure what he meant, but he was obviously right,' she said. This, Ian hadn't been expecting.

'Philip?' he asked.

'He told me you would find the letter,' Cia continued without explanation. 'That's why he taught me to teach you to read.'

'Who is Philip?' Ian asked. 'What are you talking about?'

Cia laughed and sat back down in her chair. 'We have a lot of work to do,' she said.

What you're asking me to do is very dangerous, Cia said. She sat cross-legged on a pillow on the floor of the Keep's meditation room. Her eyes were closed and her breathing was slow and even. Her hands rested palm-up on her knees. There were crystals set on the floor in front of and behind her, and to both sides. A torch burned in its sconce on the far wall. Cia was alone in the room.

She stood in her central chamber, the seat of her soul, watching the tiny, dark man who sat on the dais before her. He made no reply.

Her centre was very different from the Keep's meditation room. She had told her students over the years, as she had been taught by her first teacher, that the centre of the soul was the most beautiful place she could imagine: a private Garden of Eden. Cia had created it using all the elements that felt right to her. In it, she was surrounded by every luxury she wanted.

The walls and ceiling were of amethyst crystal, which reflected light from the diamond-and-quartz torch sconces, infusing the large space with a soft violet glow. Several doors of inlaid wood were placed at intervals about the main room, leading to other places in her centre. All of them were closed.

The floor Cia stood on was of the same inlaid wood as the doors, parqueted in elaborate patterns and scattered with silk tapestry rugs and cushions.

Cia began to pace back and forth in front of the dais. Out of the corner of her eye, she caught a flicker of something not quite there.

No! she thought. Don't look at it. There's nothing there. She breathed in deeply and exhaled slowly several times to steady herself. Turning slowly, Cia looked directly at the spot where the flicker had been. There was nothing there. She resumed her pacing.

This is our only course of action? she asked.

Amusement glittered in the little man's black eyes, but he remained silent. Philip never seemed to take anything seriously.

To Cia, he looked like someone suffering the ravages of the plague. He was thin beyond bearing, skeletal almost, and his skin was dry and taut on his bones. His clothing seemed dusty with years of disuse. Cia knew Philip was very old, but she didn't know the 'when' he came from. Every time she had asked him, he just laughed his familiar wheezing cackle and wouldn't answer her directly.

Cia bowed her head. *What do I have to do?*

Philip threw back his head and laughed a deep belly laugh that was improbable coming from his emaciated body. *Cia, you always doubt what I tell you. I too, have lessons to learn from you. The sooner we learn them, the sooner we can move on*, he said.

Cia nodded. *What do I have to do?* she repeated, seating herself at Philip's feet.

Come with me, Philip said. Taking her hand, he pulled her to her feet again and led her from her centre into the meadow that surrounded it. He pointed to the forest at the edge of the field. *There's the path. Follow it until the forest gives way to the grey area at the periphery of your consciousness. There, you will find the continuum.*

Continuum? Cia prompted.

The river of time that passes through each person, connecting them to life; to past, present and future, Philip said.

Why haven't you told me about this before? Cia demanded.

Why didn't you ever go looking for it? It's been there the whole time! Philip laughed at her. *That kind of information is given only on a need-to-know basis. It's not exactly crucial to meditation and it's not a tool most people need for their everyday lives.*

Well, what do I do when I find it? Cia asked, somewhat chastened.

You must find your way inside the continuum before we can do more, Philip chuckled.

Can't you tell me how? She was puzzled by Philip's uncharacteristic reticence.

Philip shook his head. *Each person is connected to the continuum in his or her own way. I can't help you and I can't tell you any more until you describe to me what the river of time looks like. Only then can I know that you have been successful; that you are ready to begin*.

Cia stood in the meadow staring at the forest for a long time before she became aware that Philip was gone. Taking a deep breath to square her resolve, Cia strode across the field to the edge of the woods. The path was there, as Philip had told her it would be. Cia was surprised that she had been all over the meadow but had never seen the small, distinct trail leading into the woods. It didn't seem like something she would miss. With a shrug, she set off into the forest.

Shortly, the trees thinned out and became greyer, or at least less green; the colour was being leached out of her surroundings and Cia knew she was approaching the periphery. The path faded from underfoot and the trees disappeared. The grey settled around her like fog as she continued to move through it. Gradually, her periphery darkened until it became an ill-defined band of deep black.

She was frightened by it. The blackness of it was so intense that it seemed to suck the dim light out of the greyness surrounding it. Its edges blurred, connecting her life to the river of time. There was no real barrier.

Wondering what Philip had been talking about, Cia approached the darkened area between the periphery of her consciousness and the black of the continuum. She found she could not advance. Not for many years had she found a place in her mind that she couldn't access. Frustrated, she settled back into the grey area to consider her situation. The barrier was nothing she could see, or touch. So what, she wondered, was the problem?

Cia sat on the ground as close to the blackness as she could get, closed her eyes and concentrated on the structure of the barrier. It had the solidity of an object, but no presence. There were no holes in it, but there was also nothing there. It seemed she had found the edge of her mind.

Rising, she reached for the top of the dark wall, thinking that if she could climb over it, maybe the other side would be approachable. There was no top. With hand outstretched, Cia ran along the barrier, first in one direction, then the other, but with each step, the black wall grew further and further from her fingertips.

The blackness is a void, she thought to herself. There is nothing there. That's why Philip wanted me to describe it to him. He wants to know what's there, and he wants me to tell him. Lazy bastard. He's not going to get me to do his work for him!

With that thought Cia sat down to wait for Philip to return, and eventually fell asleep. With sleep came dreams and in her dreams ran a rainbow of light. Colours flowed side by side without mixing the energies contained within them. Eight ropy strands of pure tone ran through the vast cavern of black that concealed them from the waking.

The first strand was red, the colour of life and of the first chakra. Cia could feel the power emanating from it as she passed on to the next column of orange. The depth of colour was incredible to her after the grey and black of the periphery of her mind. The second chakra colour filled her with an overwhelming sense of physical well-being. Lingering a moment to absorb the positive energies, Cia noticed that there were traces of energy between the red and orange ropes which contained elements of both colours, but weren't specifically a part of either.

Looking at the yellow strand that came next, she noticed the same phenomenon. Yellow, the colour of mental well-being and the third chakra . . . All of a sudden, the lessons her first teacher had taught her, and the lessons found in nature and those that Philip had her studying even now, began to make sense. Everything was connected through their energy patterns: life, light, time. That energy was expressed by colour.

Excited by this discovery, Cia moved on to the green river, the colour of health and growth. Reaching into it, she looked for a piece of her own life energy.

Put me down! shouted an angry voice. *We have an agreement to leave each other alone and you're violating it!*

Cia dropped the strand of energy she held, wondering who that could have been. It wasn't anyone from her own keep. With a slight frown, Cia reached back into the green energy, cautious not to pick up strange patterns. Her heart chakra had made its pattern known here. Everyone she knew was here, and they were a small portion of the total.

The blue flow of serenity and sensitivity also contained her fifth chakra energy.

Dipping into the energies between the major strands, Cia found parts of herself and others that fell into the properties of blue-green. Many of the healer's energies were concentrated in this area. Rising out of the threads, Cia saw indigo, lavender and white still before her. Most of the energies in the threads she didn't recognize. If they were in the present, she wondered, where were they?

Cia floated above, sensing the texture of the energy that she added to the river of light that fractured beneath her. With a start, she awakened.

Philip! she called in the direction of the meadow she had come from. *Philip! Is this what you meant?*

Yes. His voice chuckled at her elbow. *Now the real work begins.*

2

Ian lay face down, spreadeagled on the ground. Dirt that had been hard-packed, untilled for years, now broke apart in clods that dug into his cheek and temple, sticking in his beard and getting in his eyes and ears. He clung to the weeds even as they loosened and came up in his hands, desperately trying to remain flat against the rolling waves of earth that buckled all around him. He had been chased into a large field accidentally. He had no intention of paying for that mistake with his life.

Drove Gardner stood at the edge of the field, backlit by the sun as it sank towards the horizon. His thick arms were crossed over his chest, his feet planted wide apart. A fierce scowl of concentration drew heavy brows down over widely staring, red-rimmed eyes. A rictus grin pulled his thin lips back over stained, uneven teeth. Gardner's face flushed deep red and his neck corded with his efforts; the field continued its wild, rolling motion.

Ian tried to press his body into the dirt, but its continual heaving threatened to toss him into the air, revealing his hiding place. As the ground rose, Ian could see the jagged silhouette of the Old City on the horizon. The sun was descending as late afternoon turned to dusk. The bloody red and fiery orange of sunset behind the crumbling stone of the ancient buildings made the Old City appear to burn; as though that were the cause of its present condition. It stood in stark contrast to the rough field Ian now found himself in. Once more the ground fell away. The broken and tumbled buildings disappeared. Ian was again blind to his surroundings. He didn't even dare to raise his head to check Drove Gardner's location. Not knowing Gardner's location was what had got Ian into trouble in the first place.

It never occurred to Ian that anyone else entered the Old City, so strong were the taboos. Ian didn't have his mother's ability to hear other people's thoughts. He had no way to know he was being followed. He had left the library late that afternoon, leading his horse down the worn and cracked steps to the street. Swinging up into the saddle, he reined the large bay through the undergrowth and trees towards the outskirts of the Old City. The trees, which at one time had lined the street, had broken the pavement and road-bed with their roots. Seeds had caught hold in the exposed soil, further destroying the buckling pavement with their growth until this particular area of the Old City resembled the urban jungle referred to in the literature of the Time Before. This thought made Ian smile as he began his journey back to the Keep. It was then that he heard movement behind him.

Surprised, Ian had turned in the saddle just in time to see Gardner raise his hand. His shock at finding Gardner in the Old City evaporated as Gardner, using his psycho-kinetic abilities, uprooted a nearby sapling and flung it at Ian. Kicking his horse's flanks, Ian had fled.

A crack split the ground before him, closing again before Ian could scream or back away. All around him, cracks began to open and close while the earth continued to buckle in waves. To Ian, the only good news with this development was that Gardner didn't know where in the field Ian lay. If Gardner had known Ian's location, Ian would certainly have fallen into the first crack that opened up.

It also meant that Freddie wasn't with Gardner. Freddie was the most gifted telepath in the Keep. If Freddie had been with Gardner, Ian would have been unable to hide at all.

As it was, Ian was in an unenviable position. As long as he could stay out of Gardner's line of sight, he was relatively safe from Gardner's psychokinetic ministrations. If he could last until dark he might stand a chance of escaping unseen, but Drove would know this too, and probably take precautions against it. Nausea finally overcame caution, and Ian raised his head to appraise his situation.

Rolling to his right, he barely escaped the sharp point of a hand-beaten, metal spear as it stabbed into the ground where he had been. Ian was on his feet and running across the heaving ground, staggering and tripping as the earth alternately fell away from his feet, and rolled up to meet them again. Behind him, he heard Drove Gardner's deep, barrel-chested laugh.

This laugh usually preceded disaster. Ian flung himself headlong to the ground and rolled to his left as he pulled his leather tunic over his head and wrapped it around his right forearm. Glancing back, Ian had enough time to see the spear flashing through the air. He threw his right arm up to block it even as it tore through the leather and his arm, pinning his forearm to his side as it embedded itself in his ribs. The pain surprised him. He recognized that the tip of the spear had been treated with a poison that affected the nerves. Ian watched the ground smooth as his vision began to close in and darken. In detached and surprised calm, Ian was certain he was going to die. Then he centred himself as his mother had taught him to do and he stayed there, hoping this would help him die more easily. The last thing Ian heard as he passed from consciousness was Drove Gardner's laughter.

Cia stood at the chopping block dicing vegetables for the evening stew, listening to the women chattering and wondering how she was going to get through kitchen duty without screaming. Cia found her stints in the kitchen the most tedious part of any day. Culinary arts were of little interest to her, and the incessant gossiping was almost more than she could endure, especially since she was almost always on the 'favourite subject' list, and often discussed despite her presence.

'"No, you don't understand," I told her. "You can't do that until you've performed the smear," I says. But she says, "Mother, honestly. No one does that any more! 'Sides, it really helps with the mood to be poking each other bloody." Well, we all know who we have to blame for that."' Tiana looked significantly in Cia's direction before winking at the circle of women who were butchering a lamb that had been slaughtered that afternoon.

Cia leaned against the wooden chopping block and stared out of the window at the setting sun as she clamped down on her public mind before any of those present caught her derisive thoughts. Tiana's daughter had bedded almost every man and boy in the Keep, using Ian's efforts at re-education as an excuse not to observe tradition or propriety. Tiana, being the type who needed always to assign blame, had become one of Ian's active adversaries as a result.

Looking at the knife in her hand, Cia hefted it and briefly indulged in a fantasy of running amok, with blade and eyes flashing as she silenced the ignorant prattle . . . then she focused on the three-inch blade and sighed. The more she spoke with Philip, the more the nonsense she heard in the Keep bothered her.

Granted, these were the beliefs she too had been raised on, but the idea of continuing to inflict them on the children bothered her more now that she knew where these things had come from. Unfortunately, it wasn't her battle, or even her war. Her guide had made that more than clear. Hers was strictly an educational role. The war belonged to her son. This probably bothered Cia most:

Ian working alone against the culture and mores of an entire people . . . a people less than anxious to let go of the fears and superstitions that had held them apart from each other and at bay for generations . . . and with Drove Gardner as his primary adversary. She pushed a lock of silver-white hair out of her pale-grey eyes as she tried to refocus her attentions on the task at hand.

Bear, one of the grey, striped tabbies, had jumped up on to the counter and was sniffing at a plate of scraps.

Hey! Beth sent a thought across the room, but before Cia could react Tanner reached out with her mind to give the cat a psychokinetic swat on the bottom. The disgruntled cat saw the blow coming, leaped off the counter and ran out of the kitchen.

'That cat will never learn,' said Tiana as she hacked another joint.

Cia smiled quietly to herself as she returned to dicing potatoes. *Thanks, Tanner. I wouldn't have got a hand on him.*

Tanner giggled and several of the women looked up. *I didn't either*, she responded. *Spank him with your hand and he puts his ears back and glares at you until you're done. Turn your back and he's right back up on the counter. Try to get him with the PK, and he's a scalded rabbit for the next few minutes. He'll be back before dinner is ready!*

Cia heard the scream clearly. It might as well have happened in her ear as in her mind. She dropped her knife as though she'd cut herself and muttered a brief excuse as she pressed a cloth to her hand and ran from the kitchen.

As Ian became more outspoken on issues of tradition and societal behaviour, strange accidents began happening to him as he went about his chores in the Keep. They were too frequent to dismiss as clumsiness, but too entirely possible to begin pointing fingers and claiming harassment.

Ian might not possess psi-power, but he did have a kind of empathy with the stock animals, so it didn't ring true that a normally docile cow would suddenly kick and try to trample him during the early-morning milking. Heavy threshers did not often fall from loft storage, but it had been known to happen. One had almost crushed Ian as he was harnessing the team to the plough for his turn harrowing the field.

Cia had begun to keep a discreet watch over Ian in an attempt to catch whoever was behind the incidents. She knew they would try again, but she didn't think it would be so far from the Keep. If only she could get to Ian in time . . . she had caught the backlash of his pain as an echo in his scream. She knew the point of the spear had been poisoned.

Sarah! she called as she hurried across the open yard to the stables, scattering chickens. Cia projected the image of where she was going on a tight focus to the mind-energy she recognized as belonging to the Keep's most powerful healer. *Sarah, come quickly, please!* Cia reached the barn door and dropped the cloth she had taken from the kitchen. Grasping the latch, she wrenched the door open and slipped inside.

The horses were agitated by Cia's emotional broadcast, stamping and snorting, shying away as she came near them. She had to work at quieting them enough to get them bridled and saddled. By the time she had succeeded in this task, Sarah appeared in the doorway.

'What is it?' Sarah asked. She held the cloth Cia had dropped at the door. 'This is clean, why is it here?'

'It's Ian. I needed an excuse to leave the dinner preparations without being questioned. Take your reins, I'll explain on the way.' Cia handed the braided leather leads to Sarah and mounted her own horse.

They rode away from the Keep at full tilt, not bothering to stop and close the barn door.

After a couple of miles, Sarah finally got up the courage to ask Cia what was going on.

'Ian needs your help. Gardner's finally tipped his hand. I never honestly believed he'd go this far, but Ian is in serious trouble and you're the only one who can really help him.'

This was all that Sarah could pry out of Cia during their headlong plunge across the surrounding countryside. Sarah clung to both her reins and the mane of her small grey-dappled mare and tried to remain astride as they flew over the rough trail. Her dark, curly hair blew across her face and stung her eyes, but she dared not let go for even a moment.

Cia rode her horse at a flat run. She seemed to know already where the path lay and followed without a moment's hesitation. They left behind the Keep's orderly fields and swung out into the foothills that separated the fields of the Keep and the outskirts of the Old City. She could sense fear near her and knew that Sarah was close behind.

'What did Gardner do? What kind of trouble is Ian in? How can I help?' Sarah shouted as they sped across the landscape. 'Why are you ignoring me?'

Because you love my son. He needs more help than I can give him, but I can't follow him if I am answering your questions. He's centred himself and that makes him much more difficult to trace. Cia could hear Sarah crying, but she shut it out as she concentrated on the weakening broadcast Ian was sending. Emotional outburst would do none of them any good right now. Cia suppressed her own desire to scream as she sent out a sweep to narrow the trace she was following.

He must be near here; she couldn't have lost the trace. There was a ground fog rising in the area. Cia and Sarah

41

pelted across the meadow and into the small wood near a field no longer cultivated. Surely anyone wishing Ian harm would not have gone any nearer the Old City, Cia thought. She glanced around at Sarah to see how the young girl fared and caught a glimpse of something she had not expected.

Reining her horse abruptly, Cia halted and turned to face a young man who stood near an oak tree.

Freddie, I didn't expect to find you here, Cia thought to him.

Freddie always surprised her. He had been found in the stable one morning many years ago, when he was only four or five. Asking him where he came from, or who his parents were, proved futile. Probing his mind was even less successful; the blocks he put up prevented even Cia from questioning him. He possessed immense telepathic talent and could communicate with anything that experienced consciousness, but he was also retarded.

It was assumed that he had been abandoned by a wanderer. Wanderers were extremely rare, but strangers had been known to pass by the Keep. Sweet, but slow, he had been named Freddie and accepted into the Keep despite the group's general fear and distrust of strangers. Then, he became attached to Drove Gardner. No one ever knew why, but Freddie followed Gardner around like a puppy, devoted in spite of Gardner's abuse.

Freddie held up a string of glass beads and shrank behind them as best he could.

I wasn't supposed to be seen, he stammered apologetically.

'What is going on?' demanded Sarah as she finally reined in beside Cia. She held her own strand of glass beads before her. Cia glanced at the girl impatiently.

'Put that away and be quiet. We may find out,' she snapped as she dropped her reins, slid from the horse and started towards the young man. Sarah closed her mouth, but continued to hold the string of beads defiantly before her. She remained astride her horse and reached for Cia's reins.

Freddie, why are you here? Cia asked more directly.

Mr Gardner told me I had to stay here and keep people away from the field, Freddie responded with pathetic eagerness. *You shouldn't go near the field; it's bad.*

Cia continued to approach Freddie slowly. She radiated trust and warmth as she reached out to him. *Why is it bad, Freddie?* she asked.

I dunno, Freddie responded uncomfortably. *Mr Gardner just said to keep people away from it. He said fog would be OK. Is it OK?* Freddie's expression became pleading as he sought Cia's approval.

I don't know, Freddie. What is in the field? Cia asked with a patience she didn't feel. She couldn't find Ian if Freddie didn't release his hold on the area.

Just a guy, Freddie responded grudgingly.

Is he hurt? Cia asked, knowing full well that Ian lay injured somewhere out there in Freddie's manufactured haze.

I think so, said Freddie.

I came to help him, Cia told him. *He needs my help. May I go to him?*

Mr Gardner didn't say anything about that, said Freddie. He shifted uncomfortably from foot to foot. This conversation was rapidly approaching the point where he might have to make a decision if he wasn't careful. The thought was making him extremely nervous.

Maybe I could just look at him? Cia asked. She sensed his discomfort and pressed her advantage.

Umm, said Freddie.

Freddie, said Cia gently, *he's hurt. I came to help. Please let me see him.*

Uh, Freddie said.

Freddie, is he dying? Cia asked.

I think so, Freddie responded.

Then you have to let me help him. You have to drop the fog and let me in. Do you want him to die? Cia tried to push Freddie. She was feeling desperate. This conversation was going nowhere fast.

No, ma'am. I don't want him to die. He seems nice. He's always nice to me, Freddie said miserably.

Then you've got to let us help him, Cia said firmly. *Please, Freddie. You've got to let us see him now.*

Freddie dropped his head and nodded at his boots. The fog slowly lifted and Cia could see clearly across the field.

'Quickly, Sarah,' she said as she swung on to her horse and started into the field that appeared beside them.

Sarah was already trotting across the broken ground towards the still figure lying on the dirt. Tears streaked her face as she dropped to the ground beside Ian's motionless body and began her mental probes to determine the damage. 'Ian, oh please, Ian,' she murmured over and over as she stroked his hair back from his forehead and reached for a heartbeat or some other sign that he lived.

'Cia!' she cried.

I'm here. Cia touched Sarah's mind. She bent to examine the spear, but it was embedded too deeply to be removed in the field without risking permanent damage. Carefully, she broke the haft above where it protruded from his arm. *We've got to get him home. We can't help him here.*

With Freddie's help, they managed to hoist Ian on to the back of Sarah's saddle and tie him securely to her waist and across her shoulders. As they started back along the path they had followed, Cia turned to Freddie. The man/boy stood twisting the hem of his shirt between spatulate fingers and staring at the two women on horseback.

Thank you, she said. Then she and Sarah began the

slow journey back to the Keep. Freddie stared after them, bobbing his head.

Once Cia and Sarah got Ian back to the Keep, they had help from Lukken and Treb carrying him into the healing room and holding him while the spear was extricated from his ribs and forearm. Then Cia was able to clean the wounds with soap and water while Sarah placed quartz crystals above Ian's head and below his feet, each pointed away from his body. These would act to draw the poisons out. Then she held spheres of malachite and rose quartz against his heart to draw out the poison and begin healing the damage Drove Gardner had done.

As often as Cia cleared and balanced a new sphere, Sarah replaced the contaminated one on Ian's chest and continued to clean his blood and tissues of the toxins.

After several hours, Sarah was exhausted, but the ragged edges of Ian's wounds showed signs of improvement and he stirred restlessly. Opening her eyes, Sarah leaned back in her chair and drew a deep breath. 'We can administer a sleeping draught now,' she said on a controlled exhale. She rubbed gritty eyes with the backs of her hands and stood slowly. 'I've done as much as I can.'

Cia pretended not to hear the sobs Sarah was fighting to hide, as she raised Ian's head and placed the cup to his lips. He choked a little as he swallowed the milky-grey liquid, but didn't regain consciousness. Cia laid him back against the down pillows, bathed his wounds again and carefully bandaged his arm and chest. She pulled the blanket up to his shoulders and went to where Sarah stood at the window.

'Take care of him for me,' she told the healer. Then she left the room.

'What do you mean, "Cia took him"?' Gardner was growing apoplectic, he was so angry. Freddie didn't think

45

Gardner had ever been this furious with him before. Drove's face was a purplish-red and contorted into a frightening mask that little resembled his own face. Freddie was scared. He flinched and threw his arm up to cover his face as the chair that was suspended above him crashed down on his head again. 'How did she know he was there?' Gardner bellowed as he raised the chair up with a flick of his finger.

'She just did,' Freddie whimpered, cringing in anticipation of the next blow. 'She said he was hurt.'

'I told you to keep that field fogged!' The chair descended for another onslaught. 'I told you to keep people away!'

'But the man was hurt,' Freddie protested.

Gardner yelled incoherently in frustration and flung the chair with such force that it shattered against Freddie's body and drew blood in several places, raised welts in others. 'Next time, you will obey me! You will do exactly as I tell you or you won't live to regret it!'

Gardner wouldn't actually kill Freddie, he was much too valuable for that, but it didn't hurt to use the threat to keep him in line. Drove resented his dependence on Freddie, but the fact remained: Freddie was a powerful telepath, and Drove was not.

It had always bothered Gardner that he couldn't hear the jokes that the telepathic children told each other, and couldn't share in their laughter. His gift had never unfolded the way the telepaths' did. He was capable of psychokinetic activity, but he never heard the telepathed conversations. He was certain they were laughing at him.

His feeling of exclusion turned into a feeling of persecution, and one day he actually struck out at a boy who had been passing through the barnyard giggling, with the unfocused look associated with telepathic conversation. Drove had punched the boy in the side of the head with the invisible hand he had developed.

The boy had almost died from the blow, and after that, everyone was a bit afraid of Drove, and no one laughed during telepathic conversation in his presence. But somehow, that made Drove even angrier. Now he knew they were talking about him behind his back.

But then Freddie appeared in the Keep. Freddie allowed the women to pet him, and struggled to learn the skills the men tried to teach him, but he resisted forming attachments until the day he ran into Drove Gardner.

At first, Drove ignored the boy, but Freddie kept following him around, grinning, drooling and babbling incoherently. Drove yelled at Freddie, threatening him with psychokinesis, but Freddie continued to follow Gardner everywhere he went.

This went on for weeks. Finally, in frustration, Drove asked Freddie why.

Dada, Freddie said to Gardner's mind, and smiled trustingly up at him.

Gardner reeled under the impact of the word, and his first experience with telepathy. Freddie had been with him ever since, allowing him access to a gift he didn't possess, but that didn't make him any less angry about his lack of telepathic ability. Now he usually took that anger out on Freddie.

Gardner stomped angrily from the ramshackle front room where Freddie now crouched, trying not to cry too loudly for fear of angering him further. Wrapped up in his own misery, Freddie paid no attention to the voices in the next room.

Cia sat in the solitude of the meditation room. She sat on the floor in her centre, facing Philip. He held her hands in both of his, with amethyst and quartz crystals clasped between their palms. He rocked back and forth, black eyes staring into Cia's grey ones as she swayed with him. The energies flowed between them, amplified by the crystals, in a circle from his right hand to her left, through her body and out of her right hand to his left. As the energy passed through Philip, he modified the patterns.

Do you feel what I am doing? he asked her as he began sending the changed energies to Cia. She nodded, concentrating on the pattern, trying to grasp its significance. She felt the differences that Philip had created, sending them back to him with subtle changes of her own. *No*, he said, negating Cia's additions and sending back the one he had created. *I am not teaching you to modify energy patterns, although that was a good effort. This pattern I send you now, you must memorize. Make it a part of you.*

Why? Cia asked as she felt the energy flow back into her. The pattern was complicated and oddly twisted. Where it should have flowed freely, it was clogged and congested. There were connections where none should exist and overall, it made little sense. *It doesn't feel right. I'm not comfortable with it at all*, she objected.

This is why you taught Ian to read, Philip chuckled.

I taught Ian to read because you told me to, Cia contradicted. *Wouldn't it have made more sense to teach me how to pull the Keep together against Drove?*

Do you do everything I tell you? he asked.

Yes.

What good would it do to try and counteract a man who could lay waste to your home and family? asked Philip. *Together your PKs aren't strong enough to hold him at bay. You may not recall the effort that was made when he was still a boy?*

Cia shook her head.

Every once in a while, a really gifted psi-mechanic comes along. If they aren't taught properly, they can get out of hand. Sometimes, even good teaching doesn't help, as in Drove's case. Sometimes, a kid is just bad. It isn't anyone's fault, it just happens, and then you have to deal with it. Or maybe you should all be asking yourselves if a little kindness would have been so difficult. In any case, the Keep isn't strong enough in and of itself. You need help. That's why I taught you to teach Ian to read, and you do everything I tell you. Why? he pressed.

Because so far, you've always been right! she admitted, once again absorbing the strange distortion of energy. *Who has such a jammed-up pattern?*

Memorize it! Philip commanded as he disappeared.

I hate it when you do that! Cia yelled after him.

He had left the crystals in her hands. Closing her fingers over them, she placed her hands palm-up on her knees and breathed deeply in and out. Philip had programmed the peculiar energy into the amethyst, so Cia concentrated on it, wondering what tortures produced such blockage and unnatural distortion. Properly channelled, it could be a truly beautiful and powerful combination.

Before she was sure of every nuance, however, Cia felt the trauma of the day catch up with her and she lost her concentration. Rising out of the meditation level, she was surprised to find herself gripping an amethyst crystal of flawless colour and cut in her left hand, and a clear double-terminated quartz in her right. She stared at them a moment before tucking them into her side pockets. With a shrug, she set off towards the healing chamber.

Ian lay still in the centre of the bed. His blond hair stuck damply to his scalp. His face was pale grey in the flickering light of the wall sconce, and sweat beaded on his forehead and in his moustache.

Sarah held on to his hand. Her string of glass beads was clasped between them, pressing their shape into her palm uncomfortably, but she dared not remove them. She sat on a stool beside the bed and bent over Ian, alternately stroking his arm, and pushing her bedraggled black curls out of her eyes. Sarah looked up as Cia came into the darkened room. The tall, slender, silver-haired woman intimidated her. Cia always managed to make Sarah feel small and dowdy and incompetent without doing a thing. Sarah shifted uncomfortably. Ian, in contact with Sarah, stirred restlessly in response.

'There has been no change,' Sarah said unnecessarily. When she received no reply, she turned back to the unmoving young man. 'The last torch is guttering.'

Cia crossed to stand beside the bed and placed her hand on Ian's forehead.

'There's nothing else to counteract the poison?' Cia turned and looked down at Sarah. The girl's dark eyes were red-rimmed; the skin around her lids puffy and bruised from lack of sleep.

'I've tried everything I know. There's no cure but time and his body's ability to fight,' Sarah said, not looking up. 'Ian is strong.'

Cia nodded.

'I have been in contact with him, but he needs his strength to fight off the toxins, so I have partially withdrawn to observe.' With a small gesture of frustration, Sarah turned back to the bed.

'Gardner's forcing my hand,' Cia mused aloud. 'You'll call me if there are any changes?' she asked Sarah.

'Of course,' Sarah murmured, not taking her eyes from Ian's face.

'I'll send someone to attend the torch,' Cia said as she left the room.

Dinner had long since been cleared away and the kitchen was empty when Cia wandered in. Rummaging through the pantry she began to realize how hungry she was. She put the platter of smoked meat on the table and found a wheel of cheese and some butter to go with her bread. Setting out a pitcher of water to wash down her meal, she hitched a stool out with her foot. She stuffed a piece of meat into her mouth and sat down.

'Unnhm,' croaked a familiar voice from the doorway behind her.

Cia felt her shoulders tense at the sound. 'Good evening, Dalt,' she said through her mouthful without turning around.

'May I join you?' he asked. His voice grated like crystal on glass. He came up close behind her, breathing on her shoulder and neck.

'Must you?' she asked. She turned suddenly with her elbow levelled and whacked him in the side of the face. 'Oh, sorry,' she smiled sweetly at him. 'I didn't know you were standing there. Didn't you eat earlier?'

Dalt glared at her, rubbing his right cheek as he tried to recover his composure. He ran his tobacco-stained fingers through his sparse, wiry grey hair and tugged at his robes.

'Yes,' he said, still glowering. 'Where were you?' He retied his sash above his ample belly. He looked like a pregnant crone.

'Elsewhere,' Cia said, still smiling. She turned back to her meal, buttered a slice of bread and layered meat and cheese on it. Dalt cleared his throat again, but stayed well clear of her elbow.

'What do you want, Dalt?' she asked, trying to contain her impatience. Love, balance and harmony, she thought to herself. Love, balance and harmony.

'Well, it's just that we were worried,' he began.

Cia laughed out loud. Putting down her sandwich, she turned back to him. He backed a step away and his hand stole unconsciously to his neck for his beads. He stood twisting them as he watched her, eyes wide with fright.

Age had not been kind to Dalt. His irregular features had coarsened and drooped, so that his face looked as if it were in the process of melting. His eyes, once a brilliant and piercing blue, had faded and their whites were now yellowed and bloodshot. His eyebrows had begun falling out as his hairline receded. Now mostly bald, he had the appearance of an oddly plucked fowl.

'Dalt, the only person you ever worried about was yourself. You haven't even asked how Ian is. Why don't you go away and let me eat my dinner in peace?'

'Cia, you treat me so harshly!' Dalt objected. 'I was going to get around to the boy, of course. It's just that it's so unsafe outside the Keep at night, and when you missed dinner, well naturally we got worried. Where did you go?'

Cia inhaled sharply, air hissing between her teeth. She rose from her stool and pointed a long, slender finger at the door. 'Get out, now,' she said.

Dalt opened his mouth, closed it again and left the kitchen. He wanted to get out of this situation as soon as possible. Retreating to his room, he sat on the bed and sent a thought to Freddie.

Yes, sir? came the immediate reply. Dalt jumped. He'd grown up a Deaf, and never got over how strange it felt to have other voices talking in his head.

Freddie, tell Gardner I need to talk to him.

Cia finished her supper and wrapped a sandwich for Sarah in a clean cloth. She tucked the bundle into a pocket, gathered up her candle and the water pitcher, and walked softly through the hallways to the healing room to check Ian's progress.

Sarah looked blearily at Cia as she entered the room.

'I brought your supper,' Cia whispered, placing the pitcher on the table beside the bed. She dripped wax from the candle on to its wooden surface and set the candle into it to hold it upright, then fished the sandwich out of her pocket. 'I'll watch him for a while. You eat.'

Sarah nodded and attacked the food silently, gulping water between bites.

Cia sat on the edge of the bed and smoothed Ian's hair from his forehead. He looked much younger lying there so quietly, she thought. His skin still had a grey pallor, but he was no longer sweating as profusely. Cia felt his neck for his pulse and found it surprisingly strong.

'When you've finished that, why don't you ground and centre?' Cia suggested to Sarah. Sarah nodded, chewing a very large mouthful. 'I don't suppose it would do any good to tell you to go back to your room and get some sleep?'

'No,' Sarah said, reaching for the pitcher. 'Even if I went back to my room, I wouldn't be able to sleep, so I might as well stay here and see if I can't find something to try that I haven't thought of yet.'

Cia smiled at her. 'I still have work to do tonight, too. I'll feel a lot better about having you here with him. I know you haven't had an easy time of it. Being in love with Ian implies certain social risks and we both appreciate what you've been through on his behalf. I'm afraid that the risks have now become physical as well, and I'm not sure that Ian is the only target.'

'What are you saying?' Sarah asked. She wiped her mouth on the cloth and folded it meticulously over and over.

'Dalt was asking me questions earlier. I just want you to be careful, OK? I'm not trying to scare you.'

'OK,' Sarah nodded, wide-eyed. She slid out of her chair and sat cross-legged on the floor. She placed her hands palm-up on her knees and closed her eyes.

As Sarah performed her grounding and centring exercises, Cia watched her, monitoring quietly from the periphery. Sarah's fair skin was extremely pale, emphasizing the puffy, dark areas beneath her eyes. Freckles stood out on her short, straight nose and moisture gathered on her chin and forehead.

Cia envisioned a white light surrounding and cleansing the healing room and then the Keep. She saw Sarah and Ian bathed in the light and watched as Sarah's shoulders straightened and her breathing became more regular. Ian murmured something incoherent, his fingers plucking at the covers.

We will all be safe tonight, at least, Cia thought. She lit a smudge of sage and sweetgrass. As she blew gently on the tiny flame, she sprinkled ganja leaves over it. Making a circuit of the room, she fanned the smoke towards the centre, cleansing the energies that Sarah and Ian were drawing on. Then she passed the malachite and rose quartz spheres through the smoke, clearing them as well and rendering impotent the poison they had absorbed.

'I always liked the smell of smudge,' Sarah said. She stood up and stretched slowly. 'I'm not sure whether it's because the room always seems so clean afterwards, or because of the smell of the herbs burning.'

Cia turned. 'Maybe both. Shall I smudge you, too?'

'Yeah,' Sarah grinned. She backed away from the bed into the open space and closed her eyes. Cia bent and waved the smoke on to Sarah's feet. Moving in circles around her, Cia continued to fan the smoke on to Sarah all the way up her legs to her torso, around her chest and shoulders, face and over the top of her head.

'There,' Cia said. 'Better?'

'Much, thanks,' said Sarah.

'Well, we've both got a long night before us,' Cia said, tapping at the smouldering herbs to extinguish them. 'I'll be in the meditation room, but I'll keep an ear out if you need me.'

Sarah nodded.

'It will be all right,' said Cia gently and left Sarah to her vigil.

The meditation room was dark and silent. Cia's candle cast long, jumpy shadows on the walls and ceiling. The pillows on the floor looked like bodies. Cia suppressed a shudder as she picked her way among them to the nearest wall sconce.

As the flame of the candle blazed into the torch, light grew in the room and the pillows and shadows lost much of their malevolence. Cia drew a shaky breath and blew out the candle. She hadn't realized how much Dalt's questioning disturbed her. The undefined feeling of dread that had been growing steadily since afternoon now prickled her mind, setting off alarms she couldn't ignore.

After a brief grounding exercise, Cia centred and found Philip waiting for her, standing in the empty corner beside the dais. As she crossed the chamber towards him, she caught a flicker in the corner of her eye. She froze and caught her breath.

There's nothing there! Stop this! She closed her eyes and slowly opened them again. There was nothing there. With a small frown, Cia turned again towards Philip.

How did you get in? she demanded. No one could enter or leave someone else's centre without permission. That's what a centre was for: a beautiful, quiet, private place in which to work with the Higher Selves. Cia had never come into her centre and found it occupied except the one time she forgot to tell the person to leave. He had wreaked havoc. She had never again forgotten.

You were broadcasting for me, promising you'd be here shortly, said Philip, laughing.

I was? I did?

Everyone else heard you. You weren't aware you were doing it? Philip found this vastly amusing.

Well, I'm really worried, Cia said defensively. *Ian is very ill, and you keep giving me incompatible pieces to a puzzle and Drove grows bolder by the moment. I'm afraid that soon I won't be able to protect Ian or Sarah, or myself.*

Sit down, Philip ordered. Cia sat. Philip sat opposite her and took her hands in his. *Where are the crystals?*

Cia dropped his hands to fish in her pockets for the amethyst and quartz that he had left her with. *Here*, she said, holding them up. Rolling them into her palms, she held out her hands to him. He folded his cool, dry fingers over hers and closed his eyes.

Send me the pattern contained within the amethyst, he directed. *Send it as strongly as you can. Fill me with its energies.*

Cia closed her eyes also, and concentrated on contorting her own energy pattern into the blocked and damaged one that Philip had left her to memorize. When the last congested path was complete, she gathered all the power the pattern would permit her and hurled it at Philip through the quartz crystal in her right palm.

With a shock, she felt it hurled right back through the amethyst in her left palm.

This is not a game! Philip admonished her. *I said send it, not use it as a weapon! You asked for the other pieces of the puzzle, but you refuse to see that this is the most important one! How can I teach you if you will not learn?*

I'm sorry, said Cia. She eased the energy flowing through her and corrected the pattern where it had deviated in transmission. A picture of Nina being insolent during class flashed into her mind.

Philip laughed. *If you want to draw comparisons, that's as good a one as any!*

Intractable child? Thanks a lot! exclaimed Cia. *So when do you put some of these pieces into place?*

There are some things you must learn still, including patience, but I can shed some light on the situation, said Philip. *You can relax your energy now.*

Thanks. Cia released Philip's hands and pocketed the crystals, allowing her energies to flow back into their normal pattern. *That one is pretty cramped.*

Her name is Meg.

What?

Her name is Meg, Philip repeated. *She is an extremely powerful telepath. She is also telekinetic and a rather gifted psi-mechanic.*

Telekinetic? You mean she doesn't know how to use it? Cia asked, surprised.

She doesn't know she possesses any of it, Philip replied. *She is at present an extremely sick child and needs your help even more than Ian does.*

But what does that have to do with Ian and Drove?

You need her help to solve that problem. She has the power to defeat Gardner, but you must first heal her and then enlist her aid, said Philip.

Where is she? asked Cia.

She comes from Before, Philip answered. *The question is when is she?*

The continuum, Cia breathed. *Why can't her people help her?*

They don't understand the problem. They don't have the tools to diagnose and heal her.

She went through the Unfolding by herself? Cia exclaimed indignantly. *The poor child! Did she have any training in centring and meditation at all prior to the Unfolding? How old is she now?*

The pattern you memorized was taken when Meg was about two years old. Her mind Unfolded at birth, Philip told Cia. *You must focus on that exact pattern, because those energies are recognizable later in Meg's life in a slightly altered form.*

What do you mean 'later in Meg's life'? asked Cia. *I thought you said she was two years old.*

Time complicates things, Philip sighed. *In your here-and-now, Meg has been dead for hundreds of years. Once you are in the continuum, you can touch any point in her life by tracing her energy pattern. They're unique; no two people's are alike. Each one of us leaves a mark in the threads that make up the continuum.*

I think I understand. Next, I have to learn to work in the continuum while I'm on meditation level instead of dream-state, Right? Cia jumped to her feet and began pacing.

Exactly! laughed Philip. *It will take time and concentration, so get to it!*

3

Morning seemed to come earlier than usual. Bright sunlight shone through the window which Cia hadn't remembered to cover the night before. The crystals on the sill sparkled in contrast to the dusty panes of glass. The room was neat, if plain. A bed, a chair, a chest of drawers stood on the clean-swept, bare stone floor. The only decoration on the walls was a meditation mandala worked in silk threads. Ancient and faded, it was the only thing of beauty in the room. Three wooden pegs had been driven into the door. A blue robe of rough homespun hung from one peg; a white robe of slightly finer material hung from another. The empty peg was for the brown robe Cia had fallen asleep in.

From the activity outside her window, Cia guessed that it was still early. Morning chores, milking, feeding the animals, were well under way. Breakfast would be ready soon after. If she didn't move now, she wouldn't get a decent bath until after lessons this afternoon. She didn't want to be near herself right now. By end of lessons she would be intolerable.

She sat up and swung her legs off the side of the bed. Her head was pounding and her tongue felt thick. She'd have got more sleep if she'd covered the window, but she probably wouldn't have felt any better. Grabbing the blue robe from the back of the door, Cia padded barefoot down the hallway to the bathroom.

Several people were there, standing shivering in the tubs, pouring water from buckets over themselves to rinse off the soap. Cia picked up several empty buckets and took them to the pump to refill them. The pumping was a vigorous exercise first thing in the morning, and just the thing she liked to warm herself up to functioning. When the buckets were full, she carried them two at a time back to the tubs.

'Thanks,' said Treb, taking the bucket Cia handed him. She smiled and moved on to the next tub. The little girl stood shaking and sniffling in a tub full of dirty water.

'Rose, you know better than to climb into a tub that hasn't been emptied!' Cia scolded gently, lifting the wet child out of the tub and moving her to an empty one.

'It's not just that.' Rose's chin quivered. 'I got soap in my eyes! I was trying to wash my hair by myself. Then I couldn't find a bucket . . .'

'Here, come on, now. It's OK.' Cia went to get one of the buckets she had filled and took it back to Rose. 'Here,' she said. 'Tip your head back and I'll rinse your hair for you. That way, we can get the soap out of your eyes without getting any more in. How's that?'

'OK,' Rose snuffled, tilting her face to the ceiling.

Cia rinsed her off and flooded her eyes with water to remove the soap. 'Better?' she asked.

Rose nodded. 'Thanks,' she said shyly. She jumped out of the tub and went to get drying rags from the pile on the table in the corner.

Cia emptied both of Rose's basins and pumped more water for her own bath. Then she stripped off her dirty brown robe and stepped into a tub. First thing in the morning, the well water always felt colder than melting snow to Cia. She gasped as it coursed over her scalp and body, raising goose bumps. The soap was soft and slimy, but it lathered well and shortly, she was covered head to toe in white foam. The second bucket seemed almost warm after standing in the cold morning air sudsing up.

Mareki came by with more full buckets and handed one to Cia. 'How is Ian?' she asked.

'It's still too soon to tell, but we think he'll be all right,' said Cia. 'Thank you for asking. I appreciate your concern.' She smiled at Mareki. The girl smiled back solemnly and gathered more buckets to fill for her own bath. Mareki was close to Ian and Sarah in age, but even as a small child, had seemed old beyond her years. She was extremely beautiful with fair, unblemished skin and coppery hair, but her jade-green eyes hinted at knowledge and wisdom that a girl her age shouldn't have. Always quiet, she had drawn into herself in recent years and put up blocks in her mind that resisted Cia's attempts to penetrate. She spent long periods of time by herself.

Cia finished rinsing the soap out of her hair and off her body, emptied her tub and wrung her hair out over the sink. Without towelling or combing it out, she divided her hair into three locks and braided them together into a thick, silver cord that fell almost to her knees. Then she went to the table for drying cloths and her blue robe. Once dressed, she gathered her dirty brown robe and used drying cloths and left the bath. She stopped off in the laundry to toss the filthy clothes into a basket.

Then she went to the healing room.

Sarah lay with her head on the pillow beside Ian's. She still sat on the stool beside his bed, but some time during the night, her exhaustion had caught up with her and she slept. In the morning light, Ian's colour looked much better and his breathing had deepened and become more regular.

Sarah looked even more bedraggled than she had the night before. Her normally pale complexion was now a translucent white-blue and her eyes were sunken, darkly bruised. As Cia came into the room and closed the door, Sarah awoke with a start and rose from the pillow.

'I only just – ' she began, trying to smooth her dress and push her hair from her face. A lock caught on her cracked, dried lower lip and she gasped in pain as it tore the skin. With a gesture towards the bed, she sucked her lip into her mouth and looked pleadingly at Cia.

'I know,' Cia reassured her. 'I came to watch Ian while you go bathe and get some breakfast. Surely Jack can relieve you today so you can get some sleep?' Jack had been Sarah's teacher in healing arts after Cia had taught her everything she could. He had been glad to retire from the position of Keep Healer when Sarah was able to take over, but he still maintained his discipline and taught children who were potential healers. 'Stop in and tell him that after his breakfast, I'll need him to take over so that I can teach the morning classes.'

Sarah nodded wordlessly. She gestured towards the bed again.

Cia crossed the room in two strides and wrapped the younger woman in a bony embrace. *It's going to be all right,* she murmured into Sarah's mind. *He's going to be fine.* She held Sarah away from her again. 'Now go take a bath and get some food into you. You'll feel much better.'

Still sucking her lip, Sarah bobbed her head and left the room.

Cia moved towards the bed and placed her hand against Ian's forehead. His fever had broken during the night, but recovery was still a long way off, and the damage of the poison unknown. She pulled the stool over and sat down.

The door pushed open and Dalt entered backwards, hunched slightly in an effort to make himself unobtrusive. Silently, he closed the door again and turned around. When he saw Cia, he gasped. Then he straightened his shoulders and stood upright. 'Cia!' he said jovially. 'You look lovely this morning. I trust you slept well? I came to see how the boy was doing.'

'You saw Sarah on her way to the bathroom and thought you might spend some time alone with him?' she asked.

'Why, yes. Yes, that's exactly right,' said Dalt, crossing to the foot of the bed.

'Indeed.'

'Yes, "indeed"! Your suspicion is unwarranted. I'm surprised at you,' he protested.

Cia looked at Dalt and sighed. 'What's happened to you?' she asked finally.

'To me?' Dalt seemed more amused than angry. 'You raise a lunatic son and seem bound and determined to disrupt the Keep, and you want to know what's happened to me?' Laughing, he came around the bed and sat down on the edge by Ian's feet. He patted Ian's leg under the blankets.

'What's happened to you?' she asked again. 'Has being a Deaf been so difficult that it warped the man you were into this . . . this thing? This tool of Gardner's? You always wanted things to be easy. Wasn't our vision of a better life worth fighting for? Why do you hinder *my* fight?'

'Are you going to breakfast now?' Dalt asked, idly plucking at the blankets.

'You don't get it, do you? You never understood what this was all about. Were you just going along, hoping to seduce me?' Cia asked sadly.

'Why don't you go get some breakfast? I'll sit with the boy for a while,' Dalt suggested.

'And do what, remove his bandages and pour more nerve poison into his wounds? I'd have to be blind not to see the packet in your hand; and stupid not to recognize a surreptitious entrance! You're pathetic. Get out of here!'

'Really, Cia. You, fearful?' Dalt chuckled. 'You know, someday you'll have to let go of those strings you keep him bound with. You're much too overprotective. He's a man of twenty years now. Isn't it time you stood back and let him take his own falls?'

'I just don't want him to turn out like his father,' Cia said tiredly. 'You still can't even bring yourself to call Ian by his name. Go away, Dalt. Tell Gardner he'll have to come up with something better.'

'I'll leave, but I still think you're overreacting.' Dalt stood up and patted Cia on the arm. She stiffened and moved away from his touch. 'Fine, then.' He stalked from the room.

When Jack came at last to stay with Ian, Cia warned him about Dalt's unwelcome attention.

'Sarah will undoubtedly be back as soon as she awakens, Jack. Thanks for your help,' she said. Her first stop was the kitchen to devour a bowl of porridge before going to the classroom to begin the morning lessons.

The youngest children had lessons in the morning. Until the age of ten, their only obligation was to learn the tools of meditation and the powers and uses of crystals, and discover any special gifts and inclinations they might possess. By that time, unfolding had occurred if it was going to.

Unfolding was both a proud and frightening time for children. Their minds were opening to the special gifts that would separate them from the closed-minded, or Deaf-Mutes, enhancing their position in the Keep. But also, their minds were suddenly flooded with images and sensations never before experienced. The inability to make sense of the new information was terrifying. It usually took several days, and the constant serial vigilance of every telepath in the Keep, to pull an unfolding child through the trauma.

At the age of ten, the children who had not unfolded were set to a round of six-month 'apprenticeships', learning every aspect of Keep maintenance, including farming, livestock, carpentry, glassworks, quarrying and jewellery-making, irrigation and well maintenance, tanning and leather work, spinning and weaving, garment manufacture, cooking and cleaning. They worked at their apprenticeships in the morning while the younger children had lessons. After lunch, they went to the classroom for an hour of meditation before returning to the barns, sheds and fields.

The children who had unfolded spent their mornings in apprenticeship also, but after the meditation hour, they stayed in the classroom and studied to learn control of their gifts. Telepaths had to learn how not to broadcast their thoughts and emotions before learning how to send specific transmissions. Psychokinetics especially had to be harnessed and taught discipline and strict ethics early, and pyrokinetics also needed to learn when and where it was not appropriate to make fires.

By the time the Deaf-Mute children had reached the age of fifteen, they were allowed to choose the special area of work they wanted to pursue. Until they achieved Craftsman status, however, they would continue their six-month rotation through the other areas in the mornings, and study their chosen field in the afternoons after meditation.

Evenings were devoted to storytelling and recitation in the common room. This was the largest single room in the Keep and the best lit. Here, the elders told the children the stories of the Keep and its history. Some of the stories were only for entertainment, but most of them were to be memorized by the children. Every few nights, a different child would stand before the group and repeat one of the stories, enduring much good-natured correction and teasing in the process. The adults sat and listened as they cleaned and repaired tack, mended clothing, whittled, knitted.

At the age of twenty, adult status within the Keep community was declared. It was celebrated with a feast, and the new adult was allowed to move out of the children's dormitories into a single room. This didn't mean that psychic training had been completed, or that Craftsman status would be conferred. As adults, though, they would be entitled to form alliances and have children of their own if they chose. They were released from afternoon meditation, although many of them enjoyed it and continued to participate. They would no longer be called upon to recite stories in the evening, but again, they could do so if they wished. They were also considered fully responsible for their words and actions.

Those who had unfolded still continued their rotations through Keep chores, unless they became teachers like Cia and Jack. Even Sarah still went through rotation unless there was illness demanding her skills as healer. Telepaths were exempt when a child unfolded.

Among the Deaf-Mute, only Craftsmen no longer did rotation, but they were expected to assist in emergencies so that the Keep would continue to function efficiently.

As Cia entered the classroom, heads swivelled and small faces looked expectantly up at her.

'Good morning,' she said, pulling the door shut behind her.

'Good morning, Cia,' they responded dutifully.

Cia walked to the front of the room, pausing briefly to dangle Nina's string of beads before the girl.

'I have cleared and restrung these for you,' said Cia. 'I suggest in future you are more careful how you treat them or that you not wear them at all.'

Nina slipped the strand over her head and Cia noticed that the girl had another necklace on already. Probably her mother had given her one immediately after the original one broke. Shaking her head, she crossed to her pillow and sat down.

'Have you grounded yourselves yet?' she asked the group. The children all shook their heads no. 'Well, then.

Sit up straight, relax your muscles, hands open, palms-up on your knees. Close your eyes and breathe in deeply. Hold it. Now exhale slowly and feel the tension leaving your muscles.' Chests obediently rose and fell at her command. The children, fourteen in this group, sat in a semi-circle around her pillow breathing deeply. The group seemed to get smaller each year, and with fewer children waiting to be old enough to join, Cia thought as she sat and watched them until she sensed the energies they emanated becoming calm.

'Now, open the top of your head to the sky so that there is nothing between the air and your brain. Feel the energies from above and pull them into a column of white light.' Cia kept her voice modulated low as she spoke so that her suggestions would not distract her students from their task. 'Bring that column down from the sky and into your head through the opening you made. Feel the energy as it opens your third eye, the sixth chakra, and continues down. Remember to keep breathing deeply.'

Looking around the circle, many of the faces were tensed in concentration. This group seemed awfully young to Cia. Most of them were between five and seven. Only five of the children needed to be watched for possible unfolding, but that was probably not an immediate worry, she thought.

'Relax your forehead now as you pull the white light further into you. Feel it cleanse and open your chakras. Relax your cheeks and mouth. Let your mouths fall open. Now your chin and neck muscles. Draw the white light into your chests and feel your heart pumping, slow and strong; steady and smooth. Relax your shoulders and arms, your chest and belly. Pull the light down into your gonads and feel the white light open your first chakra, strengthening your life force. Remember to breathe.'

Cia continued to run through the litany, wondering how many times she had done this before. The names changed, but she noticed that the faces never really did. 'Let the white light flow out from your spine and through the floor into the earth. Sink the column of white light far into Mother Earth, almost to her core. Now open the light into a huge bubble in the earth. Feel all your problems and tensions coursing down into the bubble. Everything that is bothering you, making you unhappy, send it into the earth, into your bubble. When you are empty and relaxed, sit and look at the garbage you dumped in that bubble and thank Mother Earth for accepting and cleansing your garbage for you. Thank her for helping you to ground yourself.

'Right now, you look like a tree. You are drawing energies from the sky into a trunk and sending that trunk into the ground to become roots. This connects you to your higher self, and to the earth; a balance between what you are striving for and where you are now.

'OK, squeeze the bubble into a pinpoint of bright light. Squeeze as tightly as you can, until it is as small as you can get it. Bring it slowly back up the column. Feel the renewed energy in it. As you slowly rise to the surface, take a small piece of earth with you. Bring this up through the floor, into the base of your spine and up through your body until it reaches your heart. Let the piece of earth lodge there, to keep Mother Earth close to you in the healing area. Continue bringing the light up through your throat and head, back out the top and let the energy flow free. Close the top of your head. Continue breathing and open your eyes when you feel ready.'

When all of the children had opened their eyes, Cia smiled, looking around the circle at each of them. 'Today is a special day for one of you,' she said. 'Rose? You washed your hair by yourself today, didn't you?'

Rose nodded, smiling up at Cia. She sat up a little straighter.

'Do you think you're old enough to discover your own centre?' Cia asked her.

Rose's mouth fell open. She looked around the circle before looking back at Cia. Her eyes were shining as she nodded wordlessly.

'May I help you?' asked Cia.

Rose couldn't contain herself any longer. She jumped up and ran to hug Cia. 'Can I really? Will you please?'

Laughing, Cia hugged her back. 'I know this is very exciting, but you have to be calm in order to drop into meditation level. Go lie down on the pillows and do some deep-breathing exercises.' Cia rumpled Rose's hair and gently disengaged herself from the small girl.

Rose went back to the pillows and lay down. Closing her eyes, she began to breathe with a fierce scowl of concentration on her face.

'Now, for the rest of you, since you already have centres, I want you to follow along on this exercise and just spend time wandering around in your centres becoming more acquainted with them,' Cia said. 'Now, everyone, lie back and close your eyes. Rose, are you listening?'

Rose's eyes popped open. 'Yes!' she exclaimed.

'Close your eyes,' Cia told her. 'Now, you are standing at the top of a staircase in a dark so complete, you can't see your hand in front of your face. Picture your body as it is lying on the floor. Surround yourself with the colour red. Your whole body is enveloped by the colour red as you step down one step. Remember to breathe. Now you are surrounded by orange. Surround your entire body with the colour orange as you take another step down. Feel your muscles relax and your mind clear as you surround your body in yellow. Suffuse your aura with a bright-yellow glow and take another step down the stairs, remembering to breathe deeply and evenly.'

As often as she had done this particular exercise, Cia

never tired of the enthusiasm of a child visualizing a centre for the first time. Rose lay on her pillows trying hard to relax which, of course, defeated the purpose. Gently, Cia touched Rose's mind and murmured a few calming words to her. The little girl's forehead smoothed and her breathing deepened. Her fists unclenched and she smiled slightly.

'Now your body is surrounded in a rich green light. See your aura become a healthy green as you take another step down the staircase. Your muscles are relaxing more as your mind becomes clearer. You are enveloped in blue light as you step down again. You are nearing the bottom of the stairs and are almost completely relaxed. Surround yourself in lavender and feel its properties enter your body. It lifts your energies to a state where you can work in your centre and it frees your mind to accomplish anything. Take another step down and see that you have reached the bottom step. In front of you is a beautiful fountain of white light. Take the last step down and go to the fountain. Climb into it and bathe in the light. Feel it cleanse you, entering your body and purifying its energies as it clears your mind.'

Cia felt the energy in the room shift as the children altered their outputs.

'When you are finished, step out of the fountain and look around you. You are no longer in the dark. In front of you is a forest. Picture this forest. What kind of trees are in this wood? Are they densely packed, or more thinly placed? Is there a great deal of underbrush, or none at all? Can you see the sky above you, or is the leaf canopy too thick, blocking out the sun? Are there birds in the trees, and are they singing? Take a moment to explore what the edge of the forest is like. Don't enter it yet; just look at it and discover what makes it special to you.'

Rose's smile widened slightly as she developed her mental image of the forest. Cia smiled, watching her and remembering how she had felt as her first teacher had walked her through the ritual.

'Walk to the edge of the forest now. Before you is a path leading into the woods. Visualize the path. Is it smooth or rough? Wide or narrow? Does it go uphill or down? Step on to it and follow the path into the woods. Does it continue along in a straight line, or curve into the trees?

'Beside the path is a stream. Look at the stream. Again, is it wide or narrow? Rocky or smooth? Are there trees between the stream and the path, or does the path run along its banks? Are there fish in the stream? Look up as you walk. Are there birds in the branches and sky? Continue along the path and explore it as you go.'

Cia stood silently and walked around the room, concentrating on a white light, seeing it surround the children and herself. She went to the window-sill and took up the smudge pot. Placing a shredded heart of ganja in the pot, she struck a flint into the small pile and gently blew on the tiny flame. Smoke rose in a column which she fanned into the room as she walked back to where she had been sitting.

'Your path leaves the forest and you find yourself at the edge of a field. This field is the outer part of your centre. It is surrounded on all sides by the forest, and the path you have just left is the only way into or out of the field. Walk into it now. There is a pond and a rock. These are the only things in the field. Take some time to explore. Is the pond large? Small? Take a swim. Is it deep, or shallow? Has the sun warmed it, or is the water cold? Where in the field is it located in relation to the rock? How large is the rock? What kind of stone is it? Does it have a flat surface, or is it rounded? Pointed? What sort of grasses are in the field? Are they tall? Short? Green or gold?

'Visualize in infinite detail. The more you see, the more

you discover a place that is in all details unique to you. Your centre is your work-area. It is a place where you can go to be alone. It is the seat of your soul. Nothing here can ever hurt you unless you give it permission to. You can never drown in your pond. You can never get lost in your forest. You are always completely safe here, but it is a good idea to white light the field after you enter it, so that if any harmful energies follow you down the stairs and aren't cleansed by the fountain of white light, they will be unable to follow you into the field.'

Cia blew on the glowing herbs, dispersing the smoke over the inert bodies of the children on the floor.

'Your central chamber is accessible only from this field. There is no door from the outside. To get into it, just picture yourself there. It is a room, with walls, a floor and a ceiling. Walk around in it and see what the dimensions are. Is it a large room? Small? What materials is it made of? Picture the most beautiful things you can. The surfaces can be of wood, granite, diamond, crystal, anything that makes you feel good. Touch them and see what they are made of. Are there pictures or hangings on the walls? Pillows on the floor?

'There are two doors on opposite walls and beside each door is a torch in a wall sconce. They are lit and won't go out as long as you have minimal energy to maintain them. The doors are shut right now, but we will explore them later. One door is the way your guides and teachers will enter. The other is a private healing chamber, but we don't have the energy to look into them now. Remember that nothing in your centre can hurt you. If you decide to explore the healing centre on your own, that's fine. Do whatever feels right, and you will be fine.

'The door to let in other people, however, is to remain shut until we can open it together. Without knowing, you could let bad energies into your centre through the door. It's not likely, but I want to be sure you don't get hurt.

Spend some time in your central chamber now, looking around you and seeing in detail what it looks like.'

The herbs in the smudge pot had burned to ash. Cia took the pot back to the window-sill and tapped the ashes into the torch bucket that stood beside it. She replaced the pot and flint on the sill and turned to look around the room. Smoke hung in striated layers, lit by the sun coming in the window. The children lay silently on the floor, minds turned inwards, exploring their innermost beings, learning about and developing the resources that lay within themselves.

Cia sat back down again and took a deep breath. 'Now, leave your central chamber. Again, you do not go through a door. Just picture yourself standing in the field again. Go back to the path that led you here. Follow the path through the forest, back to the fountain of white light. You may bathe in it again if you like.' She paused a moment, allowing them to do so. 'When you are through, go to the stairs and climb on to the first step. You are beginning to rise up out of meditation level, now. Your mind is coming back to the conscious level. Take another step up and feel your body lying on the floor. As you continue to climb the stairs, feel yourself coming back into the classroom in the Keep. There is no need to move quickly. Remember to breathe slowly. When you reach the top of the stairs, stand there a moment and reorient yourself. Feel the floor beneath you and open your eyes when you are ready.'

When, at last, all of the children had opened their eyes and sat up, Cia looked at Rose. 'Did you see your centre?' she asked.

'Yes!' said Rose. 'It's so beautiful! The walls are smooth, polished wood with gold set into the spaces between the boards. The torch sconces are gold with garnets set into the bands and the doors have gold knobs. The floor is made of slabs of polished quartz and so is the ceiling. There are huge, thick pillows all over the floor, but there's nothing on the walls. I didn't want to cover the pretty gold bands,' she confided.

'Good,' Cia nodded approvingly. 'Are you comfortable there? Are you happy with the way everything looks?'

'Oh, yes!' said Rose.

Cia smiled at her. 'Then I'm pleased also. I will give you a few days to spend time there exploring your centre and the field around it. Then, we will introduce you to your guide. He or she will be available to you to teach you the things that are important for you to learn in this life and to answer your questions. A guide is a Higher Soul. They know many things about this world that we don't.

'The rest of you – did anyone see anything in their centre that they hadn't noticed before?'

The rest of the morning went according to formula. The familiarity of routine helped Cia to get a firmer grip on her own reality, and by lunchtime, she felt renewed and ready to face the next portion of her own task. Nardo and Kate taught the afternoon classes, so Cia would have time to practise and do more work with Philip.

Before going to the dining room, though, Cia stopped by the healing room to check on Ian. Jack smiled at her as she came in.

'He hasn't changed since this morning, and Dalt hasn't been back,' he told her. 'Sarah came back after breakfast, but I sent her off to bed. The poor child is exhausted.'

'And not able to keep her distance emotionally on this one, I'm afraid,' Cia added. 'Shall I bring you lunch?'

'I'd appreciate that,' said Jack. He looked at her closely. 'You know, you could use a nap yourself.'

Cia made a face at him and left.

'I don't know what she's doing,' Dalt whined.

'Find out!' roared Gardner, drawing himself to his full

height to tower over Dalt. 'She's vulnerable to you. Use it!'

'Yes, sir,' Dalt whimpered, cowering away from Gardner's anger. Dalt didn't like Gardner any better than anyone else did, but Drove was a dangerous man and an enemy to be feared. It was much better to bring Gardner the information he demanded. Much safer, he amended.

With one last glance at Gardner, Dalt turned and left the room, nearly tripping over Freddie on the way out.

The house was ancient, one left standing after the cities had been deserted. It had been converted and was probably lived in for a while after the exodus and then abandoned when people moved into the surrounding countryside. The roof was sagging badly and the stairs had collapsed, making access to the second floor chancy at best. Floorboards buckled and shreds of carpet stuck to them in places. The furniture appeared to be original to the place; stained and torn upholstery, rotten with age, covered couches and chairs. Tables showed scarred surfaces and some had broken legs.

The exterior of the house was in equally dismal condition. The paint had long since peeled from the boards and weather had warped and rotted the wood underneath. The garden had overgrown its original boundaries and now a riot of vegetation concealed the house's location from casual observation. This was why Drove Gardner had chosen it.

He had cleverly shored up the sagging construction inside in ways that could not be detected by cursory inspection. This made it infinitely useful.

Dalt noticed none of this as he crossed the ruined floor and opened the front door. He stepped out on to the front porch and looked up at the sky. Clouds were piling up in the west. The dark, swollen mass signalled to Dalt a cold and wet ride home if he didn't hurry. He went to where his horse was tied to a bottlebrush tree and led the animal through the undergrowth back to the main path. It was fairly close to the Old City here. The blank and empty buildings in the distance gaped at him, a warning and a threat. Dalt glanced fearfully over his shoulder at their silent malevolence as he climbed into the saddle and started back to the Keep.

OK, Cia said to Philip. *I've memorized Meg's energy pattern and learned how to come and go from the continuum while in meditation. Now what?*

Philip gave her a searching look. *Now is the most difficult task, I think. You must face your chair.*

I have no chair. Cia bristled. She felt something behind her, but as she turned towards the presence, there was nothing there.

I have let you get away with playing this game until now, but it has gone on long enough. Face it! Look at it!

No, she whined. *There's nothing there.*

How many times have you told your students that there is nothing in their centres that can harm them? Philip asked her conversationally.

Cia shrugged sullenly and said nothing.

And yet you have denied having a chair in your centre for how many years? he pressed.

Yes, but – Cia began.

But nothing! I said look at it. Philip wasn't laughing. Cia had never heard that tone from him before. It scared her more than the flicker in the corner of her eye. She had never truly angered Philip before. She started forward gingerly, willing it to appear . . .

The Chair sat solidly in the middle of the floor, a part of the parquet, but separate from it. It had a high back that curved slightly in at both sides, and wide, rounded arm-rests. The seat was deep and wide as well. The Chair was covered in a dark material, and a thick layer of dust. Cia stopped in front of it and stood very still.

Good! Philip said. *No more hiding from what you don't want to deal with. You are going to have to learn how to use this tool. It is necessary to the task ahead of you. But also, you must build up your strength. What you must do in the next few days will demand a great deal of energy. Right now relax and get some sleep.*

Philip disappeared.

Relax, he says, Cia mumbled to herself as she stood and stared at the chair. She stood that way for a very long time before backing out of her centre to wander through the meadow for a little while. She was tempted to go to the continuum, but if Philip said sleep, he meant sleep. With a sigh, she came back up out of meditation state and stretched her cramped legs before standing. She relit her candle, doused the torch in the bucket of sand that stood under it and left the room.

As she walked by the dining room, Cia saw plates whizzing through the air.

Tanner? she called. She stopped in the doorway and peered carefully around the jamb.

Tanner stood in the centre of a hurricane of plates, bowls and silverware. Cia laughed and headed on towards the kichen. Tanner was always enthusiastic about setting the tables, but it was dangerous for anyone else to get involved, since controlling that many items with her mind required considerable concentration. To interrupt her was to risk a great deal of broken pottery.

After a brief survey of work in progress in the kitchen, Cia set herself to a large sink full of dishes that needed washing. It was pleasant, she found, to stand with her hands immersed in the soapy water and listen to the conversations.

On evenings like this, she had a hard time believing that anything around her needed changing. Everything seemed peaceful and benign. Philip seemed like such an alarmist. But Ian was in fact lying in the healing chamber with poison in his body, and Gardner had a poison in his mind.

Cia shook her head and shrugged off her dark thoughts. Philip had said she should rest and relax. Just for tonight, she would allow Sarah to do her job, and not worry about what couldn't be changed. Just for tonight, she would sit by the fire and listen to the children and help with the mending, and not think critically about what was being said. Tonight, she would not try to change anything, she would just let it happen, and be happy about it. There would be time later to change things.

After dinner, Cia again volunteered for dishes. She turned the activity into a kind of ritual cleansing; the soap washed her soul, and the bad energy she had been holding on to drained away with the water when she let it out of the sink.

The evening passed quietly and Cia went to bed feeling quite a bit better than she had for several days. Philip had started to get her worked up prior to Ian's attack and she hadn't slowed down since. As she drifted off to sleep, Cia felt balanced and at peace.

In the back of her mind, she was aware that she had successfully spent the evening not thinking about the Chair.

Within her centre, Cia moved to the Chair. A thick layer of dust covered the unfamiliar material. She shuddered as she approached it, wishing she could just continue to ignore its unwanted presence. Now she had to learn to work with it and she had no idea how to go about it. Reaching out tentative fingers, she touched the arm of the Chair. With a gasp, she yanked her hand back. It had a pulse! There were three clean spots now where her fingers had been and the fur was ruffled.

Philip! she yelled. *Philip, are you there?* She backed

away from the only thing in her centre she had never understood.

The tiny, emaciated black man wheezed laughter and shook his head. He held up a hand to her as laughter continued to shake him.

Yes, of course I am here, he chuckled.

What is that? she demanded. *It moved, I swear! What is it, Philip?* She continued to back away from the Chair until she ran into the wall. Points of amethyst crystal dug into her back and palms as she pressed against it, trying to put as much distance as she could between herself and the Chair.

It's still just your chair. Haven't you experimented with it at all since the last time we worked together? Philip seemed genuinely surprised.

You never showed me how to use it and neither did anyone else, she protested.

Oh, said Philip. *I see. Just because no one ever suggested you try it, you never thought to do it on your own?*

Cia shook her head. Her back was still pressed against the wall, but her muscles were relaxing slightly. With a sigh, Philip moved to the dais and sat down.

There was a time when chairs such as this were standard issue for centres, he said as he arranged his dusty robes around his spindly legs.

Standard issue? asked Cia. She crossed the floor and sat with her back to the Chair, facing Philip.

Like the healing chamber you have behind that door. Philip waved a careless hand in the direction of Cia's healing room. *Chairs and libraries were essential areas within the centres of the People from Before. Your centre is extremely atavistic in that respect. Those two doors back there. Haven't you ever wondered what is behind them? They've always been locked, but you've never tried to open*

*them up. You're so much like the people of your Keep that
you condemn for closed-mindedness!*

What is behind them? asked Cia.

Figure it out! Philip exclaimed. *I can't tell you everything. I'm not here to lead you around by the nose. I have
to teach you to teach them how to think for themselves.
How can I do that if you want me to spoon-feed you all the
answers? How dare you have contempt for them when you
are no better!*

Well at least I'm trying! Cia yelled back. *I've laid my life
on the line for you. And my son's as well. I've done
everything you've asked of me and now you tell me you
want creative initiative as well?* Agitated, she jumped up
and paced back and forth. *Pardon me for not realizing
that I should ask questions about things I was told not to
ask questions about!*

You should always ask questions, said Philip quietly.
That is how you learn.

I know, said Cia miserably, plunking back down on the
floor in front of Philip. *It's just when I discovered my
centre, I asked my teacher what the Chair and extra doors
were for, and she said that you would tell me when the
time was right. Is the time right, now?*

The time is coming, Philip acknowledged. *Once you
have accomplished your tasks downstream in time, then we
will worry about learning how to unlock those doors. For
now, we must concentrate on your chair and the task at
hand.*

I don't want to go near that Chair, Cia objected. *It has
a pulse and it's covered with fur!*

That isn't the heartbeat of an independent living animal,
Philip laughed. *That's energy it's drawing directly from
you, amplified by the crystals. The fur comes from the
image you carry of domestic house cats. You find them
cuddly and comforting, so it is natural for you to have*

covered a threatening object in a material you have positive associations with.

That Chair is covered with dead cat pelts? Cia backed away in distaste.

No more than your doors are carved from real trees. Now, come on. Dust it off and sit down!

Reluctantly, Cia approached the Chair again and patted gingerly at the seat with one hand. Surely it moved just a little? Shortly, the dust was in the air and the Chair was the cleanest it had been since the day she had discovered her centre. She turned, placed her hands on the arms of the Chair and gingerly lowered her bottom on to its seat.

Philip smiled broadly at her. *Was that so bad?* he asked.

Cia grimaced. *You were right about the pulse, anyway. Very peculiar sensation.*

Oh, you'll get used to it, he chuckled. *Run your hand over the right chair-arm. Do you feel the buttons under the fur?*

Yeah. What are they – A light flooded the dais with the intensity and colour of a small sun. Cia gasped and jumped out of the Chair. *What the – ?* she yelled.

To her chagrin, Philip was laughing again. *What's so funny?* she demanded.

That was just a light-switch. Calm down. There is nothing in here that could ever hurt you. You know that. You teach that to the kids.

Light-switch? she echoed blankly.

As I said, your centre is somewhat atavistic, said Philip. *Chairs have not been visualized in centres for many generations, yet you have one you couldn't get rid of. The centres you have helped the children discover have a central chamber that is torchlit, and two smaller rooms that adjoin it by doors: a healing chamber and a foyer through which people may come into the centre by invitation only. Yet you have two more doors which like the chair were here when you created your centre, and electric lighting which*

*has been dead longer than most of your ancestors. These
are all things you could not have come up with on your
own, because they have not been in use in your culture for
literally hundreds of years.*

And you never wondered about it, he continued. *Never
explored it, so now when you need it most, you are terrified
by it instead. A light-switch is a way to turn lights on and
off.* He pushed her gently back down into the Chair.
*Now, can we have a minimum of hysteria during the rest
of this?*

Cia felt for the buttons and pressed the same one again.
The light over the dais went out. Her centre suddenly
seemed dark and shadowy, its normal light no longer
sufficient. Reaching further forward, Cia pressed another
button.

Silently, a panel of amethyst wall, the size of two doors
together, moved back and then sideways into the rest of
the wall. Behind it was a room lined in the most perfect
mirrors Cia had ever seen. The room was as wide and
deep as the portion of wall that had concealed it. It
contained a carved wooden bench with a tapestried seat,
and a brass handrail. A beautiful fern sat on a brass stand
beside the bench. It was illuminated by the same strange
light that had flooded her centre only moments ago. The
floor was of the same parquetry as the central chamber,
but brass edging finished either side of a gap between her
centre and this peculiar little room.

What?? Cia stared open-mouthed. *What happened to
my wall?*

Nothing, said Philip. *That's always been there. How did
you think I come and go? It's an elevator.*

Cia pressed the button again and the wall of amethyst
crystal moved smoothly back into place. She leaped up
and ran to examine the edges. Seeing nothing that she
hadn't seen before, she ran back to the Chair and pushed
the button to light the dais and the one to open the

elevator. Light flooded the room as the wall moved back to reveal the new chamber. Cia went back and examined the edges of the elevator closely.

Oh, she exclaimed almost immediately. *I see! The door is cut around the crystals in the straightest line possible. It's invisible when the door is shut. That's why I never noticed it before!*

Is that true? asked Philip. He was watching from the dais, sitting cross-legged and grinning.

No, Cia admitted grudgingly.

What is true? Philip persisted. He was rocking back and forth, patting his knees with his hands. Tiny dust motes rose from his robes as he moved.

I never noticed before because I didn't ask the right questions; I didn't explore on my own, she said. *What is behind the doors? Do the buttons on the Chair-arm unlock them?*

I can't tell you that. The buttons don't unlock the doors. When the time is right for you to know the answers, you will also know how to open them.

Now there's a conflicting message! Cia exclaimed angrily. *You yell at me for not asking questions and then when I ask them, you tell me the same thing everyone else has: Not yet! Sometimes, Philip, I could cheerfully strangle you!* She stomped across the delicate parquetry, grabbed hold of a brass doorknob and twisted with all her strength, first in one direction, then the next. The door remained stubbornly locked. With an inarticulate yell, she kicked at the door.

Do you feel better now?

Much, she spat, stalking back to the Chair. *Now what?*

Cia, I don't mean to confuse you. The doors were just an example. You will find out soon just what they conceal, but the contents of those rooms are of no use to your current search. Philip shifted on the dais and dangled his scrawny legs over the edge, kicking his heels against the side. He pointed at the Chair. *This, you cannot do without. Now sit!*

Cia sat.

That covers the two lowest buttons on the arm of the chair, doesn't it? Philip gestured at the right arm of the Chair. Cia nodded meekly. *Well?* he demanded.

She punched the button above the one which activated the elevator door.

Silently, a section of the roof, a foot wide and about six feet in length, slipped back into the recess. Again, she could see that the opening was cut around the natural crystal in the straightest line possible, but this was no 'elevator' descending from the opening. A thin, flat, opalescent rectangle emerged instead. It was taller than Cia, and as wide as the breadth of her extended fingertips, and hung directly above the dais in front of her. She sat in the Chair, her mouth forming an O of amazement.

What does this do? she whispered, not taking her eyes from the strange object.

Picture a place in its most vivid detail, Philip instructed, pivoting on the dais to observe the screen.

Cia shut her eyes and concentrated on her last image of Ian and Sarah.

See? Look! exclaimed Philip. Cia opened her eyes and stared at the screen. Sarah bent over Ian, eyes closed, waving a malachite sphere over his chest, attempting to draw more poison from him. Her glass beads dangled from the same hand between them.

Sarah, no! Cia murmured. Sarah turned with a start to look over her shoulder at the screen. Her eyes remained unfocused, searching for the source of Cia's voice. *Sarah, those silly beads will do neither of you any good,* Cia said more clearly.

Sarah dropped Ian's hand and stood slowly. Turning towards the sound, she held the beads in front of her. *Cia?* she whispered.

Of course! Cia said. *Can't you see me?*

Sarah shook her head and backed up against the bed. *I've never heard you this way before. It frightens me.*

Cia refined her mental image and altered the projection of the screen. *Does that help?* she asked finally.

Where did the mirror come from? Sarah quavered. She stared, wide-eyed, at the space Cia occupied.

I'll have to explain it to you later, Cia told her. *Right now, I don't really understand it myself.*

Cia pressed the button to shut off the screen. She turned off the light over the dais and slid to the floor. Sitting cross-legged on the fine-grained wooden parquetry, she cocked her head to one side and regarded Philip closely.

Why are you telling me to do all this? What's your stake in the success of our efforts? she asked him.

To her surprise, he sighed in relief and smiled slightly at her. *I was wondering when you would ask,* he said. *I was beginning to believe that you would continue to do my bidding without ever questioning my motivations and intent.*

Well? Cia prompted.

Well, life is a series of levels. To move from one level to the next, you must learn certain lessons. In your present form, you may live many lifetimes in order to learn all the lessons that will allow you to move on to the next level.

Is this what Ian was telling me about the philosophy of reincarnation? Cia jumped to her feet and started pacing. *That some people believe they will keep coming back in different bodies after they die?* She came to a halt in front of Philip and leaned down towards him. *Do you mean they were correct?* She sat down again.

Partly, Philip said. *But you will keep coming back in human form until you have learned all the lessons you have contracted to.*

Contracted to? Cia asked.

You essentially make deals with people on the Other Side to be a part of the life you choose for the next go around. They agree to help you learn certain lessons, you agree to teach them certain lessons. For instance: you made a deal with Dalt. He agreed to teach you that not everyone is worthy of your trust and love; that some people are shallow and opportunistic. You agreed to teach him belief in principles. You cannot be responsible for his not learning what you agreed to teach him. Someone else will have to try in the next lifetime to get the message across. He will continue to repeat the lesson until he has learned it.

Yes, but that doesn't explain – Cia interrupted.

I'm coming to that! Philip glared her to silence. *Once you have learned the lessons which need to be taught in human form and society, you progress to the next level. You become a Higher Soul, or more actually, your Higher Self. In this form, you have different lessons to learn and part of how you do that is to function as guide or teacher to those in human form.*

You mean you used to be human? Cia burst out.

Yes, Philip frowned. *And now I would like to progress to the level above mine. In fact, all of the Higher Souls would, but we've run into a serious problem. Your stagnation is causing our own. By worshipping us, you prevent us from learning what we need to from you. You don't challenge and question us the way you should. So the task fell to me to jolt you out of your complacency, and I volunteered your help. You've already run into some of the opposition, but the fight hasn't really begun.*

Now, he continued in a lighter tone. *You have some lessons of your own to perfect before you call me again, so let me out, and then get to work!*

Cia stood up, moved the step back to her Chair and sat down again. She pressed the button for the elevator, still amazed as the wall moved aside. Philip strode into the mirrored chamber, turned and sat on the tapestried seat of the wooden bench.

And get some rest! he said as the door closed between them.

It was early evening by the time Cia finished the tasks Philip had set for her. Coming back to consciousness slowly, rising out of meditation level for the first time since early afternoon, Cia stretched, enjoying the sleepy feeling she always had after working psychically for long periods.

Footsteps clattered down the hall outside the closed door, followed closely by several more. Laughter accompanied them. Shadows stretched long before the setting sun and the meditation room was dim in the gathering dusk. She could hear the sheep being driven back into the fold after a day spent grazing in the field across the river. Voices called to one another as the chores were finished up.

Cia stretched again slowly, easing the kinks out of her muscles. Rest. Hah! First do this and memorize that and work on the other . . . When did Philip think she would have time to sleep? She lay back on the pillows, closed her eyes and became aware of the rumbling in her stomach. Shutting hunger out of her mind for a moment, she infused her aura with orange, then blue, to relax and calm her cramped limbs.

Cia got to her feet and walked over to the window. On the wide, low sill were several circles of crystals that had been placed there to clear and energize. Next to these, in the corner of the sill, were a clay smudge pot, a tinder box and a small pile of smudging materials. Cia took up the pot and placed a generous pinch of the sage and sweetgrass in it. She struck the flint, sending sparks into the smudge pot until she got it lit. After fanning smoke over the crystals to clear any energies she might have transmitted to them, she made a circuit of the room, cleansing it for the next person who would use it.

By the time she finished smudging the room and had tamped out the embers in the smudge pot, the last light in the sky had died, leaving the room in darkness. Making her way carefully to the door, Cia stepped out into the hallway and shut the door on the meditation room.

Odours from the kitchen assailed her nostrils and her stomach lurched, rumbling louder than before. First, though, she wanted to check on Ian and see how Sarah was doing. With a sigh of regret, she turned away from the dining room and headed down the hallway towards the healing room.

Cia pushed the door open and peeked around the corner to make sure she wasn't going to wake Sarah up again. To her surprise, Sarah was singing softly as she rocked back and forth on her stool. Her glass beads were on the table beside the bed.

'Sarah,' Cia said, stepping into the room. 'You sound much happier this evening. Did you have a good sleep? How is Ian doing?' She came to stand at the foot of the bed.

Ian's colour was almost normal. His bandages were fresh, and much smaller than those Cia had helped apply only yesterday. Sarah looked up happily.

'I finally re-established contact. You can talk to him now, but not verbally. He's still unconscious, but he's much closer to the surface than he's been, so he's easier to reach.' She climbed down from the stool. 'I want to ground and centre while you're here, OK?'

Cia nodded and moved over to the stool. Sitting down, she took Ian's hand in her own and reached for his mind with hers.

He was groggy, but he was there. *Hi*, he croaked at her. *Sorry about this.*

You're safe now. Can you tell me what happened? Cia

asked. She could sense his weakness and didn't want to over-tire him, but she had to know how this had happened.

Gardner, Ian told her.

I figured . . . Gardner himself?

PK. He was in the Old City. Chased me. Ian was becoming agitated by the memory. Cia calmed him down and eased his mind from light to deep sleep level so he could get more rest. Then she broke contact and turned her attention to monitoring Sarah.

Buoyed by Ian's improvement, Sarah was in much better shape than Cia had expected. Possibly, Jack had done some healing on her before leaving to attend to his classes.

Cia sat back and waited for Sarah to finish.

'Why don't you go get dinner, and bring me back something from the kitchen afterwards. I'll stay with Ian tonight. Have Jack give you a sleeping draught if you need one. It wouldn't do to have the Keep's Healer getting sick because she didn't take care of herself, now would it?' Cia spoke rapidly to forestall Sarah's protest. 'Go on. It smelled wonderful and I'm starving, so hurry and bring me back a couple of sandwiches or a bowl of stew. I have a lot of work to do tonight, and I need the energy.'

Sarah opened her mouth, thought better of it and closed it again. She smiled briefly and closed the door softly behind her as she left.

Cia heard her footsteps retreating down the hallway, and turned back to the bed and the still form of her son.

Gardner in the Old City?

There was more going on than Cia had suspected, and she had a feeling that plans had best be speeded up. She would have to speak with Philip again tonight. She studied Ian's face, watched his slow, even breathing. She glanced at the closed door of the healing chamber. She hoped Sarah would bring her dinner soon.

4

Philip looked tired. Cia had never seen him look that way before. She was beginning to realize that more and more, recently, she was seeing firsts from him. Maybe, she thought, this was what he meant by the lessons he had to learn from her? She didn't ask him, though. There were too many other things on her mind.

What next? she demanded.

He sat on the edge of the dais, swinging his legs over the edge. He rubbed his eyes and then looked at her.

What do you think? he asked. *Have you done the work I told you to? Are you ready for the first phase?*

I've done what you told me, but I still don't see how I put all of the pieces together to accomplish it. Cia backed away from him and sat down in the Chair without flinching.

Have you rested?

Yes! But –

No buts! he exclaimed. *Have you rested? Are you feeling healthy?*

Yes. And I ate a huge dinner this evening. I'm ready to do it. I just need to know how. Cia felt the threat pressing in around her as she sat, outwardly calm.

You can't do it here, tonight, said Philip. He hopped off the dais and walked towards her. *I can tell just by looking at your face that you haven't rested enough.* He stood directly in front of her and leaned down until his nose was scant inches away from hers. *And one good meal doesn't build enough strength for this!* He straightened and backed away from her, turning towards the dais.

But –

No buts! he interrupted again, turning back towards where she sat. *Also, you can't do it here in the Keep. There is a place nearby that you must go to. It is safe and quiet, and there's a special quality the place has that will help you; give you power to carry out your task.*

What? Where?

In the hills above the Keep, Philip said. He walked back to the dais and sat on the edge again.

You said nearby! Cia protested. *The hills are quite a way from here. I can't take a horse without being seen and possibly followed.*

You will walk, said Philip. *This is one of the reasons you have to get some sleep.*

Great. How far into the hills is this place?

About three-quarters up the first slope, Philip replied. He scooted back from the edge of the dais and crossed his legs underneath him.

Cia sighed. *I don't suppose there will be a path to this place, like there was to the continuum?*

Of course not! That would make you much easier to track! Besides, no one has ever been there to make a path for you to follow.

Well, then, what am I looking for? Cia asked with a patience she didn't feel. *How will I know when I have found this place?*

It's covered by brush and bushes, Philip responded. *You won't be able to see it.*

Philip! How many questions do I have to ask before you tell me everything I need to know? How will I know when I've found it?

You'll feel it, he said. He held up a hand to forestall her next outburst. *The cave is like an immense geode, the walls, ceiling, even the floor are of crystal, similar to your centre chamber. This cave, however, is dirt-encrusted on the inside, as well as outside. You won't see the crystal, but you will feel their vibrations even before you get near the cave.*

A geode? she echoed. She'd never actually seen one, but a book on rocks and minerals that she'd read to Ian years ago in the library triggered a description. *Up in the hills?* she asked incredulously. *How come – ?*

How often do you go into the hills? Philip asked.

No one goes – she began.

Exactly! he cut her off. *The people who explored those hills so many generations ago weren't sensitive enough to feel the vibrations of the cave and determined that there was nothing worthwhile up there. Then one of them was killed by a wild bear and the hills were declared unsafe, correct?*

Cia nodded. *When do I go there?*

In a few nights.

At night? You want me to walk into the hills alone at night?

You mustn't be followed, Philip admonished. *Also, you concentrate better at night; less psychic static.*

OK, Cia relented. *How do I go about this?*

You will use two chakra stars: one with candles, one with crystals. Place the candles on the floor of the cave and the crystals on your forehead. The candles will help you connect to the crystals in the cave. The crystals on your forehead will help open your third eye: the sixth chakra. All of these will help generate the power you need.

Yes, but what –

Go back! Meg is in your past.

But –

But, nothing. You know everything you need to. You have all the tools. Now let me out of here and get some rest! Philip slid off the dais and walked to the portion of wall that hid the elevator.

With a sigh of resignation, Cia pressed the button that activated the door.

Philip stepped into the mirrored chamber and turned to face her. *I mean it!* he said as the door shut between them.

Cia came back out of meditation level slowly and glanced toward the door of the healing room. The stool was still in its place in front of it, where she had put it. Anyone opening the door would have knocked it down and the noise would have alerted her.

Ian lay on the bed, his chest rising and falling steadily under the blankets. Nothing in the room had been disturbed. With a small shake of her head, Cia rose and went to the cupboard to get extra pillows and blankets. She made up a pallet on the floor beside the bed, between it and the door.

With one last look at the door, she curled up under the blanket and fell asleep.

Sunlight streamed in the window when she awakened in the morning. The floor was a particularly unforgiving surface. Cia felt her bones protesting at the rough treatment as she stretched and stood up. The stool was still in front of the door in the same place she had left it the night before, and Ian was still asleep in the bed.

A soft knock on the door startled her, but Sarah's voice said softly, 'Cia, it's Sarah. May I come in?'

'Of course, Sarah,' Cia called to her. Then she remembered the chair. '*Hold on a moment!*' She moved quickly to clear the doorway. 'OK,' she said, pulling the door open.

Sarah entered timidly, looking first towards the bed. Relief was evident on her face when she saw Ian sleeping peacefully.

'Is he,' she began. 'Are you – I mean is everything – '

'Everything is fine,' Cia told her. 'Except I'm starving. Is breakfast going to be ready soon?'

'It's ready now,' Sarah said. 'Why don't you go eat? I'll

stay with Ian and you can bring me something when you finish. OK?'

'Fine,' Cia said. 'I won't be long.'

Cia found Kate in the dining room setting bowls and platters on the table.

Kate, can you teach my class this morning? she sent a feeling of exhaustion with the request.

Kate looked critically at the dark circles under Cia's eyes and nodded. *You'd better rest up. I think Jenet may unfold soon.* Kate showed Cia a mental picture of a young boy with dark hair withdrawn into his mind, and Cia asleep on the chair beside his bed.

Cia grimaced.

That's not why? Kate asked.

Well, no. Actually, I have some things to do tonight, and I didn't sleep very well on the floor of the healing chamber last night, Cia said. *I'm glad you reminded me, though. With everything that's happened recently, I'd forgotten to keep my eye on him.*

Kate smiled and handed Cia a bowl of porridge. *Here, you're also looking skinnier than usual. Maybe Sarah ought to do a healing on you!*

Without responding, Cia turned her attention to her breakfast.

Later that afternoon, feeling much better for her nap, Cia went out behind the sprawling Keep building to the sheds that housed the Keep's cottage industry.

Lidra, the jeweller, had a shed here, and Cia knew she would find her amid the litter of stone chips and metal-working tools.

The shed had large windows on the east- and west-facing walls, and fully equipped work benches under each. Smaller windows on the north- and south-facing walls provided additional light, but there were also torch sconces on either side of each bench. The close work that

Lidra did with jewellery and meditation tools required a well-lit work space.

There was a small forge and bellows under the window on the south wall because the energy there was conducive to the metals she worked with. Cia wasn't sure of this, but Lidra did extremely fine work, so she never questioned it. In the middle of the clutter was an anvil on a large stump. Several hammers of various sizes were scattered on the ground beside it.

Cia didn't understand how Lidra worked in these surroundings, but the results were undeniable. Lidra's jewellery was beautiful, as well as balanced, and her meditation tools were unsurpassed. It was for this reason Cia was looking for her.

Lidra sat at the western work bench holding a crystal up to the light and making disapproving noises with her tongue.

'Don't you see how you cut this?' she asked an apprentice, who stood quietly with slumped shoulders and bowed head. He nodded slightly and sniffled.

'You cut right across the power lines in this terminator, here,' she continued, shoving it under his nose. 'Weren't you in tune with its vibrations at all?' she demanded. 'This would have been an incredibly powerful tool. Now it's garbage!' She threw the useless crystal at the anvil. 'Denley, you have to pay attention to the stones you are working with. You can't just cut them in the easiest place. You have to feel the power in them and work with it. Move *with* the resonance, not through or against it!' She looked up and saw Cia standing uncomfortably in the doorway. 'Come on in.' She waved a hand and turned back to the unfortunate Denley. 'Work harder on feeling the resonance. We'll cut more stones later. Right now, why don't you go help with the milking?'

Denley nodded miserably and stumbled from the shed.

'He's got an amazing talent,' Lidra said, watching him

95

leave. 'He just gets so wander-minded sometimes, I could scream.'

'Sometimes my students get like that,' Cia smiled. 'I want to pinch their ears together to see if there's anything between them!'

Lidra laughed. She had a big laugh that was extremely contagious. She was a large woman, both tall and round. She wore her light-brown hair pulled back from her face and pinned haphazardly on the back of her head. Her leather tunic was scratched and showed burn marks. The sleeves were rolled back to her elbows, exposing forearms that also showed burns from the forge and sparks of molten metal. Her trousers were also well worn, and the knees were always bent, even when she stood straight.

Everything about Lidra was comfortable and familiar to Cia. She moved further into the shed and searched for a stool to sit on.

'Here,' Lidra said, sweeping debris from a chair and pushing it towards Cia. 'I haven't seen much of you lately, but I get the feeling this isn't entirely a social call.' She looked sharply at Cia.

'Well, no, not entirely,' Cia admitted. 'But I'm glad of an excuse to bring me out here. How are the new apprentices working out?'

Lidra's mouth twisted into a grimace. 'The only one who shows any promise also shows a lack of dedication. Let's talk about something else.'

'OK, then.' Cia smiled. 'How about the reason I came out here?'

'Which is?' Lidra prompted.

'A meditation tool. A very specific tool that my guide says I need for a task he has assigned me.' Cia traced a triangle in the air, and then described another one, upside-down, superimposed on the first. 'I need a six-pointed star, set with stones and crystals to correspond with the chakra system.'

Lidra nodded without comment, so Cia continued her explanation. 'The stones must resonate with each other in order for the powers to be tapped.'

'Did your guide tell you which stones must be used?' Lidra asked after thinking for a moment about what Cia had described.

Cia shook her head. 'He just said chakra stars: red, orange, yellow, green, blue, lavender, white.'

'That's seven,' Lidra pointed out.

'Well, I figure that the white should be a quartz crystal and it should be set in the centre, since white is the presence of all colour, and the light by which they are all purified.'

'OK,' Lidra said slowly. 'What order should the stones be set in?'

'We start with red as we drop into the meditation state, so probably the top point of the star should be red. And then around to the right in the pattern that energy flows.'

'Have you given any thought to what stones resonate best with you?' Lidra asked. 'I have several different types of stone in each colour. Why don't you go through and hold one of each stone so that you find the properties that will be easiest for you to work with?'

Cia nodded. 'That makes sense,' she said. She moved to the bins that Lidra pointed to and looked at the bewildering array of stones that she had to choose from. 'Might as well start at the beginning, then.' She sighed and picked up a chunk of ruby.

Lidra watched for a moment before turning back to the brass collar she was working on. She knew it would take Cia quite some time to choose the stones.

It was almost dark before Cia had picked out the types of stones that she felt most comfortable working with. Lidra examined the array and smiled in satisfaction.

'Does that mean I've chosen well?' Cia asked.

'Do you need my approval?' Lidra raised an eyebrow.

Cia laughed. 'Can you find stones in these categories that will resonate together? They're the ones that produce the most energy when I focus on them together.'

'We-e-ll,' Lidra drawled as she scratched one of her chins, 'I guess we can fake it OK. What kind of metal do you want them set in and when do you want it by?'

'Details!' Cia laughed. 'What metal will be the best conductor between these groups of stones and how soon can you have it done?'

'Always in a rush!' Lidra laughed also. 'You couldn't wait to unfold. You couldn't wait to become an adult . . . even waiting for dinner was too much for you. If I start first thing in the morning, I can have it finished by the day after. Soon enough?'

'I guess it'll have to be.' Cia tried to sound impatient, but she knew that Philip would have a great deal for her to do before she would be able to use the tool.

'Do you want it pendant-style, or on a bracelet or what?' Lidra interrupted Cia's train of thought.

'Oh, um, it's supposed to open my third eye, so I guess a pendant that will hang on my forehead. Does that make sense?' Cia frowned for a moment. She was fairly certain that was what Philip had meant: for her to wear it on her forehead.

'Come here,' Lidra commanded. She held up a piece of string and beckoned with one finger.

Cia obediently went to where Lidra stood. Lidra held the piece of string between both hands and wrapped it around Cia's head.

'What's that for?' Cia asked.

'So I know how much chain to use, silly.' Lidra knotted the string and tossed it towards the nearest work bench.

Cia had her doubts that Lidra would ever find the string again, much less make use of it, but she smiled and said, 'Thanks. Will I see you again before the day after tomorrow?'

'If you actually made it to a meal once in a while, maybe we'd see more of each other!'

Cia stood at the edge of the stony slope she had climbed into the hills above the Keep. The cave before her was the one Philip had described. On the way up the hill, she hadn't thought about the task he had sent her here to perform. Now that she was at the entrance, she felt overwhelmed by the enormity of the undertaking.

She set the cloth sack she carried on the ground and stooped to enter the low cavern. In the dark, she groped for the candle, flint and wool she had put in her pocket. Times like this, she thought, being pyrokinetic wouldn't be so bad. Lighting a candle without a struggle would be a welcome change. She crouched at the mouth of the cave with the candle between her knees as she repeatedly struck the flint into the wool.

At last a spark flared and Cia got the candle lit.

Straightening, she held the candle aloft and moved back into the cave. It was definitely the cave Philip had told her about; she could feel the crystal vibration in the stone walls. The ceiling rose steeply from the mouth to an arch overhead, high enough for Cia to stand upright. The walls were narrow and the cave was about twenty paces deep. Dripping wax on to a ledge jutting out from the wall nearest her, she set the candle in it and bent to retrieve her sack from the entrance.

First, she removed a small rug from the sack and spread it on the floor in the centre of the cave. In the dirt before it, she traced a six-pointed star, digging small holes at each of the six points. In these holes, she placed six candles: one red, one orange, one yellow, one green, one blue, one lavender. In the centre, she placed a much taller white candle.

She turned back to the rug and sat in the middle, holding her sack before her, facing the star. Reaching into the bag, she removed the six-pointed gold star hanging from a golden chain. She placed this on her forehead. The points of this star corresponded to the star she had drawn and set with the candles. Each point of the smaller star was set with a crystal: one garnet, one carnelian, one citrine, one tourmaline, one sodalite, one amethyst. In the centre of the star was a large double-terminated quartz.

This done, she reached for the original candle and lit the seven before her in the order of placement. She then blew out the one she had struggled so hard to light.

Sitting cross-legged, Cia placed her hands palm-up on her knees and closed her eyes. She drew a deep breath, held it for a few moments before exhaling, then drew several more.

Cia felt the tensions of the climb ease out as she breathed and began to run through the grounding and centring exercises which had been a part of her daily ritual for longer than she could remember.

Reaching her centre, Cia took a moment to look around the familiar space. Everything was in order. She shook herself, wondering what she had expected. Repressing a shudder, Cia turned and went to the Chair. She sat down quickly and found she was holding her breath. Feeling a bit silly, Cia exhaled and placed her hands on the arms of the Chair.

She reached out with her mind and felt for the crystals of the cave, connected them to the candles and then to the stones on her forehead. Power surged into and through her. The Souls! she thought. Philip hadn't told her to expect such . . . Of course not. She laughed and turned her attention to absorbing and directing the tremendous energy that was suddenly hers to use.

When she felt more confident with the power she had accessed, Cia left her centre chamber for the field that surrounded it. By now, the path to the continuum was well worn. She passed along it quickly, headed for the first part of her task.

Cia passed through the transition point and was enveloped in the blackness. It always took a moment for her mental 'eyes' to adjust to the complete absence of colour which gave the continuum its density. Before her were the colours lacking in her surroundings. Cia reached out into the connecting threads. The vibrant colours of the threads were a striking contrast to the dense blackness she had come through.

Back, Cia mused to herself. She had been facing forward, towards the shifting, foggy future. Now she turned and faced the direction the threads had come from. Philip had suggested that it would be easiest to trace Meg's pattern in the lavender thread, because her energies were so blocked on that line. She pulled herself over the other threads until she reached it. It stretched away from her, dwindling and thinning until she could no longer see it. Slowly, she reached out her hand and grasped the lavender thread.

Hey, let me go! said a sleepy little voice she didn't recognize.

Cia dropped the thread, startled. She had forgotten she needed to touch the threads delicately. Slowly, she reached out again. Her palm tingled as her fingers closed on the strand. Cia resisted the impulse to let go, and reached forward with her other hand, grasping further down the ropy lavender line. She could feel her environment shift, but her immediate surroundings remained static.

She let go with her right hand and pulled herself along, grasping the thread fully two feet beyond where her left hand held the glowing lavender strand. Again, the environment shifted while remaining unchanged. Is this what it feels like to travel in time? she wondered.

Cia continued to pull herself along, gradually gaining

speed as her confidence grew. Soon, she didn't need actually to hold the thread in order to travel along it, and this speeded her progress. The further Cia went into the past, however, the less she felt the influence of the crystals in the cave. She hadn't realized the tremendous amount of energy she would need to complete even this first phase of her task. Philip had been right in badgering her to rest more. She slowed her progress a moment to concentrate on breathing and relaxing her own energy flow before continuing.

Cia was casting in the dark. She didn't know where she was; she didn't know what she was looking for; she didn't know what she was supposed to do or how she should go about it.

The ropy lavender thread she had been following had dwindled down to spider silk and she seemed no closer to finding what Philip had sent her searching for. The other threads in the current were thickening rapidly. This phenomenon confused her for a moment as she fought to focus on a rapidly dwindling target. Then she realized that she had reached the point in time where the wars and plagues had taken place. More life energies were occupying the currents of time. She would just have to concentrate harder on the line she was following.

There was altogether too much riding on the success of this endeavour and Cia was feeling the pressure. She fought a panicked reaction to the uncertainty and reflexively took several deep breaths to calm herself.

This is silly, she thought to herself. Calm down and recentre, you've come too far to blow this now. The cave, her body, the stars of wax and stone all seemed so far away. She took a deep breath and held it as she concentrated on locating the energy they were directing into her centre.

There seemed to be so few people in this time who

were connected to their inner selves . . . it seemed strange in a population that surged so vastly in the other threads around her. Where they had been much smaller in her own time, the increase of these threads corresponded to the diminishing of the line she had followed here. The wars and the plague seemed to have changed everything in a very short time.

Calmer now, Cia began to closely examine the slender, silken strand before her. She closed mental eyes and ears to the static generated by the other lines in the continuum, concentrating on locating the elusive pattern that had brought her here. She channelled her mental focus through the sodalite on her forehead and the blue candle in the star on the floor of the cave. Then she amplified that energy through the white candle to the rough quartz of the cave and the double-terminated quartz, directing that power towards the lavender thread.

The thread seemed to magnify, to expand as she watched. It became many strands woven into one cord. Cia slowly began to separate the strands, methodically searching each one individually for the clues Philip had provided her. Somewhere, here, was the answer to their crisis.

So many threads . . . so many lives!

It was a for-ever sort of task. Pick up a thread, examine its energies, compare them to the pattern in the amethyst, discard, begin again. Most of these threads seemed to belong to people who were so completely unaware of their potential for psychic power that it was depressing even to contemplate. So many lives limited by ignorance; no wonder they tried to kill themselves.

Cia was beginning to feel that her search was hopeless. The population was just too great. There seemed no way she would ever find an end to the task that had been set for her. She resented Philip. She resented Gardner. She resented this impossible situation. The frustration was beginning to overwhelm her again. She knew that somewhere in the future, tears were running down her face. The candles burned brightly, but had not yet reached the halfway mark. This didn't seem possible. Cia knew she had been at this for ever.

Pick up a thread, examine its energies, compare them to the pattern in the amethyst, discard, begin again, until . . .

The darkness was complete and the only noise was deep, regular breathing. There were surface thoughts that had not yet pulled together to become a dream. The energies in this area of the thread were similar to those in the amethyst crystal.

Cia dropped her own energy into the pattern and became a part of the brain. She was actually in someone else's mind! In her excitement, she didn't stop to think.

Meg? How old are you? she asked.

The surface thoughts shifted abruptly. Nightmare shapes surged and took form around her, pushing her out of the pattern; out of the mind.

Meg? she called to the retreating entity.

What do you want? came the hostile reply.

Cia was a little hurt by the rebuff, but Philip hadn't said this would be easy. *I just need to know how old you are.*

Always the same damned question! Why can't you ask me something else for a change?

I will, later, Cia said, wondering if she was supposed to understand what was going on here. *For now, though, all I need to know is how old you are. Can you tell me? Do you know?*

Brother. Do you think I'm stupid or something? Haven't you spent enough time here to know? I'm eighteen. Now, will you go away and leave me alone? Meg demanded. She had begun to awaken.

Cia eased back out of the lavender thread and floated for a while above it, replaying the peculiar conversation in her mind. She tagged the spot with the portion of her own energy that had been expended during the contact and looked further down the line. She wondered how far . . . Of course! In her search for the right age, she had bumped (would bump?) into Meg several times. And this anger was the result of those contacts? She would have to make them as few and far between as possible.

With a sigh, Cia grasped the thread once more and pulled herself further down the continuum, further away from home.

Meg's head hurt her terribly, but she concentrated on the pain, desperately trying to drown out the words flooding her mind. She recognized the patterns of the words and understood them, but even when she was the only occupant in a room, the words didn't stop. She was unable to differentiate between spoken words and thoughts. She knew only that there was no escape from them. Ugly, frightening thoughts and sweetly spoken words confused her. They were from the same person, weren't they? The conflict never seemed to end.

At night it was quieter, but the projections of the dreams taking place around her frightened her, too. The surreal quality of the dreams made less sense than the duplicity of the words and thoughts . . . or was it thoughts and words? She was unable to sleep, but the fatigue helped to dull her mind and scatter her concentration. The voices seemed less pressing, less menacing when she was exhausted, but they never went away. Not once in her two years of life had Meg had a moment's peace from the constant barrage of noise.

She lay on her back in the darkness, chewing her fingers and staring up at the ceiling. The pain sometimes helped keep the voices at bay for a little while. She was aware that the things she did to shut out the voices bothered a lot of people, and that some of the thoughts and feelings she heard were reactions to those behaviours, but they were the only things that worked and she couldn't give them up.

Meg? Someone nearby asked her a question. She felt a strange presence in her mind. The voice was louder than the others.

'What?' she said into the darkness. She gnawed harder on her fingers as the other voices grew somehow more distant, and she tried to concentrate on the single voice that now occupied her mind.

Meg, I'm going to help you to stop the voices. A woman's voice spoke softly and reassuringly to her. *Since no one here can help you to develop your gifts, I've come back to block them away from your reach.* The woman rummaged in Meg's mind as she talked. *Some day, after you have healed and grown up, I will send someone to you who will help you learn about your talents, and teach you how to use them, but in the meantime, they are a danger to you.* She restructured and rearranged and then blocked off whole parts of Meg's mind even as the little girl listened and watched. *It's for your own good that I am doing this. You will understand some day, but that will be many years from now. When you have learned to use your special gifts, then you will be able to help us. But for now, you must grow strong and healthy with a clear mind.* The voice was soothing and calm, but Meg was upset about the parts of her mind that she could no longer reach.

Meg knew that somehow, the mind associated with the voice had made the other voices go away; that they wouldn't come back. But with them, some special portion of her was lost. She removed her bloody fingers from her mouth.

'Bye-bye,' the child said softly to herself. She drew a deep breath and wondered at the quiet surrounding her.

With a shuddery sigh, she fell into a deep, exhausted sleep.

Cia opened her eyes slowly. The candles before her were guttering in the dirt; large pools of wax formed strange shapes around the remains of the burning wicks. She reached for the common candle, relit it and dug it into the dirt.

She had been still for many hours. Her muscles were cramped and stiff with the cold of the small cave. Cia unbent her legs carefully and stretched out on the rug to begin a healing.

This time, her energies were focused through the carnelian stone on her forehead, restoring physical wellbeing to her tired body, and through the citrine, to calm her mind.

At last, Cia stood. She removed the medallion from her brow and replaced it and the rug in her sack. The remains of the candles, she gathered together and took to the back of the tiny cave. There, she dug a hole and buried the strange forms. The dirt would drain the energies from the wax and remove all traces of her presence here.

Taking a small smudge pot from her sack, she lit the sage and sweetgrass, and sprinkled ganja leaves over it to cleanse the energies of the cave. She would be back here soon, she knew. This was only the first step. She felt the smudge affecting her head. She was too tired and hungry to withstand its powers and it made her a bit dizzy as she walked the circumference of the small cavern blowing gently on the glowing, smoky herbs.

Finally, she combed her aura, gathered her sack and common candle and left the cave. The walk back to the Keep seemed to take much longer than the hike to the cave had, but at last, Cia entered the barnyard of the Keep. Dawn was lightening the sky on the horizon as she stumbled into the kitchen.

People would be up soon to begin morning chores and Cia would be able to ask Kate to take her classes again, but food was uppermost on her mind at that moment. She was munching on a large slab of bread with fruit-spread on it when the breakfast crew began to trickle into the kitchen.

Souls, Cia! Tanner exclaimed. *You look dreadful. Didn't you sleep well last night?* She rolled up her sleeves and washed her hands at the pump.

I haven't slept at all, yet, Cia replied around a mouthful of bread and jam. *Is Kate working breakfast this morning?*

No! Don't you remember, she had dinner shift last night. Tanner took a bowl to the pantry and began measuring out grains for the porridge.

Oh, right. I was hoping I wouldn't have to wake her.

Did you want her to take your class again this morning? Tanner asked as she poured the grains into the large kettle and took it over to the pump to add water. *I know Nardo gets up for the early milking, maybe he could take it for you today.* She hoisted the kettle out of the sink and took it over to set it on the hearth. She stirred the banked embers and added kindling until the fire crackled brightly in the fireplace.

There's an idea, Cia mumbled as she cut herself another hunk of bread and reached for the bowl of jam.

Tanner adjusted a spider arm and hung the kettle from it. Beth came in from the outside door with a basket of eggs and set them on the counter.

Is Nardo in the barn? Cia asked her.

I think he's below in the dairy right now, Beth said as she pumped water to wash her hands. *I asked him if he could skim yesterday's milk pans so I could make butter later this morning.*

Thanks, Cia said, sliding off her stool. Bread in hand, she left the kitchen to wander over to the barn. Below the barn, dug into the dirt, was the dairy. Always cool and dark, this was where they stored the more perishable food items. Bins of vegetables lined one wall and through the door was a room referred to as the meat locker. Sides of beef and parts of sheep and pigs hung from hooks in the ceiling, kept cool there before being smoked or salted or dried.

Nardo was in the dairy, working at a long counter of wooden milk pans. He skimmed a long-handled, large-bowled spoon across the surface of each pan, removing the cream and pouring it into the bucket he carried.

Hearing movement behind him, he looked up and smiled at Cia.

You look like hell this morning! he called to her cheerfully. Nardo was a morning person. That was why he volunteered for the early milking shift.

Cia grimaced. *Thanks very much.*

No, you know what I mean. Didn't you sleep well?

Cia walked over to where Nardo was working. *That's what I wanted to talk to you about*, she began.

You want me to take the morning class for you today? he asked.

Could you please? I was up all night last night and a good portion of the night before. I had to ask Kate to take the class yesterday, so she had to do double with her afternoon class.

Sure, I'd be happy to, Nardo smiled at her. He got a dipper from a hook on the wall and scooped milk into it. He handed it to Cia and she drank it gratefully.

Thanks, she said, handing it back to him empty. *I appreciate it. Both. Unless I'm mistaken, I'll be able to teach tomorrow*. She turned to leave the dairy. *Oh! By the way, Kate says that she thinks Jenet may unfold soon.*

I'll keep an eye on him for you, Nardo said.

Thanks. Cia smiled and left the dairy.

* * *

'Ah! There you are!' Dalt strode across the dining-room floor to the chair next to the one Cia sat in. He pulled it away from the table and sat down with a flourish of his robe.

Cia blinked myopically at him for a moment. 'Dalt, it's been a long night. Could you go away and leave me alone for now?' she asked, turning away from him and concentrating on her tea.

'That's not a very friendly greeting,' Dalt said, too heartily. 'We could just chat a little. You look terrible.'

'One more person says that, I may get hostile,' Cia said.

'Oh, you know what I mean!' laughed Dalt. 'You look like you didn't get much sleep last night. Where were you? What did you do?'

'You seem overly concerned about my comings and goings, Dalt. Until very recently, you found any excuse not to speak to me at all. Why the sudden interest? Where are you when you aren't questioning me?'

'That's not fair,' Dalt objected. 'I asked you a question first and you didn't answer it.' He smiled broadly and stroked her hand.

Cia snatched her hand away from him. 'Don't touch me,' she hissed. 'Don't sit near me, don't speak to me. And leave Ian alone.'

'I meant no harm!' exclaimed Dalt. 'I asked a simple question, that's all. You've been very busy recently, and very mysterious about it. You miss class and disappear for long periods of time. We're just worried, that's all.'

'We?' Cia asked. 'Gardner needn't worry about my activities. They're none of his business, either.' She stood up and left the dining room.

A nap. A bath and a nap. That was what she needed. After a brief check on Sarah and Ian, Cia took the white robe from the peg on the back of her door, and went to the bathroom.

It was deserted. Everyone else was at breakfast. Cia pumped several buckets of water, stripped and bathed quickly. The soap and water felt good, but she was so tired that it didn't have its usual rejuvenating effect. She dried off, braided her hair and pulled on her clean robe. Gathering up the drying rags and dirty blue robe, she dropped them off at the laundry before going to her room and collapsing on the bed. She was asleep almost instantly.

It was dark when she awoke. She came back from deep sleep slowly and as she reached meditation level, decided to centre, rather than wake completely.

It was dark in her central chamber, but Cia knew her way around. A few steps forward and – she hit the Chair and fell to the floor. She lay there for a moment, wondering what had happened. The torches must have burned out when she expended her energy tracing Meg. It wasn't often that she worked so hard that she couldn't maintain that low level of energy. She got up and sat in the Chair. The button for the light over the dais was the first one on the arm. She pressed it and light flooded the chamber. It hurt her eyes.

Philip? she called softly. She pressed the elevator button and the door slid silently open. Philip sat on the bench inside.

Yes? he asked, coming into Cia's centre. He walked to his usual place on the dais, but he didn't sit.

I ran into Meg on the way back down the continuum, she said.

I know.

Have I done irreparable harm to her? she asked.

You did infinite good, Philip told her. *But she has no way of knowing that. Ian will have to show her.*

But he isn't a telepath, Cia objected. *How will he –*

The same way you did. He'll fumble around until he figures out what works.

111

When do I have to take him?

Not for a few days, said Philip. *He needs more time to fight the poison, and you need more time to sleep and eat.*

Cia nodded, lips quirked in a wry smile that didn't soften her eyes.

Maybe you will pay more attention to me in the future? When I tell you something, it's usually for your own good.

At that, Cia smiled genuinely.

Now, let me out of here, and go get yourself some dinner. Teach your classes and put in some time on your chores. Honest labour is good for the soul.

Whose soul? Cia pressed the button for the elevator and Philip left, but the vague feeling of dread that Cia had felt after her first contact with Meg was still with her.

Sarah and Jack had been trading watch on Ian, and both of them were worn out. Cia sent them off to dinner and bed, then settled herself down for a long night alone with her still-unconscious son. Looking at him, he seemed only to be asleep. His colour was almost back to normal and his breathing was deep and regular. Cia felt his pulse and found it strong and even. Why, she wondered, was it taking so long for him to regain consciousness? She could detect no interference from another telepath. Cia had only put him into deep level sleep. She wasn't holding him there, but he showed no inclination to leave that level.

Cia seated herself on the stool beside the bed and took Ian's hand in her own. Slowly, she reached into his mind. *Ian? May I speak with you?* she asked. When she received no response, Cia descended to the next level. *Ian? Are you here?*

Mother? came the faint reply. *I wasn't sure if I had heard you or not. Are you dead too?*

What? Cia asked, shocked by the question.

I think I may be dead, Ian told her. *I can't feel my body.*

112

You aren't dead, Cia told him. *Gardner used a nerve poison on you and Sarah hasn't been able to remove it all.* Cia squeezed his hand tightly.

Ouch! Ian objected. *You really did find me?*

Yes, and everything is going to be fine.

But – Ian prompted.

But what? asked Cia.

Mother, I can hear it in your voice. Everything is going to be fine, but – Ian chuckled drily. *It must be a pretty big but if you're afraid to tell me outright.*

Well, yes, it is, Cia admitted. *Do you remember that enigmatic letter you found in the library?*

The letter from Meg?

My guide, Philip, has told me that she is the answer to our problems with Gardner. She is the one who will defeat him. We haven't been able to marshal our own strength because it still wouldn't be enough and fear of him has divided us up, Cia told him.

I know that, said Ian impatiently. *What does that have to do with Meg? And what does it have to do with me?*

Philip says I have to take you to her, leave you with her. He says you're the one who has to convince her to help us, said Cia.

Why me?

Because you're about her age; you are most directly involved, being a direct target, Cia responded.

Her age?? Mother, her letter said she'd been dead almost six hundred years! How –

Think about it! she exclaimed. *She's in the past. If you go back in time, she will still be alive. Her letter said you met, therefore, you do. You can't get to her yourself, so I will have to take you there.*

But how –

Time is a continuous flow of energy. It is possible to traverse this energy, become a part of it, travel back and forth along it.

Physically?

No, said Cia. *You'll have to leave your body here with Sarah and me to continue healing. It will take you some time to recover.*

You're going to take my mind back in time so I can convince some girl to help us? How long do I have to do this? Ian wanted to know.

As long as it takes, said Cia.

Won't that take a lot of energy? How will you keep me there long enough?

I will leave you in her mind, and come back here to keep Drove busy.

You're going to take my mind to a strange girl in the past and just leave me there? Ian was incredulous. *Why is this necessary? Why can't we just ask her for her help?*

She sort of has a thing about voices in her head, Cia said. *My voice in particular. In her time, voices in your head mean you're crazy. She unfolded at birth, and I had to go back and block her gifts so that she could grow up normally in her own time. I sort of scared her along the way. She doesn't want anything to do with us. Convincing her is going to take a lot of time and effort.*

Yeah, but I still don't get it, Ian insisted. *Why do I have to convince her there? Why not just bring her here?*

She has to come willingly, or not at all. We need her desperately. There is no better way than to involve her directly. Make our concern hers. By getting to know you intimately, she will become *directly involved. She will want to help us. That's crucial.*

Well, I still don't like it, but I guess if it's necessary . . . Ian allowed his sentence to trail off, hoping his mother would tell him never mind.

This is a turning point – a crossroad. If Gardner is allowed to dominate, we will continue to inbreed and stagnate until we are all dead, Cia said sternly.

OK, OK, I'll go. But I don't think I'm going to enjoy it, Ian said grudgingly.

You don't have to enjoy it, said Cia, smiling. *But think: Meg lives in the Time Before. You'll be seeing first-hand what you've been reading about in the library.*

Really? Ian asked eagerly.

Really, laughed Cia. *Now, I'm going to leave you to rest. I'll be here if you need me, OK?*

When are you taking me back? asked Ian.

Not for several days. It takes a tremendous amount of energy to get myself back there. If I'm to take you with me, I have to get plenty of rest and a few more good meals into my belly. Also, you and I have to talk a bit about what you will face while you are back there, Cia told him. *Now, good night!*

Good night, Mother, Ian murmured.

Cia could already feel his mind wandering off to think about the Time Before, wondering what he would really see; how accurate the books had really been. She retreated from his mind and sat for a moment, watching his eyes as they flickered back and forth under closed lids. Then she went to the cupboard for blankets and pillows. She made a pallet on the floor between the bed and door, then placed the stool in front of the door again, to act as alarm.

Without dousing the torch or candle, she crawled into the blankets and fell asleep immediately.

When Cia entered the classroom the next morning, she was greeted by shy smiles from the children.

'Jenet, how are you feeling?' she asked the slight, black-haired boy sitting on the far side of the circle. He blushed and hung his head. Nina giggled, poking at a girl sitting next to her.

'Nina, is that very nice?' Cia asked her. 'We are supposed to love and support each other. When you are

115

ready to unfold, will you want the other children to laugh at you?'

Nina shook her head.

'Do you love and accept Jenet?' Cia asked Nina. The little girl squirmed uncomfortably before nodding. 'Tell him, then.'

'I love you, Jenet,' said Nina.

'Thank you,' Jenet responded. He didn't tell Nina he loved her. Cia let it slide. The trouble was, Jenet did love Nina. At least he was infatuated with her. And Nina knew it. When the younger girl tormented him, he took it in stoic misery.

Cia walked to the front of the group and sat on her pillows. 'Have you grounded yourselves this morning?' she asked.

The children nodded vigorously. 'Yes!' they told her.

'Good. Did Kate and Nardo have you practise in your centres?'

Again they responded eagerly. 'Lots!'

Cia looked at Rose. 'Rose, do you think you're ready to begin working with a guide?'

Rose gasped. 'Oh, Cia! May I please?'

'I think you're ready,' Cia smiled. 'Everybody, lie back and let's run through our centring exercises.'

As she walked them down the stairs and along the path to the field, Cia went to the window, prepared the smudge pot and lit it.

'Now, go to your central chamber and sit on a pillow in front of the door that lets your guide in and out,' she said, walking slowly around the room fanning smoke before her. 'Give permission to the person on the other side of the door to open it. Look at their feet. Are they wearing shoes? What kind? Are their feet long, or short? What do they look like? Their legs? Move your eyes slowly up their legs to their torso. Are their hands at their sides? On their hips? Crossed against their chest? By now you should know whether this is a man or a woman. How old is he or she? What colour hair? Eyes? What sort of clothes is he or she wearing?' Cia completed her circuit of the room and sat back down on her pillow, still fanning smoke in front of her as she blew gently on the glowing herbs.

'How do you feel about the person you see standing in your doorway? Do you feel safe? If you do, invite them in. If you don't feel completely safe about the person standing in your doorway, ask them what they are there for. If you don't like their answer, you may ask them to leave. Never invite someone into your centre if you aren't comfortable having them there. They can't enter if you don't let them.'

Cia looked around at the children's faces. None of them was frowning, so she decided they must have accepted the person standing at their door. 'Ask them to sit down,' she told them. 'Ask them if they are guide, or teacher. Ask their name. Ask them anything you like. Make sure this is a person you are comfortable working with.

'Sometimes, you will get a guide or teacher who makes you uncomfortable, but it may be necessary to work with them in order to learn the lessons in this life that you need to progress to the next level. You will have many guides and teachers throughout your life. This person you are talking to now is only your first.'

Cia took the smudge pot back to the window and blew the smoke across a row of small quartz crystals that were sitting beside the flint box.

She let the children speak with their guides for a bit longer as she finished clearing the crystals. Then she walked them back out of their centres, down the path through the woods and up the stairs. When they had all opened their eyes and sat up, she pointed to the window-sill.

'There is a crystal for each of you. You will pick up the

117

crystal that most appeals to you. You will find that even the last child to go will get the stone meant for them.

'Today, we will begin to learn how crystals can be used in combination with a grounded, balanced and centred energy to amplify psychic gifts and enhance natural tendencies towards the psychic.' Looking around the circle, Cia noticed a couple of frowns on the older children's faces.

'For those of you who have worked with crystals in this way before, a little practice never hurt anyone, but you may also have specific tasks that Kate or Nardo have told you to work on, so you may use this time to do that.' The frowns smoothed away and the energy in the room lightened.

'Now, each of you in turn, starting with Rose, go up to the window-sill and pick a crystal. Don't take too long, just pick up the one that grabs your eyes first.'

'When you each have a crystal, then we will begin our new lesson.'

Cia relaxed into the rhythm of a lesson she had taught dozens of times in the past, and the rest of the morning flew by. She was surprised when the noise level outside the classroom door increased, signalling lunchtime.

'OK, I guess that will be all for today,' she told them. 'You did well. I'm proud of you.'

The children filed out of the classroom smiling to themselves and each other.

Cia spent the afternoon in the kitchen, doing dishes after lunch, and staying on to get a jump on the dinner crew. By the time Tiana came in to begin making the biscuit dough, Cia had cleaned the counters, swept the floor and chopped the vegetables for the stew.

'Well, aren't we the industrious one,' said Tiana as she took a bowl into the pantry to measure flour for her dough.

Cia shook her head and bit her tongue. *You don't have to like it, just love and accept it.* First tenet taught to all children and reinforced throughout life. Never think harsh thoughts because they will come back on you. Never speak cruel words, for you will hear them of yourself. If you are loving, you will be loved.

Horse manure, Cia thought to herself. There are small, petty people who will always be ready to believe the worst of you, no matter what you do.

'Yes,' Cia smiled sweetly at Tiana. 'I am going to the meat locker to get lamb for tonight's stew.'

'Well, now, isn't that nice,' Tiana smiled sweetly back. 'Don't get lost.'

Stepping outside the kitchen door, Cia took a deep breath of barnyard and found it an improvement over the atmosphere in the kitchen. The old shepherd dog looked up at her from his spot in the sun on the stoop. She leaned down and patted his head before going down through the dairy to the meat locker.

By the time she had returned, carrying a large joint of meat, most of the dinner crew was in the kitchen, and preparations were well under way. Beth accepted the lamb from Cia and began to cut the meat into chunks.

Cia, why don't you help me set the tables, Kate suggested, giving her a handful of flatware. *How is Jenet doing?*

He's fine, Cia replied. *It's his crush on Nina that has me worried more than anything. I know it's not my problem, and it probably won't do him any harm, but she's so awful to him I want to slap her.*

You don't have to like it, Kate began, picking up a tray of cups and following Cia into the dining room.

Oh, spare me, Kate, said Cia, plunking the flatware on to the tables and separating the forks from the knives. She moved around the table, putting them at each place.

119

Are we a little unloving today? Kate asked, following Cia with the tray, placing a cup above each knife.

We're having a bit of a time with it, yes, Cia replied. *And some trouble with Drove.*

Oh, that, said Kate.

Yes, that. How did he manage to come between so many of us before we were aware of what he was doing? Cia sat down and stuck the tines of two forks together, trying to make them stand together on the table. They fell over.

Are you saying that we turned a blind eye to his bullying for too long, hoping that love would win him over?

Cia stood up and continued setting the table. *No, I think most of us secretly enjoyed teasing him. I mean, he was never a nice boy, but we may have pushed him past the point of endurance,* she said. *There are some people who are just bad, I guess, but maybe some who might have turned out OK given a little encouragement. The question is: what do we do about it now?*

Any ideas? Kate asked.

Yeah, but it's going to take time and a lot of courage.

Anything you want to share?

Cia looked at Kate. They had known each other all their lives. Kate's hair was less brown now, more grey, but her skin was still soft and clear and unlined. Her brown eyes still laughed as they had when she was a child. Her body had grown only slightly heavier as age had slowed her down, but she was strong and supple still.

Will you give me support? Cia asked her. *Will you stand by me if things get rough?*

Cia, what are you planning? Kate searched Cia's face carefully.

I can't tell you. I can't run the risk of Gardner finding out. Freddie might search you. I wouldn't want to place you in that kind of danger.

You know what you're doing?

No, Cia told her honestly. *But I have to do it anyway.*

Well, OK, Kate said slowly. *I don't like it, but I trust you. I'll help you in any way I can.*

Cia smiled at her. *Thanks.*

Cia stood in the hills above the Keep, shivering in the late night air. She sensed the cave nearby, but there was no moon, and she was having trouble locating it in the dark. She closed her eyes and stood very still, feeling for the source of the energy. Closing in on it at last, she stumbled the rest of the way to the entrance and stooped to enter the dark cavern.

After getting her candle lit, Cia looked around to make sure nothing had been disturbed in her absence. The tiny cave was exactly as she had left it three days before. She set the candle on the ledge and began to set up her chakra star on the floor. She spread her rug before it and sat down.

Once in her central chamber, Cia pressed the button on the Chair that activated the screen. The ceiling slid back and the opalescent flat emerged. She avoided projecting a mental image, keeping the screen blank as she adjusted it to display the mirror. Satisfied that it would have the effect she intended, she left the chamber and crossed the field to the path leading to the continuum.

PART TWO

Meg

Metalogue

The little girl was on her hands and knees. She rocked back and forth, slowly, deliberately, banging her head against the bars of her crib. They had been well padded against just this activity. Silently, rhythmically, with a concentration that seemed anything but childish, the baby banged her head against the padded rails while her mother stood watching helplessly.

Autism was a word that was new to her, but this activity, this frightening reality of her baby's self-destructive behaviour, now had a name. It was common enough to have a name.

Susan Danning looked at her beautiful little girl and a shiver of fear passed through her. Doctors' voices echoed in her mind, telling her that there was really very little help for this kind of disorder. The best that could be hoped for was life in an institution. Her beautiful baby, trapped in the prison of her mind, *living* in a prison . . .

Hands closed on her upper arms and Susan started in terror.

'Oh, honey, I'm sorry. I didn't mean to frighten you,' Ted apologized quickly. His eyes caught on the macabre scene in the crib in front of them and he shuddered at the bruises beneath the fine dusting of blonde hair on their baby's scalp. She was very thin. They had been unable to get her to eat anything in days.

Her fingers were raw and bloody. She had been chewing them. The doctors had said this was normal; that mittens might help. She had choked on the yarn and they had taken her to emergency. Ted had been unable to endure the pitying stares of the people there. He paced back and forth in front of the bench on which Susan sat. Both of them shared a glassy-eyed expression as they waited for Meg's stomach to be pumped. One grandmotherly type had clucked sympathetically to Susan, and Ted wound up taking Susan to the ladies' room to calm down.

'We don't know what causes it, or how to treat it,' the doctors had told them, all looking properly sombre and concerned. 'It's a flaw in brain chemistry. One theory says that it is the brain's inability to process and interpret the signals it receives from the senses. This is normal in infants and the first part of the learning process is to sort signals into patterns and interpret their meanings according to their consistencies. We feel that autistic children never learn to process and interpret the signals their brains are receiving, and so concentrate on one specific activity which causes a sufficient level of input to override all other data. For instance, banging her head against the crib bars allows her to focus on the pain in her head and ignore the bombardment of other signals she can't comprehend. Don't forget, she sees her room and all of its colours and shapes; she smells all the smells of the house that enter her room; hears all of the sounds in her environment and feels everything she touches, but her brain can't sort out what is important and fit it into a consistent pattern.

'If this theory is true, she is failing the first lesson in her education. This is probably something she will always suffer. If you try to care for her yourself, you will suffer with her, and your marriage will suffer as well. Statistics of couples attempting to care for a severely handicapped child show that divorce is the most frequent end. It is our recommendation that you place Meg in an institution better suited to caring for her special needs.'

'No,' Susan had whispered. 'This is my baby you're talking about. There must be something you can do. My beautiful baby.' She kept repeating this as Ted led her from the office back to the car. She clutched the rigid bundle that was their baby. Meg rhythmically banged her head against Susan's collarbone.

Meg? How old are you?

She lay on her mat in the middle of the classroom floor. It was quiet-time. She didn't need to look around to see where the voice came from. She had heard it before. Quietly, she stood up and approached the teacher's desk.

'Meg, shouldn't you be lying down right now?' her teacher asked when she noticed the small blonde child standing beside her chair.

'The lady just asked me how old I am,' Meg said, keeping her voice to a whisper.

'What lady?' her teacher asked, looking sharply around the classroom. Her young students lay on towels and mats in the middle of the kindergarten classroom. There were no other people there.

'The lady in my head,' Meg responded. Her large blue eyes were pooling tears. Her chin quivered slightly. 'When I tell Mommy she takes me to a man who scares me too, but the lady in my head scares me more. Will you tell her to go away? Please?'

Elizabeth Sternan had been told she might expect this, but she'd hoped not to have to deal with it. Mental illness wasn't something she felt qualified to handle. Meg hadn't had an episode in several months, so her parents and the school board felt that she would be all right in a classroom situation. She had never posed a danger to anyone but herself. Miss Sternan took small comfort in that knowledge as she kept a close eye on the small girl. She had rehearsed in her mind what she would do if Meg came to her with this complaint.

Now that she faced the situation, the practised

responses evaporated. She looked blankly at the child and froze in her chair.

'Please, Miss Sternan? I'm scared,' Meg whispered.

Elizabeth stood and walked to the phone on the wall by the door. She picked up the receiver, put it to her ear and listened a moment.

'It's happened,' she said at last. She hung up and returned to her desk. She sat down in her chair and looked at Meg. The little girl smiled at her uncertainly through her tears. Elizabeth held her arms out and the child climbed into her lap. 'It's going to be OK,' Elizabeth murmured into the fine, blonde hair. 'I won't let anyone hurt you.'

The other children sat up on their towels and mats as the principal came into the classroom followed by the school nurse. They remained silent as they watched the Principal take Meg from the teacher. Meg looked up at him through her tears, also silent.

'Thank you, Miss Sternan,' he said, handing Meg to the nurse. She took Meg and left. The principal turned to face the children who sat on their towels and mats staring at him.

'Meg isn't feeling well,' he said to them. 'But she'll be better soon, and back in the class with you.' Then he also left.

The man with the thin moustache sat behind his desk, leaning over it to look down at Meg. She sat in the chair opposite him.

'What did the voice say to you this time?' he asked. She didn't like his tone of voice. He always spoke to her as if he thought she was lying. She squirmed under his gaze.

'Just what she always asks,' Meg said. 'She asks me how old I am. Then she goes away.'

'Do you wish you were older, Meg? Do you wish you were a grown-up so you could boss your parents around?'

128

he asked her again. He always asked this. She didn't know what it meant. It was sort of like when the mind-lady asked how old she was. The mind-lady asked how old she was, the man with the thin moustache asked if she wanted to be a grown-up. Mom and Dad got upset and everyone treated her funny.

'No. I don't want to be a grown-up. I want the mind-lady to go away. That's all,' Meg told the moustache-man. I want you to go away, she thought at him. She didn't say it out loud, though. She had once. He got very angry and told her parents. Then they got upset, too. They said he was just trying to help her. She didn't think so. He didn't make the mind-lady go away, and he asked stupid questions and didn't help at all. Meg didn't like him. He talked to her for a while, and then gave her mother a bottle of pills to give Meg. Your daughter is schizophrenic, she heard Dr Klein saying to her parents. Give her these pills and she'll be fine.

They made Meg feel dizzy and sleepy. She couldn't go out to play when she took those pills. She couldn't think when she took those pills, but at least the mind-lady left her alone for a little while.

But she always came back. She always asked the same question and she always scared Meg.

It was dark and the hallway was filled with shadows that frightened her. Her nightmare frightened her more.

'Mom?' she whispered loudly. She was terrified. She wanted her mother to hold her and make the dream go away, but she didn't want to wake her up since she was asleep. 'Mom?'

'Meg?' came the sleepy reply. She heard movement behind the closed door, and her father's grumble as the bed creaked and footsteps crossed the floor. The door opened and her mother stood in the doorway. 'Meg?

Honey? What's wrong?' she asked, kneeling and smoothing Meg's tangled blonde hair out of her face.

'The mind-lady woke me up,' Meg whispered. She felt her mother tense.

'What did she say?' Mom asked. Her fist knotted in Meg's hair and pulled so that it hurt.

'Ow,' Meg said, pulling away. 'She asked the same thing she always asks: "How old are you?"'

'Ted?' Her mother's voice trembled.

'Can I sleep with you?' Meg asked.

'No, Meg. You're eight years old. That's too old to sleep with us now. We'll take you to see Dr Klein tomorrow, OK?' Her Dad stood in the doorway behind Mom. In the dark, he was a shadow wearing pale pyjama bottoms.

'I don't want to see Dr Klein. I don't like him. He asks me the same dumb questions and gives me pills that make me tired all the time,' Meg whined.

'Go back to sleep, sweetheart.' Mom hugged her. 'Everything is going to be OK.' She led Meg back to her room and tucked her into bed.

Moustache-man leaned over his desk, staring down at Meg. She sat in the chair opposite him and squirmed under his glare.

'What did she say to you this time?' he asked.

'Just what she always asks,' Meg said. 'She asks me how old I am. Then she goes away.'

'Do you wish you were older, Meg? Do you wish you were grown-up so you could boss your parents around?' he asked again.

Meg sighed. 'No, I don't want to be grown-up. I want the mind-lady to go away. That's all.'

As they were leaving, he gave her mother a bottle of pills to give Meg. Your daughter is schizophrenic, she heard Dr Klein saying to her parents. Give her these pills and she'll be fine.

She knew what they were. They wouldn't do her any good. She resolved never to come back here again.

Meg? How old are you?

She dropped her pencil. The test was only about halfway over and long division wasn't her best subject.

Meg?

She hadn't heard the voice in almost a year. She had almost come to hope that she wouldn't hear it again. She tried to shut it out and concentrate on the problems on the board. She picked up her pencil from the floor and stared at the paper in front of her.

She could still feel the presence in her mind. She couldn't finish the test as long as the mind-lady was there.

Meg?

She gritted her teeth and shut her eyes. There was no way to block her out.

How old are you?

'Ten!'

'Meg?' her teacher asked. 'This is a silent test. You are not to give answers to your classmates.'

'Yes, sir,' Meg murmured. She bent to her paper again. The voice in her mind had gone.

'Meg,' her mother said when she got home that afternoon. 'Your principal, Mrs Deckhart, called this morning and said that you disrupted a test in class. Are you OK?'

Meg yanked the fridge door open and reached for the milk. 'Yeah, Mom. Fine,' she said. She took the carton over to the counter and got a glass from the cupboard. Her hand was shaking a little, but she didn't think her mother would notice.

'You're sure? No voices, or anything? Mr Burns thought he heard you say your age.'

'Oh, that!' Meg exclaimed a little too brightly. 'No!

131

Julie, the girl who sits next to me, kept pestering me for the answer to a problem. I finally told her just to shut her up.'

'You helped a friend cheat on a test?'

'I said she sat next to me. I didn't say she was my friend. I didn't give her the *right* answer, or anything.'

'Meg, are you telling me the truth?'

'Yes!' Meg exclaimed indignantly. 'No mind-lady, OK? You sound disappointed or something.'

Susan sat down at the kitchen table and rubbed her eyes with her fists. 'No, Meg,' she said without looking up. 'Not disappointed. I'm worried about you. I'll probably always worry about you. When these things happen, I get so scared.' She looked up. Meg was startled to see tears slipping silently down her mother's cheeks. 'You don't know,' she continued. 'When the phone rings in the middle of the day, when you're not home . . . my heart freezes. I think, oh please God, don't let this be from school. I feel so helpless. What if one day you go into your mind and never come back?'

Meg leaned against the counter. There was nothing she could say. If she told her mother the truth, she would have to go back to Dr Klein. She would spend another few weeks on a drug that did more damage to her mind than the lady who spoke to her. She would miss more school and have to lie to her friends about the reason or she wouldn't have any friends to go back to . . .

'No voice, Mom. I swear it, everything's fine.' As she said that, Meg felt a strange distance settling between them. She was certain her mother knew she was lying.

'OK,' Susan nodded. She pushed stiffly up from the table and moved towards Meg. She stopped more than an arm's distance away, an odd look on her face. She nodded again. 'OK.' She left the kitchen. If she mentioned it to Meg's father, Meg never found out.

5

Meg!

The woman's voice was strong and commanding, but it drifted towards her from a distance. It pursued her through the fog of pre-dawn, down the deserted streets of the Old City.

Glancing over her shoulder as she ran, Meg couldn't see anyone following her. The fog swallowed objects around her at only a few feet's distance, first touching lamp posts and buildings with long, wispy fingers, clutching them more firmly, and finally enveloping them possessively as she ran past.

The long tendrils caught at her, tearing like cobwebs as she fought to escape. The insistence of the voice and the footsteps behind her drove Meg along streets she didn't know. She was lost and cold and wet. She ran, terrified as she sensed the voice growing closer.

Meg! the woman called again.

Meg paused on the cracked pavement. The fog created small, round rainbows around the street lights. As she looked at them, they flickered and went out. With the darkness, her panic increased. Her chest heaved as she fought to catch her breath.

Footsteps echoed in the dark behind her, but she couldn't move. Someone else seemed to have possession of the body she occupied, and he didn't have the same sense of urgency . . . no, that wasn't it. He was terrified of the place they were in.

Meg concentrated on that terror for a moment as she managed to move closer to the empty buildings that lined the cracked and buckled pavement of the road. Desperately, she looked about. The vacant windows of the empty buildings stared back at her offering no comfort, no escape.

The fear she sensed had no grounding in the chase. Instead, it seemed to stem from a deeply ingrained belief that the place itself presented the greater danger.

The footsteps turned on to the street Meg was in. Long shadows were cast on the broken asphalt by a full, bone-white moon. The street lights were broken and had probably not worked in . . . Lord, they looked now as if they had never worked. Meg thought briefly that she ought to recognize where she was, but the blank windows stared blankly back at her as she fought to make her body co-operate. (Was it her body? She didn't think so, but that didn't make any sense.) Who was chasing her?

The feet beneath her began to move as the shadow came closer. She tried to be stealthy, but her feet (those feet were really much too large) seemed to kick loose stones so they rattled out into the street, attracting their pursuer's attention to their inadequate hiding place.

Now the misplaced fear Meg had been sensing grew to include the chase, but she still had no clear idea of where she was and why she was running in terror through streets that had been abandoned for decades.

Souls, he's come for us himself! a male voice exclaimed. The thought came to Meg unbidden as she glanced over her shoulder at the shadow.

Who? She cried as she skidded across an alley and tripped over the opposite curb. There was no answer, but a heap of rubble rose up from the pavement and came at them in a solid mass.

Almost before she knew what was happening, Meg dropped to the ground and rolled under the obstacle without slowing her headlong flight. With a great crash, the stones dropped to the cement behind her (them? The male voice was more a part of the body she occupied than she was), but there was no sound from their shadow except for his footsteps in the dark.

Meg's breath was coming in choked sobs, tearing from her (his?) throat. Fire burned in her ribs and fear constricted her heart, but still she (they?) ran on.

Meg? How old are you? the woman asked.

This is crazy, she thought to herself. A portion of her detached itself enough to wonder why none of this made sense. She realized she was in a dream, but she couldn't wake up. Something told her she had dreamed this before, had to see it through to its conclusion. What that could possibly be, she couldn't imagine, but she was powerless to escape the nightmare in which she was trapped.

A portion of a building detached itself and fell into her path. Her feet (those enormous feet) veered around the stones as they exploded and she could feel the shrapnel as it entered her leg; the warmth of the blood as it oozed out on to the leather trousers she (they?) wore. She didn't feel any pain, but that made as much sense as anything else going on around and in her. She ran on.

The female voice made encouraging sounds in her head, now. She recognized it. A part of her was relieved by its presence, but it terrified the rest of her almost as much as the person she was fleeing. There were thoughts; feelings associated with this voice that were more frightening than she could allow herself to think about.

Chaos.

This voice had something to do with chaos.

And pain.

There was a tremendous physical and emotional hurt associated with the memories of this voice. Meg was unable even to think about why the voice chilled her to the core. She ran faster. She knew she wouldn't escape its contact with her mind, but like a horse trying to outrun the burr under its saddle Meg found reserves of strength she hadn't known and she sped across the broken and deserted streets in search of sanctuary.

Rounding the next corner, the shadow that had been following her was suddenly in front of her. She skidded to a halt, a scream frozen in her throat as the barriers in her mind broke.

The scream tore raggedly from her as the chaos she had feared flooded past the broken walls and Meg knew why she was afraid of the woman's voice. Now she remembered what she had fought against, but even as the realization dawned, her ability to recognize it vanished. Once again, she was a frightened child suffering complete sensory overload. She clutched her head and sank to her knees on the hard cement, screaming as sanity and reality slipped away from her.

'Meggie?' A small voice interrupted her sleep. She groaned and turned away from the sound, pulling the feather pillow over her head.

'Go away,' she mumbled.

'Meggie,' (she hated it when he whined), 'you promised you'd take me to the fair today!'

Saturday. Bloody. So she had. She peered out from under the pillow at a small, tow-headed boy. Early-morning sunlight blazed through window shades he had apparently opened before waking her. He stared back at her through clear grey eyes. His mouth was puckered, ready to cry if she yelled at him for any reason. Mom must have made chocolate milk; he had a thin, brown moustache along his upper lip.

'I did, huh?' She squinted at the clock on her bedside table. Textbooks she had meant to study last night blocked the face. She shoved them on to the floor and pulled herself closer to it. 'Thiessen, it's only eight! The fair doesn't start for another hour.'

'The p'rade starts in half-a-hour. Mom said so.' He

looked as if he were enjoying this. Thiessen had 'six years old' down to a fine art. Meg sighed. It was too damned early in the morning to expect higher brain processes to function.

The fair was always the herald of summer. Held in early May, it was a signal to the children that freedom was pending; a signal to the adults that vacations were near – a time to relax and be young again for a little while. It was only a small fair, but the towns it visited were generally small as well. The few rides and attractions it boasted were augmented by local organizations holding raffles, and games like dunk-the-teacher/minister/mayor to raise money for community improvement. It was only in town for one weekend and practically everybody in town went.

Mom and Dad had always taken Thiessen before, but this year, they had agreed to let Meg take him. Meg felt she had scored a coup; as though she was finally vindicated in her belief that she was OK. Finally, Mom and Dad trusted her to look after her baby brother at the fair. Meg had been fourteen when Thiessen was born. Now she was twenty, a college sophomore and only recently allowed to do 'big-sister things' with him. Today, at eight in the morning on an overly bright Saturday, she wasn't so sure she wanted the privilege of being responsible for a hyper six-year-old.

'I didn't say I'd take you to the parade, I said I'd take you to the fair.' Semantic arguments don't work on six-year-olds, but Meg felt obligated to try. If she didn't do something quickly, Thiessen was going to start howling. 'OK, tell you what: you go play with your trucks while I get ready and we can ride our bikes down to the parade. Do you know where it starts?' Thiessen nodded vigorously. 'Then you can show me, because I don't remember.'

'Thanks, Meggie!' he shouted as he bounded towards the door.

'Don't – ' she started. He slammed the door behind him. 'Slam the door,' she finished to herself.

Meg rolled over on to her back and stared at the ceiling. Her eyes were sandy from lack of sleep and she wanted to close them, drift back into never-never land . . . she felt her lids shut. Ill-defined shreds of nightmare from last night reminded her there were things in her subconscious that she was still unprepared to deal with.

Freud would have something to say about that, she thought to herself.

'Can't do it,' she muttered aloud. 'Got to get up.' She threw back the covers before she could stop to think about what she was doing, and hopped out on to the bare wooden floor. Thiessen had moved her rag rug again. She pulled it towards her with one toe and stepped on to it.

Down the hall, she could hear plastic wheels rolling across the bare floor in Thiessen's room while he made engine sounds, and pans rattling on the stovetop as Mom made breakfast. She was talking to herself as she clattered around the kitchen.

Meg reached for her blue jeans and pulled them on under her nightgown.

'Hurry, Meggie!' Thiessen yelled.

'I'm coming, Thiessen,' Meg yelled back, rummaging in the drawer for a clean tee-shirt. She climbed out of her nightgown and tossed it on to the chair.

They arrived at the fairground just as the parade swung out of the church parking lot to begin its march down Main Street. Meg and Thiessen locked their bicycles at the rack beside the library and ran to find a place on the kerb. Thiessen spotted some of his friends from his first-grade class and insisted on sitting with them.

Soon, he was caught up in the kaleidoscope of costume

and colour. Meg bought him a large green balloon and tied it to his wrist. After that, he walked about with his left arm in the air as though afraid to restrict the balloon's freedom.

A man came by selling clouds of pink cotton candy and Thiessen developed a beard to complement the moustache Mom had forgotten to remove in the excitement of departure.

He laughed gleefully at the clowns and scrambled with his friends to pick up the pieces of candy that they tossed.

The high-school band marched as the centrepiece of the parade. They maintained ragged formation as they blatted out the school's fight song in equally ragged fashion. They had been arranged according to stage concert optimum, with woodwinds in front. Flutes, clarinets and saxophones were followed by trumpets, trombones and tubas. The snare and bass drums brought up the rear. As a result, only parts of the music were audible at any given time, depending upon which section was marching past the people who crowded the pavements. Thiessen and his friends strutted beside the band as it marched by, imitating the long slide of the trombone and the beat of the bass drum. They didn't look closely enough to see that the bright-red uniforms, trimmed with gold braid, were worn and stained. They stretched too tightly in most places and were pinned and tucked in many of the others. The furry hats the players wore were in many cases too big and none of the shoes matched, but the magic of a parade held the small children enthralled and they noticed none of the details that Meg felt she was seeing for the first time.

Too soon, the band turned into the grocery store parking lot at the end of the parade route and began putting instruments into the back of an old beat-up brown van. The crowds moved off in search of the wonders to be found in the booths and on the rides at the fair. Meg and Thiessen ran to follow; Thiessen clutching the sticky string which connected the balloon to his wrist, Meg clutching the rumpled bills Mom had given them for the rides and games.

They rode the ferris wheel and the roller coaster; they ate hot dogs and french fries; they played ring toss and baseball throw. Thiessen had his palm read by a Gypsy fortune-teller and Meg won a stuffed tiger for guessing the number of jelly beans in a particular jar.

As they approached the house of mirrors, Meg felt a sudden desire to grab Thiessen and run, but he jerked his hand from her grip.

'C'mon, Meggie! Martha says we should go in!' he yelled as he ran up the ramp into the attraction.

Thiessen had an imaginary friend named Martha who, it seemed, 'told' Thiessen lots of strange things. Often they were things that would ordinarily be beyond the scope of a six-year-old's knowledge and experience. Thiessen was either uncomfortably precocious, or spent more time than normal eavesdropping on adult conversation and periodically parroted it back.

Panicked, Meg thrust some tickets at the attendant and ran up the ramp after him, trying to ignore the fear that was rising in her mind. This is ridiculous, she told herself as she moved into the dimly-lit interior of the tent.

The inside consisted of a raised and railed walkway that allowed only forward movement past the warped mirrors that gave the place its name. The mirrors were set edge to edge along the sides of the walk which wound a convoluted path from entrance to exit, so that the customer wouldn't notice the relatively small size of the tent's inside. Meg tried to keep an eye on Thiessen as he moved along, watching his reflections shift and change. Meg glanced over at the mirror she was walking by and stopped, staring in horror.

The reflection in the mirror wasn't hers. Meg stood

before a mirror that was meant to distort her into a shape much taller and thinner than she actually was, but this was no shape that her body could ever become. The strangely undistorted reflection in the mirror was of a very tall, impossibly slender woman with long silver-white hair and transparent grey eyes. Meg looked about in wild desperation. No one else stood near enough to Meg to cast such a reflection. No one near Meg answered the bizarre description.

Meg glanced down at her own much shorter body. Everything looked the way it had for as long as she could remember: stocky and muscular, lean but not slender. This meant her hair must still be a pale blonde; her eyes still a startlingly bright blue. Meg looked back into the mirror.

The reflection smiled tentatively. Meg knew she hadn't smiled. She blinked rapidly several times as though to clear her eyes before looking back into the mirror. The same grey eyes regarded her as before; eyes she had never seen. Meg felt her grip on reality shift.

'No, I can't lose it here. Not now,' she muttered aloud, as if by vocalizing, she would ward off the threat implied by the figure in the mirror that wasn't herself. To test this theory, Meg reached for the apparition. A slender, translucent hand reached toward her from inside the glass, but as Meg's hand reached the surface, the hand in the mirror touched a point above her own. Meg jerked her hand back, burned by the realization that there was no way that the reflection could indeed be hers.

She whispered, 'Thiessen!'

He had wandered ahead to a mirror that made him shorter and more squat than he already was. He paid no attention to her. The crowd in the House of Mirrors continued to swirl past, unaware of Meg's distress as they laughed in delight at the mockery the mirrors made of body and face. But none of them looked into her mirror, and none of them cast an image in it as they passed by her without noticing.

With a glance back at the mirror, Meg tried to take a step towards Thiessen. Her feet were rooted to the spot; she was unable to move. Frantically, she struggled against the inertia that kept her in front of the frightening reflection. A brief image from a recurring nightmare flashed across her subconscious and she found herself struggling with the broken pavement of a dark, deserted street.

Then the voice spoke in her mind.

I've been trying to reach you.

Meg gasped. Oh God, she thought. I have lost my mind.

Her voice was familiar. Its memories weren't pleasant.

The fog began to descend on her thoughts, blanketing resistance; attempting to anaesthetize her fear. With a shudder, Meg brushed aside the encroaching tentacles and tried to focus on the woman who insisted on being the image Meg saw in the mirror. She was still there. Tall and slim, she seemed to sway as she stood with hand upraised, beckoning to Meg.

Looking Meg directly in the eyes, she repeated, *I have been trying to reach you.* Her mouth didn't move. It was the voice of the mind-lady.

Meg was overcome by a need to be as far away from the House of Mirrors and this frightening delusion as was humanly possible. She looked for Thiessen and found him still in front of the short-and-stout mirror, as though no time had passed.

Meg, we haven't much time. I won't harm you. Will you listen to what I have to say? Please, it's important. The silver-haired woman projected an aura of warmth and trust that Meg had difficulty pushing aside.

'I've lost my mind in the House of Mirrors,' Meg mused aloud. 'Mom and Dad always expected me to go crazy again, but I don't think even *they* had this in mind. Who's going to take Thiessen home safely?' She shook her head to clear the fog that seemed to accompany the strange woman. 'Who are you?' she asked.

My name is Cia Janec. I've come to ask for your help. Cia leaned forward towards the glass separating them, squinting as though the barrier dimmed her vision.

Meg swiped at the sweat on her upper lip with the back of her hand. 'Help you with what?' she asked. Again she struggled to make her feet move from the spot where she stood. Again, she failed. Arms windmilling, Meg fought to regain her balance as she screamed.

'Thiessen! Thiessen, come here now,' she cried. But Thiessen remained transfixed by the short/stout image cast by the mirror he stood before. Why can't he hear me? she wondered.

Because none of this is happening, she told herself sternly. He's not a part of your mental aberrations. None of this will affect him. You're the only one going to the funny farm for this. Stop worrying about things you have no control over.

Thiessen is fine. He just can't hear you. He won't wander off. Please stop worrying about losing your mind. I promise you're as sane as you ever were. I just don't have any other way of reaching you and as I said, I desperately need your help. Cia smiled in a way Meg felt certain was meant to be reassuring, but Meg was in no mood for coddling.

'How do I know I was ever sane?' she screamed. 'Why should I believe you that my brother is OK? Who are you and why did I make you up?'

I told you, Cia responded patiently. *My name is Cia Janec. I come from a place that is most certainly not your imagination. I have no wish nor reason to harm your brother. I am trying to save my son and I need your help to do it. If you had truly lost your mind, then you would*

143

*need my help again as when you were a tiny child suffering
telepathic overload.*

Meg gasped. 'How did you know . . .?'

*To go through the unfolding so young and with no one
to help you must have been a very frightening thing, Meg.*

Meg saw herself as a baby in her crib rhythmically
banging her head against the padded railings, but with a
clarity and perspective that could not be mistaken for
memory.

'The doctors call that autism,' she said, staring in horrid
fascination at the fading mental image. 'I was autistic.
They said my recovery was a fluke; a miracle.' Reflexively, she rubbed her thumbs against scarred fingertips.

*No, Meg. That may be what they allowed themselves to
believe, but I was there. I erected the mental barriers that
allowed you that 'miraculous recovery' and a normal
childhood.* Cia squared her skinny shoulders and inhaled
sharply. *Now I have come to ask a favour in return.*

'You're lying! I owe you nothing!' Meg clutched at the
railing and tugged furiously at one leg, then the other in
her attempt to free herself from the impossible situation.
Neither foot budged, but Thiessen was still in front of his
mirror, too. In that respect at least, the strange woman
seemed to be telling the truth. Meg pulled again at her
feet, straining thigh muscles that were trained for athletics
and swimming team, and bicycled her anywhere in town
she needed to go. There should have been no question of
their response, but she couldn't move a step. 'Let me go!'
she screamed at the reflection in the mirror. 'Leave me
alone!'

*Meg, will you keep my son? Please. He will surely die if
you don't.*

'Let me go! Let me go!' Meg wrenched violently away
from the mirror and lost her balance. She grabbed blindly
and got a handful of sweatshirt.

'Hey, miss, are you OK?'

Meg's feet came free and she staggered into the man she had accidentally accosted.

'Uh, yeah. I'm OK. I'm looking for my little brother. He's only six. He wandered off and I got worried. I'm really sorry.' Mumbling more apologies over her shoulder, Meg rushed over to Thiessen and grabbed his arm.

'Hey, Meggie, c'mon! Lemme go!' Thiessen hollered as she dragged him out of the House of Mirrors and away from the frightening reflection that wasn't hers; the voice in her head that had haunted her dreams for as long as she could remember.

Once outside the tent, Meg collapsed on the grass, unmindful of the litter of popcorn, napkins and ticket stubs. Her breath came in ragged gasps and to her dismay she began to cry.

'Hey, Meggie,' Thiessen knelt solemnly before her in the trash. 'I didn't mean to scare you,' he said. 'Martha said it would be OK.' His eyes were round in his round little face. Meg became aware that her behaviour was frightening him.

'Thiessen, I'm sorry. I just couldn't find you for a minute with all of those people and those weird mirrors . . .' She drew a shuddery breath and rubbed her cheek against her shoulder to dry her tears.

Thiessen hugged Meg. 'I love you, Meggie. I won't scare you any more.'

Meg laughed shakily and hugged him back. 'I love you too, Thiessen. Now, how about that merry-go-round ride I promised you earlier?'

'All right!' Thiessen yelled, jumping to his feet.

Cia sat slumped forward with her head on her knees. Her breath came in great, choking gasps, made more difficult by her doubled position, but she lacked the strength to sit upright. The candles in the star before her had long since

145

flickered and died. Their waxes had run together and pooled, forming discoloured swirls in the dirt. Tears of exhaustion and frustration fell unchecked; Cia had nothing left inside her to stop them.

She had failed. The blocks she had used to bring relief to the tortured mind of an infant and her inept fumbling in the continuum, searching for Meg at the proper age, had caused the distrust and fear that now thwarted her efforts to protect Ian.

The more she thought about this, the more hopeless the situation became. She cried harder, spending more precious energy on self-pity. Great sobs tore from her throat as she rocked back and forth in the dirt.

This will do no one any good. Stop it at once.

For a moment, Cia didn't recognize the voice, so stern was its tone.

Philip? she asked hesitantly. *Philip, is that you?*

Yes, came the severe reply. *Now cease this display at once.*

Cia was so shocked by Philip's harshness that she sat up immediately, swiping at her cheeks with the backs of her hands.

You will have to try again. You have not failed until you are told 'no' by this girl. Your request was not denied, Philip told her. *You will have to go back.*

Go back? Cia was too tired to understand. *But it's too late. There's nothing more I can do!* Cia was working up to tears again, feeling the hopelessness of the situation welling up inside her.

Cia, begin your healing. You need rest and food. Calm down and take care of your body's needs. We will talk later about Meg. Philip spoke with such authority that Cia obeyed him immediately, stretching out on the rug to begin monitoring her systems and performing relaxing and replenishing exercises.

It was not until she began packing up her tools that she

realized the amethyst crystal in her amulet had shattered. She sighed and shoved it into her sack without stopping to wrap it in its leather and stood to gather candle wax for burial.

Cia's vision closed around her as the blood abruptly left her head. She sat down suddenly, temples pounding and bones watery.

'I can't,' she said into the tiny cave as she slipped back into the darkness of her mind. Even food would have to wait until she had recovered sufficiently to make the journey back down the trail to the Keep. Surrounded by the trappings of her art, Cia slept soundly as day dawned outside her hiding place.

6

Meg wandered through the next day on pins and needles. She had a sense of anticipation, but the niggling worry that she was losing her mind stayed with her as she went through the motions of going to class and taking notes and paying attention.

She had grown up with the knowledge that her early childhood had been less than normal. Her parents loved her, but Meg always heard a note of recrimination when they explained that they had waited to have Thiessen because they couldn't be guaranteed not to have another child like Meg. They couldn't take that risk again. They almost hadn't got through it the last time . . .

Meg felt responsible for their troubles. She had received the message from her parents that she was somehow to blame and now all she could think of was that it was happening all over again.

One of the earliest memories Meg had was of a woman talking in her head. It was associated with unendurable chaos and incredible pain. It was the voice that had trapped her the day before; the voice that had chased her through the deserted streets of her nightmare landscape.

Meg was afraid to tell anyone about what had happened to her. The fear of being sent back to Dr Klein for more stupid questions and a thorazine prescription was all too real. Her parents always watched Meg with a wary eye anyway. This would give them grounds for their concern and she was unprepared, at present, to deal with their reaction.

Meg had never been a trusting person. She had never told anyone of her childhood illness and felt she had no one close to confide in. She was scared and lonely and very much in need of a friend, but she didn't know how to reach out for one.

She settled for hugging a protesting Thiessen at breakfast, taking a deep breath, squaring her shoulders and bicycling off to the University as though nothing out of the ordinary had happened.

Susan watched the display from behind her newspaper, but said nothing as Meg walked out the door. Small fingers of fear raised the hair on the back of Susan's neck, but there seemed nothing concrete to worry about, so she pushed it out of her mind and set about readying Thiessen for school.

Meg had so many questions that she began to write them down, intending to study them objectively later, but she misplaced the paper when she was studying for her biology exam during lunch.

'Hi, Meg.'

'Huh?' She looked up from her search, startled.

'Brilliant response. Don't I even rate a kiss, or at least a "Hi, Tucker"? Are you off in space or something?'

'Or something,' Meg answered, returning the smile of the tall, dark-haired grad student who was looking down at her. 'Sit down and stay a while. I need an excuse not to study my biology.'

'Oh no!' he laughed. 'You're not going to blame it on me.'

'I can't concentrate anyway,' Meg complained.

'That's why you were so madly searching through your notes?' Tucker grinned at her, indicating the disorderly pile of papers on the table in front of her.

'I was looking for a piece of paper.' Meg frowned slightly.

'There's lots of those,' Tucker shot back, his grin widening.

'Wise-ass. I was looking for a specific piece of paper.'

'Anything to do with bio?'

'Nothing to do with bio.'

'Why don't I sit down?'

'I thought you'd never ask.'

'Where've you been recently?' Tucker's tone changed as he slid into the chair opposite Meg's.

'Where've I been?' she echoed vaguely. 'What do you mean?'

'Well, I haven't seen you for days and you haven't returned my calls. Now it's like your mind is a million miles away. Did I do anything wrong? Are you mad at me?' Tucker asked.

'Oh, Tucker, no!' Meg said. 'I'm sorry. You didn't leave the messages with Thiessen, did you?'

'Yeah,' Tucker laughed. 'You didn't get them, huh?'

Meg shook her head. 'We can't forbid him to answer the phone because he does it anyway, but we can't seem to impress him with the importance of message-taking either.' Somehow, punishing Thiessen was like kicking a puppy. No one could quite bring themselves to do it. Meg suspected that it was all part of the six-years-old act, but she was as susceptible as the rest. 'Anyway, no, I'm not mad at you. It's just that I've had a lot on my mind and with that and finals, I'm suffering serious fry-brain.'

'Well, maybe you can recover long enough to go out with me tonight? *Mutilated Monkeys* is playing down at the Pub. How about some dancing to shake out the tension? I'll pick you up at about nine?'

'Make it tomorrow and you've got a date. I promised Mom I'd watch Thiessen tonight. Dad is pitching a grant to the Dean, so they're going out.'

'Tomorrow, then. I've got to go to class, but I'll call you tonight, OK?' He leaned over, kissed her, and then stood to leave.

'Tucker?'

Her tone checked him. 'Yes?'

'I've got a lot of studying to do tonight, and with Thiessen on my neck for horsey rides, I'm going to be hard put to get it done. Why don't you meet me at the coffee shop tomorrow at eight, instead. I'll buy you breakfast and we'll have a little uninterrupted time before class.'

Tucker flashed her a smile. 'You going to be able to wake up in time for that?'

Meg made a face at him. 'I'll manage, OK?'

'Deal,' he said. He slung his backpack over his shoulder and left the commons. Meg watched him out of sight and then returned to her notes.

Cia found herself lying on the dirt floor of the small cavern, the muddy pools of cold wax beside her. She had slept through the day, hidden in the cave on the hillside. At dusk, she awoke feeling much better for the rest and the healing.

After an extravagant stretch, Cia went out on to the hillside, leaving the interior of the cave intact as she cast about for any nearby mental activity. Finding none, she returned to the tiny cavern, folded her rug and stuffed it into her sack. She relit the common candle and examined her amulet in its feeble glow. The shards of amethyst crystal remaining in the setting had been completely drained of colour. Searching in the dirt, she found a few shards that had exploded from the setting. They had blood on them.

Cia touched her forehead, gingerly feeling the cuts made by the shattered stone. Fortunately, none of the shards had remained embedded. Soap and water would suffice to cleanse the wounds. Gathering the pieces of crystal, Cia wrapped them with the amulet in leather and tucked it into her pocket. After she buried the remains of the coloured candles and smudged the cave, Cia stepped out on to the path back to the Keep.

The walk back down the hillside gave Cia time to think about the events at the fair. She had not expected it would be so difficult to persuade this girl. Meg had put up a good fight and posed some very difficult questions. Cia would need time to prepare answers that would convince a stubborn and very frightened young woman to co-operate with a plan Cia wouldn't go along with, if she were honest with herself.

Cia was no longer sure it was such a good idea, despite what Philip said. She had not got through to the girl. Instead, she had caused such turmoil that success seemed impossible. To make matters worse, she had cracked and drained the amethyst crystal in her amulet. Now she would have to find a similar gem that would resonate in harmony with the stones already in place. Without this, her work in the past would be impossible.

By the time she reached the Keep, Cia was exhausted again. Dinner was under way and there was a cheerful commotion at the table as everyone helped themselves, passing bowls of steaming vegetables and platters of meat back and forth. Silently, Cia entered the dining room and slipped into the seat beside Sarah.

'How is Ian? Is Jack with him? Have there been any changes in my absence?' Cia asked. She snagged a chunk of roasted meat with her fork as the platter passed, and reached for a bowl of steamed vegetables.

'What happened to your forehead?' Sarah asked instead.

Cia shook her head. 'Nothing to worry about. Ian?'

'I don't know what to think.' Sarah shook her head. 'He hasn't got any worse, but he doesn't seem to be getting any better, either. He has yet to wake from the deep sleep you put him in two days ago.' Sarah shrugged helplessly. Tears pooled on the lower rim of her eyes, but she tossed her head back, blinking them away. She smiled thinly at Cia. 'This is harder than anything I've ever done. I hate waiting.'

Cia smiled. 'I don't like it much, either,' she said, giving Sarah's hand a gentle squeeze. 'He'll be fine. Whatever nerve poison Gardner used was a real shock to Ian's system. It's going to take him time to fight it off.'

'You're certain it was Gardner, then?' Sarah asked, lowering her voice. The general dinner conversation was being carried on at such a level that no one was listening to or cared much about their conversation, but Sarah glanced around surreptitiously anyway.

'Ian told me, yes,' Cia said. 'Since then, I've been working on a way to handle this mess. Gardner has got to be shown that he can't continue to frighten the Keep.'

When Cia finished wolfing her supper, she pushed herself away from the table and went to check on Ian. Jack frowned when he saw her come into the room.

'Ian is fine!' he exclaimed. 'You, however, look dreadful. Go to bed! Get some rest!'

'That's where I'm headed! Souls! Everyone is telling me that. I just wanted to see how Ian was doing before I went to bed. I haven't seen him all day and I was concerned,' Cia protested. 'Sarah is on the verge of tears and Dalt has been paying altogether too much attention to the boy.'

'Well, you've seen, now go to bed!' Jack scolded.

Cia leaned over and kissed his withered cheek. 'Yes, I know. I love you, too. Good night.'

She went back to her room and fell on to her bed. She was asleep before she could loosen her robes or pull up her blankets.

Bright sunlight in her eyes awakened Cia early the next morning, still in her dusty robe from two days previous.

Class this morning, she thought to herself. Ugh. Still, she felt better for a night's sleep in her own bed. She sat up slowly, testing muscles as she did so. Everything seemed to work with a minimum of protest so she slid out of bed, and looked at the back of her door. The three hooks were empty. She'd forgotten to go to the laundry to reclaim the ones she'd left there. With a sigh, she went to her chest of drawers and took out her leather trousers and vest. She hated wearing them, but at least they were clean. She'd have to remember to get her robes this afternoon after class. Clothing in hand, she padded down the hall for a bath.

'How did you do this without burning your brain?' The jeweller looked up from her examination of the damaged amulet. Amazement and admiration showed in Lidra's round face. Her many chins wagged as she shook her head and handed the piece back. Cia wasn't willing to have her business shared with the rest of the Keep just yet, and Lidra was a most prolific gossip, so Cia smiled mysteriously and said: 'Oh, you know me. Always testing the limits.'

Lidra shook her head again. 'One of these days, hon, you're going to test some limits that neither Sarah nor I can fix.' She stared intently at Cia for a moment, studying the marks on her forehead. 'I don't know what you're up to this time, but you be careful. You hear me?'

Cia nodded.

'Good. Now bring that around here and let me remove what's left of the damaged crystal. I'll need a couple of days if I don't have the right crystal here.' Lidra settled her considerable bulk at a cluttered and dusty work bench at the back of the shed. Light shone brightly on to the bench from the eastern window above it. With a sweep of her arm, she cleared the objects from the surface on to the floor beside her and placed the golden star on the dusty and scarred wood.

'No. Lidra, I need this back by this evening. I meant to

get it to you yesterday, but I didn't get back in time and I overslept this morning. If you can't find a resonating duplicate, do the best you can, but I have to have it for some important work tonight.'

Lidra looked up sharply, a question forming on her lips, but the look on Cia's face made her bite it back. 'This evening, then,' she said and turned her attention back to the damaged crystal she had begun to pry from its setting.

Cia went back into the main building to check on Sarah and Ian before taking a nap.

Late that afternoon Cia was back in the kitchen scrounging together sandwiches to take with her to the cave. She stopped long enough to eat two of them, washing them down with several large glasses of milk. The night before had taught her a lesson about exhaustion and undernourishment. She wrapped the remainder of her sandwiches in a clean cloth and took some apples from the bowl on the counter. She stowed these in her sack and felt in her pocket for her tinder box. Finally, she was satisfied she was ready. Leaving the kitchen by the back door, Cia crossed the barnyard, scattering chickens and fending off the dogs as she went.

Lidra was still at her work bench, soldering the last gold band over the new stone in the meditation amulet. She looked up and frowned as Cia entered.

'Well, it's done, but I can't say I'm happy with the jerry-rig. Promise me you'll bring this back when you have a couple of days to leave it with me. The resonances will work together, but I don't know how well or for how long.' Lidra held the golden star up and away from Cia as though to withhold the object until the promise had been extracted.

'I know you're concerned.' Cia smiled at her friend. 'I'll be careful, I promise. And I'll bring this back to you as soon as I can, but right now, I have to go. I have too much to do tonight to dawdle.' Taking the amulet, Cia left the Keep for the now familiar trek up the hillside. Keeping an ear out for unwanted company, she began her climb.

It was ten o'clock by the time Meg had settled Thiessen for the night. She curled up in an easy chair in the living room and opened her psychology text. With a highlighter she began to underline as she read.

Meg? The voice made her jump and the pen streaked up the page and on to the knee of her jeans. She tensed immediately.

What are you doing here? she asked tightly. *Didn't you get your quota of torture the other day?*

Meg, please. That's unfair. I have so little time. I really need your help.

Meg heard the urgency of her tone. *Why can't I see you this time? Is that a trick you can only do with mirrors?* Meg asked sarcastically.

You can if you'd like. I saw no need, Cia replied. *Please, there is much to talk about –*

Yeah, Meg said acidly. *Why don't we start with: 'Get out of my head.' If I'm not crazy already, you're going to make me crazy. You have no business here that I can see. Go away and leave me alone!*

No, Meg! You're not going crazy. I'm not trying to frighten you. I need you and there is no other way to contact you. There seemed an edge of desperation to Cia's words. They tumbled over each other in the rush to be said.

Why should I believe you that I'm not going crazy? I've been crazy before and your voice is almost all I remember about it. Doesn't it stand to reason that when I lose my marbles again, yours would be the voice I hear? Meg heard the desperation in her own voice now. As this peculiar conversation progressed, she became more and more convinced that her sanity was a tenuous thing, that her parents' fears had been justified, that they had been watching because they knew something like this would happen some day.

As her terror grew, flashes of her nightmares began playing themselves across her mind. Meg tried to shut them out. She was sitting in the living room studying psychology. There was nothing strange in that. She took a deep breath and held it for several counts, then exhaled slowly.

Meg, I'm sorry that our previous contacts have frightened you so badly. I tried to keep them to a minimum, but I had never done anything like it before, and I'm afraid I was fumbling about, Cia said.

You're sorry? Meg yelled. *You sure as hell are! Boy, this is one for the books.* Meg looked at her hands, rubbing her thumbs over the scars on her fingers and shuddered. Your daughter is schizophrenic, she heard Dr Klein saying to her parents over and over again. Give her these pills and she'll be fine.

She was running in the dark, down streets she didn't know. Her body wasn't her own. She was being chased. She was terrified. The fog reached out to claim her as the street lights flickered and died.

The woman Meg was speaking with was swept into the eddies and currents of those nightmare images. This time it was Meg who provided her with face and body. She watched as the slender, silver-haired terror struggled against the symbols of Meg's dreams, trying to maintain her hold in that portion of Meg's mind that Meg had defined as 'safe' from the maelstrom surrounding them.

Meg! Cia's voice was barely audible now. *Philip! Oh God, Ian!*

Meg had a queer feeling of eavesdropping. She no longer heard Cia's voice, but sensed thoughts that Cia seemed to be projecting elsewhere. The feeling of failure that Cia emanated, the depression and exhaustion, were emotions that Meg couldn't understand in relation to her experiences with Cia.

If she were 'making this up', if it were symptomatic of a mental breakdown, Meg wondered, would she invent another person's reactions – have them differ so radically from her own perspective? As she wondered this, she felt Cia slipping out of reach.

Cia, wait! she cried. *You haven't explained –*

But Cia was gone and Meg was sitting alone in the living room clutching her psychology text and chewing on the felt tip of her green highlighter.

'Oh, great,' she said into the silence of the house. 'I wonder what this looks like.' She stood, gingerly stretching cramped muscles, and headed for the bathroom to look in the mirror.

Meg returned to the abandoned psychology text in the living room, searched for her place in the chapter and resumed reading.

Infantile autism is a psychosis of very early onset (during the child's first year). Some consider it a prelude to schizophrenia, but its symptoms are quite distinctive . . . Autistic children often show a preference for objects that move in repetitive ways . . . One of the most serious autistic behaviours is self-destruction. These children may bang their heads against the wall until they suffer a concussion, or chew on their fingers until they are raw . . . autistic children appear to be indifferent to the reactions of others to their frustrating behaviour. Such studied indifference suggests that they have 'turned off' the world of offensive stimuli. Such a dramatic withdrawal might indicate an organic defect in the autistic child's sensory mechanism that makes him or her hypersensitive to stimuli.

(*Child Development*, Greta G. Fein, 1978, pp. 509-10)

Meg rubbed absently at the scars on her fingers. Could it be that what Cia said was true? No, that was silly. It was late and she was tired. Meg closed her book and leaned back in the chair, closing her eyes and trying not to think about it. Do people really study psychology to find out what's wrong with themselves? Granted my motivation is a little stronger than most, but if that's what I'm in this for, why not experiment by facing this head-on? It's probably just hysterical symptoms anyway, so what harm can it do?

'Meggie,' a plaintive voice called from the top of the stairs.

'Thiessen, you're supposed to be asleep,' Meg called back.

'I am, but I want a glass of water.'

'OK, but then you go right back to bed,' Meg said, walking to the foot of the stairs.

Thiessen stumbled down the stairs and followed Meg into the kitchen. She got a glass and filled it with water for Thiessen and watched him as he drank.

'Upstairs, now,' she said when he had finished. Meg took the glass from him and reached for the tuffy pad.

'Will you tell me a story?' Thiessen begged.

'Nope, I have a lot of studying to do and I already read you two stories earlier. Why don't you have Martha tell you one?'

Thiessen brightened at the suggestion.

'Come on now,' she said. 'I'll tuck you in.' She kissed him on the forehead and led him up the stairs.

After straightening out the covers, retrieving his pillow from the floor and tucking Thiessen in, Meg turned out the light and started to close the door. 'I'm right here if you need anything. Sweet dreams.'

''Night, Meggie,' Thiessen mumbled as he snuggled down into the blankets. 'I love you.'

'I love you, too,' Meg said softly.

Returning downstairs, Meg looked at her stack of texts

and groaned audibly as she dropped into the chair and reached for her psychology again.

'Well, what have you found out?' Gardner demanded.

'Nothing,' Dalt said apologetically, twisting the hem of his sleeve. He had worn two strands of glass beads this time. The old house was far too close to the Old City for his comfort, but Gardner seemed to take no notice.

'Haven't you followed her at all?' Gardner asked, incredulous. 'You are lazy and useless!'

'But she comes and goes at such odd hours!' Dalt protested. 'I can't follow her without arousing suspicion. She already distrusts me since she caught me in the healing chamber. She has told everyone to keep an eye on me.'

'Clumsy and careless as well.' Gardner rocked back on his heels and glared at Dalt through narrowed eyes. 'Are you sure no one followed you here?'

'I – ' Dalt began in protest.

'Save it!' Drove snapped. 'I'm sick of your excuses. You've bungled this at every turn. I'll have to find someone else who can get the information I need without alerting the entire Keep.'

'Please give me another chance,' Dalt begged. 'I know I can get her to tell me!'

Gardner sighed and looked Dalt up and down. The man was truly pathetic. He couldn't possibly fail any more dramatically than he had already. Maybe he could actually call on some debt of gratitude, or pity that would produce the answers Gardner needed. He didn't trust Cia's recent strange activities. There was something going on that Drove was certain he should know about. Finding Ian in the Old City had triggered his concern. Drove knew they were connected, he just didn't know how.

'Fine,' he said at last, seeing the relief on Dalt's face.

'But only one chance. If you fail this time, I'll make sure you suffer for it.'

Dalt bobbed his head. 'I'll find out, I swear!'

'Don't make promises you can't keep,' Gardner threatened quietly.

'I'll find out!' Dalt backed out of the house and ran to his horse. He mounted awkwardly and trotted back to the Keep.

Back and forth, back and forth, Cia thought to herself as she climbed back into the hills. She had begun to wear a path to the cave. That, or maybe she was more familiar with the landmarks in the dark by now.

She really felt too tired to do this tonight, but Philip had said . . . Philip had said it had to be done tonight. Time on this end could not be stretched and manipulated the way it could on the other. There was no time to waste.

So Cia climbed mechanically up the rocky slope, clutching the sack containing her rug, candles, medallion, tinder box and dinner. The cave was just around the next bend. Then she could sit and rest a moment. Eat some of the sandwiches. She was tired of sandwiches. She was tired of this cave. She was just tired.

She bent low to enter the cave, lit her candle, spread her rug on the dirt floor beside the place where she always drew the six-pointed star in the dirt, and just sat there for a long moment before digging out a packet and unwrapping her first sandwich. She nibbled at it aimlessly as she redrew her star and set her candles in the points and in the middle.

She hung her amulet over her forehead and lit the candles. She blew out the common candle and took a last bite of dinner. She grounded herself and then centred. Before she got to her central chamber, however, she veered directly off to the path heading towards the continuum.

Once she had crossed the barrier, Cia floated above the threads of the river of time. She never grew tired of looking at them, even when she was tired of everything else.

Giving herself a small shake, Cia dropped into the threads, searching each one for the traces Ian made. By removing them one by one, Cia soon had his entire imprint in her mind. She had removed all evidence of Ian's continuing existence in the threads.

Mother?

Yes, Ian. It's time to begin your part of our work, she told him. It was strange to have his conscious mind in her own.

You should try it from my point of view, he chuckled. *Why is it so dark?*

Hang on, said Cia. She made a few adjustments and then heard him gasp. *Can you see it now?*

See it! Souls, this is incredible! What is it?

Time, Cia told him. *This is what I told you about the other night. This is how I'm going to take you back to Meg.*

Cia grasped the lavender line and began pulling them back down the flow into the past.

7

Meg overslept.

She was hitting the snooze alarm for the eighth time when Susan poked her head in the bedroom door.

'Meg?'

'Mmmphgh,' came from among the blankets and pillows. The small room was a mess. Clothing was draped over every piece of furniture and piled in random heaps on the hardwood floor. Papers and books had buried what Susan could only assume was the desk. Nothing had been dusted in months; certainly no sweeping had been done. The alarm sounded again and an arm emerged from the morass long enough to slap at the clock on the bedside table.

'Meg, you must have turned the alarm on for a reason. Don't you think it's time to get up? The buzzer is sounding at one-minute intervals now.' Susan knew Meg hated to be lectured first thing in the morning (Meg hated everything first thing in the morning), but Susan hated hearing the alarm ring every ten minutes, then every eight minutes, then every five and so on until it finally shut itself off and Meg woke an hour or two later in a serious snit about being late.

'Mmmphgh,' came from among the blankets and pillows. Susan advanced to the edge of the bed and poked randomly into the covers. When nothing happened, she poked in a different place and was rewarded by general movement. Following visual cues, Susan poked what she thought was a mid-section. The bedclothes erupted as Meg surged to her feet on the mattress.

'I hate it when you do that!' Meg yelled as she lost her

footing and fell back into the tangle on the mattress. 'What time is it?'

'About quarter to eight,' Susan said as she headed for the door. 'I have to go open up the shop now. I thought you'd be angrier if you slept through your alarm.'

'Eight? Oh damn, I'll be late meeting Tucker. I promised to buy him breakfast this morning!' Meg climbed out of bed and headed towards the bathroom.

'You're welcome,' Susan called after her. 'I'll see you tonight at dinner?'

'Nope, got a date,' Meg called over her shoulder.

'Well, don't be too late then.' Susan shook her head. Whatever seemed to have been bothering Meg the last couple of days must have blown over if she was making dates before finals.

Meg was only fifteen minutes late getting to the diner. Tucker had ordered a large black coffee for her which she downed in three gulps.

'More, please,' she begged, holding the empty cup out to him.

Tucker grinned a little maliciously. 'Overslept?'

'Yes,' she admitted. 'Please?'

Tucker signalled the waitress and then sat back in the booth to examine Meg more closely. Her hair was wet, pulled into a ponytail and dripping down her shirt where it rested on her shoulder. Her face was scrubbed clean and bare of makeup. Her eyes had the sleepy, slow-to-waken puffiness he was familiar with, but there was an additional tiredness in her face that he hadn't seen before and it worried him.

The waitress arrived with a fresh pot of coffee and poured them both second cups. 'Are you ready to order?' she asked, putting the pot on the table to fish her pad out of her apron. While she was taking their order, Meg finished her second cup and poured herself a third. The waitress laughed. 'Looks like you had a rough night, honey,' she said. Meg nodded, returning her attention to the mug in front of her. The waitress winked at Tucker, took the pot and left.

'She's right, Meg. You look dreadful,' Tucker said.

Meg made a face at him and took another large swallow of coffee. 'Thanks. I love you, too.'

'No, you know what I mean. You look like you haven't slept in days. Are you OK?' Tucker looked concerned, and it was too early in the morning for her to be able to deal with it.

'Yeah,' Meg answered finally. 'I'm mostly OK. I've been having some weird nightmares, so I haven't been sleeping that well. And you know me, I don't wake up well.' She managed a grin that was closer to a grimace.

'Well, do you think you'll be up to going out tonight? I mean with finals and all.' Tucker let his sentence fade, giving Meg the out if she wanted it.

'I'm a night person, I'll be fine. Besides, we haven't seen much of each other recently. I'm looking forward to it.' Meg reached across the table and squeezed Tucker's hand. 'I'll be OK.'

The waitress arrived with their breakfast and more coffee. Meg watched in amazement as the waitress placed half a melon, eggs, sausage and hash browns, a stack of pancakes and an order of toast in front of Tucker. She glanced down at her own grapefruit and bran muffin and looked back at his plates.

'Well, I figured as long as you're buying,' Tucker laughed.

'Yeah, well, I'll get even!' Meg laughed also as she reached for her fourth cup of coffee.

After paying for breakfast and promising to be ready when Tucker stopped by at the library at nine that evening, Meg retrieved her bicycle from the rack in front of the coffee shop and pedalled off to her first class. It seemed to her there were more students on campus at finals than during the rest of the year. Bicycles crowded the streets and pedestrians clogged the pavements. Meg was late getting to her first-period English class and tried to slip into a back-row seat unnoticed. As the chair creaked under her weight, Professor Spaulding glanced up in annoyance.

Spring was in full tilt outside, but until she sat down in Spaulding's classroom, Meg hadn't noticed what a beautiful day it was. The sky was the sort of blue that reaches up for miles without a cloud to break the illusion. The trees' leaves had darkened to their pre-summer green and a slight breeze tugged at the thick, dirty-oatmeal-coloured curtains that stood open at the window.

She found herself wondering where Cia came from; if there was any possibility that Meg hadn't made her up, why Cia would want Meg to save her son and what that might involve. Why, if Meg were in fact going crazy, did the symptoms come and go and always focus on the same character with the same problem? She'd never read about delusions taking this kind of form before.

'Miss Danning!' The sound of her name brought Meg back to the classroom abruptly. The professor and her classmates were looking at her, amused and expectant. 'I asked you a question.'

'I'm sorry, could you repeat it please?' Meg asked.

A wave of suppressed laughter swept the room.

'I asked you to summarize today's lecture. Begin with a thesis statement and conclude with your opinion.'

Meg looked wildly about the room. She hadn't been listening. She didn't know what the lecture was about. Dr Spaulding was watching her, a smile pulling at his mouth under the heavy moustache. He seemed to be enjoying her discomfort.

Blushing deeply, Meg rose slowly to her feet and cleared her throat. Hesitantly she glanced around the room, and finally looked Dr Spaulding in the eye.

'I'm sorry, sir,' Meg stammered. 'I wasn't paying attention. I can't summarize the lecture.'

'I thought not.' Spaulding's smile deepened a bit. 'May I suggest you do the assigned reading and pay attention in class in the future, Miss Danning. It won't hurt you, and might even do you some good.'

'Yes, sir,' Meg whispered as she sat down.

The rest of her day went only marginally better. Meg was unable to concentrate on her lectures and her notes were mostly doodles of a slender, silver-haired woman with pale-grey eyes. The only redeeming features of the day were that it was Friday and she had a date with Tucker.

At nine o'clock, she was in front of the library waiting for Tucker.

'Hi, Meg. You ready to go?'

Meg looked up and found Tucker leaning across the passenger seat of his beat-up old Toyota, watching her through the open window.

'How long have you been there?' she asked.

'Just pulled up, but you didn't see me. You sure you still want to go?'

'Yeah!' Meg exclaimed, gathering up her books and hopping down from the stone wall she'd been sitting on. She tossed her belongings into the back seat and climbed into the car. 'Let's have some fun.'

Tucker smiled and squeezed her knee. 'You hungry?' he asked.

'You bet! And I have some ordering to do to catch up with your breakfast this morning, I do believe.' Meg smiled at him. 'Drive on, James.'

'Who's James?' Tucker tried hard to sound hurt as he engaged the clutch and eased out into traffic.

'Oh, sorry. Wrong boyfriend,' Meg teased.

The Pub was jammed, as was usual on a Friday night. Several of Meg's and Tucker's friends were there already though, and cleared space at the table for them. They sat down amid a flurry of questions and greetings.

'Where have you two been hiding yourselves?'

'Meg, do you think I could borrow your notes for anthropology?'

'Tucker, old man. How they hangin'?'

'Hey,' Tucker exclaimed. 'What do we have to do to get a beer around here?'

The pitcher and a stack of plastic cups were promptly shoved in their direction. The basket of pretzels followed. Tucker made a big show of pouring Meg's beer and proffering the pretzels. 'Your dinner, madame?'

She made a face at him, accepted the beer and grabbed a handful of pretzels. 'You won't get out of it that easily!' she laughed.

By the time the band had come out for the first set, Meg had managed to order enough munchies to satisfy everyone at the table and Tucker was bemoaning the state of his wallet.

'Come on, cheapskate, at least you can dance for free,' Meg said, tugging his arm and pulling him from his chair. On the dance floor, which was postage-stamp-sized, they merged with the press of bodies hopping up and down in place and followed suit.

'I feel really stupid,' Tucker finally yelled in Meg's ear. 'There's so many people here, I can't move without stepping on someone.'

'OK,' Meg yelled back. 'I have to pay rent on that beer anyway. Why don't I meet you back at the table.' Tucker nodded and they eased out of the congestion.

'Don't get lost,' Tucker yelled as he started back to the front of the bar.

As she headed for the back of the Pub and the restrooms, Meg began to feel dizzy and slightly nauseated. I only had two cups of beer, she thought. It shouldn't be affecting me this way. She staggered a bit and grabbed the back of a chair to steady herself.

'Hey, Meg. Are you OK?' Meg recognized Dan's voice, but she couldn't bring his face into focus.

'Dan?' Her voice sounded shrill in her ears. 'Dan? No, I'm not OK. I need to sit down.' Her knees buckled and she sagged against Dan's chair. Strong arms were about her waist and she felt herself being lowered into a chair.

'Here, put your head between your knees. Everything is going to be fine. Have a little too much to drink?' Dan chuckled as he massaged her shoulders. He was on the swimming team with Meg. He was familiar and safe.

'No. It's not alcohol. I don't know what's wrong. Get Tucker for me, will you?' Meg's vision was focused on a tiny pinpoint that seemed very distant, but she had nothing to reference it with. The blood pounded loudly in her temples . . . or was it the band? A voice was singing. There had been a singer earlier, but it was a man. This was a woman's voice and it was in counterpoint to the lyrics of the song, but what it sang made no sense at all. Michael and Beth were talking to her, but she couldn't understand what they were saying either.

'Tucker?' Meg whispered. Her thoughts were too loud in her mind. She couldn't speak; she hadn't said anything. Tucker? I think I'm in trouble.

Meg? The strange woman who had been singing? It had all been in her mind. *Meg? I had to come one last time.*

Meg clutched her ears and rocked back and forth. Oh God, oh God, oh God, she moaned, but she didn't say anything. She couldn't speak. Tucker was here now. He crouched in front of her, his hands covered hers as she clutched her ears and rocked back and forth. *Tucker, help me,* she moaned, but she didn't say anything. She couldn't speak.

Meg, please, you have to help us! Cia begged. She seemed to be doing something in Meg's mind, but Meg couldn't focus on her movements. Lights sparked in her peripheral vision adding to the blinding headache that had incapacitated her. She was aware of the small crowd that had gathered around her, but she was unable to respond to them. She couldn't understand what they were saying. Cia continued to move in her mind. Gradually, the headache lessened and Meg's vision cleared.

You've built up some pretty strong barriers in the past couple of days. I had no idea they would make you so sick. In fact, I had no idea you were capable of doing anything like that on your own. Cia sounded as if she would be puzzled by the barriers if she could see anything beyond her own dilemma.

Meg shuddered. She had known Cia would return. She had planned what she would say and how she would say it. But now that the time had come, Meg was unable even to think clearly, let alone be as verbally brilliant as she'd been in her mental rehearsals. Instead, Meg was scared to her socks and all she could find in herself was a quavery little voice which she instantly despised.

I guess the only way I can face this is head-on. What do you want me to do? Meg whispered.

Take my son, please, Cia begged. *Leaving him with you is the only way I can save his life.*

This doesn't involve changing diapers, does it? Meg asked. Memories of Thiessen as an infant crowded her mind for a moment. She shuddered.

Cia actually laughed. *No, Ian is about your age.*

So how am I going to sneak him past Mom and Dad?

'Did she say something? Meg? I thought I heard her

say something. Meg, Tucker is going to take you home. Do you think you can stand?'

Cia, we're scaring my friends. Can we just get this over with? What are you asking me to do? Meg demanded.

Just let me leave Ian's mind in yours. No one need know. I'll be back to get him as soon as it's safe.

You want to leave some guy's mind in mine? Meg asked, incredulous.

Yes! Please, we don't have much time.

Is this what's involved in facing delusions and psychoses head-on? Meg tried to remember what she had read in her psychology texts, but her brain was too muzzy to focus.

Meg, this is serious. Are you serious? Cia asked.

Yeah, if this is what it takes to restore my sanity, then it has to be done.

Thank you, Meg, Cia said. She immediately disappeared from Meg's mind. The headache was receding and her vision was returning to normal. Meg sat up and stared at the worried faces surrounding her. She smiled tentatively.

'I'm OK, now, I think,' she told them. 'Tucker, will you take me home, please?'

Tucker helped Meg to her feet and steadied her against a residual wave of dizziness before he piloted her through the crowd, and out the door into the night. Drawing a deep breath of fresh air helped to clear Meg's head further and she collapsed into the front seat of Tucker's old Toyota with a small sigh of relief. She had confronted Cia and the problem had gone away.

What problem? asked a deep voice in her mind. Meg gasped and sat up straight in her seat.

'What's the matter?' asked Tucker as he swung into the driver's seat.

'What?' Meg asked stupidly.

'Meg, just sit back and relax. I'll have you home in no

171

time. A good night's sleep and you'll be much better.' Tucker patted her knee and smiled reassuringly. Meg smiled a brittle smile and sank into the seat feeling rather like a carton of raw eggs. She closed her eyes against the glare of the street lamps and headlights and tried to think.

Somewhere, her plan had gone wrong. By facing Cia and the fears associated with her, Meg had found herself in a far worse situation. Either she had gone completely mad, or she had a man in her head.

Who are you? Meg ventured.

Ian, the voice said.

Meg was a little confused and very frightened. *I was trying to confront a psychosis*, she said. *Something went wrong. This wasn't the outcome the research said I should expect.*

I don't understand, said Ian. *I thought my mother told you she wanted to leave me with you. I thought you agreed.*

If I confront a psychosis head-on, and deny its validity, it should pretty much go away.

What are you talking about? Ian asked. *Why are you so angry?*

And why is my delusion talking back, she wondered.

I'm not a delusion! Ian objected.

What else could you possibly be? Meg cried in frustration. Her grip on reality had become a tenuous thing. *People who hear voices are crazy. I'm crazy.*

Maybe you are, he said. *But I'm no delusion. Mother asked you for permission to leave me here. It's not like anyone tricked you.*

But she didn't tell me she'd brought you, or that she'd left you behind, Meg objected.

You agreed to it, what difference does it make when I arrived?

I was on a date, for chrissakes! I was in a public place! Now everyone is worried about my health. That was embarrassing. Meg could feel tears prickling under her eyelids. Despite her best efforts, they slipped out and rolled down her cheeks.

'Hey, Meg. It's OK, we're almost there.' Tucker reached over and brushed at her tears with the back of his hand.

'I'm sorry I ruined your evening, Tucker. I thought I was feeling well enough. I guess I was wrong. I'll make it up to you, I promise.'

Who is this guy? Ian asked.

My boyfriend, Tucker, Meg said. *Try to stay out of this, will you?*

Meg felt the car pull into her driveway and began to fumble in her purse for the keys while keeping her eyes shut against the headlights. She heard Tucker rummaging in the back seat for her books, then he came around the car, opened her door and helped her out. She leaned heavily into him and he put his arm around her.

As they walked up the path to the front door, Meg felt herself involuntarily pulling away from Tucker's arm, holding herself away from his side with alien distaste. This puzzled her. When they got to the door, Tucker took her keys from her and opened it. He led her into the foyer and placed her books on the hall table.

Meg opened her eyes in the relative darkness of the house and smiled up at Tucker. 'Thanks for bringing me home. Will you call me next week?'

'Yeah, I'll call. Sleep well, Meg. I love you,' Tucker said. He pulled her to him, bent his face to hers and kissed her thoroughly.

The same strangeness in Meg fought against the embrace and when she finally managed to disengage, to her horror and Tucker's, Meg turned and spat on the floor of the hall. Aghast, Meg turned to Tucker. His face had frozen, expressionless. Then he recoiled as if slapped; hurt and anger displacing his initial reaction. Tucker

173

straightened and backed away from Meg, towards the door.

In a quiet voice he said, 'Fine. If that's the way you really feel, Meg, that's fine.' He turned and stalked into the darkness. Moments later, Meg heard the car door slam and the old Toyota roared out of the driveway and down the street in the direction it had come from.

Only when she could no longer hear it did she find herself sitting on the floor, crying.

Hey, what's the matter with you?

You did this! Meg shrieked. *You made me spit, didn't you?*

He had his arms around me, his lips on my lips and his tongue in my mouth. He was kissing me! I don't kiss other men, Ian exclaimed.

You felt that? Meg was stunned.

Well, of course I did. And I didn't care for it much!

Meg took a deep breath and pinched her arm hard.

Ow! Hey, what did you do that for? Ian yelled.

You feel everything I do? Meg asked in horror. This was something she hadn't expected at all.

And taste and smell and see and hear, yes. Don't you know sensory deprivation can make you crazy?

I am crazy! Meg yelled. *I went around the bend a week ago. That's the only logical explanation for this.*

Look, we're not going to solve this tonight. You're obviously over-tired. Let's get some sleep and talk about this tomorrow.

I'm not over-tired, I'm schizophrenic. I hear voices that aren't there. You're only one of them. Don't you dare try telling me what to do. I'll take all of us back to Dr Klein and get more thorazine.

Thorazine?? They still use that? I thought it was outlawed in twenty-seventeen! Ian exclaimed.

What? Meg laughed out loud. *This is nineteen-eighty-seven and this is the most bizarre delusion I've ever had.*

174

This can't be happening. In the morning it will all be gone,
she said and stood up. She pushed the front door shut and
turned off the porch light. As she turned to the dark
interior of the house, her hand stole out and touched the
wall. *Look*, she said wearily. *I know my way around the
house in the dark, trust me on this one, OK?* Her hand
dropped back to her side and she continued towards the
stairs. Slowly, avoiding the creaky boards, she negotiated
the steps. On the way down the upstairs hall, she paused
at the bathroom door and thought for a moment.

Her hand stole between her legs and then froze. She
felt turmoil in her mind that had nothing to do with her
own state. Her hand groped frantically at the fly of her
jeans, scrabbling at the metal zipper. She felt a fingernail
break. Panic was welling up in her and she couldn't
control it.

What is it? she cried. *What's the matter?*

Souls, he moaned. *I didn't realize . . .*

What? Didn't realize . . . She staggered against the door
jamb and slid to the floor. Her hand cupped against her
crotch as her mind was overwhelmed by a sense of loss
that was totally inappropriate. *Who are you?*

He moaned again. Her hand clenched hard on her
crotch and she gasped in pain. He gasped also. *That hurt!*
he exclaimed.

Never do that again!, she hissed. *I wonder if that beer
was spiked with anything. This is the most bizarre conversation I've ever had with myself.* She pulled her hand from
between her thighs and stood up slowly. She stepped into
the bathroom and shut the door before turning on the
light. Her reflection blinked at her myopically as her eyes
adjusted to the brightness. A wave of fright and revulsion
swept over her. Her hand clapped to her left breast and
she leaned over the sink to examine her reflection more
closely.

Her face was the same one that had looked back at her

175

for the last twenty years. What was the matter with her tonight? She was acting as if she'd never seen herself before. No, that wasn't quite right. Her actions weren't motivated by her own feelings. Somewhere during the evening, she had lost control of her mind and body.

She stepped back from the bathroom counter. Her hands closed on the hem of her cotton sweater and pulled it up over her head. She tossed it on the floor and stood staring defiantly into the mirror. In the cold of the spring night air, her nipples hardened. The areolas crinkled around them and goose bumps rose on her small breasts. Her hands reached up and cupped them gently.

Meg was surprised by a feeling of fear and curiosity. *Who are you?* she whispered. Her hands continued to move without her direction. Thumbs and forefingers rubbing against her nipples, she felt a wave of pleasure at the sensation, sending a shock of warmth to the spot between her legs . . . her hands moved slowly down her ribs to her waist and the button of her jeans.

She continued to watch herself in the mirror. She was paralysed by the scene. Her hands moved of their own accord, unzipping her pants. Again, she felt surprise at the lack of penis, surprise at the inappropriateness of her behaviour. She was over-tired and a little drunk, that had to be it. Her hands were pushing her jeans off over her hips.

Meg stood naked before the brightly-lit bathroom mirror and stared at her body. Infinitely familiar to her, tonight she was being touched by her own hands as though they had never felt her before. She was on the receiving end of emotions that were alien to her. Her fingers rubbed against the hair at the base of her belly. Again, she felt an odd sense of loss.

She told me, but I didn't think it would be like this, moaned the deep voice again.

Meg felt cold fear grip her heart. What if . . .? She couldn't bring herself to finish the thought.

Ian? she asked. Her hand slipped between her legs again. Muscles contracted and warmth flooded her as her fingers rubbed against her inner folds. Her thighs tingled and her knees felt weak.

Wet! He was shocked. Her hand jerked back roughly and he put her fingers in her mouth, sucked at them.

What did you do that for? she yelled, spitting them out. Her fingers traced saliva circles around her nipples, hardening them again. *Oh God, what's happening to me?*

Her broken fingernail scratched her belly as her hand wandered back to her thighs.

She told me, but I didn't think . . . Where is my penis? he whined again.

Wherever you left it! Meg yelled at him finally. This was really all just too much. She'd been drunk before. This felt more like a bad acid trip than a serious bender. Her fingers were stroking long and slow in the folds between her thighs. She couldn't concentrate. She moaned and spread her legs further apart. He pushed two fingers deep into her. Her broken fingernail scraped at her thigh. They ignored it, rubbing gently with the thumb.

This feels so strange, he said.

Oh, God, she moaned. *What's happening to me?* Tears slipped silently down her cheeks.

He began to rub harder and faster. *Ouch!* they exclaimed together. *Gently! See, like this*. She showed him.

Oh! Oh, he inhaled sharply and exhaled slow and shuddery. Her knees buckled slightly. She sat on the edge of the bathtub, legs wide, fingers moving in slow circles while her other hand scratched gently against her thighs.

This can't be happening, she thought to herself. She felt the wave building inside her. Sweat broke out on her forehead and lower lip. Her breathing came in rasps.

She fell over the edge. Pelvic muscles contracted hard for an endless moment, then began strong, shuddering, rhythmic contractions.

They groaned aloud.

'Meg?' Susan knocked on the bathroom door. 'Meg, are you in there?'

Oh, shit! 'Uh, yeah. Just cramps, Mom. I'll be OK. I was looking for the aspirin,' Meg lied quickly. 'Is there any in your bathroom?'

'I'll check, honey. I'll be right back.'

Meg waited until she heard Susan's footsteps retreating down the hallway, then pulled her clothes back on as fast as she could. She took the aspirin bottle from the medicine cabinet and put it in the drawer. She opened the bathroom door as she heard Susan coming back.

'Here you go,' said Susan, handing Meg the bottle. 'I could have sworn we had aspirin in here.' She opened the medicine cabinet and rummaged through it. 'Huh. Well I guess I'll have to add it to the list. You sure you're going to be OK?' She examined Meg closely.

Meg tensed, hearing the question Susan was really asking. No, she wanted to say. Mom, there are voices in my head and I'm afraid of them. This time, it wasn't just the woman asking how old I am. This time it's a man who's touching me with my own hands. She wanted to say that, but it would only frighten her family. They would take her back to the psychiatrist and he still wouldn't be able to do anything for her to make the voices go away.

'Yeah,' Meg said with a humourless laugh. 'Just premenstrual tension on top of finals. I'll be fine.' She swallowed two tablets with a handful of water from the sink. 'Thanks Mom.' Meg recapped the bottle, handed it back to Susan and gave her a quick hug. 'G'night. Sleep well.' She practically ran to her bedroom.

With the door safely shut behind her, she pulled off her

clothes again and fell into bed, exhausted. Snuggling down into the covers, Meg fell asleep almost immediately.

Morning came too soon, but in Meg's estimation, morning always came too soon. This morning, she woke up earlier than usual with an uncomfortable pressure in her bladder. As she penetrated the layers of fog between sleep and consciousness bits and pieces of last night's fiasco came back to her. It must have been something she had dreamed. None of that could possibly have happened; it was just too strange to have been real.

Could and is, said that strange, deep voice in her mind. Meg gasped and sat up. *And I think we'd both feel better after a trip to the outhouse*, the voice continued with some embarrassment.

Meg sat paralysed for a moment. 'Going to the outhouse' with a man in her head. Well, since he wasn't anything more than a delusion . . . was he a delusion? After last night, she wasn't sure of anything. Her legs swung over the edge of the bed and Meg found herself standing up.

This isn't a decision that can wait, the voice told her. She grabbed her bathrobe from the bedpost at the foot of the bed and struggled into it as she headed for the door.

Ian was fascinated by the concept of indoor plumbing.

This is incredible, he kept repeating. *An outhouse in the house. There are fixtures in the library that are like this, but I couldn't imagine they were for anything other than display.*

Library? Meg asked. *I'm going to wash my face and then we're going to get a cup of coffee and have a long talk*, she said with a patience she didn't feel. Somehow, this was feeling less and less like something she had created for purposes of delusion and derangement.

Meg stumbled downstairs and into the kitchen. As she got a coffee mug from the cabinet, she saw her mother looking over her newspaper. Meg gave Susan a deliberately unfocused look and nodded blearily as she closed in on the coffee maker.

'You were home early last night,' Susan commented. 'You're up early this morning. Is everything OK?'

Meg nodded again, maintaining the unfocused look and gulped the steaming liquid. Good, it was strong. She poured herself another mug and left the kitchen.

Once in the comparative safety of her bedroom, Meg locked her door (a concession on Ted and Susan's part when Thiessen came to the age of pest-hood) and sat on the edge of the bed cupping the mug of coffee between both palms

I've read about coffee, Ian said conversationally. *It's bitter. I'm not sure I like it.*

Get used to it, Meg responded. *I can't live without it.* With that, she drained her second cup in one prolonged swallow. She looked into the empty mug and thought regretfully of the pot downstairs, but she couldn't face her mother right now. There was this little matter of a man in her head. Real or imagined, he was something Meg had to come to terms with before she could go on with her life.

I am real. Ian sounded a bit miffed. Meg sighed and put her mug down on the nightstand. How could she explain to a delusion why she thought it was a delusion?

I had a mental illness called autism when I was a baby, she began. *And I'm a diagnosed schizophrenic. I've heard voices in my head all of my life. Why should now be any different?*

Why would hearing voices in your head mean you're sick? Ian asked. *Where I come from, that's how telepaths communicate.*

What? Meg exclaimed. *Oh, come on. This is too much! Where do you come from?*

I'm not sure how to tell you in your terms. I think the

question is more when *I come from, not so much* where, *actually.*

This is priceless. Dr Klein is going to be sorry he missed it. Meg laughed humourlessly.

Who is Dr Klein? Ian asked.

My shrink, Meg said tiredly. *The guy I always have to talk to when I hear voices in my head. I haven't seen him in a few years, though, because I stopped telling people about the mind-lady.* Meg had never come up with a better label for the woman who had plagued her life. The mind-lady was her first childhood memory and her most frightening recurrent nightmare. There was no better method of identification.

Well, I'm not a hallucination. And I'm not here because I want to be either. Frankly, I would rather have stayed in my own body, where everything is where I expect it to be, but my mother said I had to do this for several good reasons that she couldn't tell me about. Ian paused for a moment. *Right now all I can say is she'd* better *have some very good reasons!*

Meg stood up and paced restlessly around her small room. There was too much furniture and too many piles of junk to get more than a couple of strides in any direction.

'I've got to get out of here!' Meg muttered out loud. 'I need to be able to breathe. I can't think cooped up like this.' She began rummaging through the pile of clothing on the chair in the corner, coming up with a pair of not-too-dirty blue jeans and a tee-shirt that she'd slept in only a couple of times. She climbed out of her nightgown and into the clothing, found her sneakers, but no socks. Damn! She put the sneakers on anyway, anticipating the blisters they would raise on her heels. Oh well.

Going through the living room on the way to the garage, she avoided direct contact with her mother. At the door, she called generally that she was going out for a while and was taking her bike. She shut the door quickly behind her to avoid having to answer any questions.

What is a bike? Ian asked with interest.

Bicycle, Meg answered. *This, see*. She grasped the handlebars as she pushed the kickstand up with her foot and moved with the bike towards the garage door.

Bicycle? Ian repeated.

Never mind. Just remember, leave the body to me. I can't control it if you seize up on me.

OK, he agreed meekly.

Meg pushed the bike out to the driveway, hopped on and headed down to the street. Without a specific destination in mind, she turned left and pedalled towards the park.

When he discovered what a bicycle was, and how it was used, Ian retreated to a far corner, pulled into himself and watched intently. This contraption was surely the product of a sick and tortured mind.

He was certain he had been sent here to die. His mother was secretly in league with Gardner. She had smoothly double-talked him out of his body and brought him here to be tortured and killed by a girl who had no apparent problem in doing so, even at the cost of her own life. He muttered to himself as they careened around corners, in and out of immense metal-and-glass structures (some stationary, some mobile), and past pedestrians.

Curious patterns of light flashed overhead at regular intervals, but Ian was too terrified even to wonder what they signified. It was increasingly difficult to believe that Cia had a plan, or even knew what she was doing. Belief in his mother's knowledge and ability was what was keeping him relatively sane in this peculiar situation.

Meg sensed the confusion Ian was broadcasting, but said nothing, allowing him to work through it by himself. She parked the bike under a tree, locked it and sat on the grass beside it, leaning against the rough bark. In the warm sun, Meg began to feel drowsy again, despite her earlier caffeine infusion. The Saturday-morning joggers who passed by paid her scant attention as she sat splitting blades of grass with her thumbnail. She sat in silence for the better part of an hour.

It hadn't really registered emotionally that you lived in the Time Before, Ian said at last.

Before what? Meg asked.

My mother said she was taking me into the past and I've read a lot about it, but I didn't think it would be so different, Ian continued as though he hadn't heard her.

What do you mean? Meg asked. *Different from what? What do you mean 'the past'?* Meg felt her control slipping. None of these reactions felt right. If last night wasn't a bad dream or a schizophrenic episode . . .? She shut her mind on that thought and began a series of stretching exercises.

Didn't Cia tell you? Ian sounded genuinely surprised. *What are you doing?*

Tell me what? Meg cried. She was having a hard time keeping tears at bay. Never before had a voice stayed so long in her head. Having prolonged conversation was frightening her badly. She concentrated harder on her warm-up, but even her customary leg stretches seemed more difficult. *The voice of a woman with an age-fixation who's been frightening me for years told me she was giving me her son for safe-keeping. Why should I take that seriously? I thought if I said 'yes' she'd go away and leave me alone. I don't want to go back to Dr Klein, but now instead of a woman's voice, I'm hearing a man's voice and he wants to know where his penis is . . .*

Look, Meg, Ian interrupted, embarrassed. *I'm sorry about last night. I wasn't really as prepared as I thought I was to find myself in a female body. I sort of panicked. But I never meant to scare you.*

Well, you did! Meg snapped. *Just tell me how to get rid*

of you, OK? She stood and leaned against the tree, palms flat against the rough bark, and stretched her calf muscles.

I don't know, Ian admitted. *I'm not a telepath.*

Well, then get your mother back here, she demanded.

I can't: I'm not a telepath. Ian's voice changed slightly. *You are. You can call her.*

What? I'm not a telepath, I'm a schizo. Don't they have those where you come from? Meg turned away from the tree, stepped out on to the path and began jogging.

Where are we going? Meg, how can I get through to you? You aren't crazy. You're a telepath. My mother told me that there are only two ways I can get back to my body: either she will come get me, or you will figure out how to take me there.

Terrific, Meg said. *She didn't happen to tell you how I would figure it out?* She paused, *I didn't think so. Why do you think I'm a telepath?*

Mother says you are, Ian replied. *She came back to find you and put blocks in your mind. She said you unfolded when you were born, but you didn't have anyone to help you through it and everyone in your time thought you were mentally ill. If she hadn't helped you, you'd still be trapped in the unfolding.*

What's unfolding? Meg asked, trying to keep her pace steady and concentrate on her breathing. Running in blue jeans felt awkward after workouts in shorts, but there was a strange stiffness in her muscles that worried her a bit. There was a track meet on Friday. If she wasn't in top form, she would have trouble winning her events. Her sneakers were starting to chafe, but she kept running.

I don't know from experience, said Ian. *But everyone who's been through it says it's really frightening. They say it's like another dimension of sight, sound and touch suddenly opens in your mind, but you don't have the tools to understand the new information, so your mind kind of shuts down for a while.*

184

Meg tensed and missed a stride. What he was describing was entirely too familiar. There was no specific memory that she could touch, but the general feeling of the description triggered a sense of helplessness that had haunted her throughout her life. Her mind churned. *Unfolding*. Telepathy. Autism?

When your mind shuts down, the other telepaths sort of help you learn how to use your gifts, or something like that. I'm not really sure how it works. I'm a Deaf-Mute, Ian admitted. *Hey, how much longer are we going to do this? It's starting to hurt!*

A Deaf-Mute? asked Meg, ignoring his complaint.

I don't have any psychic gifts. I can't hear mind-voices and I can't broadcast my own thoughts into other people's minds. Ian spoke bitterly. *I can't move objects without touching them, or heal people and animals with crystals.*

Neither can I, Meg exclaimed. *Neither can anyone else, as far as I know. A few crackpots claim to be able to, but who knows?*

Where I come from, almost everyone can. The few of us who can't, aren't even empathic . . . well, we're just not considered very useful. They sort of pity us. Except Sarah, Ian thought to himself, feeling a wave of homesickness.

Is that what you're doing here, then? Being kept out of the way? Meg asked. She could feel the blisters rising on her heels, but she kept running along the dirt path through the park.

Not exactly like that, Ian responded, allowing the question to pull him away from his self-pity. *I'm not exactly sure why I'm here. It has something to do with Drove Gardner, and you, but I don't know what the connection is. Can we stop this now?*

No, Meg snapped. *Are you running with me? Is that why this is so difficult? Who is Drove Gardner?*

The bastard who poisoned me! He's psychokinetic and

mean. Hey, when are we going to stop? Yes, I'm running.
We're both running. What's the point of this?

Well, stop it! I can do this much better on my own. What
does he have to do with me? asked Meg.

My mother, in her infinite wisdom, didn't tell me. I think
I'm supposed to help you, but I don't know how.

Well, running isn't it, said Meg. *Please kindly leave the*
body to me. Just go away for a while. I need to think.

That was a cheap shot, Meg. Do you at least believe me
that I am not a schizophrenic delusion of yours? Ian
relinquished his hold on Meg's muscles and felt her stride
lengthen in response.

Meg sighed. *I don't know,* she said at last. *This doesn't*
feel like I've lost my mind, only like I've lost my privacy;
my separateness.

Yeah, said Ian. *That's exactly what it feels like.*

Oh, right! Meg laughed bitterly. *What would you know*
about it? It's my body we're sharing, and I didn't have
much say about it.

All you had to say was no.

I thought I was going crazy. I thought if I said yes . . .
You're right. I could have gone back to Dr Klein and got
more thorazine, and neither one of us would be in this
mess. There would be no voices in my head. There
wouldn't be much of anything in my head. Not even me.

Well then, said Ian. *I guess we both have to make the*
best of this and try to find out what Mother had in mind
when she brought me back here.

Do you have any idea how we go about that? Meg
asked. She'd only made one circuit of the park, but the
bike was just up ahead and her feet were killing her.
Rising up on her toes, she sprinted the last hundred-or-so
yards. Coming to a halt beside the tree, she dropped to
the grass and began stretching again.

No idea, Ian replied.

Look, I've got a life which doesn't include you. The

sooner we figure out what your mother has in her warped little mind, the sooner I get my mind back, Meg snapped. *So if you have anything constructive to say, say it. Otherwise, shut up!*

What! Ian yelled. *What did I say? Why do you keep getting so angry?*

You just complained through a really light workout, Meg yelled back. *I have track practice on Monday. We're getting ready for a big meet on Friday, and I have swimming team in between. During which time I also have to study for finals because I refuse to blow the end of a really great semester. I don't have time to have a man in my head!*

They sat in silence for the remainder of Meg's calisthenics and stretching out.

I'm sorry, Ian said.

It's not your fault, said Meg. *I'm sorry, too.*

They sat quietly for a while longer.

How come you keep saying you came back? Meg asked at last. *Back from where?*

Not where, Ian corrected. *The where is probably very near here. It's when I'm from, really. I'm from some time in your future.*

Oh, of course, said Meg. She lay back on the grass and stared up into the branches of the tree. *You're the guy I'm going to marry when this is all over, right?*

No, Ian said seriously. *I don't think you'll live that long. We're talking about a distance of several hundred years.*

What? Meg sat up again quickly.

I don't think you'll live long enough for us to get married. Besides I sort of have a . . .

You have a girlfriend? Meg asked. *What is she like?*

She's a healer, Ian said shortly.

You mean she has psychic gifts? I thought you said they sort of avoided you if they could.

Sarah's different, he said quietly.

She's the one you were thinking of earlier when you got homesick, huh, said Meg. *I had a boyfriend until last night. A really sweet guy: smart, good-looking, kind . . . I don't know how I can ever make it up to him for what happened last night. How would you feel if Sarah spat on the floor after you kissed her?*

Oh, the Souls! Meg, is that – . Did I – .

Yes, she said flatly. *It is, and you did. I've never told him about my history of mental illness. I know that wasn't terribly honest of me, but now I have to tell him the truth and hope that I can somehow convince him that I love him and didn't mean what I did. What you did. But I can't tell him that, ever.*

Meg, I'm sorry –

I know, Meg interrupted. *You didn't do it on purpose, but it happened and I can't undo it now. I guess my point is that I can't have you hanging around in my head screwing up my life. We have to find a way to get you back where you're supposed to be, and soon, or I really will lose my mind.*

8

Cia was late coming back to the Keep that evening. The elation she had felt at accomplishing a major part of her task carried her only as far as the return to her present. She knew she had to talk with Philip before she went home, but she was unable to pull her concentration together long enough to do so.

Even before she could perform her ritual closing, she rummaged through her sack for the remains of her dinner of the night before. After licking the last crumbs from her fingers and checking again to be sure that was really it, she did a few stretching and breathing exercises to anchor herself more firmly in the here and now. She cleansed the coloured candles, buried them with the others at the back of the cave and cleaned her aura before returning to her small rug.

Breathing deeply and evenly, Cia performed her centring routine and called to Philip. He came at once, but was smug in his vindication.

You see, he laughed at her. *You must believe me when I tell you to work harder. You must believe in yourself!*

I did do it, yes, Cia acknowledged. *Now what?* She was feeling much too tired for Philip's I-told-you-so's.

Keep your eyes open, he replied cryptically. *To keep Ian safe, you must keep yourself safe.*

What do you mean? Cia asked.

Keep your eyes open, he said again, and was gone.

Aaah! Cia yelled at Philip in particular and everything in general. She was too tired for this. Emerging from her centre, she thrust her belongings back into her sack, left the cave without smudging it, and began her descent. By the time she reached the flatlands, the sun was hovering above the horizon, reddening the clouds and casting pink in the sky. The crickets had begun their song and the path beside the river was pleasant in its solitude.

Cia dreaded her return to the Keep. She had been absent at so many of her chores, depending upon the others to pick up her share that she knew she was in for a lecture from the elders and more than a few black looks from her peers. She hoped they would at least wait until after dinner, she was much too hungry to wait, and much too tired to do so gracefully . . . just thinking about it was making her head hurt.

As she neared the Keep, the dogs came barking to find out who was trespassing so late in the day. Finding it someone they liked, the dogs leapt about Cia, nuzzling her hand and trying to get her to pet them. She stopped at the well and drew water to wash her face and hands before going to check on Ian and Sarah.

Supper in the Keep that evening was loud and cheerful. After the silence of her solitary work in the cave on the hillside, Cia was pleased to relax and take part in the talk and good-natured teasing that went on around the tables; to hear the laughter and smell the wonderful odours of the hot meal they sat down to.

Cia lingered over her tea at the end of the meal, enjoying the warmth of the dining-room, and the feeling of a full belly. As the dishes were being cleared, Cia went down the hall to the healing chamber to check on Ian and Sarah.

The healing room was empty.

A candle guttered on the table beside the bed. The blankets were in disarray; the bed was unoccupied.

Fear clamped hard on her heart and froze her bowels. If Dalt –

No. Not possible. Sarah wouldn't have let that happen. Drove – ?

Oh, the Souls.

Sarah! she screamed. She didn't bother to tighten the broadcast. Every telepath in the Keep would have heard her. She wanted everyone to know something had happened. She ran back out into the hall. *Sarah, where are you?*

But Sarah wasn't telepathic, she was empathic. She couldn't answer back. The thought took a moment to penetrate Cia's mind. She would have to do the work of establishing contact . . . Cia lost her momentum. She stood in the hallway for a moment, vaguely aware that people were crowding around her, dishes momentarily forgotten when she screamed.

'Cia, what's happened?' they asked. 'Is Ian all right? What happened to Sarah?'

She tried to focus on faces. Kate and Lidra wavered into her sight. 'They're missing,' she cried. 'Have you seen them? Where did they go? Ian was still unconscious!'

Lidra turned and snapped out some orders and the crowd began to dissipate. Kate took Cia's arm and led her back into the healing room. 'Would Sarah have moved him for any reason? For his safety, maybe?' she asked once they were alone in the room.

Cia shook her head. 'He was too ill to be moved. She would have asked me first.'

'What if she didn't have time?' Kate suggested.

'Sarah would at least have told Jack, if she were going to do something like that. Jack would have told me at dinner, wouldn't he?' Cia looked at Kate, searching her face for answers.

Kate shrugged. 'We'll find out what happened. Everything will be fine. In the meantime, you look pretty awful. Why don't you meditate on a rose quartz? Here.' She handed Cia a rough crystal.

'Souls! Everyone keeps telling me to be calm and rest.

191

My son is missing! How can I relax?' She flung the crystal across the room.

Kate flinched. Concern and fear were evident in her broad plain-featured face. She spread blunt-fingered hands, palm-up before her, raising her shoulders in a shrug.

'I'm sorry,' Cia said. She retrieved the stone and went back to where Kate stood. 'I think I just need to be alone for a bit. Will you tell me if Ian and Sarah are found in the Keep, please? I'm going to try to find their mental energies.'

'You're sure?' Kate asked.

Cia nodded. She held up the rose quartz crystal. 'Thanks,' she said with a small smile. She waited until the door closed behind Kate, then sat on Sarah's stool and closed her eyes to concentrate on locating the mental energies of her son and the healer.

Working in an ever-widening circle, she encompassed the Keep without finding them. Fear welled up in her mind, but she fought it back and tried to maintain her concentration as she began searching in the direction of the Old City, where Ian had been coming from when Gardner attacked him. Slowly, she covered the distance in a broad sweep, sensing nothing.

Then she found the wall.

There was a tap on the door to the healing room. 'Cia?' came a tentative voice on the other side. 'Cia? We can't find them anywhere in the Keep, and no one has seen them since Sarah came back to relieve Jack this afternoon.'

'Thanks,' Cia called, temporarily distracted. 'I know.' She turned her attention back to the mysterious wall she had encountered near the Old City.

'You have to do something now!'

Dalt paused in his circuit around the healing room to deliver his ultimatum.

Cia regarded him silently. A small smile of contempt twitched her lips as the silence between them stretched.

The old man began to fidget, twisting his strand of glass beads between tobacco-stained fingers, but he remained standing before her. Anger etched deep lines on his face and the torch-flame reflected in his eyes gave his expression a maniacal quality.

Cia continued to stare silently, unmoving, until at last Dalt couldn't stand it any longer. With a hiss of exasperation, he began to pace back and forth before her again.

'If you don't do something quickly, then everything we've worked for is lost!' The old man turned back and stabbed towards the ceiling with a yellowed forefinger. His voice rose to an hysterical shriek. 'Do you care so little for him that you'll sit here and do nothing?'

'Calm down, Dalt.' Cia rose slowly from her chair by the bed. She swayed slightly as she towered over the much smaller old man. The contempt that had been flickering across her fine-boned features consolidated. '*My* loyalty isn't in question. What reason do you have for wanting him back? You were going to poison him earlier for Gardner. Have you had a change of heart? Again?' Cia held Dalt in thrall, eyes locked and unblinking. Dalt was shaking now. Sweat had began to bead on his upper lip, glistening on his face and balding head, trickling slowly down his neck and back, wetting the chest and armpits of his tunic. Fear was in his eyes now, contorting his irregular features.

'Cia, no!' he pleaded. 'I swear! I wouldn't hurt him.' His tone became wheedling. 'I love the boy as much as you do.'

Cia's head jerked back as if dealt a physical blow. Her breath hissed between her teeth as the contempt turned to rage. 'How dare you?' she rasped. Too much to worry about, too little sleep. Too many people were playing too many games. Cia couldn't handle it any more.

'Tell me where Gardner has them,' she demanded. 'Where in the Old City has he taken them?'

Dalt recoiled, genuinely shocked. '*In* the Old City?' He shook his head. 'There is an abandoned house to the east of the Old City, before you get there. Maybe – '

'They are *in* the Old City. Where is he keeping them?'

Dalt shook his head again, backing slowly away from Cia. 'The abandoned house is too close to the Old City for me. No one goes into the Old City. Not even Gardner.'

'You're lying,' Cia spat. 'Ian was in the Old City, studying at the library when Drove found him, chased him and poisoned him. There is a block around the Old City now, that I'm certain Freddie is maintaining. You know where to find them. Tell me!'

'I swear, I don't know. The taboos – '

'No longer apply. I knew that. Apparently so does Gardner. How did he find out?'

'I tell you, I don't know!' Dalt cried. He had backed himself up against the wall and stood shivering under Cia's glare.

'You never told the truth to anyone in your life!' Cia said softly. 'You aren't telling the truth now. Do I have to take it from you?'

Dalt's eyes widened. He began to move sideways against the wall towards the door. He shook his head wildly back and forth. 'No, please,' he begged. 'Cia, no! I'm telling you the truth. I don't know anything about the Old City. I've never been there. To go there is death!'

Cia looked down at him pityingly. 'I loved you,' she said. Then she reached down into his mind with her own, probing ruthlessly for any information that might be of use.

Dalt began screaming as his knees buckled and he fell. He dropped his glass beads on the floor between them as he pressed his hands to his temples, then against his ears.

Finally, he crouched with his face pressed to his thighs, his hands locked behind his head, moaning.

Cia felt her anger cooling as she laid Dalt's mind open. What she found there didn't surprise her. She had always known the sort of man he was. All of this had been foreordained.

You did this for power? What power would Gardner give you? She looked down at Dalt, crouched before her, helpless and terrified, and hardened herself against the pity she felt for him. *The only power over people is the power to command their respect. Anything else is useless. Anything else inspires hatred.*

Dalt moaned. *Your son was a danger to him,* he gasped.

Even now – you are beneath contempt! she cried. She tightened her grip slightly as she sifted through the last bit she had missed . . .

They lay arm in arm, having just made love. Their breath had slowed, but their skin was warm and damp still from their exertions. Dalt smiled down at Cia as she smiled up at him. 'I love you,' she said. In response, he held her closer as the blood within him quickened. Again they made love, bodies moving together in ardent, desperate passion. He wanted to climb inside of her, become a part of her; not just send a representative to express his love for her . . .

Cia gasped and recoiled from the memory. She had blocked out her side of that afternoon long ago. But she had loved him, and he had loved her. She couldn't kill Ian's father.

With a gesture of disdain, Cia released her hold on his mind. Dalt slumped on to his side and lay whimpering softly.

Deliberately, Cia moved towards Dalt. She placed her foot on the strand of glass beads he had dropped and rocked her weight forward, crushing them. Closing her eyes, Cia turned from the scene and left the room.

* * *

'Freddie!' Drove Gardner roared at the second floor of the dilapidated old house. He stood on the damaged wooden floor, legs straddled, arms akimbo, head thrown back. Freddie scuttled quickly to the balcony and peered over the edge. The sight below frightened him and he backed away from the railing, huddling against the wall. Drove Gardner could be extremely cruel when he was angry, and he looked angry now. Freddie was afraid.

'Freddie.' Drove's voice took a more conciliatory tone as he tried to coax Freddie back to the railing. 'Freddie, I won't hurt you, I want you to do something for me.'

Freddie recognized that tone of voice and knew that things would be much worse for him if he didn't do as Gardner wanted immediately. He crept cautiously back to the edge of the balcony and clutched the railing for reassurance as he peered over it again.

'Y-yes, Mr Gardner?' he stammered, terrified.

'Freddie, I need you to contact Dalt for me and tell him I need to see him as soon as he can get away. Can you do that for me?' Gardner spoke slowly, as though to a young and slightly deaf child, but Freddie took no offence. He smiled with childlike eagerness.

'Yes, Mr Gardner! I can do that,' he said.

'Then do it now,' Gardner snapped.

Freddie's jaw slackened and his eyes went blank. He sat down abruptly as his hands relaxed and he lost his grip on the railing. Gardner had seen it often, but it always sent a shiver up his spine to watch Freddie in telepathic communication. It was almost creepy to see the young man leave his body and the conscious world; and disgusting to watch him drool. If Freddie weren't the best telepath available, Drove would never tolerate his imbecilic behaviour and disgusting personal habits.

'Um, Mr Gardner?' Freddie's abrupt return to consciousness interrupted Gardner's thoughts.

'Yes?' he said irritably.

'Um, Mr Gardner, Dalt can't answer,' Freddie said.

'What do you mean "Dalt can't answer"! How can he not answer?' Gardner's ability to deal with Freddie was limited to small amounts of time and minimal conversation. This conversation was taxing those limits.

Freddie cowered again, but remained near the railing. His mouth worked soundlessly for a moment as he screwed up his courage to speak. Drove Gardner was a powerful and angry man. Right now, he was powerfully angry at Freddie.

'Um, I mean, his mind has been opened, he can't think yet,' Freddie blurted finally.

'What are you talking about, boy? What do you mean his mind's been opened,' Gardner shouted.

Freddie whimpered and crouched behind the railing. He was going to get beaten for this. 'Um, it's, um . . .' Freddie shrugged miserably, peering through the rails. 'His mind . . .' His descriptive ability was exhausted. He had no way of explaining to Gardner that Dalt could not be found in this dimension right now.

Comprehension dawned on Gardner's face. 'You mean he's unconscious? Is that what you're trying to tell me, boy?' Drove Gardner's voice softened menacingly.

Freddie nodded slowly, fearfully. He knew a beating was coming next. Gardner always held Freddie personally responsible for any bad news the boy brought, and any mistakes made.

Gardner turned instead and strode out of the house, slamming the rickety door on the way out, leaving Freddie open-mouthed and shaking on the balcony.

The horse galloped over the rough trail as Drove Gardner switched its flank and dug his spurred heels into its sides. This close to the Old City, there were no farms, so the underbrush grew thickly along the unkempt path. Gardner was one of the few who used this particular route, so it remained mostly uncleared. Gardner didn't want anyone to become suspicious of a clear path to the warrens under the Old City. He wasn't anxious for company in this traditionally forbidden area.

He switched the horse again. The beast strained to go a bit faster and stumbled on the uneven ground. Gardner clutched the reins and dug in harder with his spurs. The horse shied from the harsh treatment, but Gardner remained firmly on his back. In anger, Gardner whipped the horse again and jerked the reins to put the horse back on to the trail headed towards the Old City and the opening of the underground halls which were his true stronghold.

Dalt's pilfered condition bothered Drove only in its inconvenience. It meant that Cia knew where Ian and Sarah were, and that she would try coming after them soon. He could go ahead with his plan. Soon, he would have Cia under his control. She and her lunatic son would no longer be an obstacle to him.

Drove jerked savagely on the reins again, pulling the horse around the bend in the path with a particularly vicious swing of the head. Rearing in protest, the horse tried hard to unseat Gardner, but failed again and received another beating with switch and spurs.

Together, horse and man pounded down the path towards the ragged buildings on the horizon. Both were so focused on the torments they suffered that they did not notice the slender, silver-haired woman who rode in their shadow and monitored their thoughts.

The entrance to the warrens was nothing more than a stairway in the middle of the pavement that descended into the otherworld that had been created before the time of the Dispersal. Survivalists had tunnelled between the basements of the buildings, and into the underground metro system. The passages went on for miles under the

Old City. It was in this area that Gardner had chosen to hide his Keep. Because of the taboos against inhabiting the Old Cities, Gardner had known that his secret would be safe from discovery.

Dismounting, Drove pulled the horse down the stairs into the darkness of the old subway station.

'You! Erhan, get up there and brush our tracks from the opening now!' he said to the man coming towards him carrying a torch. 'And take care of this horse,' he added, throwing his reins at the large man as he grabbed the torch. He strode off down the corridor, leaving Erhan and the horse in the relative darkness.

'Yes sir, Mr Gardner,' Erhan called after him. Sighing to himself, Erhan turned away and led the horse to a brass pipe protruding from the wall near the stairs. 'Treats you the same way as everybody else, don't he?' Erhan tied the horse to the pipe and ran a thick-fingered hand down the horse's neck. 'Run right over 'em, he do. He lathered you good.'

Erhan ran gentle fingers over the scored flesh of the horse's sides and flinched as he felt the animal's pain.

'We'll take you to the healer for that, but let me get the door first. Then we'll walk you a bit. You'll be OK, you'll see. I'll treat you real good.' Erhan ran his hand through his thinning, no-particular-colour hair and ascended the stairs. As he swept the tracks from the broken pavement, he thought he saw movement out of the corner of his eye, but when he looked for it, it was gone. Shaking his great head, he bent to his task, hurrying in order to get the poor abused beastie to the healer.

Gardner turned from the long passageway into a large room occupied by several individuals, all of whom flinched as his gaze swept over them. Without breaking stride, Gardner shrugged his cloak off on to the floor and threw the torch he carried towards the far wall. At the top of its arc, the invisible hand steadied its progress and tucked it safely into the sconce it had been aimed at. A tiny grey woman leaned her broom against the wall and moved to pick up the discarded cloak. Gardner whirled on the movement.

'Leave it!' he barked, pointing at the ancient offender. She shrieked in terror as the unseen hand picked her up and flung her away. She struck the wall with a muffled thump and fell soundlessly to the floor near her broom. Gardner turned on the small group who now huddled together as if that activity provided safety. 'Bring me supper. Now!' he shouted. Without waiting to see his order carried out, Gardner turned and strode through one of the many doors that lined the walls of the peculiar antechamber.

'Freddie!' Gardner yelled at the top of his lungs, both internally and externally. He crossed to a chair, sat and began to pull off his boots. 'Freddie!' he yelled again.

A beautiful young woman with long, coppery hair and clear, creamy skin peered around the edge of the door and cleared her throat timidly. Without looking up from his boots, Gardner waved her to the table against the far wall. Mareki crept in with a tray, not daring to look in Gardner's direction and hoping not to draw attention to herself. With shaking hands, she removed the bowl of stew from the tray and placed it on the table along with the utensils, a basket of bread and a pannikin of wine. Quickly, she turned to leave.

'Freddie!' Drove roared. 'Freddie, where the hell are you?'

With a whimper, Mareki fled the room, pulling the door shut behind her.

I'm here, sir, I'm sorry, sir. Freddie stammered.

You keep closer watch, damnit! Gardner yelled again. *When I want you, I expect you to respond!*

Yes, sir, Freddie said. The eagerness in his voice was apparent. *I'll watch real good.*

Freddie, Gardner began. *I need you to look in on the Keep, find out what's happening there so you can tell me.* Drove paused a moment to let this register. *Do you think you can do that?*

But, Mr Gardner, sir . . . is that stew? Freddie trailed off miserably. His belly rumbled emptily. Drove Gardner had kept Freddie in the house for the last couple of days. No one had come to cook for him, and he couldn't go into the Old City by himself. Mr Gardner had said so.

Stop snooping in my *mind and go find out what I want to know*, Gardner ground out. Idiots and incompetents. Well, soon things would be much better.

I understand, Freddie responded slowly.

Good. Go do it. Drove Gardner dismissed Freddie and settled in to his meal and his plans.

Freddie scanned the Keep stealthily, his mental touch unobtrusive, shielded from those telepaths who might detect his presence. It was suppertime at the Keep as well; everyone was occupied with food and conversation and no one noticed Freddie skulking around the edges of their consciousness. The food distracted Freddie and his belly growled loudly. It smelled so good and Freddie was so hungry that he snooped each mind slowly so that he could enjoy the taste and smell of what they were eating. Everyone was enjoying it so much that Freddie had trouble remembering the task at hand. It didn't take him long to find what he was looking for.

Mr Gardner? Freddie thrust a tentative thought into Drove Gardner's mind and withdrew quickly to observe the reaction to his interruption.

Did you find it? Gardner demanded.

Yes, sir. I think so. I think this is what you want. With that, Freddie broadcast the necessary information.

Yes, Freddie. Now go away, but remember to keep watch. Gardner dismissed him.

OK, Mr Gardner, sir! Freddie's mental projection positively wriggled with delight. Drove smiled as he turned back to Mareki, who had just come in to clear his tray. He grabbed her and tossed her on to the bed.

Freddie went to the kitchen in the ramshackle house to scavenge the cupboards in the dark.

9

Meg survived the weekend, but she was never sure afterwards just how she had managed. Tucker wouldn't return her phone calls. His mother finally suggested she leave him alone.

Her mother and father spent a lot of time watching her with worried expressions, but said nothing about her withdrawn behaviour. Even Thiessen sensed that she wanted to be left alone and didn't pester her as much as he usually did.

Meg spent the weekend studying. That was one thing Ian didn't seem to be able to get enough of. He read anything and everything he came in contact with. He was voracious. He was also indiscriminate. Meg tried to teach him to read critically, but Ian refused to believe that not everything written was worth his undivided attention and devout belief. It did, however, make it easier for Meg to catch up on her reading. By the time Monday morning rolled around, Meg felt prepared for her classes.

She didn't feel prepared for a conversation with Tucker, but she knew she had to try. Knowing he had a ten o'clock chemistry lecture on Mondays, Meg stationed herself outside the door to his classroom just before class was due to let out.

Ian, could you please go away and leave me alone for this? Meg asked.

No, Ian said. *Please, I promise I'll stay out of it. Just don't make me leave.*

I don't trust you not to screw things up, Meg told him.

Please don't make me leave, Ian begged.

It's just for a little while. Just till I talk to Tucker, Meg

203

asked. *He's so mad at me, it probably won't be very long, OK?*

Meg, please, Ian insisted.

What's the matter? Meg asked. *All I want is a little privacy while I beg for my boyfriend's forgiveness. I don't want you around for that. Is that so hard to understand?*

Will you let me back in afterwards? Ian asked uncertainly.

Of course! Meg exclaimed impatiently. *What did you think?*

I was afraid you might not let me in, he said. *You can go crazy if you're cut off from your senses.*

I promise I'll let you back in. Now will you go?

Promise? Ian asked.

I promise, said Meg.

Are you sure? You won't accidentally raise any barriers to keep me out? he insisted.

I said I promise! Now go, she begged. The door to the classroom opened and students began to trickle through.

OK, Ian said hesitantly. His consciousness disappeared from Meg's mind as he centred himself.

Meg felt him leave her conscious mind and breathed a sigh of relief, but then she saw Tucker and the tenseness in her stomach returned.

As Tucker walked through the door, he caught sight of Meg. His dazed-student expression vanished. His shoulders stiffened, his face reddened and he tried to walk past her without acknowledging her presence.

'Tucker, wait,' Meg called after him as she trotted after his long-legged stride.

'I don't want to talk to you, Meg,' he said tightly. 'Didn't my mother explain that to you?'

'Your mother suggested I not call again,' Meg said. 'She didn't say you didn't want to talk to me.'

'Well, there's nothing I have to say to you,' Tucker said, lengthening his stride.

'Not even a "how dare you?", or "why did you do that?",' Meg pushed, lengthening her own stride to keep up. 'Didn't we have enough of a relationship that you'd be willing to at least talk about what happened on Friday night?'

'I guess not!' Tucker swung round to face Meg. 'Or else how could you have done that?'

Meg smiled. 'Now we're getting somewhere,' she said. 'Look, is there some place less public we could go for just a bit? I've got something I have to tell you, and I'd rather not share it with the entire campus.'

'No,' Tucker snapped. 'Nothing you have to say could be of remote interest to me.' He started to walk away from her again.

'Tucker, wait.' Meg grabbed his arm and swung him back around. 'You may not care about what I have to say, but I still have to say it. It won't hurt you to just listen and if you won't go with me to some place more private, then I'll have to tell you here.'

Tucker sighed, but he didn't turn away, so Meg took a deep breath and began.

'Tucker, I never told you I have a history of mental illness.' She held up her hand to forestall his comment. 'I was afraid it would scare you away, and I haven't had any problems since I was about ten. Just one strange dream when I was eighteen, but I never paid much attention to it.

'For the past week and a half, I've been hearing voices again. It's really got me scared. On Friday night in the bar, I had a really bad episode, and I just wasn't in control of what I was doing.

'I know there's no excuse for what I did, but I love you, and I thought you deserved the best explanation I can give you.'

'And you expect me to believe a cock-and-bull story

205

like that?' Tucker stared at her in disbelief. 'How stupid do you think I am?'

'You can ask my Dad,' Meg said defiantly. 'You know where he is in the History Department. He'll tell you that I'm telling you the truth. I didn't tell you this because I thought it'd get you back. I thought you deserved better than the way I treated you on Friday night. I wanted to apologize. I – , I was hoping you'd at least understand that I'm sorry. I didn't mean it.' Meg shook her head and walked off, leaving Tucker standing in the middle of the pavement.

Meg waited until she reached the ladies' room before bursting into tears. She flopped on to the dilapidated couch in the corner of the 'powder room' and sobbed into a paper towel.

Ian? she called. She wasn't sure how to go about getting him back either, but at least she knew he wanted to come back. *Ian?*

Meg? he asked. *You really did let me come back!* The relief in his voice was evident.

Ian, I don't make promises lightly. When I do make a promise, I do my damnedest to come through, Meg snapped.

Hey, are you OK? he asked.

No, Meg wailed. Tears continued to slip down her cheeks. She felt utterly miserable. *I tried to talk to Tucker, but he didn't believe a word I said. I hate quitting. I hate losing. I just don't feel equipped to deal with this.*

Thank you for letting me come back, Ian said quietly. *After everything I've done to mess up your life, I'm surprised you would be so nice to me. I wish there was something I could do to make up to you for blowing it with Tucker.*

Meg smiled in spite of herself. *Who knows*, she said. *Maybe Tucker will actually go talk to my father. Maybe things aren't as hopeless as they seem. Your mother will be back for you soon, and we'll both be able to get on with our lives.*

For both of us, it had better be soon. Ian felt Meg's smile catching.

In the meantime, we've got a class to go to, and finals to study for, and track practice this afternoon, Meg said as she stood up and dried her eyes.

Ian groaned at the thought of track.

That's OK, Meg grinned a little maliciously. *Tomorrow we have swimming-team practice!*

Tiana heaved the basket of wet sheets on to her shoulder and rose to follow the others from the large washtubs to the lines that were strung behind the barns to keep the animals from getting at the drying bedding and clothing. The noon sun burned brightly down on her as she toiled under her heavy load and she thought longingly of the kitchen and the stool upon which she usually sat to do her share of that work. When she took her turn at laundry, there were no stools to sit on and the chore was much more physically demanding. Tiana was not a woman who enjoyed hard work, but she didn't shirk her responsibilities either. Not like Cia, she thought darkly to herself.

She was engrossed in thoughts of inequity when the shadow fell across her face. Looking up suspiciously, Tiana saw Drove Gardner astride his horse, blocking her path to the lines. A quick glance about told her they were alone and the fear she felt at this registered clearly on her face.

Seeing it, Gardner threw back his head and laughed his deep-throated, fear-inspiring laugh.

'You have nothing to fear from me, Tiana. We have something of mutual interest to discuss. I wonder if I may walk with you a ways?' Gardner swung out of his saddle and dropped the horse's reins, ground-hitching it.

He took the heavy basket of wet sheets from her and

placed it on the dirt beside the animal. Taking Tiana's hand, he pulled her arm through the crook of his elbow and drew her away from the Keep, on to the path to the river.

Without a sound, she allowed him to lead her away from her chores and the illusion of safety that she would have had if they remained at the Keep. She knew he could not read her mind, but she was terrified that she might do or say something to anger him. Her glass beads hung around her neck, but she was afraid to touch them even though she wanted to badly. Instead, she walked along the path at his side, not daring even a sideways glance at his face.

'Sit here,' Gardner said at last, pushing her gently on to a fallen tree trunk whose upper branches rested in the water of the river.

Tiana sat promptly and drew her robe more closely about her, but she still didn't risk looking Drove in the face. She stared instead at his knees. He wore fine leather trousers and calf-boots of good construction.

'Tiana, we have a mutual enemy. I would like to ally myself with you to bring her into hand,' Gardner said at last.

Startled by this, Tiana looked him in the face. He looked seriously back at her.

'What could I do that would be of help to you?' she finally managed to blurt out. 'I have no psi-power. Who is our "mutual" enemy?'

'I understand you have no cause to love Cia Janec. I personally loathe the woman and her son, and their disturbing ideas. I want her stopped, and you can help me.' Gardner smiled reassuringly at Tiana.

'What could I do to a telepath that she couldn't find in my thoughts before I had the chance?' Tiana was growing confused by this whole incident and longed for the safety of the Keep and the routine chore of hanging the sheets on the lines to dry. She looked over at where the leaves of the tree she sat on blocked a portion of the river. Water swirled into tiny whirlpools, and leaves and twigs carried downstream had become lodged among the branches, clogging the flow near the bank. Tiana felt as though she were trapped in a similar manner. She squinted back up at Gardner.

'With Freddie to shield your thoughts from Cia, you could administer a sleeping draught in her tea at supper; a strong one that would ensure she wouldn't awaken until in my custody.' Gardner was smiling more broadly now. Tiana suppressed a shiver at the glint in his eyes. 'You will do that for me, won't you?' he asked softly.

Tiana nodded. Of course she would. She had no wish to be hurt; if Cia should be hurt instead, only Ian would really care. Maybe Lidra and Kate, and a few others, but everyone knew Gardner hated Cia. No one would suspect Tiana of involvement.

'Yes. I knew you would.' He handed her a small wooden box which, upon inspection, contained a greyish powder. 'Here is the draught. Freddie will be waiting for you to call him. When you have the opportunity, just think his name and he will answer you. When the task is complete, tell him and I will come get Cia.'

Tiana nodded numbly and rose from the log. 'I'd better get back to the laundry before I'm missed. I will take care of it this evening, if possible.' Tiana indicated the wooden box she held, then tucked it into her pocket. She turned her back on him and walked back to where her basket waited. She didn't watch Gardner leave. She swung the basket back on to her shoulder and headed for the barns and the rest of the laundry crew.

Supper that evening was somewhat subdued. Cia's distress call when she discovered Ian and Sarah missing the day before had jolted the entire Keep. Cia sat quietly and ate with her head down. Her mind was busy with possible approaches to Gardner's lair. She didn't notice that her tea was a little more bitter than usual, but she could feel the warmth spreading through her body, relaxing muscles and nerves, taut and jangled from overwork and stress.

Tiana kept a surreptitious watch on Cia, shielded by Freddie and spurred by her fear of Gardner and the consequences of her failure. She had poured the entire contents of the small wooden box into Cia's teacup just before everyone sat down to the evening meal. She was gratified to see that Cia drained her cup and refilled it as she ate, apparently not noticing that the sleeping draught had been administered.

When supper was at last over, Cia excused herself to go to bed. She was suddenly much more tired than she had thought and she staggered a little as she headed towards her room. Tiana watched her go before helping to clear the table. After the dishes were washed and put away, she slipped off to find Cia and complete her task.

Tiana muttered to herself as she walked down the long back hallway to Cia's quarters and swung the door open. Cia lay across her bed, still fully dressed. Her mouth was open and slack, and she snored lightly. Closing the door behind her, Tiana crossed the room to the window and opened it. The evening was warm, with a gentle breeze to stir the curtains and rustle the leaves in the trees outside.

Tiana went to where Cia lay on the bed and gathered her up. Cia was extremely tall, but she weighed little more than a child, and Tiana had no trouble carrying her to the window and dumping her unceremoniously on to the ground outside.

Freddie! she called silently.

Yes, ma'am, Freddie responded.

Tell Gardner that he can come get Cia any time. I'll leave her out by the laundry lines behind the barn, understand? she asked him.

Yes, ma'am, said Freddie.

Quietly then, Tiana closed the window and left Cia's room unobserved. She went outside and around to the place where Cia lay in the dirt. Again, she lifted the limp form into her arms and carried Cia across the barnyard to the lines, where Tiana again dumped the body into the dirt. Gardner would be by shortly to claim Cia; she wouldn't be there in the morning and Tiana would have successfully discharged her responsibility to Gardner. With some haste, Tiana returned to the Keep.

The only thing that seemed to be going well in Meg's life was school. With finals half over, she had plenty of time to study because Ian wanted to read everything he hadn't had access to in the library. She questioned him closely about it, but aside from the books, he really didn't know much about it. It was just there, and his mother had taught him to read, and he went there often to read everything on the shelves.

She had overheard her father talking to her mother about the grant he had been pitching to the Dean, but paid no attention to it until Ian had begun to describe the library to her. Slowly, the pieces began to fit into place. Ted Danning was a professor of anthropology at the University, and had an interest in the present events that would be history in coming years. He had suggested that a special project be established to provide for book storage in a time-proof vault in the basement of the University library. The Dean had been interested in it as a time-capsule, to draw attention to the University; probably students and money as well.

What Ian was describing sounded an awful lot like this, so after her English exam, she hopped on to her bike and pedalled off to the library.

Ian was riveted by the sight. *Souls* he exclaimed. *It*

looks so new! I didn't recognize the street, or any of the buildings . . . I barely recognize the library, but this is it.

Meg locked her bike in the rack outside on the pavement and started up the front stairs.

It feels funny not to be leading my horse, Ian observed.

Into the library? Meg asked, incredulous.

Well, I couldn't very well leave him tied up in the hot sun all afternoon. At least once I'm inside, I pull a table across the doorway and just let Billy wander around, said Ian. *That way he's penned, but he's not.*

I can just see the librarian's reaction to that! Meg chuckled. She walked through the door and Ian gasped.

Look at all the books! he said, gazing around in awe.

Meg felt a bit stupid as her head swivelled around taking in everything, but she let Ian look as they wandered into the reference section.

I guess the ones that weren't taken in the exodus decayed here, huh? she asked him.

I guess, Ian said absently, running a hand over the bindings of a shelf of books.

Where were the books you read? Meg pressed.

Ian pulled a book off the shelf and glanced through it. *Hmm?* he murmured as he became engrossed in the pages.

Meg shut her eyes. *Show me where you found the books you read. Where did you go in the library?*

Oh! Ian snapped the book shut and returned it to the shelf. *Over this way,* he indicated the direction of the stairs. *They're in a thick-walled room in the basement. There's no windows in the room, so I keep a torch by the stairs with a flint and wool. I bring the books upstairs to read in the sunlight over by those windows.* He waved a hand towards the front of the room.

Show me where in the basement, Meg suggested. She started towards the stairs.

Don't we need – Ian began, then checked himself. *Sorry. I forgot about electric lights.*

They went down the stairs and Ian was awed by the sheer numbers of books stored in the building. *An incredible amount was lost*, he mourned.

Yeah, but a significant amount of what was lost was trash, Meg said, still trying to make her point about tabloids, bodice-rippers and self-actualization how-to books. *Where is the vault located?*

They must have walled off half the basement. The door was right over here. Or rather will be over here. Ian corrected himself.

Well, it's kind of nice to know that Dad gets his way with the Dean. This project means a lot to him, said Meg. *Tell you what. Since finals are going so well, and I have no prospect of a date in the near future, why don't we check out a novel and do some fun reading tonight, instead of studying?*

Ian agreed enthusiastically and they went back upstairs.

A couple of hours later, Meg was completely and thoroughly exasperated. Ian couldn't make up his mind on any one book. He wanted to take half the library home with them. Meg tried to explain the policy of no more than eight books being checked out at a time, but Ian was being selectively stupid.

Can't we just take these? he pleaded. They held an armload of fifteen books; all of them hardbound and all of them heavy.

No, Meg said again. *We can only take eight at a time, and we don't have time to read that many during finals. I have too much studying to do between now and the end of the semester. I still have the dreaded biology exam to study for. Pick one, and let's go home.*

But – Ian began.

One, or none, it's your choice, Meg said, unmoved. By this time, she didn't really want to read any of them.

213

I can't decide! Ian wailed.

Hey! I've got it! Meg exclaimed, inspired. *Early Heinlein is great bubble-gum-shoot-em-up-space-adventure, and I haven't read anything of his in a while, and I have all of those at home.*

But I wanted to check something out! Ian protested.

Ian, with my luck, I'd check out a book, forget I had it and have to pay outrageous overdue fines. Let's just go home, OK? Meg could feel her patience stretching past the breaking point.

I really wanted to check a book out of the library, Ian said. *We don't have to read it. It's just that I've never done it before, and I'm not likely to have the chance to do it again.*

Oh. Meg was caught flat by that argument. *Well, since you put it that way, here. We'll take this book to check out, and leave these others on this cart. Then we can read the Heinlein when we get home. Is that OK?*

OK, Ian agreed.

They put the other books down and took their one up to the circulation desk. Meg fished her library card out of her wallet and pushed it across the desk at the woman on the other side. The Librarian picked it up and scrutinized it carefully. Then she nodded and ran the computer scanner over the magnetic strip on the back. She did the same to the book and handed both of them to Meg and walked off without saying a word.

That's it? Ian asked.

Yup, said Meg. *No big deal. Now if we hadn't done that, and sneaked out of the library with the book, the metal poles there would have triggered the alarm, and security guards would have appeared from nowhere and we would have been detained and searched and all kinds of mean, nasty, ugly, horrible things.*

That sounds like much more fun, said Ian.

You have a strange sense of humour, said Meg. *Since*

we're not going to read this anyway, do you mind if I just drop it in the return slot? I know me; if I take it home, it'll stay there for at least two months. I resent paying overdue fees.

OK, Ian shrugged. He was disappointed by the check-out procedure. *Let's go home, I'm hungry.*

We're going to eat light, Meg told him. *We missed track practice, so we'll do a little running after dinner to make up for it.*

Ian groaned. *I was hoping you'd forgotten*, he said.

I never forget things like torturing the men in my head, Meg laughed. She walked back down the stairs to her bike and unlocked it. Then she climbed onto the bike and headed toward home.

Susan stood at the sink, washing lettuce, and Thiessen was at the kitchen table, colouring. Ted was in the den, watching news and sipping a glass of wine. The windows had been closed against the cooling night air and the lights pushed back the gathering darkness in a pleasant and familiar way. Meg smiled to herself as she walked into the kitchen and dropped her knapsack on the closest chair.

'How did your English exam go, Meg?' her mother asked as she shut off the water and dried her hands on a paper towel.

Thiessen smiled up at her and pointed to his picture. 'I made this for you, Meggie,' he said proudly. 'Guess what it is.'

'Better than I expected, I think,' Meg told her mother as she sat down beside Thiessen. 'That's very nice, Thies,' she said to him, looking at the squiggles on the manila paper. 'Why don't you tell me about it?'

Thiessen grinned wickedly at her. 'You don't know, and you don't want to hurt my feelings by saying the wrong thing, huh?' Thiessen could be disturbingly perceptive for a six-year-old.

Meg grinned back. 'OK, hotshot! You got me,' she said. 'What is it?'

'It's a special drawing to make you feel better,' he told her ingenuously. 'Martha said it would be good for you.'

He's a very old soul, Ian said.

What? Meg asked in disbelief. To Thiessen she said, 'Thank you. I'll hang this on my wall, OK?'

'Over your bed, Martha says,' Thiessen told her. 'She says you need to work with the colours.'

'Thiessen, what are you talking about?' Susan asked.

He's right, said Ian. *The yellow will help to relax your mind, the blue will help you with communication and calmness, and the purple will put you in touch with your psychic powers.*

Oh, come on! Meg exclaimed impatiently. *Shouldn't I use incense and crystals and weird music for that?* To her mother, Meg asked, 'Can I help you get dinner?'

Crystals are useful for many things, and drawing on psi-powers is one of them. Mother uses them to meditate, Sarah uses them to heal.

'Thanks,' Susan said. 'Why don't you finish putting together the salad while I baste the roast?'

How does a crystal heal? Meg asked as she stood up and went to the sink. She picked up a lettuce leaf, shook it dry and tore it up in the salad bowl.

It's held over the body to energize, or draw out bad energies. Sarah is using coloured stones and crystals to draw the poison Gardner used out of my system, Ian said.

Rocks to draw poison? Meg gasped in disbelief. *Your life depends on that nonsense? What are you all thinking of? Can't you analyse the poison and concoct an antidote?*

What for? Ian asked, puzzled. *We have crystals and coloured stones that will do what we need them to.*

Meg shuddered, but she didn't say anything more about it. She didn't need to get into a metaphysical argument with a man whose life depended on the success of such arcane ritual.

Dinner was pleasant enough, but as soon as she was able, Meg excused herself to go and change for a run.

'Didn't you get enough of that at practice this afternoon?' her father asked her with a tolerant smile.

'I didn't go to practice this afternoon. I went to the library instead, to look up some reference material on cellular biology for my test on Thursday,' Meg explained as she cleared her plate from the table. 'Mom, why don't you leave the dishes, and I'll wash up when I get back. Thiessen, you can help me dry, OK?'

Thiessen made a face and slid down in his chair until his head was below the table. 'I don't want to,' he muttered.

'That sounds like a good idea,' Susan said. 'Don't be out for too long. I know you're careful, but it's dark out, and I worry.'

'I know,' Meg said as she started up the stairs. 'I won't be more than an hour, I promise.'

She changed and stretched out quickly and ran out the front door, down the driveway towards the street.

Ian grumbled a bit, but he left the body to her, so Meg didn't feel as if she were fighting her own muscles.

How long did your mother figure it would be before she was able to come back for you? Meg asked as she ran along the pavement in the dark. The street lamps pooled their light at regular intervals through the neighbourhood and Meg ran from pool to pool, counting the number of steps between them, the number of steps across them, the number of steps between inhale and exhale. Running in the dark, it was easy to fall into a monotony that lulled the brain away from the chore of running. She could keep going for hours at that pace without tiring.

She didn't say, Ian responded. *But she did say that if*

she can't come get me for some reason, that you would have to figure out how to take me yourself.

Swell, Meg thought as she paced across another dark patch of pavement. She ran in and out of cul-de-sacs and around streets that meandered in and out of each other in the annoying way that suburban streets are designed.

She had fallen into a semi-hypnotized state. Her mind was wandering, not really aware of Ian's presence and not really aware of her own. Five strides through the pool of light, twenty through the darkness; around the corner and up the hill.

The lights flickered and died.

Meg ran in darkness for several strides before realization penetrated her self-hypnotized state. The pool of light had not come after twenty strides. She looked up to discover that she was in darkness except for the lights from the houses she ran past.

A shred of nightmare seized her heart and she began running faster. She looked around wildly, trying to find her bearings. She had not been paying attention to specifically where she was.

Then she heard the footsteps.

She heard them deep in her soul and felt adrenaline rush into her system, spurring her to an even faster pace.

This is backwards, she thought to herself.

Meg, what's happening? Ian demanded, fear evident in his tone. He had seen the scenes of her nightmare as she focused on them, bringing them back to the surface of her mind for comparison.

My dream, she said. *I was in a strange body, in a strange city, running through the dark. This can't be happening.*

I don't get it, said Ian.

Neither do I, Meg gasped. She lengthened her stride again and sprinted down the street towards home.

The footsteps fell away behind them, but the lights didn't come back on. Meg started to worry about tripping, or stepping wrong and falling, but her feet continued to land straight and she sped through the dark. Her breath was coming in ragged gasps that burned her lungs, but she continued to run right up the front lawn to the door.

She pushed the door open and dashed into the house, slamming it behind her and locking it quickly.

'Meg?' Ted and Susan both called from the den where they were watching television.

'Don't slam the door like that,' Susan said. 'I'm glad you're home safely.'

'Uh, yeah,' Meg gasped. 'I'll get started on the dishes now, I guess.' She walked into the kitchen and turned on the water. After splashing some on her face, she began stacking plates in the sink.

'Meggie?'

Meg jumped and turned quickly towards the sound. Thiessen stood round-eyed before her.

'I'm sorry, I didn't mean to scare you,' he said. He held up a dish-towel. 'Mom sent me in to help you,' he explained.

'Oh,' Meg said, staring at him. 'Uh, OK.' She turned blankly back to the sink and stared at it for a moment before reaching into the suds to start scrubbing.

Meg showered and changed. She read Thiessen a bedtime story and kissed him good night. At the door, she turned off the light.

'Good night, Thies,' she said. 'Sleep tight.' She left the door open a crack.

'Night, Meggie,' Thiessen murmured sleepily.

Meg stopped in her room on the way back downstairs to grab the book she had told Ian about that afternoon in the library. In the den, she settled into her favourite chair and opened the book. Ian was engrossed almost immediately, as she had known he would be. Her mother and father were talking with each other quietly and Meg slowly relaxed after the scare she had had while running. She became as involved in the book as Ian; the low murmur of her parents' voices lulled her.

She had become so relaxed and engrossed in her book, that she didn't immediately feel the energy change in the room. A chill caused her to shudder, interrupting her concentration. She looked up to see where the blanket was, and instead saw a glowing mist swirling in the corner opposite her chair.

Meg gasped and her parents looked up, eyes focusing instead on the apparition.

Slowly as the mist shifted, two faces took shape, transposed over each other and two bodies took rough form beneath them. Ian stared at them in disbelief.

'Gardner!' he yelled, jumping up from the chair where he and Meg had been reading. Meg heard a sharp intake of breath as her parents heard the recognition in her voice. There was no way for her to tell them she had no idea what was going on.

You know who this is? Meg asked stupidly as she stared in horror and fascination at the superimposed images developing in the corner of the den. One face was sweet, but vague. His nose was running and there was a thread of saliva across one cheek. The other face was the one that held Meg's attention. There was a look of smug malignancy in its eyes and an ugly curl of lip that she found frightened her beyond what she thought was normal for the expression. She realized that much of what she was feeling was transmitted to her from Ian, who seemed riveted by the appearance of the two men.

To jolt Ian into reaction, Meg sent him an image of Cia in the fun-house mirror and the feeling of terror that she had felt when she thought she was losing her mind and that Thiessen might be in danger.

Souls. Is that what it was like for you?

Ian, who are these two? What are they doing here and

why are you so frightened? Meg said, trying to get Ian back to the matter at hand.

Drove Gardner and Freddie, he responded numbly. *Something has gone very wrong. This can't be happening.*

Freddie is the telepath you told me about? Meg asked.

Yeah, he's pretty harmless without Gardner. Gardner's the one who poisoned me.

And now I've come to finish what I began, rasped a voice Meg had not heard before.

'Ted?' Susan's voice came out in a squeak.

'I heard it,' Ted replied.

Cia! Meg screamed as loudly as she could. Ian was stunned by the force of her panic and fought to control his own reaction.

She can't help you, said the strange voice. Energy surged under its broadcast and crackled in the room as it spoke. *I have her now. She can't interfere.*

What have you done with her, Drove? Ian asked, trying to sound braver than he felt.

'Meggie, look!' Thiessen came into the den holding a piece of paper very carefully in front of him as he walked. There was a purple crayon stuck behind his right ear and a look of pride on his face. His eyes never left the paper and he walked slowly so as not to disturb the object resting on it.

'Thiessen, no. Go back to bed. Get out of here now!' Meg's voice was tight with fear.

'No, look here. See? Martha said you would need this tonight.' Thiessen came to stand in front of her, holding up the paper for her inspection. Glued to the coarse manila drawing paper was a rough quartz crystal surrounded by squiggles and lines in purple crayon.

'Thiessen,' Meg began. She looked at the apparition in the corner and saw the arms raised above the heads. One pair of eyes glittered with manic determination, the other pair vacant and unfocused. Meg could feel the power building and felt Ian's fear paralysing them both.

Blue glowed in the palms of the upraised hands. Meg struggled to separate her emotions from Ian's indiscriminate broadcasting.

'Thiessen!' she screamed. As she reached towards him, the blue energy arced across the room at Meg.

Oh no, no, said Ian as he watched the bolt, steeling himself for the impact.

Time seemed to stretch out as Meg saw that Thiessen still held the paper. The crystal glittered coldly in the dimly-lit den and then sparked blue with the energy of the image's upraised hands. With a blinding flash, the crystal shattered. Tiny shards, sharp-edged and charged with blue fire, flew backwards into Thiessen's chest and stomach.

Thiessen's eyes widened and his mouth sagged open. He looked up at Meg and smiled tentatively. 'I love you, Meggie,' he whispered, as he sank to the floor. Blue energy danced along his body for a moment longer, then he lay still at Meg's feet. Meg stared in horror at his small form.

Then she looked up at Gardner. The anger on Drove's face was answered by the terror and exhaustion in Freddie's.

We will be back to take care of you! Gardner yelled in frustration as the two faded back into the mist and disappeared.

Susan and Ted crouched over Thiessen.

'No-o-o!' Meg screamed. Dropping to her knees, she picked up his limp body and hugged it to her. 'No!' she begged. 'Please, God, no.' But Thiessen didn't stir.

Meg felt something inside her give way and her mind broke.

PART THREE

The Keep, Reprise

10

He was drifting in the dark.

It felt as if he had always been there. There didn't seem to be a time of anything else. The dark was utter. He had no sensation of touch or of smell, but somewhere, a child was crying.

In the darkness, he was disoriented and couldn't trace the origin of the sound. By concentrating on it, it seemed to be coming closer to him, but there was no sensation of movement.

Hello? he thought. He was immediately rewarded with a wave of excruciating emotional pain. He gasped, recoiling from the broadcast, trying to ward off the feelings of hurt and betrayal that followed the initial blast. The crying continued, getting gradually closer to wherever it was he was.

Where am I? he asked. In return, he received the mental equivalent of a shrug and renewed sobbing.

The voice sounded familiar to him. There was a reason he was floating senseless like this. He had centred when the barriers broke.

Is this all that's left? he asked. He didn't expect a response, he was glad she could cry. Reaching out with arms he hadn't had a moment ago, he touched the child. She grabbed his hands and dragged herself to him, allowing him to pull her into his centre. Gently, he held her in his arms and rocked her frail, battered body slowly back and forth in the darkness until her sobs subsided.

There was no time-frame in this peculiar limbo. He could have held her for an hour or a week, he had no idea. Finally, she pushed away from him slightly and exhaled a long, shaky breath.

Meg?

She didn't answer. Ian stroked her hair from her face and held it between his palms. In the dark, he couldn't see her, but he got a strong impression of blankness in the touch. Taking her by the hand, he led her from his centre back out into the maelstrom of her mind. She offered token resistance, but he was firm and shut his centre to her once she was out. It was a crutch she couldn't afford right now.

Why can't I stay? she asked, plaintively.

That is no sanctuary for you, he replied.

Outside Ian's centre, chaos was brightly lit. Squinting against the onslaught, he held tightly to Meg's hand and looked around. With the shreds of Meg's battered mind swirling about them, it was impossible really to see anything. He hadn't been prepared for so much damage, and with no experience in this sort of thing, the job was daunting.

Who are you? she asked.

The chaos was complete. She couldn't distinguish anything. She clung to a hand, but she couldn't see who it belonged to.

Meg, don't you remember me? There was pain in the voice now.

Meg shook her head. Then she realized that if she couldn't see him, he probably couldn't see her. *No*, she said in a small voice.

My name is Ian. You know me almost as well as you know yourself, he told her. That didn't make any sense, though. Where was she and what was she doing here?

My guess is that you're unfolding, came the unexpected reply.

What's that? she asked.

You really don't remember?

No, she said. She was more curious than frightened now.

But you recognize your name, he said. He sounded puzzled.

Yes, she said. *My name is Meg.*

How old are you, Meg? Ian asked.

Something in her mind stirred. That question sounded familiar, but she had no frame of reference. She couldn't attach the question to anything significant.

I don't know, she said. That bothered her. She should know the answer. It should be as ordinary a question as her name.

Where are we? she asked.

In your mind, he told her. *I haven't been able to figure out exactly where, yet, but we are in your subconscious on a level that is safe from sensory overload, so we must be pretty deep, and there must be an awful lot of damage if this is safe haven.*

What does that mean?

Are you two? Ian asked on inspiration.

Yes, she said. But that didn't make any sense either. Nothing made much sense. She was older than that, wasn't she?

I was afraid of that, said Ian.

Wasn't I older than that? Meg asked him.

You were twenty when I met you, he told her. *You've begun unfolding, and I've got to help you through it. Then you'll be twenty again.*

How? she asked.

Ian thought for a moment before shaking his head. *I don't know*, he said at last. *I have no idea.*

Meg whimpered. *Ian, I'm scared*, she said.

So am I, Meg, but somehow, we'll get through this, I promise. He hugged the small child again. *Now, we have to be quiet so I can think. I'll be right here, and I'll hold your hand, so you won't be alone, but you have to let me concentrate, OK?*

OK, Meg agreed in a small voice. She squeezed his hand for reassurance.

Another timeless moment passed as Ian held Meg's hand and thought.

Mostly, he thought black thoughts about how his mother could have sent him back here to this impossible situation with no instructions on how to deal with a child unfolding.

This isn't getting us anywhere, he said at length.

Where were we going? Meg wanted to know.

That's not what I meant, he said. *I guess I meant this isn't helping any. I can't think since I left my centre. It's just too crazy out here to think, but I can't recentre without taking you with me, and I can't leave you here by yourself.*

At the mention of being left by herself, Meg's grip tightened on Ian's hand.

Don't leave me, she begged.

But without my centre – Ian began. *Wait! Maybe we could make one for you!* he exclaimed.

What? One what?

A centre. I must have heard Mother do it a hundred times in class. I'm sure we could make you a centre. That would help a lot. Both of us, Ian told her.

What is a centre? Meg asked. Her grip on Ian's hand had relaxed slightly.

It's the seat of your soul. It's a beautiful place inside you that you can go to and feel safe. You can do work there, too, if you have the gifts for it, said Ian.

Can I have one? I want to be some place pretty. This place scares me, she confided.

OK, Ian agreed. *But I think there are things you have to visualize that you don't know about, so I'll have to kind of fill in those things, and then you can change what you don't like later. Is that all right with you?*

228

What don't I know about? Meg demanded.

Well, said Ian. *Can you tell me what a room looks like?*

What's a room? asked Meg.

That's what I mean. I'll picture things for you, and then you can change what you don't like.

What's a room? Meg asked again.

A room is a space that is separate from the things outside it. It usually has a floor and ceiling and four walls. There can be doors and windows in the walls that lead to the places outside the room.

I don't understand what these words are, but I feel like I should, Meg whined.

Oh boy, Ian whistled. *This is going to be a lot harder than I expected!* He thought for a moment. *OK, let's try this: move your arms and feel the space around you, then find my hand again*, he directed.

Reluctantly, Meg let his hand go and waved her arms randomly in front of her. She immediately grabbed for his hand again and held it tightly.

You see? he asked her. *I'm still here for you, aren't I? There is nothing to be afraid of. I won't let anything hurt you.*

Meg nodded vigorously. *OK*, she said, but she didn't loosen her grasp.

Now, that space you felt? Concentrate on it and see that nothing is there. No lights, no sound, nothing but you and me. The two of us are in that dark by ourselves and the movement and noise are outside the space we are in, Ian directed.

But it's already there! Meg complained. *How can it not be there?*

It isn't supposed to be, he said. *It doesn't have to be.*

Why? asked Meg.

Because it frightens you and it's preventing you from doing what you have to do in order to heal yourself, Ian told her.

Am I sick?

Yes, you are, and I'm here to try and help you. Will you let me? Ian asked.

Meg nodded and smiled tentatively at him. *Yes.*

OK, then. Try to clear the space around us of the light and noise. Concentrate on making the things that frighten you go away. Remember that I'm here to help protect you.

Meg nodded again and squeezed her eyes tightly shut.

After a small eternity, the chaotic display of light and sound that had enveloped them receded somewhat.

That's good, Meg. Whatever you're doing is working. Concentrate harder on that and keep pushing back the darkness.

Encouraged, Meg scowled in concentration and the darkness around them grew, surrounding them both and blocking out the cacophony.

OK, Ian said presently. *That should be enough for now, Meg. Why don't you ease up and open your eyes.*

Meg's scowl deepened. The darkness became profoundly dense as she continued to push the chaos in her soul away from herself.

Meg! Ian grabbed her arms, trying to deflect her attention from her efforts. *Meg, you have to stop now. You have enough room to create your centre now.*

She showed no sign of hearing him. He shook her gently, hoping for a response, but her eyes remained tightly shut.

Meg! Ian shouted. *You have to stop this. You can't shut yourself away in the darkness and hope that everything will make itself better. You have to make yourself better. I can't do it for you, I can only help.*

Meg pulled away from his grasp and turned her back on him. She put her hands over her ears, hunched her shoulders forward over her chest.

Meg, Ian said gently. *You have to get well. Thiessen deserves better than this.*

Meg gasped. Her hands dropped from her ears and her shoulders squared. She turned slowly to face Ian.

That's not fair, she said in a voice low with pain. For a moment, Ian glimpsed the twenty-year-old Meg, but then the mask slipped and she was two again. *Thiessen?* she asked.

You can't help Thiessen until you help yourself, Ian said. *Now bring a small light into this space with us. Just enough so that we can really see each other*.

Reluctantly, Meg obeyed. A gradual light grew between them until Ian could just make out her features clearly. Her eyes were wide with terror and she was gnawing on the first two fingers of her right hand. There was blood on her lips.

Meg, no! Ian tried to pull her fingers from her mouth, but she jerked away from him and chewed more vigorously. *Meg, you don't need that any more. Your fingers are still scarred from doing that as a child*. Ian held out his own hands to her and discovered they were covered with her blood. *This can't be*, he moaned.

He sat down in the darkness and stared at Meg. How, in the name of the Souls, had Cia expected a Deaf to cope with this mess?

Then he remembered the letter. Somehow, he had succeeded. Meg had told him so herself. She had come through OK; would come through OK. He just had to find the way.

Meg was staring back at him. She had stopped gnawing on her fingers, but they remained in her mouth and blood dribbled down her chin. Her hair shone pale gold in the dim light and her eyes blurred with tears. She didn't look like a two-year-old. She had retained the mental image of herself at twenty.

Meg, will you bring the light up just a bit more? Ian asked gently.

The darkness brightened slightly, but Meg continued to stare at Ian, unmoving.

Ian chuckled weakly. *A bit more than a bit more?*

The dark was pushed back by a bright flare of light and Ian was able to see around himself for the first time. He could also see Meg more clearly.

Meg, look at yourself, he commanded. *Look into my eyes and see yourself as I do.*

Meg closed her eyes and shook her head. She began chewing on her fingers again. Ian stood up and moved to where she stood. He grasped her wrists and pulled her fingers from her mouth.

Meg, he said. *Look at me.*

I –, I'm scared I'll see the blood, Meg whispered.

You will, said Ian. *The blood is there. Your blood, my blood, Thiessen's blood. Lots of people have been hurt by what is happening. Closing your eyes won't make it go away.*

Meg opened her eyes and looked into Ian's.

Do you see what I see? he asked her.

Yes.

What do you see? he pressed.

I see a young woman and a small child.

And? Ian prompted.

And blood, she whispered. *I see Thiessen lying on the floor. I see Drove Gardner and Freddie.*

What are we going to do about this?

We have to fight, Meg said.

How? asked Ian.

You have to give me the tools, Meg responded. *You say I have the abilities, but I don't know how to use them. You have the knowledge. Teach me.*

Meg, how old are you?

You're as bad as your mother, you know that?

Answer my question! Ian couldn't help laughing.

I'm two going on twenty, how's that?

Better! Ian sighed in relief. *Now, why don't we finish making you a centre. Are you ready?*

Yeah. I think I might even be able to summon a reference or two on rooms.

Well, that's the first step, said Ian. *Picture a room large enough for you to be comfortable in with at least one other person, preferably two.*

As the walls slowly materialized around them, Ian stepped away from Meg and began to wander around the space, watching the details emerge. As he issued instructions, he heard his mother's voice in the back of his mind, walking class after class of children through this procedure. It seemed so easy. Ian said, and Meg did.

Is there much more of this? Meg asked, breaking through Ian's reverie. *Doors, rugs and pillows are all well and good, but shouldn't there be chairs? Couches? Tables? All that stuff?*

Uh, I don't know, Ian confessed, caught off guard. *Mother never mentioned any of that.*

Well, then I guess for now, we'll leave it like this, but I think that's something I'll change later. I'm not entirely comfortable with a room that doesn't have any place to sit, Meg said.

Actually, if you're not comfortable, that defeats the purpose. Why don't you do what feels right, and we'll worry about whether it is or not later, Ian suggested.

That sounds reasonable, Meg concluded as she created three deeply cushioned chairs placed around a low central table. *There. OK, what's next?*

I guess we have to start on what's outside here, Ian said reluctantly.

How do we go about it? asked Meg.

Well, if the centre is the seat of the soul, and the soul is essentially you, then I guess you have to take everything out there and bring it in, and make it yours again. Ian sounded dubious.

Won't that take an awfully long time?

What else have we got? asked Ian. *We can't leave here until the mess is straightened out. I guess we start at the beginning and end when we're finished.*

Meg grimaced. *Yeah*, she sighed. *Which one of these doors is out?*

Ian shook his head. *Which one tells you it's out?*

You people are whacked, you know it? Meg walked to the door on the right. *This one, I guess*, she said, pointing.

Well, then, open it.

Bracing herself, Meg opened the door a crack and peered out. With a gasp, she slammed it shut again. *You didn't say it would be like that!*

What did you expect? he demanded. *I said it was a mess! Now open the door and grab whatever is flying past. Don't let anything else in. Just shut the door and bring me what you catch.*

Meg turned back to the door and grasped the knob. Taking a deep breath, she opened it again and reached out. Her hand closed on something and she yanked it into her centre and slammed the door again.

What have you got? Ian asked.

Dunno, Meg said, bringing it over to him, holding it at arm's length.

Well, it's yours, kiddo. Cherish it, he advised.

Cherish it? Meg asked in disbelief. She sank into the chair opposite Ian and took a look at the object in her hands. *It's part of a nightmare I used to have as a kid*, she exclaimed with a shudder. *There's nothing here to cherish. Can't I throw it back outside and try something else?*

Ian shook his head. *No, you can't afford to be blindsided by a stray thought or memory in your subconscious. All of this stuff belongs to you, whether you like it or not.*

Swell, said Meg as she sat back in her chair.

Tell it you love it and thank it for helping you, Ian instructed.

What? Oh, right! Come on, Ian, be real! Meg said with a snort.

I'm serious, Meg. This is how my mother teaches. It works, so do it. Ian was upset by Meg's derision.

OK, uh, Meg began. She looked at the shred of nightmare doubtfully. *I love you. Thank you for helping me.* She looked expectantly at Ian. *Like that?*

It would help, I think, if you tried to act like you meant it, Ian said.

Oh, come on! This is ridiculous, Ian. I don't love this nightmare, and I don't have anything to thank it for! It used to scare me as a child, said Meg.

It served a purpose in your life?

If frightening small children could be called a purpose, then yes, it served, Meg snapped. *What's your point?*

Well, if it's no longer of use to you, then tell it thank you and let it go.

Completely whacked, Meg muttered. *Thank you for serving a purpose in my life,* she told the shred in her hands. *I don't need you any more.* She let the shred go. Before it hit the floor, it disappeared.

Ian sat up and stared at the empty space.

Hey, that's a pretty neat trick! Meg exclaimed. *Will they all go like that?*

Probably not, Ian responded. *Some will probably be harder, and some may not go at all, if you still need them. There will also be memories and knowledge that you want to keep.*

Yeah, Meg nodded.

Are you ready for the next one?

Gotta be done, hmm? Meg climbed out of the chair and went back to the door. Slowly, she twisted the knob and opened it. Reaching out, she caught another fragment.

With a gasp, she let the fragment go and shut the door, leaning against it unsteadily.

Meg, what's the matter? Ian jumped up and ran to her. *Are you all right?*

Meg drew a deep, shuddery breath and turned to him. *It was Thiessen*, she said. *It was a memory of Thiessen. He told me he loved me.* Meg's knees buckled and she sagged into Ian's arms.

Ian caught Meg and carried her back to her chair. *You'll run into things like that*, he told her, setting her into the chair and smoothing her hair away from her face. Blonde hair, and straight. Had he been expecting curly, black? Sarah seemed a lifetime away now.

Meg reached up and took Ian's hand, holding it against her cheek. *We'll get you back to Sarah*, she said. Tears slipped silently down her cheeks as she looked deep into his eyes. *I promise*, she whispered.

Letting him go, Meg swiped at her tears with the back of her hand and stood up. She drew a shaky breath, squared her shoulders and marched back to the door. With grim determination, she pulled the door open and grabbed the first thing that flew by. Shutting the door, she brought the new piece of herself into the room and held it up for inspection.

I love you, she told it. *Thank you for helping me.* She hugged it to her chest and then let go. It hovered in the air by her head. *OK*, she said with a small laugh. She went to the other door and opened it. The fragment flew through it into the dark beyond. Without shutting the door, Meg turned back to the one leading outside and approached it.

Meg, are you sure you want to take it this quickly? asked Ian.

I want to get out of here as badly as you do, she said and again twisted the knob.

Hour after hour in that timeless place, the doors opened and shut. Ian sat quietly in his chair watching Meg as she walked back and forth, struggling to reintegrate the shattered fragments of her mind.

The progress made couldn't be measured. There was nothing to point to and quantify; the chaos outside the door didn't seem to lessen.

Meg, Ian said at last. *You can't go on without rest. You can't expect to finish the entire job without taking a break*.

Meg shook her head and opened the door again.

Come sit down for a while, Ian suggested.

Meg caught a shard of memory and shut the door.

Meg, listen to me. I know you want to be done with this, but you have to rest. You're so tired you can barely stand, Ian persisted.

Meg examined the piece of herself carefully, hugged it to herself and said, *I love you. Thank you for helping me*.

When you finish that one, come and sit for a while, said Ian.

Meg let go of the fragment and it flew into the darkness of the other door.

Meg?

Only for a little while, Meg insisted as she walked over to her chair.

That's fine, Ian said.

Meg sat down and leaned back, scrunching down to cushion her head against the back of the chair. *Ooh, this feels good*, she murmured, sinking further into the soft padding.

Remember, Ian cautioned. *Just for a little while*.

Meg nodded sleepily. *Just a little while*, she repeated. In a very short time, she was sound asleep.

With a smile, Ian curled up in his own chair and also fell asleep.

I love you. Thank you for helping me.

A litany from a nightmare. It was all that Ian heard now. That, and the doors opening and shutting. Meg crying; telling the shreds of her mind that she needed them.

There was nothing he could do to help her. Periodically, he suggested she rest, but Meg was intent on finishing a job that had no end.

He had tried centring earlier, but Meg became agitated when she couldn't find his presence, so he contented himself with fantasies of seeing Sarah, and the Keep again; what he would say and do when he confronted Drove Gardner. He held conversations with his mother in which he cleverly dragged her hidden motives from her . . .

Mostly, he was bored.

He sat in one chair, then another. He walked about Meg's centre examining its contents.

Meg brought another memory into the room and smiled as she let it go. A book materialized on a shelf that hadn't been there before. Meg turned back to the door.

Ian sprang across the room and grabbed the book off the shelf. *Little Women*? He hadn't read it before. Taking it back to the chairs, he sat down, opened to the front page and began reading.

When he looked up again, Meg was sitting in the chair opposite him, watching with a bemused smile.

What? he asked a little defensively.

Nothing. Just boys aren't usually interested in books like that, she said.

Like what? Ian wanted to know.

That's, uh, considered a girls' book, Meg said.

Books are to be read, aren't they? asked Ian.

That's a healthy attitude. Meg smiled. *Books are books, yeah.*

Are you taking a break?

Umhmm, Meg nodded tiredly. *But I'm surprisingly close to being finished.*

238

Really? Ian exclaimed delightedly. *You mean you're almost ready to move on to the next level?*

No, I mean I'm almost finished. Meg giggled a bit hysterically. *Done, done, done!*

Really? Ian asked again, incredulous.

Really! She yawned hugely and sank back into the chair. *But for now, I'm going to take a nap. You keep on reading. I'll be interested to hear what you think of it when you're done.* She closed her eyes and was asleep in moments.

Ian stood and stretched. He put the book down on the table and looked around the room.

Meg had indeed been busy while he'd been reading. There were posters and paintings on the walls now. The shelf was full of books and there were several more shelves full above and below it. The wall looked like a tiny library.

There were two extra doors, both of which stood open. Ian stared at them for a moment before deciding that he would ask Meg about them when she woke up, rather than go poking into what was none of his business.

Instead, he went to the shelves and scanned the titles. There were a surprising number of psychology texts and magazines containing information on autism and schizophrenia. The remainder were stories that had been important to Meg since childhood, he guessed.

Knowing he wouldn't be able to open the outside door of Meg's centre to see how much progress she had made, Ian returned to his chair and decided to centre himself, since Meg would doubtless sleep for some time.

Ian threw himself down on the pillows on the floor of his centre and drew a deep breath, exhaling slowly. It felt good to be on familiar footing at last.

He wondered what was happening outside Meg's mind. Where was her body? Ted and Susan were probably very

239

worried about her, but there was nothing they could do either. Take care of her physical needs and wait.

Wait for what?

Just how did he expect he was going to teach her? *What* was he going to teach her?

He had no idea what she needed to know. He hadn't been in class long enough to learn what his mother taught to the children who unfolded, because he had no need for that knowledge. He would never be able to use it . . . but he needed it now. Unfortunate paradox, Ian thought wryly to himself as he sat up and looked around his centre.

It had been a while since he had been here. There was something different about it, but nothing really seemed to have changed.

This is weird, he said out loud, shuddering. *Philip, how'm I supposed to help? What am I supposed to do?*

He sat in silence for quite a while, but Philip didn't respond, and Ian couldn't come up with any answers of his own.

With a sigh, Ian left his centre and returned to Meg's. She was still asleep, so Ian picked up the book he'd been reading and slouched back into his chair.

With a muffled noise, Meg sat up and rubbed at her eyes with sensitive fingers. She must have slept many hours in the same position to have such a ferocious crick in her neck. She probed the cramped muscle and opened her eyes.

Ian leaned forward in the chair opposite hers and stared.

Good morning, she said thickly. Her mouth felt slow. She opened it slowly to stretch her facial muscles and found herself yawning widely. *Sorry*, she said as she exhaled.

Are you OK? Ian asked. He continued leaning forward anxiously, paying careful attention.

Yeah, she gasped, mid-yawn. *What?*

Nothing, Ian said quickly. *I just — well, you were asleep for a long time. Did you mean what you said about being almost finished, you know —* Ian nodded towards the outside door of Meg's centre, *out there?*

Umm. Meg continued massaging her shoulder. *Uh, yeah. Yeah, almost done. I was just so tired —*

You did the right thing, Meg. Ian watched Meg struggle against waking up. *I'm sorry there's no coffee*, he said.

Meg grimaced. *'S OK. I could probably wave myself up some from a memory somewhere if I were truly desperate, right?*

Ian shrugged. His left eyebrow twitched. *I dunno, I guess. Probably.*

Well, it will have to wait. Why does my head feel like it's full of cotton? All the camels of the desert have hiked across my tongue. My bones hurt.

I was kind of surprised that your chair never got more comfortable as you slept, but I didn't want to wake you, Ian explained.

You never told me I could change things, Meg said.

Of course you can! said Ian. *Well, not everything, but stuff like that, sure.*

Well, sorry, Meg said. *I grew up in a place where things are what they appear to be, mostly. Not what you want them to be.*

But your shoulder is going to be OK?

Meg smiled. *Yeah, I expect I probably will be too.* She leaned forward and glanced at the title of the book he was holding. *Finished* Little Women?

That was a couple of books ago, Ian told her.

Boy, I must have been asleep for ages.

It seemed like it. Ian watched Meg wriggle uncomfortably in her chair. *Why don't you do some stretching, that usually helps you relax.*

Hell of an idea, Meg said as she slid to the floor and

241

straightened her legs in front of her. To Meg's surprise, she felt muscles protest as she bent to touch her forehead to her knees. *Hey!* she exclaimed, sitting up quickly. *That hurt! I thought I was only stretching, I dunno, 'mental muscles'.*

Not if you believe the muscles you have here are real. What you profoundly believe to be true often is, said Ian. *My mother said that once in class, I think. If you can visualize something in its most minute detail and believe it is or can be, then you've taken the first step to making it so.*

Oh, Meg said vaguely as she returned to her exercise. Ian's firm belief in higher souls and mental powers made Meg slightly uneasy. It made her slightly more uneasy that he had so far been correct in everything he had told her. *Well, anyway. Got any ideas what we do next?*

You mean after you finish the clean-up outside?

Ummhmm. Meg exhaled slowly and crooked one leg behind her to begin stretching another muscle group.

I haven't really got the tools you need. I don't know how to teach you what I have never learned, Ian said regretfully. He sat watching Meg doing sit-ups.

Swell, Meg gasped on the exhale as she rolled back. She lay on the floor for a moment, panting before she sat up and pulled her legs into the lotus position. Extending her arms, she rolled her shoulders forward and back, then began swinging her arms in small circles. *Too bad your mother isn't here. Didn't she tell you anything about what we're supposed to be doing?*

Only that you're supposed to be the solution to our problem with Drove Gardner, said Ian quietly.

I'd cheerfully kill him right now. He makes me feel like the ancient Romans had something in their eye-for-an-eye system of justice! Meg erupted from her cross-legged position on the floor, jumped to her feet and began a vigorous set of jumping-jacks.

He has that effect on people. Ian smiled wryly, thinking of the number of times he'd thought similar things. *But I don't think Mother was telling me everything. I think Gardner is only a catalyst in something a whole lot bigger. I think he needs to be removed in order for something else to happen.*

What? Meg asked as she stopped jumping and began windmilling instead.

I'm not exactly sure yet.

But when you are, I'll be the first to know?

Who else would I tell? Ian asked, glancing around Meg's centre.

Ya never know, Meg grinned, doing a poor imitation of John Wayne. She stopped stretching and started jogging in place. *This really does feel good, you should try it.*

Uh, yeah. Thanks. Maybe later. Ian laughed and waved his book at her. *I've got better things to do right now.*

Well, spend some of that time trying to figure out how we're supposed to play hero while we're trapped in my mind, will you? Meg suggested as she headed towards the outer door. *In the meantime, I'm going to finish up this odious task and continue to hope that I never have to do it again!* Meg opened the door, reached out and grabbed another fragment of her memories.

Ian watched for a moment and then returned to the page he'd left off at. He stared at the page for a long time without actually seeing the print.

Finally, Ian gave up on the book and slid off the chair on to the floor. Maybe some stretches wouldn't be so bad after all, he thought to himself. He arranged his legs in front of him and bent to touch his toes with his fingers, feeling the muscles in the backs of his thighs tingle and then burn.

His mother had said that she would come for him if she could. She had also said that if she couldn't come for him, that he and Meg would have to find her.

His fingers wouldn't reach his toes, so he gave up on that exercise and tried the one with one leg crooked behind him. Cia hadn't come back for them, so they would have to go look for her. It followed that they would use the same method to find her that she had used to bring him back here to begin with.

Ian's fingers still couldn't reach his toes, so he gave up on that exercise and tried to put his legs into the lotus position. They flatly refused. He crossed them instead and began to do arm circles. There had been profound darkness, and a rainbow, he remembered.

His arms grew tired almost immediately, so he quit swinging them and hooked his feet under the nearest chair to give the sit-ups a try. He folded his hands behind his head and started to roll back, but he whacked his head against the edge of the table.

Ow! Souls, that hurts! he exclaimed, blinking back tears as he began to massage the wounded area. He glanced towards Meg, but she wasn't paying any attention to him. She stood by the door, hugging something to her chest. Her head was thrown back and her eyes were closed. Ian doubted she had even heard him.

They had travelled down one strand of the rainbow after Mother had done something to him that removed his energy from it . . . at least that was what it seemed like.

Still rubbing the back of his head, Ian levered himself up off the floor and back into the chair he'd been sitting in. Meg had done something with the piece of herself and turned back to the door. Ian watched her for a while, gingerly probing the rapidly growing bump on his head.

They had travelled along the rainbow for a long time, and while there was a sense of movement, nothing in their surroundings had changed. She had known when they were to stop. He could read the energy pattern in her mind and that was somehow the key.

Ian's bump seemed to have stopped swelling, but it still smarted, and so did his pride, even though there had been no witnesses. With a deep sigh, Ian quit rubbing it and slouched down into the chair. He didn't know anyone's energy patterns though, so finding where they were supposed to stop might prove difficult.

Then he chuckled. He still had no idea where the rainbow was, or how to get to it. They would have to solve that problem before they could even begin to worry about stopping at the right time.

What's so funny? Meg demanded. She stood straddle-legged in front of him with her arms akimbo. For a moment, Ian started. The image of Drove Gardner at the edge of the field leaped to the front of his thoughts, superimposed on Meg. *OK, then. What's wrong?*

N-nothing, Ian stuttered.

Right, Meg said. *First you laugh, then you jump half out of your skin, but nothing is funny or wrong.*

I think I know how we can get out of here, Ian said, changing the subject. *But first you have to finish out there.* Ian nodded toward the outer door.

I have, Meg said impatiently. *What do we have to do?*

See, there's this rainbow, and – you've finished? Ian asked in amazement.

Yeah, what about the rainbow? Meg asked. *Where is it and what do we have to do to get there?*

I don't know, Ian began.

With an inarticulate cry of frustration, Meg threw herself into a chair and covered her face with her hands.

Look, I'm sorry! OK? Ian leaped up from his chair and began pacing back and forth behind his chair. *Souls! He* turned back to Meg. *I don't do this stuff! I'm just a poor, stupid Deaf. I'm lucky I got a centre. I'm a farmer, not a psychic! I don't have the answers and mostly I don't know where to find them either.*

Blind leading the blind, Meg murmured from behind

her hands. *Ian, I'm sorry, too*. She rubbed her eyes and dropped her hands into her lap, rubbing absently at the scars on her fingertips. The raw places had healed as her mind had, but she would always carry the scars. *It would have been really easy for me to have stayed lost in my mind. I know it took a lot of patience and courage on your part to insist that I not just give up. We're both tired and scared.* Meg got up and went to where Ian stood. She reached up and touched his cheek with her scarred fingers.

She held both hands up in front of him. *Most of my scars don't show. I figure that's probably true of you, too?*

Ian closed his eyes and nodded slowly.

Then we're going to have to help each other, Meg said. *Now. What did you notice about the area around the rainbow? Describe to me exactly what everything you saw looked like. Maybe we'll find the clues if we sift and pool our information?*

There wasn't really anything to see, Ian said. *There was total darkness, and this fantastic rainbow. Colours like you've never seen before. Well*, he amended. *I'd never seen them until I came here. Some of your neon signs and stuff have the same qualities of the colours I saw.*

How did Cia take you there? Meg persisted.

She didn't, said Ian. *At least, once I was in her mind, and aware of where we were, we were there; hovering over this incredible river of lights. The direction we were facing was kind of silvery and it seemed to be shifting. I couldn't focus on it. It kept kind of jumping around every time I thought I had a clear fix. Then Mother turned us around and grabbed one of the colours and started pulling us along it.*

Which colour? asked Meg.

I'm not sure, but I got the feeling that it wouldn't matter so much as long as you knew what you were doing.

Great. Wonderful, drawled Meg. *As long as we know what we're doing, we'll be just fine? What did the rainbow look like in the direction you travelled? Are there more than two directions?*

Mother didn't look around much, Ian told her. *I got the impression that there was only forwards and backwards and I assume we were travelling backwards since we wound up in the past.*

Yeah, Meg giggled. *I guess that's fair.*

Her humour seemed to lift some of the tension between them. Ian's shoulders dropped slightly. He took a deep breath and exhaled slowly. Then he bent and tried to touch his toes.

Hey! Meg exclaimed. *You almost did it that time! For that you deserve a rest.*

Does that mean I can stop thinking for a while? Ian asked as he straightened up again.

Nah! I said rest, not vacation. Come on, what did the rainbow look like on the way back here? Did it ever get lighter around it? What? Meg demanded. She began doing toe-touches herself.

Ian watched Meg for a moment, wondering how anyone could be so obsessed with something so painful. *No,* he responded at length. *It never got any lighter, but the colour we were following got a lot thinner a little while before we found you.*

And? Meg prompted.

And the other colours got thicker. That was how I could tell we had actually moved. This thing is really strange. You move, but nothing changes. At least not until we got to that one point. Then, everything stayed that way until we got to where you were.

What did you do then? Meg sat on the floor again and tucked her feet under a chair. Ian waited to see if she would hit the table too, but Meg was shorter than he was and she had no trouble clearing the sharp edge as she rolled back towards the floor.

We settled into your energy pattern, he said. *When you*

*said you would take me, Mother transferred my energy
into your pattern and she left.*

Meg finished her sit-ups and pushed herself away from
the chair. *Well, that gives us something, at least.*

What? Ian wanted to know.

We know that this river of light can be found in darkness,
said Meg. *Now we have to find out where the darkness is.*

Sure, no problem, Ian said glibly. *Just start walking and
eventually you'll find it, right?*

Meg looked at Ian intently. *Were you in Cia's centre?*
she asked.

Ian was surprised by the question. He thought a
moment before responding. *Yes*, he said. *But not in her
central chamber.*

Well, then maybe that would work. Meg sat thinking,
unaware of Ian staring at her with a peculiar expression
on his face.

What? he asked when he couldn't stand the suspense
any longer.

*If we leave my central chamber and start walking, what
would we find?* asked Meg.

I don't know. Ian shrugged, dismissing the question.
You didn't take that seriously, did you? I was just kidding!

Well, I'm not, Meg said. *That can't go on for ever.* She
waved her hand towards the outside door. *There's nothing
dark enough in here to qualify for your description. If
there was, you would have spotted it by now. If you were
in Cia's centre, but not in her central chamber, then it
stands to reason that if we start walking, we'll find it
eventually.*

Oh, come on! Ian exclaimed in disbelief. *You can't be
serious! How long would it take? You could walk until the
Higher Souls claimed you and not find it.*

Or I could stay here and not find it, and never leave,
Meg said quietly. *Thiessen deserves better than that, don't
you think?*

248

OK! Ian stomped angrily around behind the furniture and shoved his hands deep into the pockets of his tunic. *Fine. We walk.* And we walk, and we walk, he thought to himself. He went to the door and stood there for a moment before turning back to Meg. *Are we ready to go?*

I guess so, she said. She glanced around the room again and followed Ian to the door. Biting her lower lip, Meg grasped the knob and turned it. Pulling the door open, she stepped outside and moved away from the jamb.

Ian followed her and pulled the door shut behind him. With a start, Meg turned and opened her mouth. Before she could say anything, Ian held up a hand.

It's never locked for you. You can go back any time. Other people need your permission to enter. If you don't want them there, they can't get in, he told her.

Really?

Yes, really. Ian took Meg's elbow and steered her away from her central chamber. *But come on, now. We have some walking to do. Remember?*

Meg smiled. *Lots quieter out here, huh?*

You did an incredible job, said Ian, smiling also. *But there should be grass out here. A meadow or something. And water and a rock. And trees and sky, and I guess we're sort of doing this backwards. You're supposed to create those things first.* He looked a little sheepish. *I'm afraid I'm not very good at this. I'm not being very much help.*

Meg punched Ian's arm lightly. *A meadow?* she asked, sweeping her arm in a semi-circle. A small field of green grass appeared around them. A small pond and a granite boulder materialized off to their right. *Where are the trees supposed to go, anywhere?*

No, there's a forest supposed to surround the meadow and a path through it leading from your conscious self to your centre, he said.

Like this? Meg asked as a tall redwood forest came into

being around the grassy area. The tall branches reached up into a clear blue sky of early spring. The air was warm, but a cool breeze rustled through the grass and somewhere a bird began to sing.

Yeah! That's really nice, said Ian enthusiastically. *There is supposed to be running water beside the path to get here.*

Is a creek OK?

Sure. Anything as long as it flows beside the path.

I wonder what's on the other side of the forest? Meg mused. She and Ian stood silent for a moment. Then they looked at each other.

The rainbow! they exclaimed simultaneously. Meg grabbed Ian's hand and began to run. She pulled him along for a few strides before he protested and she slowed to a walk.

11

The forest was growing dimmer.

It wasn't so much that the light was fading, Meg decided, but that the colour was being leached out of their surroundings.

Are you sure we're going the right way? she asked Ian uncertainly.

I'm not sure of anything, Ian snapped as he stumped along beside her. *You're the one who dragged us off on this idiotic quest. Are you leading us the right way?*

Yes, said Meg tightly. She straightened her shoulders and continued her forward motion. The forest was definitely growing dimmer. The trees were also losing their definition. *Have you ever been out this far before?* she asked.

No, said Ian.

Have you ever thought about it? she asked.

No.

Well, then we could be on the right track.

Yes, said Ian.

What's the matter with you? Meg demanded.

Nothing, it's just – Ian made a small gesture of frustration and stopped walking. *There's nothing I can do*, he said, looking miserably at Meg and then at the ground.

About what? she persisted.

Anything! exclaimed Ian. *I'm being shuffled all over the landscape and I have absolutely no control over what happens to me! I don't want to stay here, but I'm afraid to go back.*

Afraid? Meg asked. *Afraid of what? Gardner? Isn't that why you're bringing me? Isn't that my fear?*

No, not Gardner, he denied hastily.

Well who then?

Not who: what, Ian clarified. *What if I've died? Physically, I mean. What if I don't have a body to go back to?*

Sarah wouldn't let that happen. Not if she could possibly help it, said Meg. *I do wish we could analyse that chemical and get the ingredients for the antidote, though*. Drawing poison with rocks didn't seem like a very effective method of treatment to Meg, but she didn't remind Ian of this. *Come on*, she took his hand again and tugged gently. *We don't even know if we can get out of here yet. Let's just take this one step at a time*.

Ian exhaled a shaky breath. Silently, he walked beside Meg through a forest that continued losing definition and colour until they left it behind.

It's really dark here, Meg said, stretching her hand out in front of her. A couple of steps later, she came to an abrupt halt against something neither of them could see. *Oh!*

Why'd you stop? Ian asked as he stopped beside her. He reached out with his hand and encountered something that wasn't really anything.

Is this the edge of my mind? Meg asked as she continued to probe the barrier that wasn't there.

Meg, I'm really tired of saying 'I don't know'. Why don't you ask me a question I can answer, Ian complained.

Meg turned to Ian and smiled sympathetically. *Why don't we walk along the edge of the barrier and see where it leads us, since we can't seem to get past it*, she suggested. *It may take us in a big circle, but it's better than standing here talking*. She turned to the right and began to walk with her hand touching the wall.

Obediently, Ian followed. There was nothing else he could do. He thought a lot about Sarah as he walked behind Meg, and a lot about the possibility that his body had succumbed to the poison Gardner had used to tip the copper point of his spear. Ultimately, Ian knew Meg was right. There was nothing he could do about it until he had been freed from her mind, but it was logical to assume that if Mother hadn't come back for him by now, she was unable to. He and Meg would have to find their own way out. Until they did, worrying would only make him less useful to Meg. Right now, he didn't need to feel any less useful than he already did.

He walked right into Meg, knocking them both off balance.

This isn't working, she announced as they regained their footing.

What? Ian had completely lost himself in his own thoughts and couldn't think what she was talking about.

The wall, said Meg, looking at him strangely. *I keep veering to the left, but the wall is curving away from me, as though it's going around a long, continuous corner.*

Huh? Ian asked.

I think we've walked in a circle at least once, probably twice, Meg said. *This isn't the edge of my mind, it's a cylinder through it that goes upwards as far as I can reach. I wonder if it ends here at the ground, or if it goes down through it?*

A cylinder? Ian questioned Meg excitedly. *I wonder if that's – I mean could it –*

You never did say how big the rainbow was, Meg pointed out.

How big is everything in here? he wanted to know. *I always sort of assume that I am my normal size, and everything is scaled accordingly, but I don't know if that's how it actually works*, he explained. *We were floating above it, and each colour seemed a couple of feet wide, but there were spaces in between each primary colour, maybe a foot wide, that were both of the colours that were on either side.*

There are six colours in a rainbow, Meg mused. *Red,*

253

orange, yellow, green, blue, purple. They sort of all blend together in the sky and they're arced. How does this rainbow differ from the one you saw?

The one I saw also had white and lavender. The colours didn't blend together except in the special areas between them. Those areas were clearly not a part of the main stream of lights even though there wasn't a real delineation.

So eight streams of light and seven in between areas. Twenty-three feet wide if your perception is correct?

Yeah, said Ian.

Was there room around the rainbow? Meg asked.

What do you mean?

Did the walls feel close, or was there a feeling of space around you? she clarified.

Finite space? Room, but a definite feeling of limit, he said. *Does that make sense?*

Like being in the middle of a fairly large room when the lights are off? she asked.

Close, yeah, he responded. *You think the area we just walked around might be large enough to house the rainbow?*

I think it might, Meg said slowly. *But we have to figure a way past the barrier. It's the weirdest thing, it's like there's nothing there, but I can't go through it. Did Cia happen to tell you how she got past it?*

Ian shook his head. *She didn't say anything about it. Most of her energy and concentration were taken up getting both of us back here to you.*

Meg laughed humourlessly.

What? Ian asked her.

If it took that much energy, then we'd better hope that my parents got me to a hospital and hooked up to an IV or two, or we aren't going to make it very far. Probably, my parents decided I'd gone catatonic and hustled me off to the psychiatric ward. I just hope they don't try shock treatment. They did that to me once, you know. I wasn't responding to the medication, and I was having horrible nightmares about voices in my head, chasing me through empty, broken cities and men outside my head chasing me too. I would have the same dream every night, sometimes more than once. It got so bad, that I would start screaming when bedtime and sleep were mentioned and I wouldn't stay in my room alone. When I was finally too exhausted and did fall asleep, I would wake up screaming and crying. They didn't want to increase my thorazine, so they decided to try shock treatment. Meg shuddered. *I never want to go through that again*, she said.

Souls! said Ian wonderingly. *Is this what happens to a child that unfolds by itself?*

I doubt they recover, Meg said quietly. *If your mother is right, the only reason I did is because she walled off the portions of my mind that make me psychic. So now I'm just psychotic instead!*

Now who's feeling sorry for themselves? asked Ian. *They won't try shock treatment on you while you're catatonic, will they?*

We'd better hope not, huh, Meg said as she started walking around the cylinder that wasn't there. *How are we supposed to get inside this thing?*

Have you had your hand on the wall the entire time we've been walking? Ian asked.

Well, mostly, Meg said. *It kept curving away from me, so every once in a while, I sort of had to go off to my left looking for it again. What were you doing that whole time?*

Thinking, Ian said defensively. *Following you. This is your mind, remember. I don't have much to say about what we do and where we go. I just keep walking and hope that we eventually find what we're looking for.*

Well, I need you for more than that right now, Meg said. *What are the ways that you people get through barriers in the mind?*

Meg. How can I make you understand that since I'm a

Deaf, I never learned these things? I can't help you with things I don't know and don't understand, Ian said tiredly.

Maybe the same way I can convince you that I have even less expertise in this area than you do. I'm completely out of my league here. Meg looked at Ian pleadingly. *I don't even believe this crap, but here I am, and I'm trying. The least you could do is be nice about the fact that neither one of us knows what we're doing. Maybe someone said something in passing and you happened to be walking through the room at the time?* she suggested hopefully.

Let me think about that, Ian said. He started walking again. After a moment, Meg fell in beside him and they paced the outer circuit of the cylinder in silence. Meg kept her hand outstretched, but she frequently lost contact with the wall and had to move to her left to find it again.

Wait a minute. She stopped and reached out to stop Ian as well. *There's a barrier here, but there's nothing there, right?*

Yeah, said Ian. *What's new?*

If there's nothing there, why can't I stick my hand through it? she asked.

Ian shrugged and rolled his eyes.

I'm serious! she exclaimed. She pressed her hand against the wall and closed her eyes.

What are you doing? Ian asked.

Shhh! said Meg. *I'm concentrating on making the barrier not be there.*

What? Ian asked in disbelief.

If I can make a centre, and make furniture come and go and change shape, and make a forest and pond and stuff, why can't I make the barrier not be there? she demanded.

Well, I guess, Ian began.

Shhh! Meg said again. Her brow furrowed in concentration and her eyes remained tightly shut.

Ian watched her for a moment before stalking off to sit

and watch where he wouldn't bother Meg as she attempted to find a way into the rainbow. The longer she stood concentrating, the more bored he became, and shortly his mind began to wander. He saw Sarah smiling at him and felt a stab of homesickness.

He hadn't been prepared to miss the Keep as much as he did. He had never fitted in there the way he wanted to, but it was still home. Ian wondered if Sarah missed him as much as he missed her. With a sigh, he leaned back against the wall of the cylinder and closed his eyes.

He must have dozed off, because just as he reached for Sarah, who stood smiling before him, he fell backwards.

Hey! he exclaimed groggily. *What the –*

Hee, hee! Meg was jumping up and down with a maniacal grin on her face. *I did it!*

Huh? Ian sat up and rubbed at his eyes, staring around him in confusion. *What happened?* he demanded.

I got through the barrier! Meg exclaimed. *Look.*

Ian followed her pointed finger with his eyes. *Ohh . . .*

See? Meg hugged herself and danced in a small circle around him. *You were right! Nothing in my mind can exist if I don't want it to, unless I really need it for some reason I haven't figured out yet.*

The rainbow, Ian whispered. It was more beautiful than he had remembered. The colours pulsed true and bright against the pitch-black of their surroundings.

You do remember how your mother travelled on this thing, don't you?

Ian stared blankly at Meg for a moment. *What? Oh! Yes. Yes, I can remember how we travelled along it. But you're not planning on going right now, are you?*

Well, sure. Meg shrugged. *What else have we got to do? The sooner I take you home, the sooner I get my body back and can get on with my life*. She looked him steadily in the eye. *You too, hmm?*

Ian looked down and shrugged.

I know you were dreaming about Sarah earlier, Meg told him. *You have to go back. You have to find out that she did save you. You can't stay here and wonder. You have to trust that she did her job while you were doing yours.*

But I – Ian started.

But nothing, Meg said. *We got to the rainbow. You know how to travel in time and that you can teach me with no trouble. Now we go to Cia and she teaches me the rest of it. You did your job. You succeeded.*

I – Ian began again.

You succeeded! Meg cried. She grabbed his hands and pulled him to his feet. She kissed him soundly and then said, *Now, teach me how to take you home.*

Home! Ian echoed. He allowed her to pull him to the edge of the river of light. *No, wait!*

Meg stopped and waited expectantly. *Well?* she asked finally.

We didn't walk up to it, Ian said. *We were sort of floating above it.*

How?

Ian shrugged.

You don't think that just wading in will work?

No, Ian said decisively. *Somehow, I get the feeling that it would disrupt the energy flow of too many lives. We were floating above the river. I'm certain that made a difference, but I'm not sure why.*

Well, OK hotshot. How do I do that? Meg chuckled.

I don't know, repeal gravity or something! Ian exclaimed. *This is your centre, remember? I'm just passing through.*

Yeah, is that what you told her father?

What? Ian demanded, disgruntled.

Nothing. Meg laughed outright. *Hold on. If Peter Pan could do this, I guess I can give it a shot.*

Ian kept his mouth shut and waited. Meg had a scary

habit of not taking what he said seriously until confronted with the facts. Even then, she had an annoying habit of denying what she had just been hit between the eyes with.

He hadn't felt anything until his head banged against the ceiling. Actually, subjectively, that was the wall of her mind, he thought to himself as he rubbed the back of his head reflexively.

Ha, ha! Meg cackled nearby.

Ouch! Ian said, more to make Meg guilty than because his head actually hurt. *What did you do that for?*

You said repeal gravity, so I did, Meg sounded offended. *Aren't you proud of your student? We're floating now, so what's next?*

Ian closed his eyes. *I'm really tired of this*, he sighed.

What? Meg asked. *I don't have anyone else to ask, OK?*

I know, Ian sighed. *It's just, well, have you ever been to a foreign country? Everything is so different from what you're used to that sometimes you just overload. I just wish that we could be in the Keep right now, without having to actually go through the travelling to get there.*

Yeah, Meg nodded. *But unfortunately, we have to. So, how do we travel on this river, and what are we looking for as a clue to our destination?*

Mother pulled us along by grabbing handfuls of the lavender thread to start, then we just sort of flowed along until she found your energy pattern in the lines, said Ian. *We should probably look for where my energy pattern leaves the river.*

That makes sense, Meg said. She floated over to the lavender thread and grasped it.

'O-oh!' said a strange voice. 'Someone just walked over my grave!'

Meg dropped the thread. *What was that?*

A life you touched? Ian suggested. *Maybe we should do this more carefully.*

Meg nodded and reached for the thread again, gingerly.

Well, come on, she added when she noticed that Ian had not followed suit.

Ian moved reluctantly to join Meg, and grasped the thread just below where she held on to it. He took a deep breath. *Are you ready?* he asked.

Ready as I'll ever be, Meg replied. She grasped the lavender line with her other hand and pulled herself forward. She felt her perception shift, but her surroundings remained unchanged. *Boy, does that feel weird!*

Get used to it, Ian said from somewhere behind her. *We'll be travelling for some time.*

His voice was slightly distorted, Meg guessed from the discrepancy in time and position, but she understood him clearly enough. Meg set her mind to pulling herself along on the threads of the continuum, blocking out thoughts about her parents, and what they must be going through right now.

They travelled for what felt like hours. Neither of them said much. They kept pulling themselves along the lavender line. At first, Meg had felt a tingling on her spine as she touched the thread, but gradually she got used to it. Now she didn't notice it. She looked ahead at the river and called back to Ian.

What on earth is that? she asked. She moved aside to let him have a look.

The holocaust, Ian said. *This is where the plagues and the wars took their greatest tolls.* He stopped beside her and they stared at the drastic change in the flow of energy.

The thread they followed grew larger and stronger as the remainder of the continuum dwindled.

So this is where the switch in life focus occurred? Meg asked.

You could call it that, said Ian. *We always saw it as the way our ancestors got society back on track.*

So much for that thought. I guess we'd better get going. Meg reached again for the thread and began pulling herself along. Ian fell in behind her and they continued their silent journey.

Meg was certain days had passed. She continued to pull herself along the threads. She had not figured out a way to float above them and still move forward, and Ian was no help at all. The closer they got to his present, the quieter he became. She had tried asking questions to draw him out, but he didn't seem to hear her.

For quite a while now, Meg had been searching the energies for a trace of something recognizable, but everything seemed the same. The time continued to shift as it had in the beginning of their journey, but the energy no longer seemed to flow. It had become static.

Pardon me, said a strange voice as a woman sped by her on the blue thread.

Meg looked up, startled. She hadn't even seen her coming. *What on earth was that?* she asked. *Ian?*

There was no answer. Meg stopped and turned around, still holding on to the lavender thread.

Ian had stopped a short way back and was starting to fade into the lavender energies.

Ian, wait! Meg exclaimed, feeling a sudden urgency. She began to pull herself frantically back downstream. *Ian!* she called again.

He looked up at her and began to sink faster into the continuum.

Meg cast herself free of the thread and hurled herself at his disappearing form. *You can't do this!* she shrieked as she grabbed his arm and yanked on him hard.

Let me go! he gasped as he tried to shake her grip. *Leave me alone. You wanted to be rid of me, just let me go*, he pleaded.

No! Meg said vehemently. *This isn't where you belong. You have unfinished business in your own time. I can't let you sink into the past and hide from your fears!* She gave another yank and pulled him free of the threads.

Let me go! he cried again, struggling.

No! Meg held on tightly. *You can't use Sarah and a happier time to escape from Drove Gardner. He'll still be there, and eventually, you'll have to face him anyway. You can't postpone the inevitable!*

Ian said nothing, but his shoulders sagged and he sighed softly.

How far are we? Meg asked.

Not too far, he replied.

Well then, come on, she said, giving his arm a gentle tug. *We're in this together, remember?*

Ian nodded.

Sarah wouldn't let you die, Ian. She loves you, Meg said as she drew him forward on the continuum. She searched for the place where his energy ceased to be in the threads and murmured softly, as though comforting a frightened animal. Ian yielded to her and allowed himself to be pulled in her wake.

Ian had been right. Meg travelled a relatively short distance along the continuum and came to the place where Ian didn't exist. When she reached it, she felt a brief moment of panic, wondering if Sarah had in fact been able to keep his body alive once the life force had been removed from it.

Meg dipped into the energy directly at the end of Ian's and sank both of them into the flow. She felt their energies spreading to each of the other colours in the threads as they became a part of the present.

Cia? Meg called tentatively.

There was no immediate response, so Meg cast about with her mind, trying to get a handle on her surroundings.

She was certain that she and Ian were currently in his body, because it was totally dark and there was no sensation of physical awareness. He was still under the

262

effects of the poison and therefore unconscious. There was someone beside the bed on which the body lay, but Meg could get only the vaguest impression of healing energy and another male mind.

She decided that someone must have relieved Sarah. Hers was an energy Ian would be immediately in touch with if she were nearby, so she must be asleep right now.

Casting her mind out into the room a ways, Meg decided to try again. *Cia?* she called.

There was a gasp nearby, but she didn't recognize the source. From somewhere, a barrier was thrown up and Meg found herself surrounded; walled off from the other energies she sensed in the area.

Hello? she asked.

The barrier seemed to grow stronger.

Oh, swell, she muttered. Withdrawing from the barrier, Meg spent some time considering her situation.

This wasn't the type of wall her own mind had constructed, so the methods she had used to find the continuum wouldn't work. Meg wondered if she should wait until Cia decided to explore the wall of energy, or try to punch her way through.

Ian? she asked. *What should I do about this?*

About what? he asked. He was delighted to discover that they were able to re-enter time's mainstream just after he and Cia had left it. Being in his body during its fight against Gardner's poison made him feel better about the outcome. He hadn't been paying any attention to what Meg was doing.

How do I get your mother's attention? Meg asked.

Can't you make the energy not be there? he suggested.

No, she explained. *This is outside my mind. I have no control over its existence. It feels like several minds are maintaining it. If I can't break through it, how do I contact your mother?*

Well it's just my mind they have contained, he said. *And*

263

your mind inside it. Why don't you go back into the continuum and look for Mother's energies directly. They can't follow you there, I bet.

But I don't know her energy pattern, said Meg. *How will I know what to look for?*

Meg, you're starting to make excuses, Ian told her. *You've had contact with her before. Look for what you remember from those encounters and you'll probably find her.*

But what if I don't? Meg demanded.

Then you keep trying! Ian sighed. *Look, Meg. I can't tell you how to do this. You'll have to go trial-by-error, the way Mother did looking for you. You probably won't drive her crazy, but you may surprise a few other people along the way.* He grabbed Meg by the shoulders and shook her. *We can't have come this far to let some paranoid individuals stop us!*

You're right, Meg said. *I'm just so tired.*

It must be the poison affecting our minds, Ian suggested. *I can feel it too. Since we left the continuum, we've been supported by the energy that my body has to spare. It ain't much. Maybe you'd be better off in the continuum, or at least in Mother's mind. Neither you, nor I, are in that great a shape right now, and you're a long way from home.*

That makes sense, Meg allowed. *Do you want to come with me?*

No, he said quickly.

Meg smiled at him. *Tell Sarah 'Hi' for me,* she said. Then she retreated from his conscious mind and drifted back into the river of time.

Energy, Meg found, had nothing to do with genetics. The 'fingerprint' of an individual had nothing to do with familial ties or bloodlines.

She started to look for Cia by searching for patterns that were similar to Ian, but she kept coming in contact either with Ian himself, or a man who said he knew no one named Cia and finally asked her please to leave. Embarrassed, Meg withdrew and settled above the continuum to rethink her approach.

The river of lavender flowed strongly beneath her. Meg knew there was no way she could search each energy pattern in the river individually. There were too many of them. It would take for ever. What had there been in Cia's contact with Meg that would help Meg locate her?

Meg found herself wishing that she had not been so abrupt and insistent during those visits. She had been so intent on making Cia leave, she hadn't paid attention to her at all.

Then Meg was hit by a thought. Cia's energy was still in the threads of Meg's early childhood.

Oh, God, Meg said out loud. She looked at the thread again.

Either way, it seemed she was destined to spend a lot of time in the continuum. She could travel back to her childhood and find the energy pattern she was looking for, or she could use the trial-by-error search in the here-and-now. Meg resisted an impulse to sweep her hand through the energies in the lavender thread and sighed.

Meg found Ian's pattern again. As she started to sink into it to tell him what she was doing, she reached back just a bit and found that Cia was just breaking contact with his mind. She grabbed for the last retreating wisps and followed them out of Ian, down further into the threads.

Meg maintained her grip out of sheer desperation and plunged after the rapidly disappearing consciousness.

Cia! she called. *Cia, wait!* She felt a hesitation, then a shrug. Cia wasn't really aware of her tag-along. She was completely preoccupied with something and moving much too quickly for Meg to keep up. Meg concentrated instead on the portion of Cia's mind she had touched. She thought

265

she would be able to remember what to look for in the threads to find Cia's conscious mind. She hoped that, with this information, she wouldn't have to travel back to her own childhood to find it.

Reaching into the threads again, Meg travelled backwards a short way and dipped into the energies below her. Ian had been right in stopping her before she waded through the entire spectrum to get to the lavender portion of the flow. She touched the lives of people who were as unhappy to see her as she had been to see Cia during her childhood.

Parts of Cia were everywhere. There had to be a specific configuration that made up her total energy pattern, but Meg only had a bit to go on, so she tried to limit her contact with individuals in the threads.

As she continued pulling strands out of the flow for scrutiny, she entertained a thought of going back to find Cia's trace, but a glance over her shoulder at where she had come from was enough to convince her that she had enough to go on here.

Meg, you're going about that all wrong, a voice said at her elbow.

Startled, Meg swung around and gaped at the tiny, wizened black man who floated beside her. He threw his head back and loosed a surprisingly powerful belly-laugh.

Wh − , who are you? Meg asked. She had seen pictures of people who looked like him, in magazines and on news programmes. He was starving to death and grinning ear-to-ear.

You may call me Philip, he told her, still laughing. He acted as if startling her was the best joke he'd had in a long time. She wasn't sure how his fragile body withstood the exertion.

Are you the Philip Cia mentioned? Meg asked him, remembering the night Cia had come to her before the night in the bar. She shuddered reflexively at the thought.

She mentioned me? Philip asked, delighted.

Well, Meg recanted. *She called to you for help when I tried to drown her in my mind. I just remembered the name because I thought . . . Well, never mind what I thought. What are you doing here?*

I came to help you, Philip said. He held out his hand, fingers closed, palm-down, and nodded at Meg.

She held her hand out under his, open and palm-up.

Philip opened his fingers and a huge, flawless amethyst dropped into her hand.

Meg gasped. *What is this for?*

It contains Cia's energy pattern, Philip told her. *It is the only help I can give you. That and a piece of advice: don't try to mess with the time continuum.*

What do you mean? Meg asked, puzzled.

Time is less flexible than the continuum would lead you to believe. There are some things that you simply cannot change. If you try, you will find you are unable to. I just thought I would tell you in advance and save you some time and energy. Philip laughed as though he had told a particularly funny joke.

What things can't I change? asked Meg.

Things that have already happened, for instance. It would do you no good to try and intercept Gardner on his way down-time and stop him from killing your brother. It's already happened. If it hadn't, you wouldn't be here. Also, you can't be in the same time twice. The continuum won't let you back in. Look, he continued, seeing the expression on Meg's face. *I don't make the rules, I just thought I'd save you some frustration.* He disappeared.

Meg floated above the continuum with her mouth hanging open and her fist tight around the beautiful amethyst, trying to figure out what had just happened.

Opening her hand slowly, she gaped at the large stone. It had been cut in the shape of a tear-drop and was faceted on both sides as if they were the bottom of the stone.

How on earth did Philip expect her to find an energy pattern in a stone?

Mother uses them for meditation, Ian had told her.

Maybe if she concentrated on the stone . . . Taking a deep breath and feeling more than a little silly, Meg held the stone between her palms and closed her eyes. She continued to inhale and exhale slowly as she concentrated on the stone.

She sat like that for a very long time, feeling sillier and sillier. Nothing was happening. Nothing was going to happen. Philip was having a good joke at her expense and none of this was helping find Cia.

Having forgotten to concentrate, she felt a surge of energy enter her through her left hand. The strange feeling coursed through her body and back out through her right hand. It tingled the stone in her palms and she felt the cycle begin again.

She almost dropped the stone she was so startled by it. Now she knew what she was looking for.

12

Cia? Meg had found the pattern just before a major fall-off of output, and decided that would be the best place to make contact. It was just ahead of where she had left Ian, so at least she could tell Cia that she had brought her son back safely. Also, she wanted to find out if Cia knew what had gone wrong; why Gardner had been able to find the exact place and time Ian had been secreted.

Cia knew the voice sounded familiar, but she was unable to place it immediately. She had too many things on her mind. She had just returned to the Keep from the Old City and was shaken by what she had seen.

The man who had brushed Gardner's footprints from the rubble in front of the stairwell was someone she had never seen before. Had people wandered past and been snared by Gardner? Kept there somehow and forced into his service? And to what purpose?

Cia? The voice asked again.

Cia made an effort to drag her concentration back to reality. *Hello?* she asked.

Oh, good! I found you, the voice said.

Meg? Cia hadn't been prepared for this. She had planned to go back for Ian, and hopefully Meg as well, in a few days, when she had figured out how best to deal with Gardner . . . Something had gone wrong.

You bet it did! Meg snapped, and set off on a litany of complaints, ending with Thiessen's death. *So here I am*, she finished.

Where is Ian? Cia asked.

I left him off back at his body, said Meg. *It made him*

269

feel a lot better about the war he's fighting against Gardner's poison. Sarah wasn't there though. He won't feel really OK until she gets back.

Gardner has them both, Cia said.

What?

Gardner kidnapped them while I was up in the cave taking Ian's mind back to you. They aren't in the Keep, they're in the Old City.

When Gardner appeared in our den at home, Ian and I knew something had gone wrong.

Wait a minute, Cia said. *Gardner was in your time?* She had been so caught up in her own problems that she hadn't really heard what Meg had been saying.

Yes! Meg snapped. *What did you think I said?*

Then something is about to happen that we won't be able to change, because neither Ian, nor Sarah, knew where I was taking him, said Cia.

Your energy level drops drastically just beyond the point where I've contacted you, Meg said quietly. *There are portions of the future I guess we just can't change.*

Well, I can't say I'm glad to hear that, but I'm glad you're here and Ian is safe, said Cia.

Thiessen is dead, Meg repeated. *Gardner killed my little brother. This would never have happened if you had left me alone.*

And he would kill our future if I did, said Cia. *I didn't know that would happen. I'm sorry.*

Well, where can I find this bastard? Meg demanded. *I want him to know how it felt for Thiessen. I didn't come here to help you. I came to hurt Gardner.*

That's not a very healthy attitude, Cia observed.

What do you care? Meg cried. *As long as your ends are served, what difference do my motives make?*

Anger is a good motivator, but it needs to be tempered with good judgement to be effective, said Cia. *I can teach you some things you will need to know, and take you to*

270

him, but you will have to figure out the best way to strike. If what you say is true about my own energy flow, I will be unable to help you when you attack.

That's fine, Meg said tightly. *Just teach me Gardner's energy pattern, and what you think I need to know. I want to get this over with.*

Fine, Cia began. *Ian taught you to centre; did he teach you how to ground yourself? You'll need this to draw on the cosmic energy and balance it with the earth to cleanse you and lend you strength.*

Several hours later, Meg returned to the continuum armed with knowledge and an energy pattern to search for.

Sarah sat in the corner by the bed, trying to make herself as small as possible. She gripped Ian's hand tightly in her own and watched with wide eyes as the door to their cell swung open.

Freddie entered carrying a body and Gardner strode in after him.

'Put her there,' Gardner commanded, pointing at a pallet of straw on the floor.

Freddie stooped and gently placed his load on the makeshift bed, straightening garments and limbs to make her rest more comfortable.

Sarah recognized Cia at once, and was shocked at her condition. Her robes were dirty and rumpled. Her hair was dishevelled and old straw clung to it. She looked as if she had been thrown into the back of a hay waggon. She was thin and drawn, her fair skin paler than usual in the flickering torchlight. Sarah gasped.

Gardner swung towards the sound and Sarah cowered back against the wall.

'She can't help you now,' Gardner leered at her. 'You have no one to help you. No one who cares!' With a harsh laugh, he turned his back on her and concentrated on

Freddie. 'You be sure to keep her mind enclosed, Freddie. No one goes in, and she doesn't come out. Is that clear?'

Freddie gulped miserably and nodded.

'Good,' said Gardner. He turned back to Sarah and smiled a blood-chilling smile. Then he left the room, bolting the door behind him. His footsteps echoed down the hallway and shortly they were left in silence.

Sarah looked at Ian and then at Freddie and Cia.

Cia was in bad shape. Her breathing was shallow and rapid. Her eyelids flickered as though she were fighting to regain consciousness. Her fingers twitched sporadically, but she didn't awaken.

Freddie just looked terrified. He stared at Sarah, mouth open, saliva threaded down his chin. His clothing was no cleaner than Cia's and he too had hollow cheeks.

Sarah tried to smile reassuringly at him, but Freddie flinched and looked down.

'Freddie, I don't mean to frighten you,' Sarah said. 'I won't try to keep you from doing what Drove told you to do, but you both could use a healing. I can do that without touching your mind, if you let me. I can do the same for Cia. She has given me permission before. I'm sure she would agree that her body needs attention, even if her mind is trapped.'

Freddie didn't say anything, but he looked up at her again.

'I promise I won't do anything to get you in trouble with Drove,' she said again.

Slowly, Freddie nodded.

Glad to have something to do, Sarah let go of Ian's hand and stood up. Crossing to where Freddie stood, she placed a hand on his shoulder.

'Sit down beside Cia and just concentrate on what you have to do with her. I won't interfere,' she said, pushing him gently to the floor. Fishing some crystals out of her

272

pockets, she concentrated her mind on their healing powers and set to work, first on Freddie, then on Cia.

The block Freddie held on Cia's mind was strong. Sarah could not have penetrated it even if she had not promised Freddie to leave them alone. She could feel Cia fighting against the intrusion with every fibre of her being. By healing Cia's body, she gave Cia's mind something to draw on, but judging by the block, Cia wouldn't win. Gardner would keep putting sleeping draughts in her mouth, washing them down with a little water, and Cia would continue to lose her battle.

Sarah finished her work and went back to her stool beside Ian's bed. She could sense his mind, still in deep sleep, and took small comfort in the touch of his hand.

Gardner had not treated them badly. She had been given food and water, and the chamber pot was emptied each morning and evening. But Sarah had grown up believing all the tales of the Old City, and the dreadful things that would happen to any child foolish enough to stray near it. To be held in the tunnels under it was more than she could bear. She had given up hope that her glass beads would protect her from the diseases and creatures that surely lurked in the buildings and passages, waiting for their moment to attack.

When they had first been brought here, Sarah spent several hours screaming and crying and pounding at the door, but no one had paid any attention to her, so gradually, she stopped and went to sit beside Ian. She didn't dare relax her vigilance for even a moment.

Now, she was exhausted. Ian looked so peaceful lying on the bed, breathing deeply and regularly. Freddie sat quietly beside Cia, who had subsided a bit since the healing. Sarah hadn't slept since their capture and she could barely keep her eyes open. She moved Ian over in the bed a bit and climbed in beside him. Pulling the covers over her, she snuggled down into the pillow and fell asleep almost immediately.

The creak of the door awakened her with a start several hours later. She looked up to see Mareki enter with a large tray and set it on the floor. There was no table, and only the one stool beside the bed.

Sarah sat up and rubbed her eyes. 'Mareki?' she asked.

The girl started as if she had been struck.

'Mareki?' Sarah asked again. 'Is that you? What are you doing here?'

Mareki shook her head and backed out of the room. The door was shut and bolted again. The footsteps that retreated this time were much swifter and quieter.

Sarah rubbed her eyes again and stared at Freddie. He still sat where she had left him earlier. He didn't look up, nor did he glance at the tray of food on the floor in front of him.

Sarah climbed out of bed and went to see what had been left this time. Lifting covers, Sarah discovered a tureen of stew and two bowls, a loaf of bread and some butter, two apples and a pitcher of milk. Also, there were two large cups of a rich broth.

Before she ate, Sarah took a cup of broth and lifted Ian, supporting his head and shoulders with her own body and left arm. In this position, she was able to pour the broth into his mouth a little at a time and he swallowed most of it reflexively. Wiping his mouth with a corner of the sheet, she laid him back down on the pillow and went back to the tray.

Taking the second cup of broth, she approached Cia. Freddie had seen what she did with Ian, so he didn't object when she repeated the procedure with Cia.

After that, she ladled two bowls full of stew and broke two hunks of bread from the loaf. She handed one of these to Freddie and brought hers over to sit on the floor beside him. Silently, they ate their dinner.

When they had finished, Sarah put cups and bowls back on the tray and put it beside the door. Then she went back to the stool beside Ian's bed and picked up his hand again.

They sat like that for the rest of the night. Sarah beside Ian; Freddie beside Cia. Silent and still; practically unmoving, they had no idea when the sun rose, but eventually a tiny old woman came with a tray of breakfast and took the dinner tray with her when she went. Sarah was too dispirited even to ask her about Mareki. She went through the routine of feeding Ian and Cia, then prepared breakfast for herself and Freddie.

The porridge sat leaden in her stomach and her brain felt heavy in her head. She was certain that sleeping draughts were being put into the cups of broth, but neither of the unconscious patients could survive without food. She wondered what Gardner had in mind, but she didn't have to wait long to find out.

His arrival was announced by the thudding of his boots in the passageway outside their door. They echoed loudly at his approach and stirred Sarah from her stupor. She sat back on the stool, leaning against the wall and gripping Ian's hand more tightly.

Freddie sat up straighter and looked intently at Cia, as though that were necessary to convince Gardner he was doing as he had been told.

The door banged open with a flourish and Gardner strode into the small chamber.

'Freddie.' His voice rang loudly in the quiet of the cell.

Sarah flinched. So did Freddie. Ian and Cia didn't stir.

'Yes, s-sir?' Freddie stammered. He looked up at Gardner obediently.

'You will now let me into Cia's mind, but you will not let anyone else in, and you will not let her mind escape,' he commanded. 'Is that clear?'

'Yes sir,' Freddie said. He closed his eyes and his jaw went slack.

Gardner sat down abruptly, his eyes also closed. He and Freddie sat that way for a long time while Sarah sat and watched.

The door to the cell stood open, but she made no move towards it. There was no place for her to go. She couldn't take Ian with her, and she couldn't hide from Gardner anywhere. It was much safer to stay right where she was and wait to see what was going on.

She could guess that Gardner was searching Cia's mind, but she had no idea why, or what he hoped to find. Sarah continued to sit by the bed, clutching Ian's hand and watching the tableau on the floor in front of her.

Cia stirred restlessly, but her eyes remained closed. Freddie sat quietly with his mouth hanging open and his eyes screwed shut. Gardner sat with his eyes closed, but his lids flickered rapidly and his jaw worked as his face grew slowly more red.

Then suddenly, the tableau broke. With a roar, Gardner leaped to his feet. Freddie's eyes snapped open and Cia ceased to move at all.

'Keep her here!' Gardner snapped. 'Remember: no one in, no one out!' Then he turned and strode from the room, slamming the door and bolting it behind him.

Sarah waited until she could no longer hear his footsteps before moving. She found she had been holding her breath.

'Freddie, what happened?' she asked finally.

Freddie looked at her uncomprehendingly.

'What happened?' she asked him again.

'Meg,' said Freddie

Sarah questioned him for several more minutes, but Freddie refused to say anything more.

'How does he expect you to sleep?' Sarah asked him at last.

Freddie shrugged. He turned to Cia and silence returned to the small room.

Sarah settled back on her stool and looked at Ian. She hoped this would be over soon. She was terrified and lonely.

Meg attacked the threads. She didn't pick them up and sort through them so much as she grabbed, yanked and scrutinized.

She was angry and hurt; determined that Gardner would be made to pay, and imagining the dreadful things she would do to him. She felt strong for the first time in her life.

Strong at least in the emotional sense. She had worked her muscles until they delivered an exacting performance on demand. Her mind had never really been very healthy. She had never been certain it would be there when she really needed it.

Now, she was sure. She continued her reckless search through the continuum, not caring that she was disrupting the lives of the strangers she was touching.

You may not care, but others do. Tread lightly through other people's lives. They also have the power to steamroller you.

Meg jumped and turned towards the voice, but she was alone in the continuum. She was certain it had been Philip who had spoken but he didn't show himself this time.

Philip? she called. She received no answer. Frustrated, she turned back to the threads to renew her search. *Damn!* she exclaimed to herself and gently touched a strand. Her wholesale rampage through the threads meant inconsistent coverage. She wasn't sure where she still needed to look.

The touch brought a wave of hostility. Meg dropped the strand immediately and floated above the river of time, wondering what to do next. She had wreaked such havoc here, that perhaps if she moved upstream a short way, people would have calmed down a bit and wouldn't mind her gently poking around.

She floated a bit further forward and began her search again, much more slowly and calmly. She was still angry at Gardner, but her anger wasn't helping her, so she put it aside for the duration of her task.

She had been sorting for hours, she was certain. She reached for thread after thread, but none of them was the one she was looking for. She picked up another thread and . . .

Jenet unfolded.

His mind came apart in her hands.

Meg screamed, but she was unable to let go. Every telepath within range of his broadcast must have heard him. Probably heard her too, since she was so closely in contact with his mind.

Unable to silence his chaotic squalling, Meg inadvertently put a barrier around his mind. She was the only one with access to his mind now.

Jenet cried in fear and clung to her touch. He couldn't make contact with any mind he recognized and all of his external senses had shut down when his brain overloaded. He was alone in the dark and at the mercy of a strange woman who had closed him off from the rest of the Keep.

Who are you? he quavered.

Meg was unsure how to respond. She tried to lower the barrier, but she didn't know how she had erected it. She couldn't make it go away, and she couldn't concentrate on it with a frightened child clinging to her mind.

I'm Meg, she told him at last. *I am a friend of Ian and Cia's.*

She felt him relax a bit, but his grip didn't loosen. He held on to her for his sanity.

Help me, he whimpered. *I'm scared. What have you done to my mind?*

I don't know, Meg told him truthfully. *I think I blocked off your broadcast because it was scaring everybody else. At least it scared me. Now I can't make it go away.*

Where is Cia? Jenet asked.

I don't know that either, Meg admitted. *I came here to help her, but maybe I can help you, too.*

Where are you from? Jenet asked, curiosity getting the best of his fear.

A long time ago, Meg said. *I just went through something like this, and Ian helped me.*

Ha! Jenet said, pouncing on the word. *Ian is a Deaf. How could he help you?*

He just did, Meg told him. *He held my hand and talked to me like I'm talking to you right now. He took me to my centre and told me how to love and accept everything in my mind after it fell apart. When I was done, I came here.*

Is that what I should do? Jenet asked.

Well, probably something like it, she said. *But I don't think you have as much to work on as I did. Is it just your senses, or did your whole mind break?*

What do you mean? Jenet was clearly puzzled by her question. His grip tightened on her hand, and he moved closer to her.

Well, you seem pretty coherent for a kid unfolding, said Meg.

Light a torch, Jenet suggested. *I think we're in your centre.*

Meg reached out and found the wall. Moving her hand along it, she ran across a switch. She flipped it on and the room was flooded with light. They were in fact in her centre.

This won't do, she said. *We have to work in your centre, since this is your problem.*

We have to? he whined.

Yes, Meg said firmly. She tugged on his hand to pull

him towards the door. He resisted, but Meg remained adamant.

OK, Jenet said grudgingly, moving with her towards the door. He was tall for his age, with sandy-brown hair and a shy smile. His dark eyes were wide with fear, but he squared his shoulders and allowed Meg to pull him through the door into the chaos beyond.

Here, his courage failed him and he cowered against her, but she gave his hand a quick squeeze and smiled at him.

Everything will be OK, I promise, she said. *Now, do you want me to come with you to your centre, or would you rather be alone for this?*

Will you please come with me? he asked.

Sure, Meg smiled down at him. *How do we get there from here?*

Just hold on to my hand, Jenet said, feeling a little more in charge.

Meg laughed. Jenet had not let go of her hand yet. *OK*, she said. *I'm ready*.

And then they were in Jenet's centre. It was much more austere than she had expected a child's centre would be. The walls and floor were bare. There were no chairs or pillows, no wall hangings; only two torch sconces on the plain wooden walls and dust everywhere.

Jenet, this is the seat of your soul. Shouldn't it be as beautiful as you can make it? Meg asked, puzzled.

Cia always told us to discover what was there, Jenet said. *This is what I found. I don't come here often. When Cia says to go to our centre, I go to the field outside and stay there. My guide and I talk while we sit in the grass.*

Why don't you change it? asked Meg.

Jenet shrugged. *It doesn't matter.*

Well, it should matter, Meg said. *If this is what you discovered in your soul, why didn't you try making some changes in yourself?*

280

Again, Jenet shrugged. *Do you think it would make Nina like me any better?*

This is about a girl? Meg laughed.

Jenet turned red and looked at the dusty floor. *So?* he demanded sullenly.

Nina doesn't like you? Meg asked gently.

Jenet shook his head. *She laughs at me and makes fun of me with the other kids*, he whispered.

How old is she? Meg asked. God, she thought to herself: now I'm starting to sound like Cia!

Eight, Jenet said. *She's two years younger than I am. But I've always loved her.*

Meg stifled her laughter this time. *Jenet, it seems to me that little girls of eight tease the boys they like because they don't know how else to express the feelings they have.*

Jenet looked up, hopeful. *Do you think so?* he asked.

I think so, she said. *Would you want Nina to see you in a centre that suggests you don't like yourself? Don't you think that would send her a message that you don't think there is anything about you worth liking?*

Well, maybe, Jenet began.

Definitely, Meg said. *Why don't you start by cleaning up this place? Maybe a chair or two, some pillows. Something to make this place look like someone lives here and cares about it.*

Jenet set to work and shortly had all the dust picked up. *Now what?* he asked.

What are you comfortable with? Meg countered. *This is your centre. I've already done mine.*

Jenet made a face at her, but returned to his task.

Meg placed her back against the wall and slid down it until she was sitting on the floor with her chin on her knees. She had been completely sidetracked in her search for Gardner by Jenet's unfolding. Now she was committed to finishing this task before she could continue her own.

She felt even less equipped to handle this than Ian had.

281

She didn't know what to tell this boy. It would be so much easier to believe this was a psychotic episode and just quit, pull into herself and give up trying.

Then she heard her mother and father talking to each other when Gardner had appeared in the den. They had heard him too. There was no question that this was really happening.

There, what do you think? Jenet stood in front of Meg, arms folded across his chest and a rather smug expression on his face. Meg glanced around the room and then looked again more slowly.

Wow! she exclaimed. *Not too shabby.*

What does that mean? asked Jenet in a rather aggrieved tone.

That means I approve. Nina would be impressed.

Really? Jenet almost squealed. *I tried to think of what she might like to see, and what I like too.*

You did a good job, Meg said looking around again. The floor was now covered with a richly coloured, thick blue carpeting. Huge beige pillows were scattered all over the floor. The walls were still wood, but the boards had been polished to a high gloss and stained a shade darker than their natural pale tone. Pictures of the land around the Keep, and his favourite animals hung on the walls in between gold-banded torch sconces. There were now two on each wall, burning brightly. There were two doors on opposite walls that had crystal knobs. *For a ten-year-old you have very sophisticated taste*, Meg commented as she took in the details.

What does that mean? Jenet asked.

Not too shabby, Meg said again and grinned. *Are you ready to figure out what we have to do to get you healed so you can show this off to Nina?*

Yeah, Jenet grinned too. *What's my gift?*

Your gift? asked Meg. *What gift?*

My psi-power, he clarified. *Don't you know?*

282

I have no idea. Don't you have to straighten up the mess outside before you can determine that?

Jenet shrugged. *I dunno. I've never done this before.*

Well, neither have I, so let's just take this one step at a time. Go open the door to outside and tell me what you see, Meg suggested.

Obediently, Jenet went to the door and opened it. He stuck his head out and then jumped back, slamming the door quickly.

Stuff is flying around out there! he exclaimed. *I nearly got my head cut off by something going by.*

Meg sighed. Then she explained to him what Ian had told her to do. She set him to his task, and closed her eyes. She was going to be here for a long time. She settled back against the wall to wait it out.

Jenet didn't take anywhere near as long as she had taken. There was less lifetime-accumulated junk, and less trauma lived through. He finished so quickly, in fact, that Meg made him show her.

Well, you're OK, now. I guess we can both go? she suggested.

I still don't know what my talent is, Jenet objected.

Can't you get someone in the Keep to help you with that? Meg asked.

No, Jenet said definitely. *When kids unfold, they come back and know what their talents are. Then they get trained in them by the adults who have those gifts. You have to test me.*

I don't know how to do that, Meg said.

You'll think of something, said Jenet confidently. He sat down on one of his pillows and settled in to wait for Meg to figure out what she was supposed to do.

OK, she said at last. *Lift one of those torches out of the sconce. Tell me which one you're going to try to lift.*

That one, Jenet pointed. His face screwed up in concentration and he turned red in his efforts, but the torch stayed put. *I knew that would happen,* he said.

Did you know that was going to happen because it's impossible to lift things with your mind, or because that didn't feel like what your talent might be? Meg questioned his response.

Everyone knows it's possible, Jenet scoffed. *It just didn't feel right for me.*

Think about it then, Meg said, looking intently at Jenet. *What feels right to you?*

The animals, he responded immediately, indicating the pictures on his walls.

What about them? asked Meg.

I think healing them, he said wonderingly. *Also, talking with you this way. I think I'm also a telepath.*

If I doused a torch in sand, do you think you could light it again? Meg asked.

Jenet shook his head. *No, I don't think I'm a pyrokinetic. I also don't think my healing will work on people.*

Do you feel anything else? Meg asked him.

No, he said. *I guess that's it. That's what I feel strongly.*

Meg thought about what she had just done. It made sense in a large way. *Are we done now?* she asked him.

You need to drop the barrier around my mind, he reminded her. *Neither one of us can go anywhere until you do.*

Oh, hell, said Meg. *I'd forgotten about that.* Reaching deep into her mind, she found that the psychic static had finally cleared up and she was able to concentrate on what she had done automatically in response to the noise.

The barrier was solid, but by focusing on a portion of it, she was able to dissolve it fairly quickly. The rest of the wall fell once it had been breached.

OK, she told Jenet at last. *You've given me a lot to think about. Thank you for letting me help you.*

He grinned shyly. *Thank you, too*, he said, ducking his head. He took Meg's hand and led her from his centre.

Goodbye, he said. He left her and started towards the path at the edge of the field.

Goodbye, she called after him. She centred and returned to the continuum.

Floating above the strands, Meg stayed in her centre and sat in one of her over-stuffed chairs. What did her gifts feel like, she wondered. She hadn't known she needed to give it any thought, and Cia hadn't been able to concentrate on that aspect of her training. She had been in too much of a hurry, and too worried about Ian and Sarah.

Meg sat for a long time concentrating, and what she discovered amazed and alarmed her: telepathic, psycho-kinetic and a minor healer. The healer was empathic. She would feel the pain and sickness of anyone she came in contact with unless she could learn to block it out. This could be a major handicap in any battle against Drove Gardner.

She floated above the continuum and thought about that for a long time.

13

Meg thought about what Philip had said, what Cia had taught her, what she had been through with Jenet, and what she had discovered about herself as a result of those contacts.

Then she thought about what she had been brought here to do. All of a sudden, she was assailed by doubt. She wasn't sure she would be able to be strong enough when the time came actually to confront Gardner. Her anger was now tempered by the discovery of her own vulnerability to anything she might do to him.

Ian and Cia counted on her. Thiessen wouldn't know the difference, but Meg felt that his death deserved an acknowledgement of some sort from Gardner. If she let them down, she would also let herself down. So Meg continued to float above the continuum for a while longer, thinking about failure; her resolve paralysed by fear.

Then she saw Thiessen's face when the crystal shattered and heard him say 'I love you, Meggie', and she found the courage to pick up the threads and begin searching for a new energy pattern.

She had to move forward on the continuum, because there were too many places she had been in the present, and too many things that couldn't be changed in the past. Philip still made her wonder what that had all been about, but he had been so insistent that Meg decided to take him at his word.

After a small eternity of mucking about in the threads, Meg found what she was looking for, only to discover that she had run up against another barrier. Gardner's mind was being protected from outside intrusion. Meg suspected it was Freddie who had stopped her, so she investigated the energy a little closer.

Freddie's energy was intertwined with both Gardner and Cia. He was stretched almost to his limit. Also, Meg noted, Gardner would be unable to use his psychokinetic abilities without having Freddie drop his barrier first. Meg hoped that information would come in handy later, but for now, she filed it away and continued to search for a way to get into the present without drawing attention to her presence and giving Gardner the edge.

Meg had been secretly hoping to find Sarah, since she had picked up some of her energy in talking to Ian about her, but before Meg had searched much farther, she found a minor telepath who was more than willing to share her mind and the dangers of confronting Gardner in the Old City.

If anyone noticed a new light in Mareki's eyes, they failed to point it out. They probably wouldn't have noticed the difference anyway, because she had always spent so much time with her eyes fixed on the ground. There were more important things to worry about. First Ian and Sarah had disappeared. Now Cia was missing.

Mareki walked with her head up and her shoulders squared. A small smile twitched the corner of her mouth occasionally.

No unusual behaviour, Meg warned her. *We can't afford discovery. We have to take Gardner by surprise.*

That shouldn't be a problem, Mareki said grimly.

It will be if you give us away, Meg pointed out. *When does he expect you back next?*

Not until tomorrow afternoon, said Mareki. Always before, she had dreaded going back to Gardner in the Old City. Recently, he had been spending most of his time there, and he expected her to be there as often as she could get away from her chores around the Keep. She felt she was constantly working for someone else. Mareki hated the Old City. She hated Gardner, but she was afraid.

Now she had hope that her trips to the Old City could end. Never again would she have to submit to the invisible hand or Gardner's sweaty hands and hot breath; feel his touch burn her skin. With fierce joy she said, *We could go tonight, if you like.*

Nothing out of the ordinary! Meg reiterated. *There are enough suspicious things happening around here. We don't need to have you added to the list. The fewer people who know about what is going on, the fewer will get hurt. I get the feeling Gardner doesn't lose gracefully?*

Mareki laughed and shook her head. *No. We have surely got our work cut out for us.*

You're sure you don't mind the risks? Meg pressed.

Meg, if I die in this, I'll be better off than I have been. I'll be able to move to the next life. If I survive, then obviously I still have lessons to learn in this life.

God! Meg exclaimed in exasperation. *Do all of you talk like this?*

Like what? asked Mareki, sounding hurt.

Crystals and reincarnation and the power of meditation? You people are whacked! Meg exclaimed. *If you die, you're dead. That's all.*

Are you sure? Mareki asked slyly.

Oh, I give up! Let's get something to eat and get a good night's rest. Tomorrow may very well be a long day.

Tomorrow was even longer than that.

Meg had never been fond of mornings, but this particular morning, she got up with Mareki at dawn to slop the hogs and wash up before beginning work on breakfast.

To her dismay, the bath was communal. Mareki was completely unconcerned about standing in a tub and soaping up in front of anyone who happened to be washing at the same time. Meg was unused to sharing her bath, except most recently with Ian, but that had been a necessary evil.

Don't think this isn't, Mareki said drily.

Meg found herself fighting not to point out that Mareki had chosen this and found herself chuckling silently. It was too early in the morning to be awake, let alone pick a fight.

After breakfast, there was laundry, then lunch and a stint in the weaving room. Meg was certain they would never be free to travel to the Old City, but after weaving for several hours, many of the women got up and left to begin dinner preparations.

Mareki also got up.

Is this it? Meg asked.

Yes, Mareki said. *But we have to be quiet about it.*

They left on foot. It took almost three hours to walk into the Old City. By the time they got there it was dark and they were hot, dusty and thirsty. Mary met them at the first doorway and shooed them into a corner as quickly as her old bones let her.

"E's in a fine mood tonight,' she said in a stage whisper. 'Better be extra-careful, he's findin' fault in everyone and everything.' With a nod and a wink, she shuffled off across the huge room, leaving Mareki and Meg wondering.

Mareki wondered if she had done something to displease Gardner.

Meg wondered if he had already tried to kill her and failed. If so, she had better tread lightly. Freddie might be working at capacity, but he could still find her energy if he looked carefully.

After a moment's thought, Mareki crossed to the fire and began setting out Gardner's dinner tray.

Meg smiled to herself. She would need to know him a

bit better before feeling confident in attacking Gardner in his own territory. She was still uncomfortable enough with the idea of psi-powers to want experience with them first-hand.

Travelling in the continuum, she was sure had been a fluke. There was no connection between that and the use of mind capabilities which, in the twentieth century, were associated with witchcraft and hobgoblins. Watching Gardner in action might give her the incentive she needed to continue with the task so many people were counting on her for.

Myself included, she thought to herself. If none of this was real, she was likely to find herself strapped to a hospital bed when she came to. The idea didn't appeal to her much.

Mareki laughed.

What's so funny? Meg demanded.

Just listening to you! she said. *You've been fighting so hard against believing that this could really be happening, you haven't even considered a plan against Gardner. Are we really in that much trouble?*

Evidently, Meg grimaced. *Look, where I come from, this stuff pretty much died out with the Salem witch-hunts; except for a few nutcases who think that drawing poison with rocks works. Then I come here and find out a whole culture bases its behaviour on these facts??* Meg left the remainder of her thoughts unsaid.

Mareki shrugged and continued setting up Gardner's dinner tray. She'd seen altogether too much. She kept her counsel. Meg would find out soon enough on her own.

Gardner was in a foul mood when Mareki slipped into his room to place his dinner tray on the table. He didn't even look up when she opened the door. Usually, this act produced at least a frightening leer. Tonight, she made it back to the door unnoticed. With a grateful sigh, she pulled it shut behind her and started back down the hallway.

Meg was surprised at the level of feeling she sensed from Mareki. She didn't know the situation between the two of them very well, because she had declined to snoop, and Mareki had been reticent about sharing information.

Meg couldn't blame her. From the level of relief, Meg decided their relationship wasn't the healthiest one around.

Mareki hurried back to the central chamber to have dinner with the rest of the people there. Meg looked around, but refrained from asking questions until after they had finished their meal.

Who are these people? she asked finally. *Where did they come from? Are they all from the Keep?*

No. Mareki seemed reluctant to answer the questions, but Meg got the feeling that it was more for their safety, than her own, that she was worried. *Many of them blundered into this place. They wanted to leave, but Gardner made them stay.*

How? Meg asked.

The same way he makes me come back, Mareki admitted miserably. *You can't travel farther in a day than Gardner can search for you telepathically using Freddie. His punishment is constant pain and physical disabling. Mary, who met us at the door, is no older than I am.*

But she looks sixty! Meg gasped.

You grasp my point, said Mareki. *You know what death means to us. He would never kill us. He would never allow us to kill ourselves. Even if we did kill ourselves, we would have to learn all over again, the lessons we didn't learn in this life. I'm not prepared to go through something like this again. I might as well get it over with now.*

Is that how Mary feels? Meg asked, horrified.

Of course, Mareki responded. *How else could she feel?*

291

Was she a part of the Keep before this? Meg wanted to know.

No. She was part of another Keep. She left them on the advice of her guide. She wound up here.

Does that happen often? asked Meg.

Often enough, Mareki said defensively. *Well, no. Not often. Every few years, a stranger passes by the Keep. We never take them in, even for a night. They usually end up here, and Gardner won't let them go.*

Do people like this leave your Keep?

No, Mareki was quick to respond. *Not in my memory. Not that anyone talks about. I don't think anyone has left in a generation or two.*

Why? asked Meg.

I don't know, answered Mareki. *I have no idea.*

Is that the truth? Meg asked.

No, said Mareki. Meg was unable to discover what the truth was. Gardner came storming down the corridor ranting about small children.

Meg was reasonably certain he had just killed Thiessen.

After supper, they helped clean up the large chamber that served as kitchen, dining room and sleeping quarters for the people who lived here. Then they started off down a different corridor carrying a torch against the darkness.

Where are we going? asked Meg.

To collect the dinner tray and the chamber pot from the cell, Mareki responded almost blankly. She stopped at a door and pushed the bolt aside.

The door swung open silently and a rush of stale air met them. The light in the room was dim, as the only torch was guttering in its sconce. Meg looked around in horror. There was a bed, a stool and a pile of straw on the floor.

Cia lay on the straw, unconscious. It was obvious to Meg that she fought an inner battle against Freddie's hold

292

on her mind. She was dirty and bedraggled, hardly resembling the beautiful and remote woman she had seen in the fun-house mirror. Her eyes had withdrawn into their sockets, casting dark shadows in her face. She looked skeletal.

Freddie sat beside her on the floor. He looked little better, not having slept recently enough. Despite his apparent physical age, he looked very young and frightened.

Then Meg looked at the bed.

Sarah sat on the stool beside it, staring at her intently, her terror momentarily forgotten.

'Mareki?' she asked tentatively. Her eyes were wide, dark in her pale face. She was as bedraggled as the two on the floor, but there was a dignity about her posture that belied her circumstances. 'There is something about you . . . I can sense a difference. Are you all right?' Her concern was evident, but Meg couldn't afford to let Mareki answer. Sarah was empathic and might detect Meg's presence if given a chance.

Meg looked instead at the bed.

Ian lay in the middle of squalor untouched. His pale hair shone in the flickering light of the torch, unrumpled. His skin was clear and his expression untroubled.

Meg stared at him for a long moment, taking in the face of the man with whom she had shared . . . well, everything. It didn't seem possible.

You've got to stop thinking in those terms, Mareki chided. Shaking off the inertia of Meg's wonder, she took the torch from the sconce and replaced it with the one they had brought. Then she retrieved the chamber pot and balanced the dinner tray on top of it.

We'll have to get someone else to bring the chamber pot back, Meg said to Mareki. *Sarah started to pick up my energy from you. We can't risk her finding out about me.*

She might accidentally warn Gardner, and I'm not ready to face him yet.

Mareki pulled the door shut and slid the bolt across. *OK*, she said. *But you'd better think of something soon. You can't hide here waiting until he finds you.*

I know, said Meg with a sigh. *I just don't know how to go about choreographing a battle using psychic powers. I've never used them before, and I've never seen them in use. Maybe you could give me some help in that department?*

I could try, Mareki said.

They returned to the main chamber.

This place must have been rebuilt, Meg observed, looking around the room. *It must have been part of the subway system once, but I think it's been rebuilt since then. I recognize the general structure, but it doesn't look like this in my time.*

Many things are different now, said Mareki drily. She gave over her burdens for others to take care of and went back to Gardner's room to get his tray.

To her surprise, she made it out of his room unmolested again.

He must be dreadfully angry with you, she said.

Mmhmm, Meg agreed. *But I'm pretty angry with him, too. And so are you. Does he rape you that often?*

A shiver passed down Mareki's spine, giving Meg her answer.

Then you've got to help me, she pressed. *Tell me what you know about this psycho-stuff, and everything you can think of about Gardner and Freddie.*

Sarah sat for quite a while thinking about the difference she sensed in Mareki. It was the first time ever that Sarah had seen Mareki not look like a beaten animal. She had been carrying herself with an unconscious grace and confidence that were not naturally a part of her.

She thought long and hard about it, but none of the strange pieces fitted into the puzzle she thought she had been working on. She had nothing to do here but sit and think.

Ian's strange behaviour, Gardner's strange behaviour, Cia's strange behaviour, and now Mareki. None of it seemed to make sense. The longer she mulled things over, the more confusing they became.

Giving up for a while, she found contact with Ian again. He wouldn't tell her what was going on, but it was pleasant to share his thoughts. It helped time pass. Freddie was too absorbed in his efforts to shield both Gardner and Cia.

Gardner seemed to be expecting something, but Sarah wasn't able to figure out what from his external cues. He had been back once, in a terrible mood, and kicked Cia in the head. Then he left again, without saying a word.

Hope! That had been what was different about Mareki. Maybe she wouldn't be in this cell much longer after all. When Cia had been brought in, Sarah's hope had vanished.

But that was also what was different about Ian. Just before they had been kidnapped, he suddenly became almost serene.

Something was going to happen soon. Sarah could feel it in her bones. She looked down at Ian, peacefully asleep on the bed. His smile told her everything she needed to know.

After a restless night spent under thin blankets on a hard stone floor, Meg and Mareki awoke with a muzzy and disoriented feeling. They stretched and felt every muscle and joint protest the rough treatment.

Do you always feel this way after a night here? Meg asked, testing general movement.

No, Mareki said quickly. *The muscles usually hurt less, the dignity more.*

When do we have to be back at the Keep? Meg changed the subject quickly.

Not until later this afternoon. I'm expected to help with the dinner preparations, said Mareki. *I ought to be helping in the weaving room early this afternoon, but they will excuse my absence, since I work so quickly.*

Meg nodded. *We have to pick our fight this morning, then. Freddie will be especially tired after two days and nights without sleep, guarding Cia. I believe Gardner will also be distracted because he failed to kill Ian and me. He'll be planning a trip back rather than searching for a threat in this time.*

Do you really think so? Mareki asked hopefully.

It's our best hope, isn't it? said Meg. *In the meantime, what's for breakfast, and what do we have to do around here while we wait for Gardner to put in an appearance?*

The huge chamber was slowly filling with the odours of Mary cooking breakfast and both Meg and Mareki could hear their stomach rumbling.

Mary? Mareki asked as they approached.

The old woman slowly turned from her pot and smiled tentatively.

May we help you? asked Mareki solicitously.

Mary bobbed her head and gestured vaguely at the table beside her cook-fire. She turned back to her pot and said nothing more.

Mareki looked at the table, figured out what needed doing and set to work. The breakfast trays for Gardner and the prisoners needed fixing, and she cut up fruit to go with the porridge. Then she folded and stored the blankets they had used as bedding. When the tray for the prisoners was ready, Mareki started to give it to Erhan, but Meg stopped her.

I need to see them again, she explained. *I think seeing*

*them caged and scared like this will help me get angry
enough to carry this through. Avenging Thiessen isn't
enough of a reason any more.*

Mareki nodded and they carried the tray off down the
hall balanced on her left shoulder and hand. The right
held aloft a torch to replace the one from last night, which
had probably gone out by now.

The room was exactly as they had left it the night
before. Sarah sat beside Ian, and Freddie sat beside Cia.
He looked up when the door opened, flinching as if he
expected Gardner to stride through instead of Mareki
with breakfast. Sarah looked up more slowly. There was
a defiance in her expression that hadn't been there last
night. Ian and Cia lay still.

Mareki set the tray on the floor, exchanged the torch
and left quietly.

Inside, Meg seethed. No one had the right to treat
other people this way.

They bolted breakfast while Mary prepared Gardner's
tray, then they took it and started down the other corridor
towards his room.

He heard them coming. In anticipation, he turned back
the covers next to him. As Mareki came through the
door, he smiled and patted the bed invitingly.

'Why don't we have a morning romp?' he suggested,
leering at her as she moved to the table to put her tray
down. 'Come on over here.'

Mareki turned around slowly, but Meg spoke before
Mareki could. 'No,' she said. She turned Mareki towards
the door and by main force, made her start walking.

Are you crazy? Mareki hissed.

I'm picking a fight, Meg clarified. *You saw how tired
Freddie was. We're best off striking while he's off-guard
anyway.*

I'm not ready for this! Mareki exclaimed.

Neither am I, said Meg.

'What?' Gardner asked, his voice becoming dangerously low.

'No,' said Meg again, before Mareki could interfere. 'I don't like you, and I don't want to be raped by you again.'

Meg could feel Mareki tensing inside, flinching away from the anticipated attack.

The invisible hand reached towards them from across the room. Meg could feel its approach and fended it off fairly easily. Gardner hadn't been expecting resistance, so it was a simple matter to brush it aside. She smiled slightly and continued towards the door.

Meg could feel Mareki frozen inside herself. She had given over complete control to Meg. She had withdrawn in terror and watched what was happening to her from a corner of her mind. Meg felt a surge of power and drew from it, letting it fill her.

The hand was more insistent this time. Gardner put more of his energy into maintaining it and Meg felt its fingers closing around her as she raised a barrier. It prevented Gardner from closing his psychokinetic fingers on her, but not from surrounding her in the process.

This won't do, she thought to herself. She still wasn't sure where the barrier had come from. There were many things it seemed her mind could do, but she was unaware of. Maybe Ian and Cia had been right, but this was an awkward way to find out. She couldn't move, but Gardner couldn't touch her either.

Interesting trade-off, she said to Mareki, even though she knew that Mareki had withdrawn. Meg needed someone to talk to, even if that someone didn't respond. She stood and waited for Gardner to tire of trying to close his fist on her barrier.

'You've never resisted,' he said at length, releasing his grip on Meg's barrier. 'Be reasonable, I don't want to have to hurt you. It would be a shame to mar such beauty.'

'I loathe and detest you,' Meg said. 'You're a pig.' She felt Gardner tense and strengthened her barrier, but instead of grabbing at her, he shot a bolt of blue energy from his fingertips.

Meg's barrier didn't hold against the onslaught. She could feel the skin on Mareki's arm and right side burning. She slapped at the flames as she ran for the door.

'I don't want to hurt you,' Gardner said again. 'Come to bed, and we'll forget this all happened.' There was a force in his voice that Mareki wanted desperately to obey.

Please, she begged Meg. *It will be much worse if we don't!*

You wanted to help me in this attack, said Meg. *We can't back down now. You have lessons to learn from this. Remember what you told me? Are you going to back down on that too?* Meg hated losing. She hated quitting even more.

She turned back to Gardner, glancing at the charred flesh of Mareki's right arm. 'You can damage me,' she said, 'but you can't harm me more than you already have. I will not be raped by you ever again.' Still cold with anger, Meg raised her own hand and felt the energy tingling up and down Mareki's injured arm. Green danced on the palm and she willed it outwards, visualizing Gardner as the target.

Lightning stabbed across the room only to shatter harmlessly against Gardner's shield. It started a small fire in the bedclothes, but Gardner slapped it out with PK.

Meg smiled when she saw her efforts deflected. Freddie had been called in on that one. He would tire even more quickly now. He wouldn't be able to maintain Gardner's defence.

Meg was close to the door. While Gardner was diverted by the fire, she ran to the door and pulled it open. He tried to push it shut again before she got out, but Meg slipped through and ran down the hallway as fast as she could.

'It's begun!' she shouted as she re-entered the main chamber. Heads swung towards the sound of her voice, but the eyes which regarded her were blank and uncomprehending. No one reacted. They turned back to their breakfast. 'Get clear!' Meg fairly screamed, brandishing Mareki's burnt arm for their inspection. 'He might do worse to you if you get caught in the crossfire!'

That provoked a response. They shuddered at the sight of charred flesh, but they still didn't move.

It would be worse for them if they did, Mareki said. *Right now, Drove's anger is directed only at me. If they move, they become targets*.

Meg shot them one last glance as she fled down the corridor towards the steps leading out of the warrens. Her best chance, she thought, might be outside. Also, she wanted to get Gardner as far away from Ian, Sarah and Cia as possible. If Freddie could track a runaway more than a day's travel away, she couldn't do anything to diminish his protection of Gardner.

As she reached the stairs, she heard Gardner's roar from the main chamber. She scrambled up the stairs and burst out into the bright daylight.

Temporarily blinded by the glare of the sun on the broken pavement, she stumbled away from the entrance to what had been the subway in her time. She tried to focus on the buildings around her to get her bearings, but nothing looked familiar to her. She turned up a side street and continued running away from the warrens. Somewhere behind her, she knew Gardner was pursuing. She could feel Freddie tracking her consciousness, but did nothing to stop him. Gardner would have to find them to inflict damage.

As Meg continued to run, her vision cleared and she made an effort to pace herself. Mareki was not in bad shape, but she was unused to running. Meg knew they would need as much of their combined strength as they could marshal when the time came to defend themselves while she searched for Gardner's weakness.

Footsteps echoed on the pavement behind her. They were the only other sound in the Old City besides Mareki's own. On the uncertain footing, Meg didn't dare glance over her shoulder to see if he was in sight yet.

I'll be damned, she said as she rounded another corner without slowing her pace. *This is backwards too!*

What are you talking about? Mareki asked. She had returned, although she still left muscular control of her body to Meg. She sensed Meg knew how to maintain energy while leading Gardner as far from the warrens as possible.

My dream, Meg said as she glanced around her to see if she recognized anything yet. *Part of it took place at home while I was out running with Ian on the night Thiessen was killed. Part of it seems to be taking place here. Neither of the two are completely like my dream, but they each contain essential portions.* Meg returned her concentration to her breathing for a moment. *I hope this doesn't mean he's going to be throwing parts of buildings at us.*

What? Mareki gasped. She could feel the fire burning her arm and ribs. There was an internal fire burning in her muscles as she ran. She hadn't realized there would be so much pain involved before the fight really got going.

Wait a minute, Meg corrected. *In my dream, I was running in Ian's body. This is too weird.*

That, said Mareki, *I'll agree with*.

Suddenly, Meg recognized the library ahead. It was the only building on the street that looked remotely familiar. She listened to where the echo of Gardner's footsteps emanated.

As soon as she figured out where he was, she turned

away from the library, and Gardner, and continued running, drawing him away from the precious books. Ian would be very unhappy if they got caught in the middle of the conflict. Especially since things had a nasty habit of getting burned.

Books? asked Mareki. She had clearly never heard the word before, and didn't understand any of Meg's mental images.

Assuming we make it, Ian will be happy to explain when this is all over, said Meg. She turned her head slightly, so she could listen behind her and still be able to place her feet safely on the rubble of the street.

Gardner's breath came in great gasps, which Meg could hear over the sound of his footsteps. She slowed to a jog and listened more closely.

Then she realized she was sensing his exhaustion. She couldn't actually hear belaboured breathing. She made an effort to shut her mind to the empathic reception of his fatigue.

She dropped to a walk, and then stopped completely. Looking around, she saw empty buildings gaping at her, but nothing stirred. There was no place to hide, so she stood in the middle of the street and turned to face the direction she had come from.

Mareki, you've done this all your life. Please help me to ground and centre myself. I need to be completely in possession of myself by the time he gets here, Meg said.

Here, Mareki took over. This was something she was familiar with. She slowed her breathing and began the exercises she had done daily for her entire life.

Meg allowed herself to fall into the ritual and relax with it. She continued to keep her ear tuned to Gardner's approach. As the white light came into Mareki, Meg connected with it and felt the sudden surge of power again. Drawing it into her, Meg felt it growing, feeding her with the energy she had depleted in her cross-town run.

When Mareki sent the energy into the ground, Meg felt the connection and remembered what Cia had said about that being the key to her battle against Gardner.

Mareki, she gasped, feeling the power increase. *You'll have to concentrate on maintaining that contact for me. Please? It may be our best chance of winning this thing.*

Mareki said nothing, but signalled her understanding and agreement.

Meg centred herself, feeling the connection of the seat of her soul to the energy in earth and sky. The power coursing through her filled her with confidence. She opened her awareness to her surroundings and heard Gardner's footsteps grow loud.

He's coming, she said unnecessarily. She felt Mareki nod and opened her eyes.

Gardner rounded the corner and saw Mareki standing in the middle of the street with her legs straddled and her arms akimbo. Her chin up and shoulders squared, she looked formidable. Gardner slowed and walked closer to her.

'Freddie tells me he senses something new about you,' he said conversationally.

Meg met his eyes. 'Do you sense something different as well?' she asked.

'Meg, are you there?'

'With permission,' said Meg. She was not surprised that he knew who she was. Mareki would never have had the courage to stand up to Gardner and he knew it. 'Mareki wants me to kill you,' she told him.

At that, Gardner threw back his head and laughed loudly. The sound echoed off the tumbled buildings. 'Does she?' he asked, delighted. 'Well, you're welcome to try.' He raised his hand and jabbed a finger at her. Blue energy crackled in a bright bolt that glowed even in the harsh sunlight. As it stabbed towards Mareki, Meg waved it away, allowing it to shatter harmlessly on the stone street.

'You'll have to do better than that,' Meg said. Drawing on the powers she had been infused with, she sent several bolts of her own green energy at Gardner.

He fended them off with equal ease. He had regained his breath and stood before her unintimidated. His mind guarded by Freddie, he remained unreadable. With a flick of his hand, rocks began flying about the street, striking at Mareki with stunning force.

Unprepared for this, Meg wasn't able to block the first few stones. She felt a rib break as the wind was knocked out of her. A stone cracked against her temple and she fell to the ground. In the moment that it took to regain her wits, several more stones pelted Mareki's unprotected body, but at last, Meg established a field around her that repelled the attack. Sitting up shakily, she drew a long breath, trying to ignore the burning of the broken rib, and tested her head gingerly with her fingertips. She could feel Mareki struggling to maintain the contact with earth and sky energies.

Drawing from those, Meg stood carefully and faced Gardner again. The look on his face froze her mind for an instant. The smug malevolence that she had seen just before he killed Thiessen smiled at her.

With a scream of frustrated anger, she grabbed him with a psychokinetic hand and held him aloft. Before she could throw him to the ground, however, he brushed aside her grasp and landed lightly on his feet.

'*You'll* have to do better than *that*,' Gardner laughed at her. Again, rocks began to fly. Whole pieces of buildings broke loose and added to the confusion of debris in the air.

Meg continued to hold her barrier, but the battering it took drew energy from her.

Gardner raised his hand again and added blue lightning to the fray.

Meg felt it strike her barrier and for a moment, she tensed against it. But then she felt the energy crackling against the screen, and the energy from earth and sky that Mareki strained to provide. It was all the same thing, wasn't it? If energy was energy, what difference did it make what the source was?

Meg relaxed her tension and probed the barrier. She could feel the energy there. Instead of treating it as a weapon, Meg revised her visualization and saw the energy as a source of power to draw from.

The shield absorbed the bolts and strengthened itself.

Gardner's eyes widened as he saw that the energy no longer coruscated around Mareki's body. Instead, it disappeared completely. He redoubled his efforts. Freddie was almost at the end of his energy reserves and would then be unable to protect Gardner.

Meg reached out to touch the barrier. It had strengthened several times beyond what she had been able to generate on her own with the power supplied by Mareki. Now she felt the energy enter through her left hand, adding to the energy in her body. She surged with power now. Her whole being was electrified by it. She felt as though her hair was standing on end.

Mareki could feel the change. She tapped into the new resources of energy, which aided her connection to earth and sky. They were both more firmly grounded now. Meg could feel her fingertips burning with green fire. Her temple and ribs burned. Her arm and right side ached where they had been scorched, and yet she felt incredible. She could run for days; swim for miles.

Is this better? she asked Gardner. She could feel him flinch at the touch of her mind. Gathering her power to her, Meg raised both hands above her head and struck out. Flames of green surged across the space between

305

them, and consumed Gardner's barrier, drawing the energy from it and turning it back on itself.

Gardner crumpled.

As his mind became open to hers, Meg found that she was unable to shut off the empathic healer. She felt his pain as searingly as her own. Stunned by the impact, she reeled away from him and broke contact with his mind. Dropping her barrier, she stood in the street amid the rocks that had fallen when Gardner did. She panted, trying desperately to regain her breath and her wits.

Mareki fought to maintain the grounded state as Meg stumbled to where Gardner lay.

He didn't move as she bent over him. Tentatively, she reached out with her mind and touched his. Since she was expecting the pain this time, she was able to defend herself against it better, but she couldn't shut it out. She knew he wouldn't be able to strike at her again for some time.

Probing into his mind further, she set out to accomplish the final task. She searched for the portions of his mind that made Gardner a psychokinetic, and made sure they did nothing else for him.

Once she had determined that no physical or mental damage would result, Meg systematically destroyed Gardner's psi-power. There would be emotional damage, but that was a small price to pay for his life, Meg thought.

No, Mareki corrected. *It would have been much kinder for you to kill him. Then he could have moved on to the next life and its lessons.*

Meg heaved a sigh and felt broken ends of the rib grinding against each other. *You people are completely whacked*, she said, shaking her head. *We can't just leave him here.*

Call Erhan, Mareki suggested. *He's empathic. Call Freddie, too.*

So Meg did. Then she sat down on the ground beside Gardner and waited for help to arrive. There was a price to pay for commanding such energy. She was too injured to move and too exhausted to care.

14

Erhan found them first. Mareki was curled into a ball and lay a few feet from Gardner on the street. They were both in bad shape and he was reluctant to move either of them, so he stood and waited for additional help to arrive. Gardner lay still, breathing deeply and evenly, but Erhan stayed on the far side of where Mareki lay, just in case.

Freddie rounded the corner, face red with exertion, and stopped short.

Mr Gardner? he whispered. Gardner didn't move. *Mr Gardner?* he repeated more urgently. Freddie began walking slowly towards the bodies on the street. His mouth moved silently.

Mareki stirred, and moaned as she felt her injuries. *Freddie?* she asked, confused. *Where's Meg?*

Erhan backed away a bit and continued to watch first Freddie, then Mareki.

Freddie looked at Mareki uncomprehendingly.

Mareki struggled to sit up, gasping as the ends of her broken rib ground together. *Meg?* she asked again.

Meg is gone, said Freddie. He looked back at Gardner. With a small gesture of frustration he said, *What happened?*

I don't know, Mareki answered, fighting against the pain for a deep breath. She felt as though she were suffocating. Her eyes wouldn't focus, and a sheep had slept on her tongue. *Drove can't hurt you any more.* She squinted up at Freddie, blinking back tears. *Where is Meg?*

Freddie shrugged. He knelt beside Gardner and put a gentle hand on his shoulder. *His mind is different*, he said.

Erhan risked moving closer to Mareki. 'Are you all right?' he asked her shyly.

Mareki jumped at the sound, and then winced in pain. 'I didn't know you were there,' she gasped.

Erhan backed away again, mumbling apologies.

Meg did something to Drove's mind, Mareki told Freddie. *She took away his psychokinetic abilities. He can't hurt you any more.* She turned back to Erhan. 'I can't walk back to the warrens,' she said. 'Freddie can't carry Gardner alone. He's in worse shape than I am. Move me into the shade of those buildings and help Freddie. Then come back for me, please?'

Erhan smiled at her, glad that someone had taken charge of the bizarre situation. He moved to her uninjured left side and lifted her carefully from the street. Walking as gently as he could, he took her to the shade and settled her on the ground.

'I'll be back as soon as I can,' he promised. Then he helped Freddie pick up Gardner and they trundled off down the street back to the warrens.

Mareki leaned back against the building and listened to their footsteps fade.

Meg? she called again. There was no answer. The presence she had felt was gone. Gritting her teeth against the necessity of breathing, Mareki settled down to wait for Erhan's return.

He wasn't long in coming, but to Mareki it seemed for ever. She couldn't find a comfortable position sitting or lying down, and she couldn't get enough air into her lungs. Her throat was dry and gritty, her head ached and her right arm and side throbbed. The raw flesh blistered and blackened.

She was utterly miserable, but she couldn't even cry because it hurt too much. Laughing at the ridiculousness of the situation was also out of the question, so she sat in the shade and tried to be patient.

When she at last heard footsteps, there were more than one pair. Erhan rounded the corner and Sarah came into sight behind him. Sarah still looked exhausted, but the hope Mareki had seen on her face earlier had been changed to happiness.

'You look dreadful!' she said cheerfully as she looked Mareki up and down.

'Thank you. So do you.' Mareki mustered a smile. She tried not to cry out when Erhan lifted her again. He felt so badly about hurting her, she didn't want to make him feel worse. 'You came with Erhan to cheer me up, did you?' she asked Sarah.

'Of course!' Sarah was positively grinning by now. 'I also wanted to get a look at this place. Erhan said you'd wrecked it. What on earth happened?'

'I wish I knew,' Mareki answered truthfully. 'It might make up for these bruises. By the time I woke up, Meg was gone, so I couldn't ask her.'

'Meg?' asked Sarah. 'I caught that name in Ian's thoughts, but it didn't seem to be associated with here. Who is she?'

Mareki closed her eyes against the jarring of Erhan's footsteps and bit her lip.

'Let's concentrate on healing you. I'll ask my questions later,' Sarah said.

Meg had fled Mareki's mind as they slipped into unconsciousness. The pull of her own body, and the desire for familiarity drove Meg back along the continuum.

She had almost no energy left for the journey, but she continued to haul herself back down the lavender thread towards home by main force. Evidently the small amount of energy being supplied to her body had been used up during the reconstitution of her mind and her sojourn in the future. Her confrontation with Gardner had sapped her remaining strength. The need to be among people she knew and understood was overwhelming.

She clung to the thread, knowing if she let go, she would float in the continuum, unable to re-establish contact. She pulled herself along mechanically. There was no thought involved. She barely noticed the transition in the continuum, sensing only that the handful of lavender she grasped was much smaller than it had been.

Without making a conscious decision, Meg slowed her pace. She sensed her own energy in the line, but wasn't sure where the point at which she had left it was. She crawled along the continuum trying to concentrate . . .

I can't, she cried at last. Past caring, Meg sank into the threads, and back into her own mind. With a feeling of relief, she let her consciousness go and slipped into the blackness she had fought since leaving Mareki.

Erhan settled Mareki on a pallet of clean straw covered with a blanket. She smiled at him and he backed away, embarrassed.

Mary fed her a cup of tea that had a small amount of a sleeping draught in it. It didn't really make Mareki sleepy, but it did relax her muscles and her mind, making it easier for Sarah to heal her.

Sarah worked on the burns and broken rib for quite a while, and gradually, Mareki felt comfortable enough to drift off to sleep.

When she finally awoke she found Cia, freshly bathed and looking much better, sitting in a chair near the straw pallet watching her.

'How do you feel?' Cia asked.

Mareki tested various muscle groups before risking a deep breath. 'Much better,' she responded, surprised. She sat up carefully, feeling only a twinge from her rib and her temple. Her arm was bandaged, as was her side, but they didn't hurt.

'You look much better than when I saw you last,' Mareki observed. 'How long was I asleep?'

'Almost a day and a half,' Cia said. 'Not quite as long as I was. Freddie says Meg has gone.' She changed the subject.

Mareki nodded. 'When I woke up on the street with Gardner, she was already gone. Where is she now?'

Cia shook her head. 'I hope she's gone back to her own time. I would have liked to say thank you, though.'

'What happened?' Mareki asked finally.

'Who knows,' Cia shrugged. 'The telepaths say all hell broke loose shortly after Jenet's peculiar unfolding. They say the energy could be seen at the Keep. It was probably felt for miles. I felt it, even through the drug Gardner gave me. It rocked Freddie to his centre, and I felt that too.'

'She used Gardner's energy against him,' said Mareki. 'Beyond that, I don't know.'

'I wish I could have seen it.' Cia smiled. 'It must have been incredible.'

'How is Gardner?' Mareki asked, suddenly feeling guilty that she hadn't remembered before.

'Still in deep sleep,' said Cia, frowning slightly. 'His mind is in shock after what Meg did to him. He may not recover, but Sarah is still working on him. We aren't giving up yet.'

'I told her it was the most cruel thing she could have done to him,' said Mareki. 'Killing him would have been a kindness.'

'She did the right thing,' said Cia. 'If he lives, he will learn a powerful lesson from this. It might make subsequent lives easier for him.'

Mareki smiled. 'When I told Meg that, she said we were completely "whacked". She said when you're dead, you're dead and that's all.'

'Do you believe that?' Cia countered.

'No,' Mareki responded immediately. 'I think she's "whacked", but I didn't tell her so.'

Cia laughed. 'She would have liked that, I think. Are you hungry? I helped Mary make a stew earlier, and I baked a loaf of bread to go with it. Can I get you some?'

'Please!' Mareki exclaimed, suddenly ravenous. Then she felt suddenly guilty again. 'How is Ian?' she asked.

With a smile, Cia said, 'Awake and extremely weak, but he's getting stronger by the hour and feeling much better. We know this because he's so incredibly cranky.'

Mareki laughed. The sound surprised her, but it felt good. She couldn't remember the last time she'd had anything to laugh at. Settling back on the blankets, she waited for Cia to bring her meal.

The Keep was in an uproar when they finally returned late in the afternoon of the next day. They had waited until Drove reached a plateau before risking taking him back to the Keep. It had also taken a while for Cia and Mary to dismantle and pack up the items they would be taking back with them.

They were met in the barnyard by everyone who could be spared from chores, and by a barrage of questions.

'Please!' Cia tried to make her voice heard over the tumult of voices. 'We have sick people to attend to first. Then we'll be happy to answer any questions we can.'

Her words drew attention to her companions. She could feel the climate change when it was discovered that many of them were not from this Keep. The distrust overrode the curiosity and the crowd was drawing away from the strangers.

'Nardo,' Cia said quickly, before the situation became too tense. 'Will you please give Erhan help with Gardner? He needs to be taken to the healing chamber.'

Nardo smiled at her and stepped forward immediately.

'I'd be glad to,' he said, loudly enough to be heard by almost everyone there.

As Erhan slid from his horse's back, the muttering increased, and Cia saw many hands reaching for strands of glass beads. Fear of Gardner and the strangers showed in their eyes, and in the way they shrank from them as Gardner was carried by.

'Most of you know by now that something unusual took place in the Old City several days ago,' Cia said, drawing their attention back to her. There were nods and more mutters, so she went on quickly. 'During that strange occurrence, Gardner was stripped of his psychokinetic abilities. He no longer has the power to harm us, or terrorize us with that threat.'

The noise level in the barnyard rose again. Cia sat on her horse and let them talk for a bit. 'Mareki has paid the price for that,' she gestured at the injured girl who still sat on the horse behind her. 'But now you have a decision to make about whether or not Gardner will be allowed to live among us. He has acted without love towards all of you. Mareki has forgiven him. Can you?' Cia looked around at the faces looking up to her. 'You don't have to make your decision right now. Gardner may not live, but if he does, he may not have let go of the attitudes which we dislike. Think about it and talk about it.' She swung out of the saddle and led her horse off to the barn. The others from the Old City followed her.

Philip?

Cia had finally slipped away from the endless debate taking place in the common room, and gone to the meditation chamber to ground and centre herself. She had been away too long.

Without thinking, Cia sat in her chair facing the dais. She pressed the button for the elevator and watched as the door slid open.

Philip sat on the bench inside. He was unchanged, but there was a subtle difference about him as he walked into her centre and stood before her. He smiled at her fondly.

You did what you were certain couldn't be done, he said with a chuckle.

He was no longer laughing at a private joke. At last Cia understood.

Was I that amusing? she asked with a small giggle. *It didn't seem funny at the time.*

You have grown, Philip said. *You have learned a great lesson from this, and allowed me to learn the lessons that had been set for me. I, too, have grown.*

Cia smiled. *I sensed a change. The Keep has changed also. There are strangers among us for the first time. There is a feeling of freedom from Drove's tyranny and a sense of unity that I don't recall ever being present. The glass beads have been put aside, and several people have made the journey to the Old City to see where the battle took place.*

Philip grinned and nodded. *Now the ground is prepared, your real task begins!* he exclaimed gleefully.

But it's over! Cia cried in dismay. *What more can I do?*

It hasn't even begun! Philip laughed so hard he began to cough.

Philip, damn your dark little soul, what more is there?

The continuum, he choked.

Cia looked at him with her eyebrows drawn together more in question than in a frown.

Don't you remember touching lives you didn't recognize? he asked when he had stopped choking.

Yes, Cia prompted.

Contact them! Philip said impatiently. *If you idiots keep inbreeding, you'll be dead before too many more generations. Pool your minds and resources. Grow!*

What? Cia was appalled. *Oh, come on. Haven't I done enough?*

Nope, said Philip.

Well, you'll help me, won't you? she demanded.

Nope, said Philip again, grinning ear to ear. *I've learned everything I have to. I get to move on. You'll have a new guide after this visit. My work here is complete.*

I won't see you again? Cia asked, distressed. She had worked with Philip for most of her adult life. She didn't feel ready to let go.

Not in this form; not in this life, said Philip. *You've learned everything I have to teach you, I came back to give you these instructions and to say thank you and goodbye.*

Surprised at herself, Cia blinked back tears. She stood slowly and walked to the dais where Philip sat. She bent and hugged him. *Thank you*, she whispered. *Goodbye.*

Philip rose and went to the elevator. He sat on the bench and looked at her, grinning widely.

As the door slipped shut, Cia could hear his laughter.

Slowly, Meg rose from under the layers of fog.

She could hear the low murmur of voices and the background hum of machinery. She opened her eyes and blinked against the unaccustomed glare. Everything around her was white.

'Meg?' a male voice asked.

It sounded like her father. She looked around, trying to find him, but there wasn't anyone in her field of vision. There was a bank of monitors beside her and an IV needle taped to her arm.

Daddy?

There was no response.

'Daddy?' She tried again. His face appeared at the foot of her bed.

'Meg? You're awake!'

Her mother appeared beside him, and they came around to the side of her bed. Susan took her hand and

316

squeezed it gently. 'We were so worried,' she began, but her voice wobbled and she stopped speaking.

'Thiessen?' Meg asked.

Her father shook his head. He placed his hand on her forehead, smoothing the hair from it. 'We were afraid we would lose you, too,' he said, his voice rough with emotion.

Meg took his hand and placed it on her mother's, holding them both between her palms. 'I love you,' she said. A tear slipped from the corner of her eye and into her hair. 'I won't go away again.'

With a deep breath, she blinked back her tears and smiled at her parents. 'How long have I been here?' she asked.

'Almost a week,' said Susan.

Meg thought for a moment. 'Damn,' she said at last. 'That means I blew finals.'

Ted managed a sickly smile. 'I bet I could talk to a couple of your professors and arrange some make-ups when you feel better,' he offered.

'Thanks,' Meg smiled back.

'There's someone here to see you,' Susan told her. She and Ted disengaged from Meg's grasp and stepped away from her bed.

Meg looked towards the foot of her bed and saw Tucker move into view.

'Meg,' he began. He looked awkwardly at Meg's parents.

'Mom, Dad?' Meg looked at them pleadingly. 'Could we please have some time alone?'

They smiled at her and left the room.

'Meg,' Tucker began again. He looked miserable. He probably hadn't slept recently.

Meg smiled encouragingly, but said nothing.

'I went to talk to your father,' he said, gesturing towards the door without looking at it. His eyes remained fixed on hers. 'He wasn't at the university. The department secretary told me I would find him here.' Tucker's eyes searched her face. He twisted his fingers together, rubbing his knuckles and pulling the joints. 'We had a long talk.'

Meg nodded, but stayed silent.

'You were right,' he said finally. 'Our relationship is important to me and I'm sorry I overreacted. I didn't know you were under so much pressure. I can't say that if you were honest with me from the start that I wouldn't have reacted in exactly the way you were afraid I would, but I love you too much to just let you go.'

'Do you forgive me, then?' Meg asked.

'I will if you will,' he said smiling.

'Well, I will if you will,' Meg laughed. 'I love you, Tucker. I'm sorry I hurt you. The best I can do is tell you this will never happen again.'

She held out her hand and Tucker came around the bed to take it.

'How can you be sure?' he asked.

'I just am,' she said. Pulling him down to her, she kissed him thoroughly.

Epilogue

Dear Ian,

It seems strange to be writing to you. So much has happened that you know nothing about, but will play an important part in . . .

My name is Meg, and we haven't met yet, but in your time, I have been dead for almost six hundred years.

Writing you now is difficult, because I know you as well as I know myself, and we've been through a tremendous amount of awkward and painful stuff, but I can't tell you about it.

This time-travel business is tough, because everything I say seems to be a paradox. You will understand my frustration better when you have to explain it to me. (See what I mean? When we meet, I won't know what I am telling you now!)

In the beginning, you expressed frustration and wondered how a Deaf-Mute young man could possibly help a mentally blocked and impossibly stubborn young woman to realize her potential. You didn't see what you could possibly have to offer me.

I can't tell you what you said or did. Some of it I will never understand, but for all our inept fumbling, something worked. I'm not saying we enjoyed it. Quite the contrary.

Most of the time, I was frightened and very angry. You didn't know how to deal with that, especially being so far out of your element, but you managed to overcome your frustration and help me realize my potential. For that, I can never thank you enough.

Was it worth it?

I hope so. We suffered heavy losses, for which there is no consolation. Perhaps what we have gained from them will help lessen the pain. Sarah will be able to help you somewhat to realize that being a Deaf is not such a curse after all.

Love,
Meg